REST IN CHOCOLATE PIECES

"Hasn't it occurred to you that Gemma Rose might know that you're with *me?* She's smart. Maybe she's using you to find out what I've learned while investigating Jeremy's murder."

Danny's expression looked incredulous. "Not bloody likely."

"It's possible," I insisted, unmoved by his sardonic use of that British slang. I could be stubborn too. "Watch out."

"You watch out," my bodyguard shot back irritably. He didn't look at me, but most of his earlier gleefulness had left his face. "I'm seeing Gemma later, and you can't stop me."

"I'm seeing Liam later, and you can't stop me."

"I don't care about stopping you." Danny touched my elbow, steering me backward. I was dangerously close to the yellow line that marked the platform's edge. One overeager commuter, one overzealous bump, and I'd be toast. "I'm too happy to bother."

I studied him and saw that it was true. "Just be careful," I relented. We could handle an argument. We always did. "Keep an eye out for tricks. Or murder plans. Or evidence! I need some."

"I could say the same to you, about Hulk Hands."

"I don't think Liam is guilty. Just misguided about sugar."

Books by Colette London

Criminal Confections

Dangerously Dark

The Semi-Sweet Hereafter

•

Published by Kensington Publishing Corp.

The Semi-Sweet Hereafter

COLETTE LONDON

KENSINGTON PUBLISHING CORP.
http://www.kensingtonbooks.com

KENSINGTON BOOKS are published by

Kensington Publishing Corp.
119 West 40th Street
New York, NY 10018

All Kensington Titles, Imprints, and Distributed Lines are available at special quantity discounts for bulk purchases for sales promotions, premiums, fund-raising, and educational or institutional use. Special book excerpts or customized printings can also be created to fit specific needs. For details, write or phone the office of the Kensington special sales manager: Kensington Publishing Corp., 119 West 40th Street, New York, NY 10018, attn: Special Sales Department, Phone: 1-800-221-2647.

Kensington and the K logo Reg. U.S. Pat & TM Off.

ISBN-13: 978-1-61773-349-9
ISBN-10: 1-61773-349-0
First Kensington Mass Market Edition: October 2016

eISBN-13: 978-1-61773-350-5
eISBN-10: 1-61773-350-4
First Kensington Electronic Edition: October 2016

10 9 8 7 6 5 4 3 2 1

Printed in the United States of America

To John Plumley, with all my love

One

When most people find out what I do for a living, they have one of two reactions. Either they think my life is a nonstop vacation (because of all the traveling I do), or they think I must have a sweet tooth the size of Texas (because of all the chocolate I sample). The truth is, those people are not wrong.

I *do* visit my share of exotic locales. The Taj Mahal. The Eiffel Tower. The Great Wall of China. All of them (and more) have starring roles in my Instagram feed. And I *do* taste more than the typical amount of chocolate. Caramel truffles. Triple mocha brownies. Cocoa cake with raspberry buttercream.

I'm guilty. Guilty as charged.

But that's not because I'm an incurable vagabond *or* because I'm a glutton for *Theobroma cacao*. It's because—in the first case—my eccentric Uncle Ross's will stipulates that I keep moving . . . at least if I want to supply myself with couverture spoons and Converse (and I do). It's also because—in the second case— sharpening my renowned taste buds with all the latest chocolaty treats is my job. Seriously. It really is.

See, I'm the world's first (and maybe only) official

chocolate whisperer. You've probably never heard of
me. That's exactly the way I like it. My clients hire me
on a discreet—often undercover—basis to troubleshoot
their floundering cakes, cookies, and confections . . .
to fine-tune their frappés, mousses, and mendiants.
That means that if you *really* like your favorite candy bar
or frozen mocha drink, *I* might be partly responsible.
Think of a famous confectioner, restaurant, or international chocolate conglomerate. I've probably consulted
with them.

They'll never admit it, though. Neither will I.

In my business, discretion trumps all.

At the moment, I was in London on a job, but you
wouldn't have known it to look at me. I don't carry a
briefcase or consult via conference call. I don't brag
about my prowess or troll for customers. I don't carry
five-kilo bars of chocolate with me and whip up
ganache on demand. I simply travel the globe at least
six months of every year, fixing things for my ap-
preciative client base and enjoying life while I'm at it.

I've always had a knack for *le chocolat.* I don't know
where it came from. I simply *know,* precisely, how any
given chocolate should taste, how it should smell, how
it should snap and melt, and how it should best be
enjoyed. (Slowly, at body temperature, in case you're
curious.) My specialty is taking any given chocolate
from "okay" to "excellent" to "ohmigod *amazing*!" I'm
happy to say that I've never disappointed a client, no
matter how problematic their issues (or they themselves) were.

Which wasn't to say that I wasn't considering
doing exactly that at the moment. Disappointing a
client, that is. Because my latest consultee, Phoebe
Wright, had just popped up on my cell phone's
screen, demanding that I answer her call. And I just

couldn't bring myself to do it. Not immediately, at least.

I glanced at her image, seriously debating pocketing my phone instead of getting down to business. I hemmed. I hawed. I frowned at Phoebe's pretty brunette image. She was nice. *Very* nice. Thirtysomething, pink-cheeked, polite to a fault, and very, *very* British. Phoebe was prone to tea breaks, crumbly Cadbury Flake bars, and marathon viewings of soapy BBC historical dramas like "*Poldark*"—not that she'd admit such a plebian pastime to any of her posh acquaintances, of course.

Phoebe wasn't someone I would call a friend. Not exactly. We were of similar ages. We were sociable, too. And I do make that transition with some of my clients. But I didn't see it happening with Phoebe. She was a bit *too* pinkies-in-the-air for me. She wouldn't have been caught dead pub-crawling with me on a typical Tuesday, for instance—unlike my best pal, Danny Jamieson, my sometime security expert, who was working back in the States while I enjoyed Guinness, West Ham matches, and Maltesers without him. Not necessarily in that order.

But Phoebe was—temporarily, at least—my boss. Duty was (literally) calling. In my business, there's no such thing as "after hours." I'm always on the hook.

I stopped in the midst of the shopping I'd been doing and picked up the call. Before I could say hello, Phoebe spoke.

"Hiya, Hayden!" she crowed cheerfully, her bonhomie amped by years of privilege and elite schooling. "Listen, I'm sorry to trouble you this way, but I can't quite remember if I locked up the shop properly today. Hugh bollixed up a whole batch of brownies, the poor thing, and I'm afraid I was very distracted when I dashed out. He didn't understand what went wrong. Of course, coming from his background he wouldn't, would he? So anyway, we mustn't say anything more, given the circumstances, mustn't we? So let's just never mind that." She inhaled. "Anyway, the thing is, would you mind checking on it for me? Just pop over and wiggle the doorknob a bit, that's all. Primrose really oughtn't be left open all night, now should it?"

Couched in Phoebe-speak, that meant *get your butt over to Sloane Square and lock up my chocolaterie-pâtisserie for me.* I knew that. Phoebe might be full of *shouldn't we?* and *mustn't we?* and other courteous fillers, but she was the daughter of a peer. Technically, she was the Honourable Phoebe Wright. She had no compunction about telling me what to do—no *oughtn't*s required.

As far as Phoebe knew, I was right around the corner. Hers wasn't an unreasonable request. Not really. But I was much farther from Sloane Square than that. I was supposed to have been meeting friends in Leicester Square to see a show. Having planned for the vagaries of London Underground service, I'd arrived in the West End—the "Broadway" of the U.K.—earlier than was strictly necessary. So I'd decided to kill time with one of my favorite jet-setting activities: browsing for groceries.

I know, it doesn't sound glamorous. But bear with me.

I've been *all* over the world during my (barely) thirty years of life. If there's one thing I've learned, it's that nothing else gives you a sense of the culture of a place more than the local grocery store. It doesn't matter if it's big or small, fancy or utilitarian, a bodega or a supermarché. All that matters is that it's *authentic*.

And, in the case of the Marks & Spencer store not far from Covent Garden, that it carries black currant jam, one of my absolute favorite British foods.

My delight with grocery stores doesn't stop with jam, though. I'll happily pick up anchiote seeds in Yucatán, samsa in Kashgar, or unrefrigerated eggs in Monoprix ("Monop" to the French). In Tokyo, I always hit up a *conbini* for cherry-blossom-flavored KitKat bars (provided it's springtime), and when I'm in Oz, you'll find me stocking up on delicious Capilano honey.

Phoebe, unaware of my zeal for foodstuffs, waited on the line. Hey, I'm a food professional. I was (sort of) working.

"Of course, I will." Silently, I began composing a texted apology to my friends. "I'll stop by Primrose right away."

"Would you? That's fab! Thanks ever so much, Hayden!"

"It's all part of the service." I sidestepped a harried Tube commuter. They swarmed shops like M&S and Pret at lunchtime and after work, moving with proto-typical city speed. "I'll let you know what I find when I get there. You can count on me."

I heard Phoebe exhale with relief. Her worrywart tendencies could be tough to manage—mostly because I'm not a world-class worrier myself, so I can't relate. I leave the teeth-gnashing to Travis Turner, my trusty financial adviser. He's good at fretting. He's good at everything. Gallingly, he's younger than me, too. It hardly seems fair that Travis should be so organized, so responsible, and so brilliant . . . while I'm still trying to figure out all the intricacies of my favorite uncle's will.

I'd been fortunate enough to inherit a great deal

of money when Uncle Ross died. It had definitely
come with strings. I still missed him, though. I missed
his laughter. His wild hair.

"Are you at a party?" I asked Phoebe, distracting
both of us as I picked up on the sounds of a gathering.
Glasses clinked. Music played. Conversations waxed
and waned. "Having fun?"

"Oh, absolutely! Must dash, though. Kisses! Bye!"

With an amplified *smack,* Phoebe hung up. Now
that she'd gotten me to do her bidding, I guessed, she
didn't have time for chitchat. That was my life, though.
I wasn't soul mates with my clients. I was a consultant.
An expert one. But that was all.

Ooh, were those McVitie's Dark Chocolate Hobnobs?

They weren't. They were a knockoff of the famous
cult cookies. But I was hooked, all the same. I grabbed
a box, added it to my stash of British goodies, then
headed for the tills.

It wouldn't be easy tromping all this stuff back
across London on the Piccadilly and Victoria lines,
but it would be worth it. I'd miss the show with my
friends, but I'd have a few of my favorite goodies to
comfort me while I texted them to reschedule. I'd be
in London a while yet. I had plenty of time.

In the meantime, I'd almost forgotten my daily
phone call to Travis. As a woman traveling solo, I
couldn't be too careful about safety. Checking in with
my financial adviser meant that at least one person
knew whether I was happily gridskipping or unhappily
being mugged at any given moment. Ordinarily, I like
to savor my phone calls to Travis. I like to settle in,
focus, and really melt into the experience. If you
heard Travis's deep, sensual, faintly raspy voice, you'd
do the same, believe me.

But given the time difference between The Big Smoke and downtown Seattle, where Travis's office was located, I sometimes had to compromise. That meant, in this instance, pocketing my colorful pound-sterling banknotes with their pictures of the Queen and heading for the closest Tube station while waiting for the man who held the purse strings to my fortune to pick up.

Promptly, he did. Hearing the call connect, I couldn't help smiling. Travis had that effect on me, despite everything.

"So, Travis . . . what are you wearing right now?"

It was my usual gambit. I couldn't shake Travis's financial leash, but I *could* let him know that I didn't intend to toe the line all the time. That's what my teasing opener was all about.

That . . . and the under-the-radar hope he'd (some-day) tell me.

I'd been curious how things stood between us, but it turned out I hadn't needed to wonder. Travis's deep chuckle let me know that everything was copacetic. Despite the . . . incidents . . . in San Francisco and Portland that I'd run into, despite the borderline sketchy things that Travis had done to help me out of some dangerous situations in those cities, we were still buds.

"Hayden Mundy Moore." His sexy, sonorous voice induced shivers. As usual. I imagined all the associates and admins in his office glancing up from their spread-sheets and swooning. "Shouldn't you be working? You don't have time to call me."

"I *always* have time to call you."

"No, you don't. You have clients to see, chocolates to improve, cacao farmers to meet." He knew my job as well as I did. I pictured him ticking off items on his talented hands. "Reports to write. Expenses to file. That reminds me—"

He broke off, shuffling papers in the background. Yep. Papers. Evidently, financial management required old-fashioned tree killing. I wouldn't know. I'd never been to Travis's office in person. I'd never met *him* in person, believe it or not.

"Have you been using the app I recommended?" he asked.

I frowned, remembering. "The anti-procrastination app?"

"That's the one." Crisply, he recited its name.

"Nope. I didn't have time. I forgot. I mean, it broke." I picked up the pace, jogging as I spotted a roundel—the iconic red, blue, and white symbol of the London Underground. "Anyway, my cell phone battery died. I don't think it was meant to be."

"And your dog ate your homework?"

"Exactly!" I paused outside the station, adding one of those tawdry free tabloid papers to my bag. "You get me."

This time, Travis laughed outright. "Nice try. Don't make me enlist the enforcer on this effort. I'll do it, believe me."

"No. I still have nightmares about the last time you two collaborated on something." *On me.* "I'll use it. I promise."

The *enforcer* nickname made me grin, though. He meant Danny, of course. My on-call bodyguard and longtime platonic pal.

I'd known Danny for ages. He was my frequent traveling partner, my favorite plus one for occasional fancy events, and my most trusted confidante. People tended to take Danny at face value. They saw six-plus feet of musclebound, sporadically tattooed security expert and nothing else. But I knew better.

I knew there was more to Danny Jamieson than sticky fingers, a shady past, and a scowl that intimidated even the most hardened criminals . . . maybe because he was one of them at heart, no matter how far he'd moved from his bad old neighborhood.

Recently, "the enforcer" (Danny) had teamed up with "Harvard" (Travis) to make sure I took matters appropriately seriously while on assignment in Bridgetown—the up-and-coming foodie nirvana of Portland, Oregon. Having the men in my life, the two of them archenemies, team up to "help" me had been . . .

Well, let's just call it *unnerving* and leave it at that.

"See that you keep your promise this time. I vetted that app myself." Travis was still doggedly dealing with the issue of my procrastinatory tendencies. The idea of him needing to "vet" a productivity app was laughable. He *was* a productivity app—a living, breathing, authoritative machine. "It will help."

"I'll add it to my to-do list," I promised, reaching past the trusty Moleskine notebook that held that very same list as I dug around in my favorite crossbody bag for my Oyster card. I'd entered the Underground station. From here, it was push or be pushed as everyone surged toward the barriers that divided the ticket hall from the escalators and stairs leading down to the various platform levels. The hubbub almost drowned out Travis.

I was pretty sure he was laughing, though. The nerve.

Was he really convinced I wouldn't to-do-list that app? He, more than anyone, should have known how much I value my running to-do lists. They keep me on track even more than Travis does.

"I'll do it," I insisted. "I have a system."

Despite open skepticism, I always get things done.

Travis didn't reply. He was laughing too hard.

I decided to take the high road. "Gotta go, Travis." I touched in with my card and headed for the escalator, juggling my phone and groceries. "Try to stay out of trouble, okay?"

"You do the same, Hayden. I mean it." My financial adviser overrode my flippancy with stern sobriety. It was his go-to approach to everything. "You be careful out there."

Aw. See what I mean? Travis is a championship-caliber worrier. He worries like a boss. He'd probably get on well with Phoebe, in fact. They'd make adorable fussbudget kids together.

If Phoebe weren't already married to the U.K.'s most famous celebrity "sexy chef," Jeremy Wright, of course. Details.

All the same, the fondness in Travis's voice warmed me.

You be careful out there.

We both knew there were reasons I needed to watch out. We weren't talking about the dangers inherent in my unconventional line of work, either— although chocolate whispering does come with certain complications. That's just life.

Sometimes I meet unsavory types during my consulting gigs, for instance. Sometimes I'm offered a bribe to wreck a competitor's product line. Or I stir up hurt feelings by helping one company and not another. Or I outright refuse to work with someone. I have standards. I don't perform chocolate magic for just anyone who comes to me with substandard sweets and the ability to pay my (modest) consulting fee.

Rex Rader had been proof of that much in San Francisco.

But Travis wasn't talking about the chocolate biz. He was talking about murder . . . and the unpredictable ways I'd become involved in it lately. It had been a while since my latest foray into the rougher side of beating buttercream and making fudge. Everything was fine now. I figured it would stay that way.

"I will." I rode the escalator downward, glancing at ads for Lloyds Bank, the Royal Botanic Gardens at Kew, and "fatigue reducing" Floradix iron-and-vitamin supplements. "But I don't have to. I mean, what are the odds of something happening here?"

"About twelve per million."

"Come again, Mr. Wizard?"

"Given a population of around eight and a half million people and an average of two homicides per week, that's—"

I groaned. Leave it to my wunderkind financial adviser to compute the chances of my getting killed while in London.

"Your predecessor, old Mr. Whatshisname, would never have settled for 'about' twelve per million," I interrupted drily. Until Travis had taken over for his firm's older associate, my required check-ins had been . . . *enervating.* "He would have known—"

Travis interrupted with a to-the-decimal-point calculation.

"That seems really low," I countered, feeling encouraged.

"It is. There's a reason your current assignment is there."

There . . . in Safetown, aka London, where being

murdered was statistically less likely than meeting Her Majesty, the Queen.

I strode through the tunnel, shaking my head as I realized Travis was trying to protect me—was hinting he *had* protected me.

"Did you nudge the Primrose bid to the top of the pile?"

He didn't admit as much. But Travis handled all my requests for consultations. He was the one who decided where I went, aside from me. It was a broadening of his role, but he hadn't minded. It wasn't as though Danny could take on the job. He was so eager for me to "succeed"—that is, grow my business—he would have let me consult for anyone with a pulse and a bank account.

With him there to back me up, for sure. But still.

Danny was terrific. But tough times changed people. They changed their priorities and their willingness to follow the rules.

"Aw. I love you, too, Travis." Saying so with over-the-top sentimentality, I pulled a goofy face. "I'm definitely coming to the Pacific Northwest after this job so we can meet in person."

As if that would ever happen, I groused silently. Travis is as elusive personally as he is proficient professionally. I knew more about his dog than I did about him. Which wasn't saying much. I'd only found out about the dog recently. From Danny. My security expert had a talent for sussing out details. And for punching people. But in this case, he'd only snooped. On Travis.

He'd gotten woefully little information, though. Darn it. "Speaking of which, I've been wondering," I pressed, seizing the moment, "what kind of dog do you have, Travis?"

A moment passed. Nada. I should have expected that, I guessed. Then I realized the phone had gone dead in my hand.

There was no service on the platform. Foiled again. Even the London Underground was stymying my efforts to find out more about Travis. I sighed and queued up along the yellow line with everyone else, headed to Primrose to set Phoebe's mind at ease.

By the time I made it to Chelsea, the tony neighborhood not far from the Thames where Primrose drew crowds every morning, I regretted my earlier shopping expedition. Sure, I'm strong. I can hoist burlap bags of cacao beans and handle heavy stainless steel sauciers in a restaurant's back-of-house with the best of them. But even in a typically cramped bakery kitchen, it's possible to turn around. That wasn't true of an Underground train during rush hour. I'd gotten a *lot* more intimate with my fellow travelers than I wanted to be. Stepping aboveground afterward, I exhaled with relief and headed for the chocolaterie-pâtisserie.

I'd been consulting at Primrose for a couple of weeks now. Phoebe had entrusted me with a set of keys and access to the shop's secret recipe journal—a notebook full of various bakers' formulas, its pages splattered with cream and dusted with cocoa powder. Most establishments treated their "books" with utmost secrecy, but Phoebe had practically thrown Primrose's at me.

She'd been desperate to sort out Primrose's quality problems. Lately, the shop's sweets hadn't been sweet enough, their cakes hadn't been tender enough, their chocolate treats hadn't been creative enough. Those issues, combined with competition from newer artisanal chocolateries, threatened to squash Primrose's longtime supremacy in the neighborhood.

Like many of my clients, Phoebe had come to me via referral. I had a feeling my previous consultee might have been a little *too* effusive in his praise, though, because Phoebe seemed convinced I could work miracles at her shop.

I was convinced I could, too, of course. I'm generally pretty confident. Honestly, all Primrose needed were some new suppliers and a few technical improvements—tweaks I could easily teach the staff, given time. But usually it's best to manage clients' expectations. I didn't want Phoebe thinking I could turn her ramshackle team of bakers into geniuses overnight.

I'd come pretty far in tutoring them—in getting a feel for what was working well at Primrose (brownies, fudge) and what wasn't (cookies, single-origin bars, cakes). But the staff were green. I'd need more time to achieve a full turnaround.

As expected, Primrose was locked up tight. The shop's brick walls and Georgian façade stood sturdily against the encroaching sunset, an event that streaked the sky orange and lent a faint rosy glow to the neighborhood. On the corner, locals gathered for a pint, most of them standing outside the pub chatting. In the distance, I heard cars and Routemaster buses roaring down Chelsea Embankment. Here, though, everything was peaceful.

I hadn't really expected anything else. The problems at the chocolaterie-pâtisserie didn't include rampant carelessness, despite the mistakes Phoebe had alluded to with Hugh Menadue, one of the apprentice bakers. Overall, Primrose was a cozy and inviting shop. Its café-style tables and chairs were immaculate, its floor spotless, its windowpanes streak-free. Through those windows, in front of me, passersby could be lured inside with views of cocoa-marbled "slices" (Britspeak for pieces of cake), malted chocolate cream pies, semi-sweet cream buns, and more.

Now, though, after hours, Primrose's display platters and vintage cake stands had been removed. The windows stood empty.

I beelined down the tight alleyway behind Primrose and double-checked the back door, too. It was similarly secure.

I called Phoebe and left her a message saying so, trying not to feel irked at having been sent on a wild-goose chase. She didn't pick up, probably because her upper-crust soirée had taken a turn for the raucous. Don't let anyone tell you that the English aristocracy don't know how to party. The dark circles under my eyes proved otherwise. I hadn't gotten a truly solid night's sleep since coming to London to consult at Primrose.

See, I'm not just chocolate whispering for Phoebe. I'm staying at her place, too—at the guesthouse adjacent to her fancy-pants Georgian town house a few streets over, in fact.

The accommodations came with the job. While I can hold my own in the financial department, I can't just conjure up an eighteenth-century crash pad full of antiques and luxuries for myself. So when Phoebe offered, I accepted. She hinted there'd be cocktails and tea parties, an introduction to her sought-after celebrity chef hubby and an opportunity to network with her well-connected friends. But I'd been sold at the words "four-poster in the bedroom" and "claw-footed tub in the bath."

I might be a sneaker-wearing, chocolate-whispering bohemian most of the time, but I'm secretly a Jane Austen heroine at heart. Aren't all women, given the opportunity? So I said yes.

Now, with visions of that old-timey bathtub swimming in my head, I rearranged my grocery bags, left the alleyway, and headed east. The Wright residence stood only a few streets from the chocolaterie-pâtisserie, on a quiet avenue chockablock with similarly grand terraced town houses equipped with white Doric-columned stone façades, dentiled cornices, wrought-iron railings, and enormously imposing six-paneled front doors.

Not that I was going in by the front door, of course. I ducked into another passageway, maneuvered past a fading lilac bush, and pushed open the Wrights' back gate. Their walled garden ("yard" to a Yank like me) was green and welcoming, bordered by primroses (get it?) and cushiony with grass. I trod past that grass on the graveled path, my footsteps crunching in the lengthening shadows. The guesthouse wasn't far, but reaching it always felt like invading a private space meant for family.

Me, I'm at home in hotels, in hostels, in yurts, and in bed-and-breakfasts. Growing up with a pair of globe-trotting parents and no siblings, I'd stayed in accommodations ranging from five-star resorts to remote Swiss cabins, from hammocks on a Balinese beach to cramped sleeper cars on European trains. But I hadn't stayed in anyone's home for years now. Including my own.

That's because I don't have one. Not really. Not anymore.

Not that I regretted my wayfaring lifestyle, I reminded myself as I stepped into the guesthouse's foyer, switched on the lights, and strode to the kitchen to put away my grocery-store finds. I was privileged. I was independent. I was secure.

I was staring at a dead man on the floor.

Again. *Oh, God.* No no no no.

I blinked, but he was still there. Unmoving. Unbreathing. Unlikely to be simply napping in that awkward slumped position on my guesthouse's blood-streaked tiles. On the verge of freaking out, I hauled in a deep breath and tried to evaluate the situation calmly. That's what I'd promised myself I'd do in the (very) unlikely event that anything like this ever came up again.

I failed. Mostly because of the blood. It was just . . .

Too much. I dropped everything and grabbed my phone.

I needed help, and I needed it now. Because if I wasn't mistaken, Travis's homicidal-incidence-per-population odds had just been illustrated in the worst possible way. On my floor.

It looked as though I, Hayden Mundy Moore, had stumbled upon a murder. All over again.

TWO

"And what time was it again when you arrived?"

At the sound of the detective constable's voice, I started. I'd been drawn away from our interview, pulled inexorably toward the sight of the London Metropolitan Police officers who were currently dealing with the evidence. With the body.

With *him*. Jeremy Sebastian Wright. Dead at thirty-seven.

Phoebe will be devastated, I thought to myself. Jeremy was—*had been*—her husband. I had to call her. Right away. What if no one else had? What if she was partying away, oblivious to this?

Numbly, I reached for my crossbody bag. For my phone.

The constable closed her hand on mine. "Ms. Mundy Moore, I need you to concentrate right now. Just for a little longer."

Her calm demeanor was soothing. I nodded, then let my hand fall away. It trembled. My mouth felt dry, my mind full of shock. How could this be happening? Why here? Why now? Why him?

"I'm sorry." I shifted my gaze to the DC's white starched collar. Like the rest of her, it was pristine. "Where were we?"

"With you, just as you arrived here this evening."

Duly reminded, I nodded again. Detective Constable Satya Mishra watched me intently, her dark eyes inscrutable and her features composed. I couldn't begin to guess what she was thinking. Her overall air of command was impressive.

I *felt* impressed. Also, dazed, disbelieving, and shaky.

I told Detective Constable Mishra what I knew. It wasn't much. I hadn't seen anyone fleeing the scene—hadn't seen anyone inside the place, either. Trying to help, I described my arrival at the Wrights' guesthouse, my approach from outside through the garden, my turning on the lights, and my practically tripping over Jeremy Wright's inert body as he lay in the kitchen.

Recalling the scene, I shuddered. I'd never forget that grisly sight. Part of Jeremy's skull had been . . . well, *crushed* was the best way I could find to describe it. Gruesomely, the rest of him had looked just as handsome as ever. His light brown hair had crowned his face as appealingly as it had when he'd been alive, accenting his blue eyes and his square, stubbled jawline.

Those famous eyes of his had looked blank, though. Horribly blank, devoid of the liveliness they'd possessed the one and only time I'd met him on the day I'd arrived in London. Now he'd be unshaven forever, too. His mother would be so disappointed.

At that moment, as DC Mishra continued questioning me, I wished *my* mother were there. She and my father lived in London—in Mayfair, to be precise—

but they were working in France. We were divided by the English Channel and hundreds of miles.

Much closer to me, officers dressed in the Metropolitan Police force's black uniforms with white shirts, black ties, and vivid yellow "high-vis" vests performed their duties. Two loaded Jeremy's body onto a stretcher, guided by a medical examiner. Others took photographs and (I presumed) gathered forensic evidence. I couldn't be sure. I couldn't even be sure how much time had passed. I've witnessed dead bodies before. Sadly. But I'll never become inured to the awful unreality of it all.

An officer wearing a bowler hat with a distinctive band of Sillitoe tartan wrapped around it—you've probably glimpsed that black-and-white checked pattern somewhere—cataloged my fallen groceries as though they too were evidence. My Dark Chocolate Hobnob wannabes merited a tag. My blackcurrant jam got another.

The jar had smashed on impact. I eyed the purple goop my preserves had become, feeling disconnected from it all. I didn't even remember having dropped my grocery bag. I was lucky I'd had the wits to dial 1-0-1, the English nonemergency services code.

I told Constable Mishra as much. She nodded graciously.

I didn't know why she was spending so much time questioning me. I was a bystander. That's all. Yes, I was staying in the guesthouse temporarily, I confirmed when she asked me. But no, I hadn't really known Jeremy Wright. I'd been working for Phoebe.

"Did your work involve all this?" DC Mishra's wave indicated the kitchen and the equipment currently cluttering it.

I recognized most of it. I've consulted on film sets

and commercials, helping to make the chocolate "hero" (the subject of the filming) look its best. Professional lighting rigs stood ready to illuminate the work area with the help of filters and reflectors. A boom pole with a muff-covered shotgun mic affixed to it leaned against the refrigerator. A portable audio recorder waited on the countertop next to a stack of boxed cake mixes.

I squinted to read the labels. *Hambleton & Hart Molten Chocolate-flavored Dessert Delight,* one read. I glimpsed *Strawberry Surprise* something-or-other on another box. Hm.

Want a professional tip? When a food product uses lots of ambiguous terms like "delight" and "surprise," watch out. That generally means it's more manufactured than baked. Not yummy.

"No, this wasn't mine," I told DC Mishra, returning my full attention to her. "Phoebe had told me that Jeremy might be in and out during my stay, though. He sometimes filmed in here."

What I didn't want to disclose was that the reason Jeremy Wright filmed in the guesthouse's kitchen—which masqueraded as his home kitchen on television—was that his *real* kitchen was much too fancy to be relatable to his everyday viewers. Jeremy was a real "bloke"—a guy's guy—who'd come from nothing to build his foodie empire. He couldn't risk alienating any of his fans.

Satya had noticed those Hambleton & Hart boxes, too. But her expression as she studied them was markedly different from mine. She smiled. "I used to *love* those things as a kid."

Her open nostalgia surprised me. But it only lasted a moment. I might have imagined it. Her expression hardened again.

"Process those," she instructed her partner with a nod to the mix-and-bake treats. "Find out who's in charge at Hambleton & Hart and get them to come to the station to give a statement."

"Right away," came the response, followed by scurrying.

I wasn't the only one who respected Satya Mishra.

My gaze wandered again to the scene behind her. One of the officers had bagged something as evidence. Something gray, blood-stained, and shaped like a smallish American baseball bat. He held it up in his gloved hands, peering perplexedly at it.

"What do you reckon?" he asked his colleague, frowning.

The lull that followed was too much for me. I wanted to *do* something. At the best of times, I'm an ants-in-the-pants kind of gal. I've got a rampant monkey mind and a need to keep moving. The officers on hand obviously needed my assistance.

"It's a metlapil."

Several interested gazes swerved toward me. I couldn't help feeling on safer ground. This I knew. This I understood.

Murder? Not so much. But kitchen equipment? Sure. So I kept talking.

"It's a heavy stone tool used for grinding, usually in conjunction with a metate." More baffled gazes focused on me. "You know, like a mortar and pestle?" I mimed a grinding gesture, cupping my palm for a metate and curling my fingers around an imaginary metlapil. "They're typically made of volcanic rock. They're virtually indestructible. Before the industrial age, they were used to pulverize grain, seeds—"

"Heads?" Two of the officers—unbelievably—chuckled.

A harsh look from Satya Mishra put a stop to that.

Then she returned her attention to me, eyebrows raised.

I recognized her unspoken question. "Yes, maybe." I didn't want to think about that. I raised my palms in a defensive *hold on* gesture. "I've only ever seen metlapils used to make bean-to-bar artisanal chocolate. It's pretty complicated, though. First you have to remove the cacao beans from their fruit, then you have to ferment them, then comes roasting, cracking, winnowing—"

I stopped short, realizing that DC Mishra was staring at my hands. Why would she stare at my hands, especially so fixedly?

Realizing one possible explanation, I froze. "I've only used a metlapil once, on a plantation in Venezuela," I clarified hastily. Have I mentioned that I tend to get chatty when nervous? "I've never even noticed that gigantic one before."

I pointed at it and immediately wished I hadn't. Doing so seemed to draw an unmistakable connection between it and me.

That was the murder weapon. What was I, crazy?

I clammed up, but it was too late.

"Yet you live here, isn't that correct?" she asked me.

I swallowed hard. Reluctantly, I nodded. I couldn't help noticing that the rest of the officers had also become very interested in what I had to say. Uh-oh. I wished Danny were there. I wished Travis were there. I wished I'd stayed in a nearby hotel and not been lured by promises of beds and baths.

"You've stayed here for . . . ?" Constable Mishra consulted her notes. Her calm demeanor no longer felt comforting. It felt entrapping. "Almost two weeks now. Isn't that correct?" Her laser attention fixed on me. "But you claim you've never seen that particular metlapil? I find that hard to believe."

Frankly, I did, too. Had that (unusually large) metlapil been here all along? Or had someone brought it? The film crew?

The killer?

"You can't think *I* did this!" I blurted. "I'm innocent!"

Her tightly pursed lips suggested she remained unconvinced.

"I didn't have any reason to want Jeremy Wright dead."

Blithely, DC Mishra asked, "You were a fan?"

"Of course! Who wasn't?" Anxiously, I barked out a laugh. Hey, it's not easy being interrogated. *You* try holding up under that much pressure—that much intense scrutiny. Satya Mishra might have the beauty and poise of a Bollywood actress, but she also had the severity and formidable authority of a police officer. They're trained to be daunting. "Weren't we all?"

If they didn't want to acknowledge the truth, I would. Jeremy Wright had been the U.K.'s most famous celebrity chef for almost a decade. He'd eclipsed all his rivals with his rough-hewn charm, Essex-bred accent, and culinary charisma. He'd done several popular TV cooking shows. He'd done sold-out tours in England and abroad. He'd authored multiple best-selling cookery books. He'd married the daughter of a peer! He'd made it.

His fans would probably bawl in the streets when they heard the news. They'd queue (politely, of course) to lay tributes to Jeremy at his jam-packed city restaurants, as fans had done in Camden Square when Amy Winehouse had died. They'd be devastated.

The police offers appeared less distraught. "Nothing he cooked could beat a nice takeaway chicken vindaloo," one said.

"Or a doner kebab," confirmed another with a nod. You might think that Londoners nosh on fish and chips and pints of ale exclusively. But the city has a robust food scene. Jeremy Wright had been at the forefront of it. Cheap takeaways notwithstanding, he'd done his share of proper English grub.

"I don't cook," Constable Mishra told me. "My freezer is stocked with ready meals from Waitrose, like a normal person."

Ugh. "Well, you're busy. You have an important job."

I hoped that job wouldn't include arresting me.

"I could give you a few cooking lessons sometime." I'd already told Satya Mishra what I did for a living. "Free of charge."

"Bribing an officer is a crime, Ms. Mundy Moore."

"Or you could pay me." I was floundering. We both knew it.

To my relief, DC Mishra did not choose that moment to incarcerate me. Instead, she wrote something in her notebook, gave me another evaluative look, then stood in the guesthouse's kitchen. She frowned at me. "Don't leave town, Ms. Mundy Moore."

I gulped and tried to look guilt free.

Don't leave town. Wasn't that what the police said to their prime suspects? Was I a prime suspect? All I'd done was stay in a place where I had plenty of opportunity, report finding a dead body, identify the until-then-unknown murder weapon, and loudly proclaim my innocence. Maybe more than once. I wasn't sure.

Hmm. If that last bit didn't implicate me, nothing would.

"We may need to speak to you again, after we've finished processing the crime scene." DC Mishra eyed her colleagues in what seemed to be her typical no-nonsense way. Then, me. "You should find somewhere else to stay tonight. Possibly for the next forty-eight hours. It all depends on what we find here."

"I hope you find a murderer!" I said urgently. I was under suspicion of murder. Officially under suspicion. Oh no.

"We'll find who did this." The detective constable pierced me with a deadeye look. "You can be assured of that." Then she conferred with her fellow officers, nodded, and left the scene. If I was supposed to feel comforted, I didn't. While it was somewhat reassuring to know that the police were on the job, they were pointed squarely in the wrong direction.

They were pointed at me. I wanted to escape, but I wasn't sure where to go. I wanted to forget about this, but that was impossible. I wanted to break down the situation with someone who wasn't mentally fitting me for handcuffs and prison stripes.

Muzzy-headed, I stepped outside into the encroaching darkness. In the garden, I could still make out the faraway sounds of laughing pubgoers and summertime traffic on the embankment.

I pulled out my phone and dialed. It would be afternoon in L.A., where Danny lived and worked. I pictured sunshine and smog, traffic and tacos. He picked up on the first ring.

"The margaritas here are horrible," I told him in my best upbeat voice. "Can you FedEx me some tequila right away?"

Danny wasn't fooled by my fake bonhomie. He's known me too long for that. His voice took on a hard edge. "What's wrong?"

My throat burned. I gulped some air and blinked hard. I was afraid I might start crying. I like to think I'm pretty tough—pretty live-and-let-live about things—

but at the familiar, cherished sound of Danny's voice, everything rushed at me.

"It happened again," I croaked, unable to say more.

A moment of silence stretched along the line. I imagined Danny at work, wearing a tuxedo and a skeleton-style, two-way radio earpiece on a red carpet somewhere in La-La Land. He made (most of) his living as a private security expert, ushering Hollywood types to movie premieres and fancy charity events.

"I'm on the next red-eye," he told me. "Sit tight."

That's when I started weeping, of course. All the stress of the past few hours blubbered out of me in fits and starts. I stared at London's skyline, hoping to regain my composure. I could glimpse the very tippy top of the Shard, lighted for the nighttime, but that celebrated view didn't help. I was a wreck.

"The police think *I* did it," I confided, calmer now.

Danny never left my (telephonic) side, not even while handing off whatever protection job he'd taken on. Knowing him, he would arrange air travel, grab his go bag, and intimidate L.A.'s infamously grid-locked traffic out of his path while driving. When engaged in a mission, Danny was a fearsome sight.

He was *my* fearsome sight. I needed him.

"You'll just have to prove you *didn't* do it, then," he said now. "You're not a murderer. You like everybody. They like you."

Just like that, everything became clearer. Count on Danny to get down to brass tacks. He didn't usually add in mushy stuff about my personal likability, of course, but this was a crisis.

He might be built like a muscleman, but he wasn't made of stone. When it came to me, Danny was sur-prisingly schmaltzy.

I mean, not that we were dating, or anything. God

forbid. We'd tried that once and lived to regret it. Now we knew better.

"I'm not paying you overtime for an overnight flight," I joked, still searching for my equilibrium. I started walking.

"I'm not flying coach. Those seats will squash me like a sardine," Danny shot back. "Business class. Deal with it."

Despite everything, I smiled. I sniffled. I smiled again, knowing he was doing his best to divert me from all the drama.

I didn't know how. Or when. But I knew everything would be okay. Eventually. Because I intended to make sure it was.

One way or another. But first, now that I felt calmer and readier to deal with everything, I needed to call Phoebe.

After news broke of Jeremy's death, chaos descended.

I wanted to leave London altogether, but I couldn't. For one thing, I was a suspect in Jeremy's murder. For another, I was under contract to work at Primrose until Phoebe pronounced the shop's problems solved. That was our agreement. I typically keep my consultations open-ended, taking on one at a time and working it from analysis to enhancement to report, step by step.

I'm methodical like that. I'm also a stickler for details *and* an unrepentant procrastinator. You'd think those qualities wouldn't go together. You'd be wrong. However kooky, my methods work. My clients are always satisfied. But this was different.

Phoebe would be different. Maybe she'd want to cancel.

Most likely, just then, she wouldn't care about Primrose, its pastries, or its soon-to-be-decadent chocolate treats. She'd be absorbed in mourning the man she loved. In gathering with Jeremy's family and friends and remembering him. In crying and questioning and making funeral arrangements for her husband.

I kept on as best I could, taking refuge in what needed to be done. I needed to get up early (hideously early) to arrive at Primrose. I needed to oversee the morning bakers' work. I needed to taste-test chocolate chunk cookies and chocolate cherry scones. I needed to keep my mouth shut and listen when the curious and surprised Primrose staff gossiped about Jeremy.

They had a lot to say, actually. Which brought me to . . .

You'll just have to prove you didn't do it, then.

Danny had been right when he'd said that. He'd said it again when he'd come in from Heathrow to join me, too.

You'll just have to prove you didn't do it.

I did. So, as much as I wanted to take refuge in chocolate whispering, I had to keep my eyes and ears open for clues. I couldn't wait for DC Mishra to catch the killer. I had to do a little sleuthing myself. Just on the off chance I could succeed.

The idea wasn't as crazy as it sounded. I've been mixed up in dangerous situations before and emerged unscathed. A little bruised, battered, or scared, maybe, but mostly okay. I'd survived, *and* I'd brought justice to some people who needed it.

I knew I could do it again. With Danny to help me and Travis on call, I figured I could clear my name and troubleshoot Primrose's problems . . . and comfort Phoebe, too. I hadn't seen her in person yet. But when I did, I meant to offer my sincerest condolences.

I hadn't known Jeremy well, but I'd respected his accomplishments. He'd seemed nice. He hadn't deserved to die.

Not that anyone did. You know what I mean.

In the immediate aftermath of Jeremy's death, I crashed overnight on a friend's sofa in Shoreditch. Even that was a tight squeeze, though. She had other guests to accommodate—including Danny, who roughed it on the floor beside me without complaint for a night after he hit town. After that, neither love nor money could secure us another place to stay—not one that hadn't recently hosted a murder, at least. I was stuck.

I had to return to the Wrights' guesthouse. Today.

In a black cab hurtling across London, I made another go at it anyway. Despite needing to be near the scene of the crime to do a little snooping, I wasn't wild about the idea of sleeping a measly few feet from where someone had bashed Jeremy's head in.

That had been the official cause of death, by the way. Jeremy had been bludgeoned to death. Likely with that oversize stone metlapil. Likely by someone tall, strong, and left-handed.

"It all comes down to the evidence, doesn't it?" said DC Mishra's colleague, George, when I inquired. "That's what the fellas in forensics tell us, anyway." He'd dropped his gaze to my hand, then scratched his head musingly. "Yep. Left-handed."

I'd clutched my crossbody bag harder in my right hand and then skedaddled, finished with the "few questions" DC Mishra had summoned me back to the police station to answer. Now I returned my attention to the cab driver. I smiled at him.

"You wouldn't happen to know of a hotel with rooms available, would you? You black cab drivers have the Knowledge of London. If anybody can tell me where to go, it's you."

"Nope. Wimbledon's in town, innit?" Cheerfully, the driver eyed me in his rearview mirror, nodding to recognize my familiarity with the Knowledge—the grueling, comprehensive test that all licensed cab drivers were required to pass. It was rumored to detail more than 25,000 roads and 20,000 attendant land-marks and businesses. That's why the drivers of black cabs are so skilled. "Everyplace is blocked up solid this time of year. My missus makes extra money renting out our son's room. He's away at university. We split the take with him."

"That's enterprising of you," I said, disappointed. I'd forgone public transport today on purpose, hoping to pick the brain of a black cab driver like him. If you ever find yourself in a strange city, needing a tip about where to go, what to see, or where to eat, ask a cab driver where he or she likes to go. You'll get the real skinny on what's good (and cheap) anywhere.

"Every little bit helps," he said with a shrug and an-other grin. "I've got a vacation villa in Spain to pay for, don't I?"

"It's smart of you not to leave money on the table, then."

"Can't afford it. London's an expensive city."

It was getting more expensive all the time, I knew. Every year, more and more people were squeezed out of living in the capital. Even the royal household was subject to scrutiny. Its treasury had been criticized for

spending beyond the yearly Sovereign Grant allotted
to pay for the royal family's expenses.

The driver rounded a turn and stopped at a busy
crosswalk, his cab idling in the sunshine. We watched
the people flooding across the designated zebra crossing. Its helpful instructions—painted on the pavement
in white—instructed pedestrians to LOOK RIGHT or
LOOK LEFT, as was appropriate for those who weren't
used to traffic coming from the "wrong" direction.

I couldn't help imagining all those people returning to snug hotel rooms—rooms they'd providentially
booked *before* tennis, murder, and flower shows had
descended on the capital.

I wouldn't have believed the crowds if I hadn't seen
them for myself—and had the situation confirmed by
a concierge I trusted. Evidently, the championship
tennis tournament—held in a borough southwest of
London—was even more popular than I'd realized.
Combined with the usual tourist crush and the throngs
of people in town for festivals and events like the
RHS Hampton Court Palace Flower Show, London
Town was busy, busy, busy.

I'd tried appealing to Travis for help. My financial
adviser's hands had been tied. Even with his myriad
connections, he hadn't been able to secure a room for
Danny and me. Not on a last-minute basis. Not even
for gobs of Uncle Ross's money.

I'd called my parents, too. While they'd been upset
on my behalf, they'd already sublet their Mayfair flat
for the next few months while they worked in France.
Both experimental archaeologists, they were busy on
a castle-rebuilding project.

I wished I could have seen them while I was in
London.

More than ever, I was aware that life was short. You

never knew when it would be the last time you saw someone you loved.

For Jeremy's relatives, the *very* last time they'd see him would likely be a few days from now. I'd learned from the police—after a few pointed (possibly fool-hardy) questions—that a postmortem exam was required. That was customary in cases of unexpected death. That would take a few days, I'd been told.

All in all, I *didn't* want to return to the guesthouse. I was sensitive enough to be bothered by sleeping where Jeremy had drawn his last breath and sensible enough to worry about the killer coming back. But I didn't have a choice. I did hope to see Phoebe, though. I was starting to get concerned about her.

She hadn't been to work, of course. That was understandable. Primrose could function without her for a while. But according to news reports, she hadn't even left the town house. She and Jeremy hadn't had any children. Phoebe might be alone in her grief, I knew, solitarily wandering her huge house.

That fact was what had finally drawn me back. If I were in the guesthouse nearby, I could keep Phoebe company. Just in case being a member of the privileged class was lonelier than I knew.

Yes, I'm a softy. So what? I know better than most that money doesn't solve all problems. Sometimes it creates more.

An exclamation from the black cab driver startled me.

"Oi! What's going on here?" He braked, making me sway.

My daily quota of tabloid papers almost slid off my lap. Their headlines screamed about Jeremy's "TRAGIC MURDER!" so I'd grabbed several. Then I steadied my always-packed wheelie suitcase before it toppled to the floor, taking my duffel bag with it. Those two items were the entirety of my luggage. At least I hadn't had to enlist the help of a burly porter before leaving the guesthouse/scene of the crime. I like traveling light.

With my things secured, I craned my neck to see outside the cab's expansive windows. We'd arrived in Chelsea, in Phoebe's exclusive neighborhood. Unlike the other evening, though, the area was anything but peaceful or glowing. Today, groups of distressed people blocked the street. Some of them carried homemade banners; others, posters and pictures of Jeremy. A middle-aged woman near the cab held a tall, unlit candle. Her daughter clutched a bouquet of flowers. Some people were crying.

Jeremy's fans. I'd never been that attached to a celebrity, so I didn't understand their grief. But their anguish seemed genuine. Their gathering had created as effective an obstruction as any roadworks project would have, too. We were jammed.

"That's all right. Here is fine." I handed the driver enough pounds to pay the fare, along with a chocolate bar. I always travel with them. Thanks to my job, I'm gifted with more samples than I know what to do with. "If you try to get any closer, you might not be able to get out again. Thanks!"

After trading "cheers!" with the driver, I grabbed my stuff and jumped out. Instantly, the sounds of the crowd swamped me.

Public mourning is a curious thing. Jeremy's fans seemed to have been drawn here in the hours since his death. Being with other people who also missed and admired Jeremy probably comforted them. For me, their vigil felt weirdly moving.

Jeremy must have been quite a man to have stirred such a reaction, I couldn't help thinking as I weaved my way through the bereaved fans. There must have been more to him than I'd realized during our three-minute, nice-to-meet-you conversation.

Spurred by that realization, I wanted to find his killer. Not just so that Phoebe and his family could find some peace. Not only so that I wouldn't be under suspicion anymore. But just because, in that moment and in that place, it felt right.

"Eh! Get off! Get away from my garden!" someone yelled.

I swerved to see what was going on. I'd followed the private alley path, just as I'd done on the night of Jeremy's death. Now, from my vantage point near the Wrights' garden gate, I glimpsed an elderly man, clad in neatly pressed trousers, a button-down shirt, and an argyle cardigan, wielding . . . a rake?

He swatted at some reporters with it. *Paparazzi.* Ugh.

They laughed and took photos. A few filmed videos, too.

"*Leave,* I say!" the man yelled. "This is private property!"

He was getting nowhere fast. I hurried forward, hauling my luggage. I plastered on a big smile. "Gramps! Grampsy! Wooo!"

"Eh? What's that?" He peered at me suspiciously.

He didn't recognize my clever plan for what it was.

"I'm so glad I got here in time!" I breathed. "Follow me!"

Then I pushed open the garden gate next to the Wrights' and bustled us both inside, safe from the paparazzi swarm.

Three

For an elderly man in need of assistance, he didn't take kindly to my rescuing him. The moment we got inside the garden, he irritably shook off my helpful arm.

"Who are you?" His suspicious gaze examined my usual working wardrobe—a pair of jeans, a gray T-shirt, comfy Converse sneakers, and a jacket. "Never mind. I can tell by looking at you that we're not related." He gave an imperious sniff. "'Gramps,'" he mimicked. "I've never heard such nonsense."

"You didn't even look at me until I tried 'Grampsy,'" I reminded him, still a little worked up from the hubbub.

He harrumphed. "You 'woooed!'" he said with disdain. "Americans. Always whooping over this, that, and the other."

I was a little surprised he identified me as such, given how muddled my accent was these days. I didn't mind, though.

"We're enthusiastic, that's all." I watched him with concern, half expecting a heart attack. He'd probably been out running some midmorning errands and had been caught in the mêlée coming home. With a rake. I nodded at it. "What's that for?"

"For teaching those buffoons they need to show some respect, that's what." His white hair stood on end. He would have looked comical if he'd seemed the least bit lovable. But he only seemed irascible. "This neighborhood used to be respectable. It used to be orderly. It used to be peaceful and quiet, until *your* boss moved in next door with his monstrous friends and all-night parties. And now this! The press." He flung up his hands. "It's mayhem!"

I felt a glimmer of sympathy. Also, confusion. "My boss?"

I guess he assumed that no one else would be in the alleyway except Jeremy and Phoebe's staff and employees? Or someone staggering home from one of Jeremy's all-nighters?

I definitely wasn't kitted out for a boisterous party.

He hooked his thumb toward the Wrights' house. "All respect to the dead, you understand, but I was utterly fed up with that dreadful man before he turned toes up. Now I'm apoplectic!"

A gob of spittle flew from his mouth to prove it. Gross.

He also waved around his garden rake in a very threatening manner. He looked more than willing to use it to beat someone. Because he'd already used (and misplaced) his metlapil?

Doubtful. Jeremy's next-door neighbor seemed hostile, for sure. But a murderer? Only if he could do the deed via proxy. I wasn't sure he was hearty enough to bludgeon Jeremy to death.

Maybe he could give me some information, though. I stuck out my hand. "I'm Hayden Mundy Moore. Pleased to meet you."

He ignored my offer of a handshake in favor of shooting death glares at my wheelie suitcase and duffel bag, both of which were temporarily parked near his garden wall. "Don't get comfortable," he grumped. "Your kind never last around here."

I felt affronted on my own behalf. "I don't—"

Work for Jeremy, I was about to say. But he cut me off. He glared beyond his brick garden wall toward the Wrights' yard as though hoping to make it burst into flames.

"You can tell them next door that if things don't change soon, I'll sue. Nobody pushes around Ellis Barclay. There'll be consequences. I've lived here more than forty years!"

"I'm sure this madness won't last," I soothed. I needed allies. I wanted to make friends with him. My only source of intel couldn't be the chatty bakers at Primrose. Plus, if the killer came back, I might need crabby old Mr. Barclay from next door to rush to my rescue with his rake. "As soon as everyone has mourned Jeremy's death, things will be back to normal."

Another skeptical grunt. "They'd better be."

"I'm sure they will be." They had to be. Right?

Sure, the tabloid press was interested in Jeremy's story now. But that fervor would naturally subside once he was buried.

Guiltily, I tucked my free papers more securely under my elbow. Yes, I was adding fuel to the fire by reading them. But I had good reason to follow the story. It wasn't as though I was the only one, either. Jeremy's death seemed to have brought renewed interest to the tabloids. They'd long been a fixture on the Underground (for instance), but lately commuters had shunned papers in favor of using their cell phones. I wouldn't have been surprised if tabloid circulation had plummeted in recent years.

The papers were probably delighted by Jeremy's untimely death. Covering all the lurid details would boost readership.

Mr. Barclay gave me a suspicious look. "You're not like the last girl. She was a mousy little twat. Always scurrying in and out of here, making sure things went smoothly for *him*."

I didn't appreciate his offensive language. Or his rampant sexism. But I bit my tongue. I wasn't here to enlighten an elderly gentleman about modern times. I didn't have to ask who he was referring to. "Was Jeremy difficult to work for?"

He sniffed. "Everything about that man was difficult. He didn't belong here. We all knew it. Something had to be done."

So you . . . bludgeoned him to death? "Something . . . ?" I led him.

"Yes. Something." Mr. Barclay rolled his eyes in evident exasperation. "Legal action, perhaps. Or a community meeting." He narrowed his eyes. "What are you, thickheaded? You won't last any longer than the other girls. Not that you'll need to."

Now, lay unspoken between us. We both knew it.

He thought I was a (now) unemployed assistant. I thought he might be an unrepentant murderer. We were at a standstill.

I was curious to learn that Jeremy had cycled through multiple assistants, though. I wondered what that was about.

Beyond us both, the media stakeout continued. I heard journalists talking into their cell phones. Smelled cigarette smoke and takeaway coffee—maybe even from Primrose. The nerve.

"Is there another way to the Wrights'?" I asked.

"Only through the front door, and that's far worse. I couldn't even collect my copy of the *Daily Mail* this morning."

I wasn't surprised he read that notoriously scandal-mongering paper. "Well, that *would* kick off a bad mood, wouldn't it?" I asked sunnily, still trying to win him over.

"Bad mood?" He clenched his rake. "What bad mood?"

Uh-oh. I decided tomorrow would be soon enough to make nice. "I'm sorry to have disturbed you, Mr. Barclay. You have a nice day, all right? I hope to see you again sometime soon."

Maybe without your rake next time.

He grumbled and watched me leave. I wrangled my suitcases.

"You'll leave that house in tears!" Ellis Barclay shouted as I closed the gate behind me. "Same as the last girl did!"

Last girl. I hadn't met Jeremy's assistant, but I felt sorry for her already, if she routinely left work bawling.

Feeling grateful not to be working for Jeremy—or living next door to Mr. Barclay on a permanent basis—I weaved my way between the tabloid journalists outside, then opened the Wrights' familiar guesthouse gate. Just as I stepped onto the tidy graveled path wending through the grass, though, I heard something crash. Then, a woman wailed. *Phoebe.* Oh no.

It took me maybe twelve seconds to abandon my luggage on the walkway and sprint across the garden to the terrace. Through the white-painted French doors leading from it into the Wrights' expansive town house, I glimpsed Phoebe in the kitchen.

At least she was still standing. Thank God. I knocked. She started. Her pale face flashed toward mine.

I couldn't help blanching. She looked terrible. Her eyes were red-rimmed, her cheeks hollow, her brown hair askew. She'd twirled it into a haphazard updo, but the overall effect was less boho chic and more rat's nest. Ordinarily Phoebe didn't wear much makeup, but ordinarily she didn't need it. Today, her appearance was disquieting. I'd never seen her so unkempt.

Commiseration shot through me. I gave a cheering wave.

During the few moments that Phoebe needed to cross the kitchen and reach the breakfast nook that lay beyond the French doors, I assessed the situation. From where I stood, I glimpsed kitchen implements and groceries strewn about the countertops. I saw Phoebe's jacket and designer purse slung uncaringly over a chair. I saw dirty dishes on the table, dead flowers in a vase on the sideboard, and no sign of anyone there to care for her.

The situation was worse than I'd imagined. Poor Phoebe. I intended to do what I could, so I gave her a bolstering smile as she opened the door. The fragrances of stale perfume and burnt baked goods rolled out to greet me. I did my best not to recoil.

"Phoebe, I'm so sorry." I took a step nearer, studying her face. Her lower lip wobbled. Full of sympathy, I opened my arms. I can't say I wasn't a little surprised when she stepped into my embrace. "I'm so, *so* sorry about Jeremy. This so awful."

"It is, isn't it?" She sniffled. "Oh, Hayden."

Her moan of grief coincided with her full acceptance of my hug. Dropping her upper-crust façade altogether, Phoebe sagged in my arms. She felt like a sparrow, slight and skittish. I was afraid she might snap back into mannerly mode at any second.

I hoped she wouldn't. Understandably, she seemed to need company. I wondered why no one else was there with her. Family? Friends? The timid assistant cranky Mr. Barclay had mentioned?

"I'm here for anything you need," I promised. Her silk shirt felt ridiculously luxe beneath my fingertips. I'm not hard up for money, but I don't tend to spend it on fancy clothes. In my line of work, nice things only get chocolate spattered and ruined. I inhaled, chancing a glance at the disarray beyond her. "Are you making some breakfast? I can do that. Here, let me."

We parted. Glad to have something useful to do, I strode to the peninsula, then surveyed the kitchen. It was spacious, with white quartz countertops, white custom cabinetry, and hardware done in copper. It was obvious that no expense had been spared in outfitting it, from the glossy sealed teak floor underfoot to the professional-caliber appliances. But the farmhouse-style sink overflowed with dirty dishes. The quartz countertops were littered with bowls of batter, baking pans that had been dropped higgledy-piggledy, and ingredients ranging from chocolate chips to sugar.

I eyed three pounds of butter, arranged in a lopsided pyramid beside a carton of double cream, and realized this was no ordinary breakfast. It wasn't even a supercaloric full English breakfast. Phoebe wasn't making herself a fry-up.

She was baking sweets. For a hundred people, it seemed.

She caught my questioning look and gave a sheepish wave. "I'm just working out a few new ideas for the shop, that's all."

I raised my eyebrows. We both knew that Phoebe had neither the inclination nor the training to "work out ideas" in a culinary sense. She wasn't a professional chef. She wasn't an experienced baker. What she was, to put it kindly, was an enthusiastic hobbyist. She'd opened Primrose on a lark, hired talented bakers to work there, and chanced into wild success.

Her shop was both homey and welcoming. It was a place to pick up a loaf of good English wholemeal bread for a picnic and some muffins, besides. Primrose had sold handmade chocolates before anyone else in Chelsea had thought to do the same. The trouble was, the chocolaterie-pâtisserie had been coasting on its reputation for some time now. I suspected that tourists formed the bulk of its business. That was why Phoebe needed me.

Her hobby had hit a roadblock. It was threatening to run off course altogether. Now, with Jeremy gone, I wanted to make sure that Phoebe could count on Primrose to be there for her.

"Aha." I tried to look reassuring about the disarray. Whatever she needed to distract her from her sadness, I figured. "That explains the mess in here. It's creative fire."

It was more than that, though, I saw. On the breakfast nook table were a laptop and a cell phone, a box full of knickknacks, and a travel mug bearing an image of the London Eye. Phoebe was cleaning house, I realized. Had those things belonged to Jeremy?

That seemed doubtful. The London Eye on the travel mug was bright pink, and the cell phone was in a bejeweled case. Hmm.

"It *is* a mess, isn't it?" Phoebe blustered over to the other side of the kitchen as though hoping she could still carry off her baking charade. Her face crumpled, though, as she stood helplessly over a blob of spilled batter on the floor. A broken bowl lay in pieces nearby, explaining the crash—and the wail—I'd heard earlier. "The truth is, I'm supposed to be doing a live baking demonstration on one of those TV chat shows ten days from now, and I'm not the least bit prepared for it, am I?"

"I'm sure they'll postpone," I soothed. "Won't they?"

"I promised to do it ages ago, then what did I do? I forgot all about it, didn't I?" Phoebe wailed again. "Now I'm completely up against it, with no idea how to manage." She broke into raspy tears, then covered her face with her hands. The jeweled rings on her fingers glimmered. "It's all fallen apart, hasn't it? I thought I had so much more time than this."

Her obvious despair moved me. "I know. We all did."

Neither of us were talking about cakes and cookies.

"What am I going to make?" Phoebe stared at her kitchen. "Everything I try falls apart. I'm supposed to be demonstrating traditional British sweets in less than two weeks! I can't even make a simple strawberry Eton mess or Victoria sponge, can I?"

"Those aren't exactly simple dishes to do well," I pointed out, grabbing a nearby tea towel. I crouched to deal with the spill on the floor while Phoebe helpfully moved out of the way. I couldn't expect her to do it. She employed a cleaning service to come in twice a week. She'd probably not even recognize a mop.

There. All done. "Why don't I help you? I can teach you. Then, when the time comes, you can do the demo on TV."

"Would you?" Phoebe gazed at me as if she were mentally outfitting me with a marble pedestal in Trafalgar Square. I was her hero. "That would be brilliant, Hayden! It really would."

"I'm happy to do it," I told her truthfully. Teaching people about chocolate and baking comes naturally to me. Plus, I like a challenge. I gestured at the mess. "If there's anything else I could do, I'd be happy to do that, too, Phoebe. It looks as though you're getting things sorted around here."

Discreetly, I nodded toward the breakfast nook table full of items. If she were cleaning out Jeremy's things already, that would be surprising but not completely unexpected. Everyone dealt with grief in different ways. I'd noticed earlier that Phoebe hadn't been wearing a wedding band among her sparkling jewelry. Maybe she was planning to bury it with her husband?

"Oh, those are Nicola's things. Nicola Mitchell, Jeremy's personal assistant. I can't imagine why they're still here, can you? No one goes anyplace without their phone these days."

Nicola . . . the "girl" who'd left here crying?

"I'll handle returning them." It would give me a chance to ask Jeremy's assistant a few things. "Anything else? Maybe some breakfast that doesn't include three pounds of butter?"

Phoebe actually smiled. Faintly. But still. I felt glad.

"I couldn't eat anything now, could I?" she demurred. "Those vultures outside might catch a glimpse. They've got telephoto lenses, don't they? I'd find myself in the tabloids in an instant, caught in one of those dreadful 'who's gained three stone' articles." She gave an aristocratic shudder of distaste.

Her mention of camera lenses reminded me of the equipment in the guesthouse. I didn't want to be indelicate by discussing mundane details, but I wanted that stuff moved out of there. The more I could do to return the place to normal—with the approval of the police, of course—the better. Policeman George had already cleared my return to the guesthouse. Danny was meeting me there later.

"I'll make sure all the curtains are closed first, then I'll whip up some breakfast and call the cleaner to take care of this mess. Whenever you're ready, we'll start our lessons, too."

Phoebe brightened. "You're a wonder, aren't you, Hayden? You really know how to take charge. I'm so glad I hired you."

"I'm glad, too." For the first time, I thought maybe we could become friends. Speaking of which . . . "Is there anyone else I could call to come stay with you? Your family? Your friends?"

She shook her head, her expression distraught. "No. I don't want them worrying about me, do I? If they see me this way, they'll think the worst. For now, let's just muddle through."

I nodded. They call it a stiff upper lip for a reason, right? I figured British people were made of pretty stern stuff.

"If that's what you want," I agreed. "But if you change your mind, please let me know. I really do want to help."

Conspicuously, Phoebe perked up. I wanted to think it was because I'd arrived to keep her company.

But it was something else entirely. Phoebe had an idea, I learned an instant later.

"Could you make me a proper full English breakfast?" she asked with her eyes alight. "Fried bread, brown sauce, bangers, and all? I might even have some black pudding and mushrooms around here. I really fancy a fry-up. I haven't eaten since—"

She broke off. *Since Jeremy died,* was obviously what she'd been about to say. Tactfully, I nodded. I patted her arm.

"Anyway." Phoebe tossed her head imperiously. I could easily imagine her at boarding school somewhere, taking riding lessons and learning how to curtsy. "Jeremy quit making them for me after he started training and eating 'clean.' He wouldn't so much as touch a fried potato or Primrose's pastries." She gave a moue of distress. "Once you're past thirty, it's all downhill, isn't it? The pounds simply want to pile on, don't they?"

I was already rummaging in the enormous side-by-side refrigerator by then, looking for all the necessary supplies. Eggs, of course. A couple of rashers of back bacon. Sausage. One sad tomato—but that wouldn't matter, since it would be broiled.

Phoebe watched as I worked. She seemed pretty comfortable with her role as spectator. I experienced a flicker of concern about that, now that I'd taken on the role of her baking tutor.

"Do you have any tinned beans?" I asked, searching.

"Of course. Don't we? Somewhere." She gave an airy wave. "Amelja puts away all the groceries. Just don't tell Liam."

Her giggle gave me pause. I wheeled around. "Liam?"

"Liam Taylor. Jeremy's personal trainer." Phoebe gave an eager look at the tinned beans I'd found.

A fry-up isn't my cup of tea—I like the Euro approach to breakfast, with coffee and a slice of baguette or pastry—but Phoebe seemed over the moon at the prospect. "He explicitly forbade all processed foods for Jeremy. No tinned beans. I wonder how he's dealing with—"

She broke off on a sob, her eyes filling with tears.

That was grief for you. Here one minute, gone the next. It was surreal to be discussing routine details when something so monumental as losing a husband had happened. But there we were.

"I'll check on Liam," I volunteered. "Don't you worry."

For a moment, Phoebe sharpened. "I'm not paying you extra. Just your agreed-upon consultation fee. For Primrose, not me. You know that, don't you? If you think this is some sort of—"

"Of course not." I smiled at her. "I only want to help."

A moment passed. Very faintly, I heard the members of the media outside, shouting to the fans who'd gathered. I wondered what Phoebe thought of the world's adoration of Jeremy. Did it comfort her? Did she resent sharing his memory? Or did she have a reaction I couldn't even guess at? After all, I've never been married. I've had three ex-fiancés, but that's it for me.

"In that case, I'll lend you Jeremy's cell phone." Phoebe settled in at the peninsula, arranging her lithe frame onto one of the expensive-looking stools. "You can find whatever you need on that thing. DC Mishra gave it to me, not long after they—"

Processed his body. That's how the detective constable had described the scenario to me. It all sounded so cold-blooded.

Necessary, of course, in light of the circumstances. But I still wished everyone could have been spared the investigation.

"She's very impressive, isn't she?" I interrupted, lapsing into Phoebespeak before I could stop myself. "I don't know where some people get such a sense of authority and command."

"It's called breeding," Phoebe sniffed. "And education."

Her haughty tone stopped us both cold. Evidently realizing (too late) that she wasn't conversing with one of her snobby friends—who would understand "breeding," of course—Phoebe blinked at me. I guessed maybe we weren't destined to be pals, after all. She seemed to view me as the hired help. That's it.

"I'll have a friend staying with me in the guesthouse for a few days." I decided to take advantage of the situation. Even if it didn't show, Phoebe must have felt a modicum of embarrassment to have spoken to me that way. "You don't mind, do you?"

Just as I'd anticipated. A headshake. "Of course not."

And that's how I secured lodgings for myself and for Danny, during Wimbledon, in one of the busiest cities in the world. I'd wondered if Phoebe might object to my having a guest, but now I'd handily leveraged my way out of that delicate situation.

Yay, me. Now all I had to do was catch a killer.

Later that day, with Phoebe's craving for a greasy fry-up temporarily (and deliciously) assuaged, I slipped out to a nearby Italian-style café to meet with Jeremy's assistant. I wanted to return her things, of course—the box of knickknacks, the London Eye mug, the laptop computer, and the cell phone, which

I'd used to ask one of Nicola's friends to have her contact me to make meeting arrangements—but more than that, I wanted to speak with her. I hoped Nicola Mitchell could shed some light on Jeremy. The man. The myth.

"The arsehole!" Nicola blurted, having navigated down the narrow stairs to the café's lower level, where I'd waited with the box and everything else. I'd admired her ability to do so while carrying a tray full of mocha frappé latte, a slice of Limoncello mascarpone cake, a cookie, a cello pack of almond biscotti, and a diminutive shortbread fruit tart. All just for her. "I'm sorry, but he really was insufferable to work for."

She shook her head and forked up an angry mouthful of cake. Tall, angular, and possessed of a headful of curly auburn hair, Nicola was twenty-five at most and not at all mousy. Not now.

"Jeremy Wright was a bully, plain and simple." She glanced at the cafégoers enjoying Milanese hot chocolate and Loacker wafers nearby, then lowered her voice. Her gaze met mine, full of unequivocal certainty. "If Jeremy got his way, he was fine. If he didn't, you'd better run and hide. He was a complete egomaniac!" She rolled her eyes. "Don't even get me started."

"All I said was, 'have you worked for Jeremy long?'"

"I know. I'm sorry. But grrrr!" Nicola stabbed up more cake. I felt sorry for that beleaguered slice. "When he picked me to work for him—just for *him*, I mean, not at the restaurant—"

Aha. She must be a former server. That's how she'd managed to carry that loaded tray with such agility. Most people couldn't do the same. Which didn't explain why nearly everything in a quick-service environment in the U.K. was presented that way. Tea, coffee, cake slices, scones—they all came served on a tray.

It was a uniquely English thing. Just like queuing, a lack of eye contact on the Tube, and enthusiasm for old-world outdoor Christmas markets stocked for the holidays with carnival rides, mulled wine, and music. I'd experienced the latter last year.

"I thought I'd made it. I truly did," Nicola confided. "I was underemployed as it was, with my degree. I didn't want to deal with hungry, demanding customers for years to come."

I nodded, understanding. I've held my share of ordinary jobs all over the world. Before embarking on chocolate whispering, for instance, I'd worked for a while at a café near the Leidseplein in Amsterdam. I understood Nicola's position.

Just as in America, the youth of Europe tend to be underemployed or even unemployed. Economies are tough all over.

"But the joke was on me." Nicola slurped her frappé. "I wound up dealing with hungry, demanding Jeremy instead."

I winced at the force of her irritation. First cranky Mr. Barclay, now irate Nicola Mitchell. Jeremy Wright had definitely rubbed a few people the wrong way. Not everyone would be lining up outside one of Jeremy's restaurants with tears and a candle.

"Well, all successful people tend to be demanding," I said.

"Not like Jeremy." Nicola scowled at her plated cookie, then bit into it. She chewed with relish. "Sure, he *seemed* nice. He played that 'Essex boy makes good' business for all it was worth, too, believe me. He *loved* being England's 'sexy chef.' He loved being asked for autographs whenever he stepped outside."

I thought of the tabloid press assembled outside the Wrights' town house. Jeremy might have loved all the attention.

"What he didn't love was being contradicted. Or being reminded he'd forgotten something. Or being corrected." Nicola shook her head. "That's what ultimately got me sacked. Can you believe it? I had the temerity to point out that Jeremy had made a mistake on the inscription he'd written for a donation to his charity. He completely flew into a rage. I thought he was going to smack me! He was screaming. Red-faced. I ran for my life! That's why I didn't have my phone with me. Or anything else."

Her tone was dramatic. But maybe it was called for.

Nobody liked being fired ("sacked," in U.K. vernacular), especially in such a dramatic way. Apparently, Jeremy had calmed down afterward—at least enough to collect all Nicola's things for her—but they'd obviously never had a chance to reconcile.

"Sounds scary," I said. "Jeremy had a temper, then?"

"It was terrifying! And yes, he did," Nicola divulged, clenching her fork. If Jeremy had suffered multiple tiny stab wounds, I would have thought Nicola could have been the killer. She was definitely carrying a grudge. "Jeremy wasn't as posh as he wanted to seem, despite being married to Phoebe and all. Underneath his swanky clothes and nice hair, he was a brute. You know he grew up on a council estate in East London, right?"

I did. I nodded. If you're not familiar, a "council estate" is what public housing is called in the U.K. It sounds much fancier than it typically is. The upshot was, Jeremy came from a wrong-side-of-the-tracks background . . . and maybe hadn't left all of his more combative instincts behind him. That didn't bother me as much as it might have, though. Danny was very similar.

"That's where Jeremy's charity is based," Nicola informed me as she put down her stabbing fork and unwrapped her biscotti instead. She seemed resentful. Also, in need of a commiserating ear. Fortunately, I have a knack for listening. People tend to open up to me. "It's supposed to help show less fortunate kids that they can make it out of the old neighborhood, too, just the way Jeremy did." She rolled her eyes. "Those dumb kids idolized him. Or maybe they just wanted a shot at one of his restaurant apprenticeships. Those were pretty lucrative."

"An apprenticeship like Hugh's?" I asked, encouraging her. Jeremy and Phoebe had run separate businesses, but they must have collaborated. Plus, Nicola needed to know I was listening.

"That's right." Nicola offered me a biscotto. I demurred. She shrugged and kept eating. It was remarkable that she managed to pack away so many goodies. Unfortunately, she caught me noticing and gave me a defensive look. "I haven't tasted sugar for months. Jeremy had all of us on his 'clean eating' plan."

Aha. The same healthy-eating kick Phoebe had mentioned—the one championed by Jeremy's trainer, Liam Taylor. I doubted we'd get along. His approach to eating would give me nightmares.

"Come by Primrose," I offered. "I'll hook you up."

Nicola laughed, that awkward moment between us forgotten. "I might just do that, if you've managed to improve things already. I heard the baked goods really went downhill at the shop after Jeremy hired away all Phoebe's bakers. But maybe he wanted to get a jump on consolidating their assets for himself before the divorce papers were served. Who knows with him?"

I almost choked on my latte. "*Divorce papers?*"

"You didn't know?" Nicola looked perplexed. "I thought that was why Phoebe needed your help— because Jeremy had poached all the talent on her staff. She was at risk of being exposed as a talentless fraud. They had epic fights about who owned what, who was responsible for what, and whose fault everything was."

"Fights?" I hadn't known about any marital discord. Even the staff at Primrose hadn't gossiped about Phoebe's marriage.

Of course, I didn't know if Nicola was trustworthy or simply bitter—eager to bad-mouth her former boss. I *did* know that I didn't much care for her take on Phoebe. Calling Phoebe Wright a fraud was putting a pretty harsh spin on things.

Wealthy people routinely started boutiques, candy stores, art galleries, and more—businesses that produced an income but were actually hobbies. If you could do the same, wouldn't you?

On the other hand, the staff at Primrose *was* surprisingly green. And they *were* mostly newcomers to the shop. Hmm.

Maybe, just as Phoebe had pretended to be "working out" new recipes, she'd pretended to be "temporarily shorthanded," too. That had been her excuse for needing my troubleshooting skills.

I didn't like the idea that she'd hidden her true problems from me. But then, someone like her would value privacy and propriety, wouldn't she? Her personal life wasn't my business.

"As I said, Jeremy wasn't an easy man to deal with. I'm sure he stole away those bakers out of sheer spite."

Nicola looked me square in the eye. "He was mean, Jeremy was. Before he died, he found time to black-ball me in the industry, just because I corrected one little typo. Now I'm unemployable."

"But you have other skills," I tried. "Your degree?"

"Didn't get me a job before Jeremy and can't now, either."

"Can you bake?" I hoped to cheer her up. "I'll hire you."

"Thanks, but I need to think about my next move more carefully this time. I jumped into that job with Jeremy, and that was a disaster, to say the least." Nicola shifted her gaze to the tabloid paper lying beside my latte. She gave me a semi-smile. "You're lucky you never knew him, Hayden. I certainly wish I never had. We're all better off now that Jeremy is gone." Then she thanked me for bringing her things, took them upstairs with her, and left me behind with more questions than answers . . . and more food for thought than I'd counted on getting.

Also, a major appetite for cake. I ventured to the café's counter and bought a wedge of triple-layered mocha, then savored that slice while considering my suspects. So far, no one stood out. But maybe meeting Liam Taylor would change that.

Four

I couldn't get away to meet Jeremy's trainer. I was called back to Primrose instead, to troubleshoot a batch of failed brownies. Those are the breaks of chocolate whispering, though.

When I arrived, the shop was nearly devoid of customers but chockablock with the dizzying fragrances of chocolate, butter, and sugar. Also, a faint undercurrent of burnt brownies. Uh-oh.

It hadn't been a false alarm, then. I'd hoped that my high standards might have affected the staff's assessment of the situation, leading them to call me to deal with a minimally flawed batch of crumbly or overly moist sweets. I guessed not.

I stepped past a mother with a portable pram and a businessman with a copy of the *Financial Times* tucked under his suited elbow. I spied a customer with a tabloid paper, too.

The press's take was that Jeremy Wright had been murdered (IN COLD BLOOD! the headlines hollered) by any number of suspects. An angry employee. A deranged fan. A jilted would-be lover. One "source" even envisioned a secret plot by MI6. (Now known as "SIS," the British Secret Intelligence Service, by the way. James Bond movies had been altered forever, it turned out.)

The tabloid press definitely stood to gain from an event like Jeremy's suspicious death. After all, nothing stoked the public's prurient interest as much as a celebrity's untimely death did. The free papers given away on street corners would benefit from increased ad sales—sales that would buy them another year or two of operations, despite the encroachment of Wi-Fi on the Underground luring away their (former) readers to cell phone games and texting. The legitimate press would benefit from runaway sales, period. Even TV broadcasts were going crazy.

For all kinds of media, Jeremy's demise was a win-win.

That macabre situation brought up more than a few ghoulish questions. Could someone in the press have been desperate enough—or motivated enough— to have engineered Jeremy's murder, I wondered? Or, given Jeremy's supposedly legendary temper, to have actually bludgeoned him to death themselves? I doubted it.

But seeing those tabloid papers at Primrose, I couldn't discount the possibility altogether. The next time I returned to the Wrights' guesthouse, I needed to talk to a journalist.

In the back of the house—where the shop's kitchens, work space, ovens, walk-in refrigerator and freezer, and office were all shoehorned into far too little space— the bakers all made room for me. I grabbed an apron and pulled it over my head.

The full sheet pan of brownies in front of me was . . . abysmal. The brownies smelled nicely chocolaty, so that was a plus. But they lacked the glossy, crackly surface that all good brownies should have. When I cut one, it mushed to bits, too soft to hold together. When I sniffed it, I detected hints of charred sugar.

That might not have been all bad. Technically, caramel is burnt sugar—expertly burnt sugar—mixed with cream and butter. But these brownies had not been expertly made. Not in the least.

The assembled bakers shifted, staring hopefully at me. I couldn't bear to disappoint them. That was no way to teach.

"Not bad," I told them with an encouraging smile. "Ten minutes less baking time, a slightly heavier hand with the flour, and more time spent whisking the eggs with the sugar, and you'd have a wonderful fudgy brownie here." I tasted a crumb. "The chocolate must have burned in the bain-marie." That was the first step—melting at least two kinds of chocolate together with butter in a bowl set over simmering (never boiling!) water. I rolled up my sleeves. "Let's try again. Together this time."

Hugh Menadue hesitated beside me, tall and broad-shouldered in chef's whites. He'd tied a bandanna on his head. "Don't see the point, me." He frowned. "We're all bloody doomed anyway."

"No, we're not!" disagreed the petite, plump baker beside him. No longer an apprentice, Myra had been through the fire. Her grit and experience showed. "Phoebe will set things right."

There was a general murmur of agreement over that. Except for Hugh, who was the newest apprentice, they all seemed to have the opinion that Phoebe would be able to right the ship.

Largely, I figured, with my chocolate-whispering help.

"It's a matter of time. You're all a bunch of blind

idiots, if you can't see that." Hugh's sinewy muscles flexed beneath the rolled-up sleeves of his whites, showing off multiple tattoos. Beneath his bandanna, he had wild hair and a pierced eyebrow. In his combat boots, he carried a knife. I'd seen it when he'd hoisted some trash. "I never should have come here."

He whipped off his apron, untying it with nimble fingers. He hurled it away. His knuckles bore multiple tattoos, too.

On a stream of swearing, Hugh stomped toward the back door.

Myra nudged me. "Shouldn't we go after him?"

"Nope." Hugh needed time to cool off—time to regain hope that his apprenticeship would work out. "He'll be back."

Everyone looked dubious, but I was certain. I've known people like Hugh Menadue—proud, hot-headed, and impervious to the dangers of fire, knives, and 115-degree heat—for years now. He was born to work in the restaurant business. He was family now.

We all were. That was my rule. When consulting, my first order of business was diagnosing interpersonal problems in any given environment and dealing with them. Only after that did I tackle brittle cookies, failed viennoiserie, or fallen gâteaux.

With Hugh momentarily left to his own devices—and, most likely, the comforts of a cigarette in the alleyway—I set about assigning tasks. One baker chopped chocolate with a sharp chef's knife, turning it from a solid block to uniform tiny shards. Another cracked room-temperature eggs, kept that way so they'd blend uniformly with the batter and not "curdle" it—basically, overchill the butter in the mix, and make it harden into small lumps. Another sifted flour. A fourth added hot coffee to cocoa powder, melting the cocoa butter trapped within those particles and enabling them to meld smoothly with the brownie batter.

That's a trick you might not have heard of. Although it seems efficient (and obvious) to combine dry cocoa powder with flour, it's almost always better to mix it with a liquid first. Otherwise, you're leaving flavor untapped. Just take one whiff of the resulting slurry—as I did then—and you'll be a convert.

As the (lackadaisical) business went on in Primrose's front of house, we went on with our (umpteenth) brownie lesson in the back. I might have despaired of ever teaching the beginner staff the best ways to grind almonds for macarons or beat eggs for genoise, but their mistakes were the best way to learn.

I can tell you twenty times not to overbeat the sugar and butter for chocolate chip cookies, to substitute part bread flour for cakier results, to add more salt than you think you need, to chill the dough before baking, and not to reuse a sheet pan before it's cool . . . on and on and on. But until you've spent forty-five minutes laboriously mixing chocolate chip cookie dough—only to scoop it, bake it, and wind up with a lavalike spread of greasy, flat, sadness-inducing cookies—you just won't get it.

While the resulting (refined) brownies baked, I got busy checking with Primrose's resident chocolatier. To my relief, the department that handled truffles, fudge, and handmade bars full of cacao nibs, nuts, and dried fruit was doing just fine. Evidently, Phoebe had lucked into someone skilled to handle her confectionary—that, or Jeremy hadn't been interested in stealing away the person responsible for ganache and molded candy.

I helped to troubleshoot a batch of chocolate-cream filling that was destined for chocolate and vanilla trifles, making sure it contained the correct balance of dark and semi-sweet chocolate. I tasted a fresh sample of pain au chocolat and pronounced it acceptable. I oversaw the production of loaf cakes studded with chocolate and frosted with spicy ginger icing.

All the while, I listened. Carefully. There was no mention of marital disharmony between Phoebe and Jeremy. In fact, several employees asked me how Phoebe was getting on. Their concern for her well-being seemed genuine. I was touched.

Hugh lumbered inside, smelling of tobacco but full of newfound equanimity. I knew it would be better not to dwell on his earlier outburst. Men like Hugh—proud, bellicose, and new to the task at hand—needed space to thrive. I was happy to give it.

"I can handle that." Hugh nodded at the Breton-style sea salt caramels I'd been wrapping. His gaze was forthright, his hands reddened by recent washing. He angled his shoulder toward the other side of the chocolaterie-pâtisserie's kitchen. "You'll be wanting to check on Poppy's buttercream, anyway."

His approach was an invitation for us to start fresh. I recognized that. With Hugh, a lot of things remained unspoken.

He caught my eye and grinned. "I'm serious," he nudged. "It's a disaster situation of sugar and egg whites over there."

I laughed and nodded. "Good eye. Thanks for the tip."

Although Hugh was new at Primrose—brought to the shop via Jeremy's charity program—he had all he needed to succeed: good instincts and a willingness to learn. Despite his inherent cynicism, I knew he could succeed. Anything else was a bonus.

Almost two hours later, I'd successfully reset the kitchen. The bakers were turning out the last orders of the day, filling the rolling metal baker's racks with confections and baked goods to sell to the after-school students, post-yoga mums, and stockbrokers from The City who needed "homemade" tarts for dinner parties. Their wives, who generally didn't work in the Square Mile, wouldn't mind the subterfuge. Happy wife, happy life.

Speaking of which . . . with Phoebe away from Primrose, I was free to do a little well-intentioned snooping. I needed to know if the divorce rumors Nicola Mitchell had mentioned were valid.

Whipping off my (now chocolate-smeared) apron, I exhaled a satisfied breath and ducked around the corner. Phoebe's office was tiny, hopelessly cluttered, and (blessedly) deserted. With the place to myself, I examined the computer and bulletin board, the calendar and filing cabinet, the desktop diary ("planner," to you and me), and the cardigan Phoebe had left hanging on the coatrack. Her perfume clung to it. Reminded of her, I hesitated.

Was prying in here really the right thing to do?

Even DC Mishra and the police hadn't come to Primrose.

The clatter of baking pans in the kitchen made me jump and decided the issue for me. I might not have this chance again. I had to act. For myself. For Jeremy. He deserved justice.

I grabbed the cardigan. My fingertips encountered ultrasoft cashmere in a suitably Londonesque shade of inky blue, with a discreet sewn-in label denoting the garment's bespoke origins and a crackle in one of the pockets. I withdrew a paper scrap.

I expected . . . well, I'm not sure what I expected to find, actually. A receipt for a marriage-ending extravagance, maybe. A matchbook with a lover's phone number. A top secret recipe.

Instead, it was a Crazy-for-Coconut Vitality Bar wrapper.

That's all it was. One of those "power snacks" targeted at women. An engineered pseudo-food that used empowerment buzzwords to sell precisely 150 calories of "energy" and "indulgence."

I frowned at it with antipathy, reminded of Phoebe's fear of being caught eating breakfast on camera. Obviously, keeping her willowy figure wasn't easy for her. Was it for anyone?

I started to replace the wrapper where I'd found it, not wanting Phoebe to realize that anyone had uncovered her secret stash. Then I did a double take as I recognized the wrapper's logo. Hambleton & Hart. The same company whose ready-to-bake products had littered the guesthouse's kitchen counters.

Someone from Hambleton & Hart was supposed to have given a statement at the London Metropolitan Police department, I recalled. Neither George nor DC Mishra had clued me in to the results. Nor were they likely to. I'd assumed Jeremy had been filming one of his TV cooking shows in the guesthouse, given the A/V equipment that was (still) on hand. Had he incorporated "molten chocolate-flavored dessert delight" and "strawberry surprise" into his latest (inevitably successful) venture?

I made a note to look into it. I wasn't sure how I'd gain access to Hambleton & Hart, but I was a food professional, wasn't I? I didn't usually seek out clients, but maybe I could get an appointment to discuss chocolate whispering on the company's behalf . . . *if* they used any genuine chocolate, that was.

Wondering if Phoebe's "vitality bar" counted as

evidence that I ought to report, I studied it. Then I shook my head and replaced the wrapper where I'd discovered it. Satya Mishra would be unlikely to consider Phoebe's snack attack relevant to her investigation. But that didn't mean *I* shouldn't speak to someone at Hambleton & Hart about their work with Jeremy. At the least, I might be able to find out where that metlapil came from.

With that decided, I took one final look around. I'd have to enlist Travis to have a comprehensive look into Phoebe's finances. But even if I didn't get another opportunity to scrutinize the office, I'd done a thorough job of inspecting the place. I'd done my due diligence. I'd found nothing. No evidence of divorce papers. No suggestion of anything underhanded or even vaguely questionable. Nothing at all to do with Jeremy.

Nothing that would motivate a murder, certainly.

I guessed Nicola had been deliberately stirring the pot, doing her utmost to smear Jeremy. Exactly the way, she'd said, that he'd slandered her. But now I doubted that I could trust Nicola, no matter how unfairly ill-treated she'd seemed to be.

I'd felt sorry for Nicola earlier. But, going forward, I needed to remain skeptical, I reminded myself. When dealing with suspects, I needed to stay detached. Wary. In San Francisco and in Portland, I'd (almost) taken too long to identify who was responsible for all the wrongdoing. This time, I didn't intend to make the same mistake. This time, I planned to remain deeply suspicious of *everyone* in Jeremy's life, no matter how innocent they might seem. To me, no one could be above suspicion.

If Jeremy had a sweet, loving, gray-haired old granny

who knit scarves for the less fortunate, she was on my suspect list.

Danny and Travis constantly insist that I'm too nice—too inclined to always think the best of everyone. I knew they were exaggerating the situation. All the same, I couldn't let my (potential) blind spot trip me up. I had to be smarter. I had to stay alert to possible subterfuge—which seemed likely to be what Jeremy's assistant had employed at the café today.

In hindsight, Nicola had obviously had other motivations to meet me than simply retrieving her things. She'd also wanted to instill doubt about Jeremy's character and his marriage. Because she'd wanted her boss dead? Because she'd wanted him for herself and had been spurned? Because she'd disliked Phoebe for some reason—maybe resented her privileged status— and wanted to implicate her? Maybe Nicola was the one who'd sneaked into the guesthouse and bludgeoned Jeremy to death with that metlapil, and she'd needed a scapegoat (like Phoebe) for her crime.

I shook my head at the supposition. I didn't think so.

For one thing, Nicola would have had a hard time hoisting that metlapil effectively, much less fighting off Jeremy's inevitable defense. For another, despite my mostly favorable impressions of her, I'd only ever heard Nicola described as "mousy." That hardly made her sound like a cold-blooded killer.

On the other hand, even the mousiest person could be pushed too far. Couldn't they? I sighed, knowing it was still possible I was barking up the wrong tree. Had Jeremy's murderer known him at all? It might still have been a random, anonymous killer.

Maybe I ought to leave the investigation up to DC Mishra, I debated as I pulled my cell phone from my bag. After all, the detective constable hadn't called me back in. Maybe she told all her witnesses not to leave town, as a matter of course. Maybe I didn't need to worry about winding up in a British prison.

I didn't know. But I did know I was supposed to have checked in with Danny by now. I wanted him nearby, for protection and (frankly) for comfort. For a sounding board, too.

My quick-thinking, longtime pal was invaluable for that. But we'd decided it would be too weird if my on-call bodyguard shadowed me during my chocolate-whisperer duties. That was a distraction no one needed—not while the bakers were still baffled by buttercream and confused by chocolate chip cookies.

Listening to the distant drone of the gigantic standing mixer as it mixed a batch of pillowy Swiss-style icing at that moment, I dialed. Trying to look as though I hadn't just been riffling through Phoebe's office on purpose, I wandered toward Primrose's storeroom, where the shop kept stacked bags of flour.

I sat on one of the piles, those fifty-pound bags easily supporting my weight. They were dusted powdery white and wouldn't do my jeans any favors, but those were the breaks. I'm fastidious with work but not too concerned with fashion. I did like Phoebe's cardigan, though. With London's sometimes drizzly weather to contend with, an extra layer was definitely needed.

I wished I'd found something more incriminating in that pocket. A receipt for a metlapil bearing Phoebe's credit card number, perhaps. Or a "how to cudgel your husband" manual.

I couldn't afford to be naïve about my consultee. I knew that. But it was still difficult to think of Phoebe as a killer. The most horrific crime she seemed capable of was unrepentant snobbishness. Besides, Phoebe had an alibi: her party. George had already let slip to me that they'd confirmed her presence at some la-di-da private soirée near Westminster that night.

Danny didn't pick up. Uneasy, I disconnected my call.

Had my best (platonic) friend arrived at the murder scene and become a victim himself? There *was* a killer on the loose. Danny had been planning to "secure" the guesthouse (whatever that meant) before I joined him there. In a former life, he would have been casing the place for a burglary. But those bad old days were behind him. Now he only used his powers for good.

I took advantage of my relative solitude to write myself some investigatory notes in my trusty, omnipresent Moleskine notebook. It was something I wished I'd done more of in San Francisco and Portland. I guessed the third time was the charm, because I actually managed to put down some cogent observations and theories while sitting on the flour-sack piles with the reassuringly familiar hum of restaurant work going on nearby.

With that done, I put away my notebook and pencil. Yes, paper and lead, nothing fancier. While my friends encouraged me to use a more modern, technologically savvy means of making my to-do lists (and sometimes suspect lists), I knew better. It wouldn't do to run out of batteries or encounter a malfunction while globe-trotting. There aren't a lot of power outlets on the road to Machu Picchu. Internet reception isn't as reliable on a cacao plantation in Madagascar as it is in downtown Los Angeles.

I'm happy to stick with something I can count on. Like Danny. Usually. Where *was* he?

Irked, I texted him an exclamation point. Just that.

It was our own private emergency code, designed to bring him running.

I knew I shouldn't have been the girl who cried wolf, but rules were made to be broken, right? Besides, I'd just uncovered a serious flaw in our alert system. How was *I* supposed to know if *Danny* was okay? Short of tagging him with a secret GPS tracking device—which he'd probably find, laugh at, and crush beneath his big-booted foot anyway—I didn't have many options.

I slung my crossbody bag over my shoulder, brushed the worst of the flour from my backside, then said good-bye to the staff. Everything at Primrose was under control. That meant I had a few hours to myself. I needed to spend them investigating.

I stepped outside the chocolaterie-pâtisserie with my phone to my ear, breathing in the assembled scents of sugary goodness, damp pavement, and faraway exhaust. A double-decker Routemaster chugged past me, vibrant in iconic Bus Red. A nearby square beckoned with green grass and trees. Shops lined the street, full of chichi merchandise geared to the upscale neighborhood and bearing centuries-old frontages that had been meticulously maintained. There weren't any other bakeries or confectioners in the area, but there were those corner pubs and some cute cafés.

I pondered stopping in some of them to study Primrose's competition. I was, after all, still responsible for seeing the shop succeed. But then my call connected. I stopped to listen.

Liam Taylor's voice-mail message rumbled into my

ear, nearly as full of depth and sex appeal as Travis's out-of-office dispatch. I seldom heard the latter. My financial adviser rarely quit working. Maybe he'd only turned on voice mail the one time, purposely to titillate me. If so, it had definitely worked.

I may or may not have called in three or four more times.

"I'm out training another client right now," Liam's message continued, full of rounded British vowels and certainty. "But leave a message, and I'll get back to you with the best way to—"

. . . *kick sugar, gluten, and fun out of your life,* I imagined but didn't technically hear. That's because I suddenly found myself gripping empty air. Someone had snatched away my phone.

A mugger? London was home to a few of them, of course.

I inhaled hard, ready to unleash my patented antimugger maneuver. It was physical, fast, and (almost) foolproof. I'd learned it in Barcelona. If I haven't mentioned it before, I make all kinds of friends while I'm traveling. Spanish, French, and Italian men seem to be especially concerned with making sure I know how to handle myself. Partly thanks to them, I could.

Scarcely thinking, I whirled. There was a man close to me. *Too close.* I aimed a sturdy kick at the side of his kneecap. It would at least momentarily incapacitate him, long enough for me to grab my cell phone. Not that I recommend attacking someone for a mere possession. I don't. But I couldn't help acting.

To my amazement, the man stepped out of range. I looked up.

Danny towered above me, looking irate. "Hey. Watch it."

I smacked him on the shoulder. "Where have you been?"

Secretly, I was flooded with relief at finding him safe. Officially, I was panicked that he'd been off-line for so long.

"Shadowing you, dummy." His affectionate gaze meandered over me. Maybe a bit too lingeringly. "What's the emergency?"

His scowl returned. Passersby caught sight of it and purposely detoured around us both. Even while not annoyed over a false-alarm summons, Danny tends to be menacing. He's taller than most men, full of (well-deserved) swagger, and willing to throw down at the merest provocation. Remember how I said Hugh Menadue was bellicose? Danny Jamieson is like twenty Hughs.

With me, he's a teddy bear. Mostly. With other people?

Let's just say Danny never backs down from a fight. Not of any kind. He fought to go back to school and earn two college degrees. He fought to establish his own personal security firm. He fought to be put on my payroll as beefcake on call—a decision he was probably regretting just then, by the looks of him.

I couldn't help gawking, though. With pleasure, not fear. Danny is gorgeous, muscular, and devoid of the kind of ego that typically destroys the positives in those two attributes. He loves birthday parties and *Antiques Roadshow,* dive bars and fast cars, hanging out with me and pestering "Harvard."

He didn't have any reason to go toe-to-toe with Travis. I think he just enjoyed skirmishing. Travis was the same way.

Danny caught my affectionate look and deepened his scowl.

What's the emergency? reverberated between us. Whoops.

I went on the offensive. "You were supposed to pick up all my calls," I reminded him. "You were supposed to guard me!"

"I was. I am." He crossed his beefy arms. "I always will."

Okay. Before you start imagining some dreamy bodyguard-meets-chocolate whisperer scenario here, let me set you straight. Danny and I are friends. That's it. Yes, he sometimes spouts mushy stuff like *I always will,* but he's all business.

"You were guarding me how, from a pub? With a pint in hand? Come on, Danny," I shot back, undaunted. "I was on the lookout for you all day." He was hard to miss. "I never saw you."

He smiled. Fearsomely. "I'd make a pretty bad tail if you saw me, now wouldn't I?" He handed back my phone. "Liam Taylor is at The Green Park right now, making a client do a million burpees. That's why he didn't answer your call. Try later."

"I don't see how you could possibly know that."

"Yet I do. You're not the only one with skills. And that's the way we both like it, isn't it? *Mysterious.*" Teasingly, Danny waggled his eyebrows. I laughed. He sighed, then got serious. His gaze probed mine. "You're okay? No emergency?"

"Nothing your being here can't solve. How about a drink?"

"Best idea you've had all day," he said. "Come on."

Maybe, I decided, I could find out about Jeremy in the pub.

Five

I wasn't the only one who had the bright idea of finding out about Jeremy in the dark, oak-paneled, decorated-with-soccer-banners pub that I scouted for us around a corner and down an alleyway. No sooner had the publican served us our bitters—a whole pint for Danny, a half for me—than he went right back to the conversation he'd been having. About Jeremy Wright.

It took a few seconds for that reality to filter in, though. The pub was noisy, filled with rough-and-tumble builders ("construction workers," to us Americans) there for an after-work pint. One of them delivered a fresh round to his mates. In return, he was greeted with hearty cheers and manly laughter.

Danny locked eyes with him. The builder looked away first. Apparently satisfied, Danny raised his glass to me. "Kanapai!"

It meant (roughly) "cheers!" in Japanese—something you might hear in an *izakaya*, the Japanese equivalent of a pub. I recognized it. I was the one who'd taught it to Danny. But I wasn't sidetracked. I returned his toast and duly took a sip.

Then I nodded at the builder. "What was that all about?"

"Nothing." Danny rotated his shoulder, then took a big slurp of his pint. Our bitters looked dark and tasted darker.

"Come on, Danny. I know something was going on just now."

He relented. "That guy was eyeing you. That's all."

I almost burst out laughing. "So what? Maybe I like him."

Danny's knowing, lopsided grin said he doubted it. "Maybe."

Anyone else would have thought Danny was jealous. I knew better. Defiantly, I sneaked a glance at the bloke in question, intending to prove my point. He was short and stout, clad in grimy work clothes and steel-toed boots. He looked rough, like the kind of guy Jeremy would have become if he'd stayed in his East London neighborhood. Jeremy was . . . lucky he'd gotten out.

I probably shouldn't have thought so. Especially given the unfair advantages Jeremy had enjoyed since marrying Phoebe and finding culinary success. But I couldn't help it. The builder, as he sauntered over for his turn at the dartboard, had the same cockiness, the same virility, and the same accent Jeremy had had. Not the stereotypical British accent Americans thought of—the cultured, short-voweled, clipped-consonant dialect heard on *Downton Abbey*—but something earthier. Realer. Happier.

I liked it. But I didn't fancy that builder. Danny was right. Not that I intended to admit as much. Fortunately, that was the moment I caught wind of the conversation going on between the pub's barman and the woman standing a few feet away.

"Did you ever see him with this guy?" She turned her cell phone's screen toward the barman. "Were they here together?"

Impatiently, the barman spread his palms on the scarred wooden bar, his face a study of creases and bushy gray eyebrow hairs. He frowned and shook his head. "Don't think so."

"But he *did* meet people in here," she nudged. "Women?"

I pegged her as a journalist. Medium height, midtwenties, possessed of a dark bob and all-black clothes. She was probably from the East Coast, maybe New York. She'd bought a gauzy scarf since coming to London, but its exactingly tied folds marked her as an outsider as clearly as did her insistence on grilling the reluctant barman. A Londoner would have thrown on that scarf with a lot more insouciance. A Londoner would have known, too, that most publicans don't respond well to being interrogated.

I leaned nearer. "Maybe I can help," I suggested to her, indicating her cell phone picture. "I'm Hayden Mundy Moore."

"Oh, thanks." She smiled. "Are you from around here?"

I gave a careless wave, blessing my travels for the jumbled accent they'd given me. Maybe Mr. Barclay had pegged me for a gauche American, but she hadn't. I gestured. "Let's see that."

She hesitated, but not because she was wary. She'd noticed Danny. He had a way of making most women lose their composure.

I could practically feel the charisma rolling off him. When he turned it on, he *really* turned it on. Good thing, too. He must have realized what I was up to and decided to help.

Carelessly, the journalist handed me her phone. I could barely grab it before she edged past me to cozy up to Danny.

"I'm Ashley Fowler. Are you from around here, too?"

Too. She'd definitely bought my loosely contrived cover.

I peered at the phone's screen while Ashley and Danny made small talk. He said he was from L.A. She squealed with delight and announced that she was "so psyched!" to meet an American.

"Nobody ever talks to you here!" Ashley exclaimed. "Forget about a nice little chat over drinks. It's not happening. Plus, they're all so terribly proper, aren't they? Ugh! Ridiculous."

I knew the builders nearby were probably rolling their eyes at her sweeping (and inaccurate) notions of British propriety—not to mention her over-the-top rendition of an English accent. But I was busy examining the photo she'd shown the barman.

The man pictured looked rumpled, awkward, and vaguely clammy. Although he wore a nice suit and tie, his sandy hair was unruly. His cheeks looked ruddy. Overall, he seemed . . . harmless.

That was my overwhelming impression. I didn't recognize him, but I stored away his likeness in my memory, just in case.

"Nope, sorry. I'm afraid I've never seen him before." I handed Ashley her phone while the pub grew noisier around us. We should have had our pints outside. "Who is he? What did he do?"

"Oh, nothing. He's not a criminal or anything, if that's what you mean." She waved blithely, briefly transferring her gaze from Danny to me, then mentioned his name. I'd never heard of him before. "He's part of a story I'm working on."

"Mmm." Lazily, Danny smiled at her. "You're a journalist?"

He made it sound like the most desirable occupation ever. I almost guffawed. But first I (briefly) considered a career in journalism. Hey, I'm only human. It had been a difficult week.

I can't be on guard against Danny's charm 24/7.

"Yeah. I'm assigned to the Jeremy Wright story. I was over here on vacation for a wedding and got called in on it. Just my luck, right?" Ashley rolled her eyes. "I know he was famous and everything, but seriously? All this fuss over one guy?"

I felt slighted on Jeremy's behalf. "He was beloved around the world. Didn't you see all the mourners? All the memorials?"

I'd passed by one of Jeremy's restaurants on the way to Primrose earlier. Its portico had been piled with mementos.

"I guess so." She shrugged and twirled her hair, eyes fixed on Danny's broad shoulders. She licked her lips. "All I know is the British press is rabid about this story. I'm only an intern right now, but if I get a scoop, I can get some real attention. Maybe a permanent position. And a big, fat paycheck, too."

I doubted that's how journalism worked, but what do I know? I melt chocolate for a living. I taste truffles for money.

It's a nice career, but I'm aware it's not rocket science.

"You deserve it, if you're tracking down leads all the way to an out-of-the-way place like this one," I told her.

She brightened. "I know, right? Turns out, Jeremy Wright loved going to skeevy places like this one, though."

As she aimed her chin toward the (doubtless)

antique carved oak bar and its polished brass fittings, she didn't notice one of the customers of that "skeevy place" staring lustfully at her. Danny did. But he didn't leap to her rescue as he had mine.

I knew he would if things got dicey. But until then . . .

"How did you uncover that tidbit?" I asked, wide-eyed.

You've probably already guessed that *disingenuous* is a poor fit for me. But you've got to do what you've got to do, right?

"This pub was in one of his cookbooks," Ashley told us. "I was supposed to be combing them for material—for pictures that hadn't already been seen a million times in other publications—but I knew I could do more. That's why I came down here."

I made a mental note to examine Jeremy's cookbooks myself. It was possible they would yield some clues, either to Jeremy's true nature or to his relationships with the people around him.

"He did this one book about regional British cooking." The reporter flirtatiously stroked Danny's bulging biceps. "It was packed with pictures of dingy, old-timey pubs like this one."

Nearby, the barman frowned. Danny soothed his hurt feelings by buying two more rounds—one for the three of us, and one for the table full of builders. That perked up the publican nicely.

"And one for yourself?" Danny offered in lieu of a tip.

That was Danny for you. Generous to a fault. Especially when it came to the regular working stiffs of the world.

"I could show you some of the pubs sometime." Ashley was snuggling closer to Danny when I checked back in. She gazed up at him expectantly. "I'm planning to hit up all of them for clues. You know, all except the ones really way far away, in, like, Newcastle, or whatever. I don't have an expense account or anything, but I have a feeling you won't mind treating us both?"

Oh, great. Danny's largesse had gotten her more excited.

"The local media pretty much have things locked down around here anyway," Ashley confided with a toss of her sleek bob. She pouted her lipsticked lips. "I've got to be creative to get by. But, you know, I can be very, very creative when motivated."

"I'll bet you can." Danny's voice rumbled under another shout from the dartboard. "I wish I could come with you."

"You can't? Really?" She looked crestfallen. "Why not?"

"I'm booked on another job." He meant me, I knew.

"Is it dangerous?" Ashley breathed, clutching him harder.

He must have told her about his bodyguard-to-the-stars gig. That detail was like catnip for a certain kind of woman.

"I don't think so." Danny shrugged, outlining his pub mat. "So far, it's pretty routine. The risks might be exaggerated."

I frowned, knowing he still meant me. That had probably been a dig at my false alarm earlier. Maybe I deserved it, but . . .

"It sounded dangerous to me," I argued in my own defense. "Really dangerous. People have already gotten"—I broke off, unable to say *killed* without alerting Ashley that we were both investigating the same murder—"seriously hurt."

For the first time, she gave me her full attention. Her pretty face filled with disbelief. "Are you a bodyguard, too?"

Ha. I tried not to spit out my mouthful of bitters. "No."

Unless the bad guys needed an expert opinion about Trinitario cacao beans versus Forastero and Criollo—or a hands-on demonstration of melting chocolate using an ordinary household hair dryer— I wasn't equipped to do the same things Danny did on a regular basis. Detect threats. Disarm threats. Rinse and repeat as needed, all while remaining inscrutable.

Even I couldn't tell if Danny was genuinely interested in Ashley, and I've known Danny for ages. He was just that enigmatic. For better or worse, that quality was part of his appeal. Women seemed to go crazy for Danny's unknowable side.

And his physical side, too. All except me, of course.

Speaking of me, though . . . I was getting antsy. I was pretty sure Ashley wasn't leading us anywhere close to finding Jeremy's killer. Members of the U.K.'s tabloid press were the ones desperately in need of lucrative stories, not journalists in the U.S. If anyone in the media had gotten murderous with Jeremy, I doubted Ashley would know about it. Aside from her seeming lack of experience and insight, if the way she'd been fondling Danny for the past few minutes was any indication, Ashley was right-handed.

The killer, George had said, was probably left-handed.

It looked as though we were back to square one. Even if Ashley Fowler had despised Jeremy more than she hated "skeevy pubs" and a lack of chitchat, she probably wasn't our killer. I doubted she had the wherewithal to discover who was, either.

Silently, I gave Danny our top-secret SOS signal: a barely detectible head scratch. Originally, we'd used it to ditch dates that weren't going well. Lately, we'd been forced to adapt it for more multipurpose use. Our circumstances had changed a lot since the days when we'd trawled SoCal watering holes together.

I wasn't talking about the "circumstances" of my inherited fortune, either. While that's not exactly Danny's favorite subject to deal with—even though it had brought me (wonderfully) into orbit with Travis—it wasn't relevant to the second (ahem) head scratch I delivered.

My longtime buddy caught on. We excused ourselves.

On the way out, I had an idea. I motioned for Danny to wait, then caught the barman's attention. I watched him lumber over with chary eyes and a bar towel thrown over his shoulder.

"I already told your friend everything I'm going to."

I smiled. "I know. Thanks." It was time to play my hunch. "I want to settle up for Jeremy Wright. Somebody has to pay his bar tab, right? All the beer for his parties wasn't cheap."

For a long moment, the barman only glowered at me. I held my ground. If what Mr. Barclay had said before was correct, Jeremy had thrown a lot of wild parties at his town house. His drinks had to have come from someplace. The local (Jeremy's "favorite neighborhood pub" to you and me) seemed a good bet.

Eventually, the barman's head for business won out. He gave me a nod, then went in the back. While a puzzled Danny looked on, I waited. Then I watched the barman return with a notepad.

He licked the tip of a pencil, did some calculations,

then squinted up at me. The figure he announced was mind-boggling.

Let's just say it's a good thing I'm financially secure.

Knowing I'd have to explain this expense to my keeper (aka Travis) later, I handed over my credit card. While the barman processed it, I had another brainstorm. "Who was set to pick up the next order?" I asked while performing the usual ritual with a hand-held POS terminal. "I'm going to need to cancel that."

The barman took back the device. "You're different from the other girl," he observed, chipper now that he'd gotten a big payment. "She was a mousy little thing. Wouldn't say boo."

Hmm. This wasn't the first time I'd been mistaken for Jeremy's personal assistant. It wasn't the first insinuation I'd heard that Nicola Mitchell was timid, either. That opinion was definitely the prevailing one. Yet she'd been plenty forthright with me at the café. That must have been a ruse. Right?

Or maybe it had been a sugar surplus, overloading Nicola's (normally reserved) circuits and making her talk brashly.

I couldn't help wondering . . . which Nicola had Jeremy known?

Before I could defend my own assertiveness, the publican consulted his notepad. "Hugh Menadue," he said. "He usually picked up orders for Jeremy. Good Cornwall lad. He'll be gutted that Jeremy's gone—not just for the extra work, either."

Hugh. I guessed he'd done odd jobs for Jeremy after getting hired at Primrose. Maybe he'd needed the money.

"Is that so?" I leaned on the bar. "They were friendly?"

"Yeah." A nod. "Hugh's a good kid. He's had some hard times. Got done for having sticky fingers at a shop. Asda, I think. Nothing bad. I knew his dad. Used to run a pub himself."

Hmm. He meant Hugh had been in trouble for shoplifting.

We chatted about the business for a few minutes. I learned that the elder Menadue had come to East London from Cornwall to look for work after losing his job. He'd had to go on the dole.

"Proud bunch, though," the barman told me. "Tough, too."

I nodded, having learned more than I expected.

"Jeremy was the same, God rest him. He was a good man." Soberly, the barman picked up something from behind the bar. A heavy glass tankard. He offered it to me, leaving empty the space it had formerly occupied on the bar's shelf—a space marked with a discreet engraved brass nameplate. "You might as well have this, too, I reckon. Maybe take it home to his missus?"

I figured Phoebe would rather jump off Tower Bridge than allow an old-fashioned dimpled pub glass to become part of her décor. But the barman seemed pretty emotional, all of a sudden. So I accepted it anyway, nodding solemnly at his thoughtfulness.

"Thank you," I told him. "I'll take good care of this."

I hadn't known Jeremy well. But as I accepted that personal pub mug of his, I felt something shift inside me. When he'd last used it, he'd probably never dreamed it would be the final time.

I hoped the fact that it had had its own place on the pub's shelf meant that Jeremy had lived his life to the fullest. You never knew how long you had with your family and friends . . . and your regular pubgoers, some of whom kept their own mug on site.

That's how I'd suspected Jeremy had probably kept an open tab. I'd caught sight of that row of mugs, different from the typical conical, tulip-shaped, or nonic glasses Danny and I had gotten, and had wondered if Jeremy Wright had had a designated one.

My intuition had played out. That's because, in the U.K., a corner pub isn't really the same thing as a bar in the U.S. Likening the two does a grave disservice. To its regulars, a pub is more. It's part living room, part sanctuary; part camaraderie and part relaxation. You can do more than drink. You can talk with your friends, play snooker, throw darts—even triumph as part of a weekly quiz team. A pub is a true home away from home.

I had a feeling this place had felt more like home to Jeremy than his fine terraced town house ever could have done.

"Come back anytime," the publican told me. He included Danny in his invitation with a tilt of his chin. We both nodded.

"Nice of you to pay off a dead man's tab." Danny studied me as we stepped outside into the sunshine. "How did you know?"

I explained about the shelf of glasses that were kept behind the bar for regulars. After the dim snugness of the pub, the city streets felt twice as bright and three times as impersonal. I dodged an oncoming pedestrian commuter who was headed for the closest Tube station, then grabbed Danny.

"Come on," I told him. "I've got another errand to run."

My clever distraction technique almost worked.

I nearly diverted Danny before he started grumbling at length about my big payout on Jeremy's pub tab that afternoon. But by the time we'd returned to the guesthouse, my luck had run out.

"Must be nice to dish out that much money without even blinking," Danny remarked in a too-casual tone. "Are you going to get Harvard to expense it? You could get away with it. Investigating murders is practically your part-time job now."

I shuddered at the thought. I didn't want another "job." Especially not one that didn't concern *Schokolade*.

"No, I'm not going to expense it." Paying off Jeremy's bill had been expedient. Now I knew that he *had* thrown wild parties—parties that included regular-Joe beer drinkers, not hoity-toity cocktail or wine sippers—and that Hugh Menadue had been involved in those parties, however tangentially. That was more than I could say for any of the other apprentices or crew at Primrose. "I'm going to move up Hugh on my suspect list, though."

I'd shared with Danny my scheme to be extra suspicious of all my suspects. His hoot of laughter hadn't been encouraging.

"That's a lot of cash to drop for a few hints."

I didn't want to get into it. We both knew I'd lucked into my inheritance, just because Uncle Ross and I had been close. I'd loved my uncle's spirt; he'd loved my energy. I missed him. But it never did any good to dissect the issue with Danny.

"I can afford it," I said, just in case Danny was sincerely worried about my cash flow. We'd arrived at the guesthouse a few minutes ago and were settling in. "Now, about what's next—"

"I don't want to. I'm not going to do it. Not again."

"You always say that." I gave him a sassy grin. "Right

before you cave in. Let's just skip the preliminaries, okay?"

My muscle-bound buddy furrowed his brow. "No means no."

"You'll like it once we get started," I cajoled.

He glanced at me. That meant he was weakening. "Hayden."

I tossed my shoulder-length dark hair. "We both know where this is going. Telling me 'no' doesn't get us anywhere." I grabbed his hand and then pulled it to where I wanted it. "Go ahead," I coaxed. "Don't deny yourself any longer. Let's go."

Danny bit his lip. "I'm serious. This is a bad idea."

"It's a great idea."

"I can't believe you're asking me to do this again."

"I ask you to do this every time. Please. For me?"

He sighed, and I won. "Where do you want me to start?"

I swept my gaze over the . . . accoutrements . . . I'd brought back to the guesthouse with us. They lent an indulgent spark to the place's straitlaced, chintz-and-corgis atmosphere. Some loosening up was needed, especially in the bedroom, where we'd been deciding who got the gigantic four-poster bed (me).

I'd tried to get Danny to take turns. He'd opted out.

Finally, he made his choice. Dubiously, he eyed me.

Feeling breathless with victory, I nodded. "Go on."

He screwed shut his eyes. He took a bite of flapjack.

On a surprised moan, he opened his eyes. "This is good!"

"See?" Triumphantly, I selected my own treat—a "millionaire" shortbread bar layered with chocolate and caramel. It was, I suspected, far better than the granola-bar-style sweet that described a U.K. flapjack (hint: not a pancake). "Yum."

At the same time, we both stopped chewing. We'd gotten these takeaway treats from an assortment of local shops. While they weren't quite artisanal-bakery quality, they were good.

That meant my work at Primrose was cut out for me. Uh-oh.

As though simultaneously sensing as much, Danny put down his nut-and-dried-fruit-studded flapjack. He gave me a sarcastic look. "How about it? Want to talk about Jeremy's bar tab now?"

I didn't. It would only make Danny mad. He resented the gulf that Uncle Ross's money had opened between us, no matter how much I tried to gloss over it. He resented the strings that were attached to my fortune—the strings that kept me on the move for at least several months per year—no matter how much I laughed them off. He didn't understand the same things I did.

Things like . . . Uncle Ross had believed that growth was paramount. That stretching boundaries was crucial. That not getting stuck meant more than not being comfortable. He'd given me a chance, in his will, to live life to the largest. I hadn't had to take it—especially with all the stipulations attached—but I had. I'd done it with my eyes open, too. I was a big girl.

I could handle my finances. Danny, my friend, was trickier.

In simple terms, my eccentric Uncle Ross had made a fortune but had never found a wife or children to share it with. He'd regretted making his work his life. He'd wanted me to live big.

To make sure I would, he'd required in his will that I travel, widely and often. He'd enlisted Travis's firm to make sure I did. In return, I got more money than

I'd ever told Danny about. Enough to keep us both pretty comfy while investigating.

Or while tasting chocolate. Which was what we were doing, in the guesthouse's elegant bedroom, as a means of furthering my chocolate-whispering job. I got back on track. "Cupcake?"

Danny frowned at the delicacy I offered as though it might explode. "Maybe later. You know this is the worst part for me."

That's right. He said it. Tasting cupcakes was torture.

"I don't even like chocolate," he added in an unbelievably long-suffering tone. "You know that. I. Don't. Like. Chocolate."

And that's why Danny and I aren't soul mates. Because I'm a person who lives for a perfectly made mousse or a delicately spun chiffon cake, and he . . . well, he would rather eat pork rinds.

Danny's affinity for the salty/spicy/savory end of the snack spectrum baffled me. Why would anyone eat Sriracha hot wings when chocolate pecan pie existed? Why nosh on nachos when you could go for devil's food layer cake? Why eat jalapeño poppers when you could fire up some melty, marshmallowy, scrumptious s'mores, and really treat yourself?

I've tried to woo over Danny to the dark side for years. Dark chocolate bars, cookie bites, cheesecake, hot-fudge sauce . . . they've all failed. Every time, I die a little bit on the inside.

Okay, just kidding on that last part. But still. I wished Danny could enjoy the same things I enjoy. Isn't that part of friendship? Savoring experiences together?

Thanks to Danny's flawed taste buds (there was no other reasonable explanation), we had to get our friendship groove on in other ways. I wished, just then, that one of those ways was visiting a club I'd heard about near Borough Market. I could have used a night out. But we weren't in London to enjoy ourselves. We were there to solve problems.

Jeremy's murder first among them now.

Phoebe's chocolaty Primrose treats second.

But since I'd done all the chocolate whispering I could for the day, that left only one topic to deal with: Jeremy.

"Okay, fine." I sat up straighter, leaving our assembled "research" treats unfinished. "Let's get down to it, then. Tell me what you found when you 'secured' this place earlier today."

Danny perked up. He likes talking about perimeters, windows, and dead bolts the way I like talking about triple-fudge ice cream and chocolate ganache. "I thought you'd never ask."

Six

The thing I love about London isn't just that it's a bustling, cosmopolitan city full of skyscrapers, historical buildings, and a tremendous variety of people. It's also that it's full of green spaces. It's counterintuitive in a city of almost nine million people, but London is a city with lungs.

It's all thanks to the presence of the city's commons—a combination of squares, royal parks, grassy canalside spaces, riverfront greens along the Thames, and a variety of gardens.

I paced through one of them early the next morning, after having gotten a late-night phone call from Liam Taylor, Jeremy's personal trainer. I'd been surprised to hear from him, given that I hadn't left him a message, but he'd cheerfully explained that.

"Lots of my clients are 'hang-ups' the first time they contact me." Liam had sounded hearty and alert, even given the late hour he'd called. Maybe that's what kicking sugar did for a person. *I'd* never know. "They get nervous and hang up before asking for help. They usually appreciate it when I call them back, though, so I thought you might, too."

I'd been on the verge of asking how he'd gotten my number when it hit me: caller ID on his cellphone. Of course.

"I'm used to it," he'd gone on, sounding burly even over the phone. His voice had been deep. Jocular. Confident. "It's all part of dealing with people who need help. Sometimes I have to goose them along. But there's nothing to be afraid of."

"I hear you. I'm in the 'helping' business myself."

"Well, I'd love to hear more about it, Hayden," Liam had assured me, after I'd divulged a brief cover story about working at Primrose with Phoebe—and hence having been referred to her husband's personal trainer. "And about you and your fitness goals, too. Let's say, six AM? Victoria Esplanade Gardens?"

I'd agreed, which explained how I'd come to be striding past early-morning joggers and people feeding pigeons while the sun had barely peeped over the top of the "Cheesegrater," the tower otherwise known as the Leadenhall Building in The City.

I'm used to keeping unusual hours, though. Professional baking is a predawn activity. It has to be. Nobody wants to think about *how* their favorite morning muffins turn up at breakfast, fresh (not merely thawed) and ready to go, before they head off to work. But if those muffins are any good, there were some dedicated bakers behind the scenes making it happen.

That didn't mean I hadn't grabbed some fortifying coffee first. I'm not crazy. Somewhere behind me, too, was Danny. He'd insisted on tailing me to my meeting with Liam. Again, you might think he was being possessive, given that I was about to get up close and personal with some professional man candy, but that wasn't it. Danny also had been caught flat-footed by the whole *Murder, She Wrote* routine I'd inadvertently fallen into. He'd been a step or two behind, once or twice, during our time at Lemaître Chocolates and at the Cartorama food cart pod. I think my freelance bodyguard wanted to make up for those lapses.

Not that I could tell for sure, of course. The minute we left the Wrights' guesthouse and trundled through the streets of Chelsea toward the Thames Embankment, I lost sight of Danny.

I felt reassured knowing he was there, though. Especially once I caught sight of the gigantic man headed toward me along the winding path. He stood out like a colossus amid the genteel flower beds and green-leafed trees, moving with purpose and a clear sense of vitality—and a frightening frown on his face, too. I almost balked. His expression looked that forbidding.

Then he caught sight of me and grinned. He waved.

The greyhound leashed beside him sensed his mood and picked up the pace, paws clicking along gracefully on the sidewalk.

I melted. I love dogs. Cats, too, although you won't see them obediently being walked through a public garden. I know a greyhound is probably nobody's idea of a particularly endearing pet, but this one looked especially sweet, with big brown eyes and a lolling tongue. Helplessly, I cooed. "Aren't *you* sweet?"

I stopped to let her greet me, tail wagging. At her side, Liam Taylor watched us both with evident pleasure. "Hayden?"

Already in a crouch to make friends with the dog, I nodded. I rose and extended my hand, keeping my cup of takeaway coffee safe in the other. "That's me. You're Liam, right?"

He nodded too. His right hand engulfed mine to

perform the usual handshake ritual. His hand wasn't "usual," though. It was enormous.

Was it wrong that I instantly envisioned it wielding a metlapil? A man the size of Liam could have easily overpowered Jeremy, who, while not exactly small, couldn't begin to compare.

Liam Taylor was, I saw, the size you'd image a bona fide superhero to be. Tall, broad-shouldered, and so tautly muscular that his workout clothes—a pair of track pants and a tank top, with a jacket and sneakers—looked comically skintight in places. Like his bulging biceps. His gigantic thighs. His barrel chest.

Wow. I could scarcely imagine the effort it must have taken him to build a physique like his. I mean, Danny is well built; you already know that. But Liam Taylor was in a class by himself. Literally. Another weight class altogether. He was a walking advertisement for his training methods. I was impressed.

Maybe I should have been alarmed, too. But except for that brief flicker of hostility I'd glimpsed before Liam had noticed me, Jeremy's personal trainer seemed to have a real Mary Poppins disposition, coupled with a scientist's knack for observation.

Was he observing *me* just then? Looking for physical flaws? Areas to improve? I hadn't signed up for that. Not yet. I squared my shoulders and got the preliminary chitchat over with.

"That is the sweetest dog," I couldn't help saying, noticing her placidly sitting on her leash at Liam's feet. Not even the numerous squirrels could rattle her. "What's her name?"

"Goldie." Liam scratched her head. She almost purred. "It's short for Goldie Goes for Gold. She's a rescue from the track. You know, greyhound racing? When the race dogs get old—"

"They retire?" I chimed in, not wanting the harsh reality. I'd had enough of that lately. Jeremy's death haunted me. "They go to live on a beautiful farm somewhere in the Cotswolds?"

Liam laughed. "Sure, why not? Let's go with that."

I parsed his earlier comment about "the track" full of racing greyhounds, wondering if he was a betting man and therefore might have gambling debts to settle, while Liam gave me another evaluative look. I tried to stand straighter. Hours spent hunched over chocolates doesn't exactly do wonders for a person's posture. My faux ramrod-straight military stance probably didn't fool anyone, but I had to do something.

Speaking of which . . . "Why don't we walk and talk?"

I needed to move. Despite my crack about my chocolatier's hump, I tend to think best on my feet. Aside from which, Liam had been giving my innocent Americano the stink eye since we'd met. I wanted to show him I was more than an over-caffeinated potential dog napper with a crossbody bag full of chocolate samples and ideas for future decadent treats I intended to make.

I didn't need to make a good impression on Liam Taylor. Strictly speaking, he was a suspect in Jeremy's murder, just like (almost) everyone else I'd met in London. But he was a suspect who'd rescued a lovable dog from certain death. That earned him some brownie points, right?

As far as I was concerned, it did. Because I'm an unequivocal dog person. Just as Danny's incomprehensible dislike of chocolate puts him squarely in the non-soul-mate category, Travis's (new?) dog put him firmly in the maybe-soul-mate zone.

On the other hand, Travis does have that pesky air-travel phobia of his to deal with. That throws a monkey wrench into our make-believe long-term happiness. Because I'm always on the move. And I'm not going to limit myself to cars to get there.

Amid my Travis-centric daydream, I caught myself staring at Liam's streaky blond hair, blue eyes, undeniably handsome face, and crazy-hot bod. I shook myself and got back down to business.

I was there for a concrete purpose. Sadly, that purpose wasn't coaxing away Goldie to come and live with me. I'm afraid my chocolate-whispering lifestyle doesn't mesh with pets. But I definitely want a place to hang up my wheelie bag for good someday. You know, eventually. Way far into the future.

"I really appreciate your meeting me like this," I told Liam as we walked side by side. His idea of a walk-and-talk was considerably brisker than mine. I huffed. "Especially on such short notice. After what happened with Jeremy, you must be devastated. Phoebe said you'd worked together a long time?"

He'd been smiling, having caught me admiring his muscles. But now a shadow passed over his face. "Jeremy and I went way back." His voice sounded gruff, but he kept moving. I examined his profile but couldn't detect any obvious subterfuge. Or any noticeable culpability. "He wasn't the perfect client, but he kept me busy. Now that he's gone, I'm looking to rebuild."

"I'm so sorry for your loss. It's such a shock."

He cleared his throat. "I just want to move on, yeah?"

Liam walked faster, coaxing Goldie to pick up the pace. Because he was trying to outrun his guilty feelings? I had to stay on the alert for deception, no matter how nice he seemed.

"That's why I called you back," Liam went on, scanning the nearby trees instead of meeting my eyes. "I need to stay busy."

I understood that. If he was innocent. That was—had to be—a big *if*, if I were to find out who'd killed Jeremy. I hated suspecting everyone I met, when all I wanted was information.

Honestly, there could only be one killer. That meant I would unavoidably suspect several people who were innocent.

Liam inhaled, then glanced at me. "What about you, Hayden? I get the impression Phoebe told you all about me, but I don't know anything about you. Jeremy never mentioned you." His scrutiny deepened as he said it. "You're not English, are you?"

"No. I've lived all over the place. My parents always traveled for work, so when I was a kid, I did too." I named some of the places I've lived while traveling with my adventure-loving mom and dad. "I guess all the gridskipping grew on me."

Liam nodded, pausing to let Goldie sniff delicately at a leafy London plane tree. "I like traveling too. A quick holiday to Ibiza, a stag weekend in Majorca . . . whatever, whenever."

I liked his attitude. Willingness to travel? Check. Dog companionship? Check. Physical attractiveness? Check, check.

It was too bad I wasn't in London to have fun.

It was too bad Liam was a suspect, I reminded myself. All the same . . . "What do you do with Goldie while you're gone?"

"She stays with friends. So . . . you're not a journalist?"

"A what?" I couldn't help laughing. "No, definitely

not. Poking into people's private lives? Chasing stories? Not me."

I was surprised he'd mentioned the press. Especially given my own doubts about them. When Danny and I had returned to the guesthouse last night, the crowd of paparazzi had diminished—at least at the back door. The front door had been another story.

Interestingly (or not), Ashley hadn't been among them.

Liam looked embarrassed. He was definitely English. "It's just that a few people from the media have contacted me. About Jeremy." He shrugged his massive shoulders. "I guess they thought I might have something to say about his death."

Now *I* felt uncomfortable. But I pressed on. For Jeremy.

"Did you?" I pushed. "Have something to say, I mean?"

"Only that he's gone too soon." Liam hastily rubbed his eyes, ignoring Goldie's pull at the leash. "I'll miss him."

He seemed genuinely bereft. I felt sorry for him. Commiserating, I touched his forearm. It felt like one of the marble statues lining the exhibit rooms at the British Museum. "I wish I'd known him better. Were the two of you close?"

Liam cracked an appealing grin. "You get pretty close, watching someone sweat." He inhaled deeply, then looked around. The Embankment had become busier now. Bankers and businesspeople strode to work in a perpetual Londoner's hurry. "How about you? What are your goals? Improve cardiovascular stamina, of course?"

He said it leadingly, encouraging me to own up to

the theoretical physical shortcomings that had brought me to him. I felt new sympathy for my chocolate-whisperer clientele. I'd always found it frustrating when they wouldn't tell me what was wrong. Or, like Phoebe, when they'd omitted information that I'd inevitably discover later. But now, standing there with my empty coffee cup and my belly full of chocolate-chip crumb cake (you might have guessed that I hadn't only stopped for coffee), I knew what it was like to feel evaluated. Needy. And lacking.

Of course, what *I* lacked were solid leads about Jeremy's murder, not six-pack abs and the ability to bench-press fifty-kilo bags of cacao beans from a Venezuelan plantation.

"Don't be offended," Liam rushed to add, undoubtedly seeing my expression. "I set a pretty fast pace back there. It's on purpose, to get an idea of your current condition, that's all."

My "condition" was breathless, vaguely sweaty, and hungry for another slice of crumb cake. In short, I'm someone who perfects chocolates for a living, and it shows. It was going to catch up to me someday. But today wasn't my day of reckoning.

Except in one particular sense, that was. Trapped in my "I want to shape up" ruse, I bought time by watching Goldie. The dog sat happily at Liam's side, tongue lolling, eyes taking in a bulldog walking near some fading daffodils. I lifted my gaze to Liam's similarly openhearted expression and big, blue eyes.

I decided I could trust him. "I want to get in the best shape of my life," I said firmly. "Starting right now."

Well, what did you expect? That just because I felt I could trust him, I'd spill everything? Not me. Not the new Hayden Mundy Moore. This (part-time) amateur sleuth was wising up.

I suspected Liam of maybe murdering Jeremy, after all. I didn't intend to get close to him. I was keeping my eyes open.

My goals were finding Jeremy's killer and clearing my own name—preferably while remaining unbludgeoned myself. I still wasn't comfortable staying in the Wrights' guesthouse, despite Danny having vetted it. He *had* turned up some interesting information about the place, though. It seemed that Phoebe's property was located in a pretty old part of London. It was close by the Thames, where cargo would have been moved, so—

"I can definitely help you get into top shape," Liam interrupted before I could finish the thought. His eyes sparkled at me, practically overflowing with eagerness at the notion of making me run wind sprints, do crunches, and plank myself silly.

He outlined a program. It sounded about as much fun as endlessly baking cookies and never getting to eat any of them.

"How long before all of this starts to work?" I asked.

I was doing this to tease info from Liam, but I wouldn't mind if I got some results, too. There had to be some benefits to simultaneously consulting at Primrose, tutoring Phoebe, chasing a killer, *and* embarking on a strenuous workout regimen.

It occurred to me that I might have bitten off more than I could chew. Could I send in a body double to meet Liam? At the chocolaterie-pâtisserie, Poppy was almost a dead ringer for me.

You know, if I'd had zero chocolate knowledge and was six years younger, with an eyebrow piercing and a love of leggings.

Okay, so there was no way out of this. Whoops.

I had to make the most of my cover story. "Just kidding," I amended with a grin and a "just joshing" poke to Liam's sturdy ribs. "I can't wait to get started, and I don't care how long it takes. Maybe I'll train for a marathon!"

Hey, in for a penny, in for a pound, right?

"In that case, you'll want to follow my clean nutrition program, too." He looked thrilled at the prospect. "You wouldn't believe how sugar, gluten, and alcohol affect your performance."

He meant adversely, of course, something that was anathema to me. Somewhere, Danny was laughing his head off at the predicament I'd gotten myself into. As far as I was concerned, bread (with chocolate, natch) really was the staff of life.

If you haven't had a grilled chocolate sandwich, made with some quality brioche, good dark chocolate, and a sprinkle of fleur de sel, you haven't really lived, as far as I'm concerned.

Liam was busy outlining the plan that Phoebe and Nicola had alluded to. It sounded positively Spartan. Poor Jeremy. "But surely there are exceptions, right? For birthdays? Christmas?"

"No." Liam's expression hardened. "Either you're all in or you're all out. I know you'll have some unique challenges while you're spending time with Phoebe at the bakery, but you can do it. I don't tolerate doing things halfway. Jeremy could have told you that much."

Yikes. At that moment, Liam looked fully capable of whacking to death someone who didn't adhere to the "program." I shivered, wondering exactly how well Jeremy had obeyed Liam's regimen.

Could noncompliance have cost Jeremy his life?

"A glass of wine now and then is okay, though,

right?" What can I say? I'm a born rebel. "My favorite restaurant in town serves a very nice Montepulciano D'Abruzzo. It's so good."

I named the specific vintner and vintage—one served only at Jeremy's restaurants. Liam tightened his mouth. And his fist.

Uh-oh. At his side, Goldie whimpered. I had a bad feeling.

Towering above me, Liam narrowed his eyes. He appeared to be considering walloping the memory of Abruzzo's tasty central Italian red wine right out of me. I might have overplayed my hand, I realized, by bringing up Jeremy one too many times.

But then Liam suddenly grinned. "That's *my* favorite restaurant, too! Jeremy's place at Covent Garden, right?"

His expression glowed at our newfound similarities. He was happy we liked the same place. I practically passed out with pent-up anxiety. Or maybe with the exertion of our speedy walk.

It was hard to tell. I'm relatively new at being sneaky myself. I found it stressful. Also, I could have sworn I glimpsed Danny moving closer to me. We should have devised an "all clear" signal. Given Liam's size, strength, and agitated demeanor—and my own tense posture—my security expert probably thought I was in imminent danger. He might rush in to save the day at any moment. I had to let Danny know I was all right.

"I know it's not everyone's idea of fancy," Liam was saying in a remarkably easygoing tone, "but it's a special occasion place for me. I grew up on a council estate in East London, see. Same as Jeremy. Things were rough. I'm successful now, but—"

"But a part of you will always remember that. I get it."

Behind my back, I tried surreptitiously shooing Danny away.

"Yeah." Liam's face eased even further. I began to wonder if I'd imagined his menacing demeanor earlier. "I'm pretty lucky. Mostly thanks to Jeremy. After he got out, he took me with him. But you probably don't even know what a council estate is, do you?" His quizzical look probed me. "Since you're not—"

English, I figured he was about to say. But I was already ahead of him. An idea had occurred to me. I was running with it.

"I do, but only because Jeremy invited me to invest in his charity," I fibbed. I figured he would have done so, if he'd lived long enough. "Are you familiar with its work?"

I wanted to keep Liam talking about Jeremy in particular, not British public housing in general. I needed to keep control of the conversation, but I wasn't sure how to do that without seeming as though I was interrogating him. That would surely spook him. I'd never find out what information Liam could share.

This all would have been much easier if I were DC Mishra. She had the authority to grill people, no questions asked.

But Liam didn't seem to suspect a thing. "Sure, you could say I'm familiar with it—since I'm on the board of directors."

"Really? Then you're probably not an impartial source."

I was joking, but Liam creased his brow. "I don't have to be uninvolved to see the good work they're doing at Jeremy's Jump Start Foundation." He crossed his arms, the self-appointed defender of Jeremy's charity. "Are you planning to invest? Now that Jeremy's gone, we'll need more support than ever."

"I haven't decided yet." I'm stubborn that way. You don't want to back me into a corner. "I need to find out more first."

That was the first excuse that came to mind. Not that I don't like to support good causes. I absolutely do. All the time. But I didn't like feeling strong-armed into doing things.

Besides, I had an undercover agenda here. Liam bit on it.

"Why don't I take you for a visit?" he offered. "I'm going out there soon anyway. The kids need an explanation for Jeremy's death. They need to hear from someone besides the media."

His dislike of the press seemed to mirror mine. I wondered why. Had the paparazzi followed Jeremy on his workouts, too?

"I'd love to go with you." Doing so would give me an inside glimpse into another part of Jeremy's life—and any people within it who might have wanted him dead. My suspects were piling up quickly. "Just tell me how and when, and we'll go together."

Skeptically, Liam angled his head. "You're not afraid?"

"Of a bad neighborhood?" I shook my head. Even if I'd been terrified, I knew I'd have Danny nearby for protection. "I know how to handle myself. Besides, who'll bother us with you there?"

At my overt flattery, Liam grinned. "I'm a pussycat."

"I'll bet those kids love you. Sometimes when people make it out of the neighborhood, they don't want to ever go back."

"Not me. Or Jeremy. He wasn't like that."

"I wonder how Phoebe felt about that. Did she visit, too?"

Liam chortled. "Phoebe? At the council estate? No

way. She thought she'd get stabbed if she stepped east of Knightsbridge."

"She didn't support Jeremy's foundation?"

"Sure, she did. By getting her fancy friends to donate." Liam paused. "Speaking of which, how involved are you at Primrose?"

How involved? That was a tricky question. I didn't want to give away the real troubleshooting work I was doing on Phoebe's behalf. As far as her staff knew, I was nothing more than a knowledgeable new hire, brought in to help Primrose benefit from my experience. *Why* I'm at a particular business is always undisclosed; the *fact* that I'm there can't be. I have to be on site to do a consultation.

I wished more of my consultees would be open about needing my help. It would make things much easier for me. I'm skilled at evaluating ganache and gianduia, not at hiding my raison d'être.

"Pretty involved." I crouched to pet Goldie, hoping to hide my impending smokescreen. "I'm aces at chocolate." All good cover-ups contain some truth. That's what Danny had told me. "I spend a lot of time at Primrose. But taste-testing three-layer German chocolate cakes isn't exactly a cardiovascular workout, is it?" Trying to hone my poker face, I rose. "Why do you ask?"

"Because if you're one of Phoebe's rich friends, I have to be extra nice to you." Liam smiled. "To convince you to donate."

His motivation was so obvious, I almost laughed. "I don't think you're supposed to tell me that's what you're doing."

He gave an offhand shrug. "I guess I'm bad at being devious."

I hoped so. "I won't tell anyone if you won't."

A broader smile. "It's a deal."

Playfully, we shook on it. Newfound solidarity rose between us. I really wanted Liam to be innocent—and not just because he had dog-rescue skills and the physique of a Greek god, either.

I liked him. I know, you're thinking I'm being gullible. So would Danny. Maybe Travis, too. But I can't help being me.

I don't want to believe the worst of everyone I meet.

As though validating my optimistic impulses, Liam made plans for us to visit Jeremy's Jump Start Foundation together in a few days. He'd been planning to go anyway, he confided.

A guy who'd just bludgeoned his friend to death wouldn't spend a day working with disadvantaged youth in a bad neighborhood, would he?

"So." With that accomplished, I looked around, ready to get on with my day. "Now I've got my program." Liam had given me his personal-trainer marching orders—regular cardio, "conditioning" sessions with him a few times a week, and the aforementioned anti-carb, anti-sugar, anti-booze, anti-fun regimen. That was the real sticking point for me. I didn't really have to stick with the program, since I was only there to get information. In fact, I couldn't "eat clean" and do my chocolate-whispering job.

But when I was with Liam, I'd have to pretend to have done exactly that. And hope he never, ever found out. "What happens if I blow it?"

"You won't blow it," Liam assured me. His face took on a scary seriousness. "None of my clients ever let me down."

At his dire tone, I gulped. "Come on. A few must. Right?"

"Nope." Liam shook his head. "All I have is my reputation. That depends on compliance. So I make well sure I get it."

Ooookay. Maybe he *wasn't* a pussycat, after all. "I'm on it, then! Thanks for your time. See you later." Then I skedaddled.

You know . . . before Liam could make an example of me, the way he might have done with Jeremy on the night he'd died.

Seven

"He was playing you."

Danny made that announcement in his usual cock-sure tone, settling back against the banquette at Jeremy's Covent Garden restaurant as though he owned the place. He eyed me silently.

I knew he was waiting for my inevitable defense. I don't like being wrong. Who does? But I paid Danny for a reason. I respected his expertise far beyond that paycheck, too. So I had to put aside any knee-jerk rationalizations and be smart.

"What makes you think that?" I asked. It was hard to ponder deception (much less murder) after having just enjoyed the most mouthwatering truffled mushroom risotto ever, but I tried.

Mostly for the sake of keeping Danny at the restaurant until our pudding arrived (to those of you who are stateside, that's "dessert"—*any* kind, not just pudding). Flourless chocolate cake for me, and a deep-fried, batter-dipped Mars bar for Danny. He was trying to eat chocolate, which I found heartening, but I was skeptical about its probable tastiness. I'm all for a retro dessert now and then, but fried sugar? No. None for me, thanks.

And yes, I know that donuts are fried. But here's the thing—I don't like them, either. If anyone ever claims I've consulted for your favorite donut shop, they're pulling your leg. Because I just don't have the stomach for a job like that.

"Liam Taylor is hiding something," Danny insisted. "Halfway through your conversation with him, his whole demeanor changed."

"He's upset about Jeremy's death. They've known each other for years. People behave erratically when they're grieving."

"They're predictable as hell when they're *not* grieving. What makes you think Hulk Jr. is really sorry about Jeremy?"

I quirked my lips at his nickname for Liam. "He's sorry."

"Unless he's the one who crushed Jeremy's skull."

"I still think Hugh might have done it," I maintained, not wanting to revisit my mental picture of that night. I hated to say so, but . . . "Hugh has the size, the impulsivity, and the bad attitude to attack Jeremy. Maybe it was an accident," I mused, toying with my wineglass. "Maybe he didn't mean to do it."

"Right." Danny compressed his mouth. "Pick on the kid from the wrong side of the tracks. Nice going, Hayden. I'm sure Harvard will agree with you. You'll wrap this up by teatime."

"Come on. You know I'm not biased that way."

My friendship with Danny—and my understanding of his sketchy background—was proof of it. Reluctantly, he nodded.

Smartly, he didn't bring up any of his friends from his old 'hood—buddies who could always count on

Danny for a helping hand, a sofa to crash on, a hot meal, or a ride someplace.

Above all, Danny was loyal. But his ongoing relationships with people I thought were bad influences on him was a touchy subject between us. I admired his dependability. I also feared his "buddies" and the slip-slide into trouble they embodied.

"Either way, I don't feel any closer to identifying who might have killed Jeremy than I did yesterday." I sighed, then perked up as I noticed the server approaching with our desserts.

For the next few minutes, we were absorbed with pudding. I considered it my professional obligation to focus completely on the soft, dark, über-chocolaty slice of cake in front of me. My motto is, if it doesn't deserve my complete attention, it's probably not worth eating at all. So I savor every mouthful.

"Hey, what was with you waving me off when you were with Liam this morning?" Danny put down his fork and gave me a quizzical look. This question must have slipped his mind while we'd canvassed K&C (the Kensington and Chelsea neighborhoods) earlier, picking up the requisite free tabloid papers after my meeting with Liam. "I can't protect you if you won't let me."

Before I could answer, my phone buzzed. Ordinarily, I wouldn't interrupt an in-person conversation for a phone call, but this was different. "It's Travis. I've got to pick up."

"Of course you do. Can't keep Captain Calculator waiting."

I couldn't tell if Danny was being sarcastic or not. With him, cynicism is like breathing. That's one reason he's a good security expert. He's as ready to suspect the worst of people as I am to think the best. He's really persistent. Tough, too.

But I was already being transported across the Atlantic, a few thousand miles and several hours into Travis's downtown Seattle office. I hustled toward the restaurant's exit, leaving Danny to hold down our table until I returned. All around me, Jeremy's loyal customers and fans kept up a steady background hum, competing for attention with the place's lively music.

Danny and I had waited almost an hour for a table—at lunch, no less. It seemed that Jeremy's untimely death had only made his already thriving dynasty of restaurants even more popular. The servers were hopping. Unless the back-of-house staff were unusually skilled, they were probably deep in the weeds by now.

But back to Travis. Putting my restaurant persona on hold, I stepped out into Covent Garden's neoclassical market hall. Its immense green-painted steel beams arched gracefully above me to support the former fruit-and-vegetable market's glasswork ceiling. Below me was another level of the Italianate arcade. It dominated the piazza, each level and passageway featuring charming brickwork along with shops where the former sellers' stalls had been. It was bustling, but understandably so. Covent Garden packed a variety of retail and dining outlets into its spacious, open-air complex. Its visitors were entertained by street performers and lured by all kinds of food and flowers.

I was lured by the promise of another chat with Travis. I wished it didn't have to happen amid such distracting hubbub.

"Travis! This is a surprise." Cheekily, I lowered my

voice. "You're calling to tell me what you're wearing, aren't you?"

"Only if an expression of indignation counts."

His usually deep-timbred voice had dropped even further. I'll admit, that sound gave me chills. The good kind, of course.

"Don't be that way. You know you love talking to me." I broke off to consult my phone's clock. Uh-oh. The time zone shift was brutal. "Even if it is before dawn there. Sorry."

Travis, being Travis, didn't quibble about unalterable factors like time zones. He accepted what couldn't be changed and worked diligently (and intelligently) on what could.

"Why didn't you tell me you were a murder suspect?"

I froze. Foreboding washed over me. "DC Mishra?"

"Called me with a few 'off the record' questions just now."

I tried to laugh. "At least *I* apologized for the time change. Detective Constable Mishra and the London Metropolitan Police Service aren't quite as thoughtful as I am, I guess."

My attempt at misdirection failed. "What's going on, Hayden?"

Travis sounded beleaguered. But sexy. He just couldn't help it. He's so . . . *capable.* Of all kinds of things, I imagined.

"I should have known something was up when Danny flew over there to join you," Travis groused, interrupting my reverie. "I thought you were bored with your consultation at Primrose."

"Bored? With *you* to talk to? Never. You know that."

"I made it as safe as possible. The location, the job at Primrose, the people involved . . . they were all factors pointing to an assignment that would not put you in danger again, damn it."

"Danger of incarceration isn't danger per se," I reasoned. I'd never heard Travis swear before. I was freaked out. "There's no need for you to blame yourself. You *tried* to bore me. Okay?"

As reassurances went, it was admittedly lame. But maybe steady-to-a-fault Travis would *like* being aces at boredom?

"I mean it." His newly flinty tone stopped me cold. "Jeremy Wright. What happened? I want to know every detail, right now."

"Right now?" Still trying to laugh off his concern, I mimed looking at my (nonexistent) watch. "I'm pretty busy right now."

"Tell. Me. Everything."

Whoa. When he talked that way, I was afraid not to. Sparing only the grisliest bits, I brought Travis up to speed with everything that had been going on since I'd found Jeremy Wright dead on my guesthouse floor. ". . . which explains all I know so far."

Silence took up all the space on the line. I gripped my phone and paced among the Covent Garden visitors, glancing back at Jeremy's restaurant now and then to make sure Danny hadn't sneaked away from "pudding" to grab a quick junk-food sausage roll, Cornish pasty, or Turkey Twizzler when I wasn't looking.

Hey . . . was that Nicola Mitchell ducking out of a jewelry store? She vanished into the crowd before I could be certain.

"And it never occurred to you that *I* could help you?"

A hard edge had slipped into Travis's seductive, sonorous tones. Too late, I realized that he wasn't just worried about me. I've experienced that before. This time, Travis was hurt.

And he was mad. Mad that I hadn't turned to him sooner.

Maybe even mad that I'd called on Danny, but not him.

"Well . . ." I groped for an explanation, feeling awful to have upset him. I churned my arm, still seeking. "It's not as though I needed to have my taxes done ten months early, Travis."

I waited for his usual chuckle—the one that would let me off the hook. But my financial planner wasn't humoring me.

"Or are we on a quarterly plan now?" I quipped, getting desperate. I no longer cared about my abandoned chocolate cake or Danny's junk-food jones. "Help me out, here. You know I'm—"

I suddenly became aware of dead air on the line. Had Travis actually hung up on me? I pulled my cell phone away from my ear and goggled at it. Yep. Naturally, I dialed straight back.

My call connected. My heart pounded an extra beat. I could fix this. "If I wind up needing bail, you're first on my list."

Click. Oh no.

I dialed again. Connection. "I'm sorry. I'm *really*—"

Click. What the heck? I *had* to make this right.

Another call. Another eternal, expectant pause. I hauled in a deep breath. "If Jeremy had needed fiscal advice, I would—"

Click. I was starting to get frustrated. I thought Travis and Danny both understood their roles. Most of the time, Travis was the brains—and the brakes, when necessary. Danny was the brawn—and the backup, when called upon. Wasn't that good enough?

I dialed. Travis picked up. He didn't speak. That was just spiteful of him. He knew how much I looked forward to hearing his voice. "It's not as though you would have hopped a plane."

There was a long, almost interminable pause. Have I mentioned that I sometimes put my foot in my mouth?

Then Travis spoke. I've never felt more grateful for an audible intake of breath followed by eight raspy words in my whole life as I was in the next few seconds. I waited.

"You didn't give me a chance, did you?" he said.

Galvanized and repentant, I gripped my phone. I didn't dare speak. I didn't want to interrupt Travis if he wanted to talk.

Besides, I'd already said a few things I regretted. It was better to quit while I was ahead. Plus, I needed time to think.

Had Travis really just suggested he might have battled his chronic air-travel phobia . . . for me? To help *me*?

While I grappled with that possibility, my trusty financial adviser reverted to his usual detail-oriented form. "Jeremy Wright's financials come up clean. As far as I can tell, he was thriving. He'd just signed a lucrative contract with a company called Hambleton & Hart. They make cakes, cookies, dessert toppings . . . the kinds of things you'd find in a convenience store."

Aha. Interesting. Travis had obviously been busy since his call from Satya Mishra. "Can you get me a meeting with them?"

He remained silent. Whoops. I'd really upset him.

"I mean," I amended, "will you *please* get me a meeting?"

I heard him typing. "I'm on it."

Wearily, Travis exhaled. I imagined him squinting at his computer screen, dressed in a suit and tie even in the murky predawn hours, and felt repentant for the trouble I'd put him to. I wasn't the one who'd made DC Mishra call. But I should have been more up front with Travis. I truly valued him.

He must have hated being caught without all the facts.

"Other than that, Jeremy's financial and legal activities look legit," Travis told me. "He was working on a new cooking show and an accompanying cookbook. His charity was thriving. His biggest expenses were a new house in Kent for his retired parents and an underground addition to his own town house in Chelsea. Both appear to have been completely routine."

I paused, confused. While it was nice that Jeremy had generously bought his parents a house, these weren't the kinds of details Travis and I typically covered during our usual pre-consultation phone briefing. "Underground? What do you mean?"

"Technically, it's what's known as a basement extension. Those historic town houses are protected. They can't be knocked down, expanded upward, or outward. There's only one way to go."

Down. That made sense. But I'd seen no signs of construction. I guessed it would never happen now. I steered us away from real estate and renovations toward Jeremy's Jump Start Foundation and my scheduled visit there with Liam Taylor.

"Don't let Jeremy's physical trainer get you alone," Travis warned in a gravely, slightly warmer voice. "Just in case."

"You sound like Danny. He doesn't trust anybody."

"Neither should you."

I ducked into a bricked alcove. "I trust you."

The sound of typing stopped. I imagined Travis lit by the golden glow of an old-fashioned desk lamp, his face . . .

Humph. That was where I drew a blank. I've never met Travis, remember? I've never so much as seen a photograph of my notoriously private financial adviser. I knew he was blond. He'd told me so once. I knew he was brilliant and fond of suits.

"Next time," Travis told me, "trust me sooner."

Then he informed me of a few more financial and legal details about Phoebe, Primrose chocolaterie-pâtisserie, and my consultation, asked me who I wanted him to check next (Nicola, Hugh, and Liam topped the list), and told me good-bye.

I didn't want to hang up. "It's not even teatime here."

Finally, I heard a smile sneak into his voice. Hurrah. "Have a cup of tea for me later. Earl Grey. Hot. No sugar."

I smiled too. "Are you a *Star Trek* fan, Travis?"

I wasn't a particular aficionada. But almost everyone has seen those clips of Captain Picard ordering his favorite drink.

Travis didn't indulge me. "You're trying to keep me on the phone. You know better than that. We both have work to do."

"You always have work to do. Humor me. I want to talk."

More than that, I wanted to make sure things were okay between us. I wished I hadn't accidentally upset Travis.

"You know you're just going to go reconcile some

accounts or something," I pushed. "What's a few more minutes?"

He paused. "Who says I'm not doing something fun?"

"You never worry about fun. Just numbers. And facts."

Travis laughed. "There's a lot you don't know about me, Hayden. I'm hanging up now. Keep me in the loop from now on."

I promised I would. But I suspected the tail end of my declaration wound up vanishing somewhere over the Atlantic.

Travis was a hard man to know, I reflected as I hung up and headed back to Jeremy's restaurant to join Danny. In some ways, my supersmart financial adviser was even more cryptic than Danny.

On the other hand . . . sometimes Danny was pretty up front about things, I saw as I reentered the hectic *osteria* and saw him at our table. From somewhere, he'd procured a beer, a cheese plate, and a flirtatious server's phone number. My pudding was still there; his sat ignored on the table with a single bite gone.

Some things would never change. But a few other things might. I shook off the memory of Travis's phone call and went to rejoin my friend. It was time to move forward. For Jeremy.

Moving forward wasn't easy. Not in any sense.

Not for me, and not (as it turned out) for Phoebe Wright, either. That much became clear the following sunny afternoon, when I joined my current consultee (and brand-new student) for our very first lesson in traditional British cookery.

It should have been easy. We couldn't have been more stocked with state-of-the-art equipment or (thanks to Amelja) all the necessary baking supplies. But Phoebe and I struggled from the get-go, from deciding what to bake first to staying focused on our lessons to figuring out what to wear.

Phoebe eyed the apron I offered with dismay. "That won't be necessary, will it? Not for me." She waved. "You go ahead."

If this was indicative of her usual level of cooperativeness, I was concerned. "You'll want to protect your clothes. Baking is messy business." I gave her an encouraging smile. "At least it is when done properly. Flour everywhere!"

"I will *not* appear on television dressed in *that*."

She sniffed, indicating that the subject was now closed. I was reminded that Phoebe probably hadn't encountered much adversity in her privileged life. Born wealthy, educated well, welcomed into every exclusive circle, just by virtue of birth . . .

I couldn't imagine what that was like. It made me wonder how Phoebe and Jeremy had ever gotten together—or gotten along.

But maybe I was the only one who butted heads with the Honourable, etc. Maybe Jeremy had given his wife everything she wanted, including his own sex appeal and street credibility.

What I'm saying is, on her own, Phoebe was pretty starchy.

"What are you going to wear, then?" I envisioned pearls.

An airy wave. "A friend of mine is whipping up something."

She meant something couture. Made to measure. Expensive.

Of course. "Besides, these are my running-around clothes."

"Okay, well . . ." I examined her outfit—perfectly

fitted trousers, another silk shirt, fashionable high-heeled sandals, and gobs of jewelry. She looked outfitted for a dinner date, not baking. "If you're happy, I'm happy. So, what do you plan to make?"

"On television?" Phoebe blinked. "Well, it's got to be something traditional, doesn't it? That's what they asked for."

"Do you know the producers?" Maybe they would cut her some slack. Baked goods for TV were usually premade, then stashed beneath a counter for the big reveal. She wouldn't really have to bake something from start to finish, but she would have to appear competent. "Are they the same crew who did Jeremy's show?"

She narrowed her eyes. "I'm more than Jeremy's wife. You can't possibly believe I was only asked because of him."

"No! Of course not." I held out my palms, wary of offending her. "I was only thinking that maybe they would let you talk about traditional British baking, rather than demonstrate it."

Phoebe's cheeks flushed. Uh-oh. "Look, Hayden. You're here to help me, aren't you? So if you aren't up to that task—"

"I am. No worries." Proving as much, I put on my own apron, then surveyed the deluxe kitchen. "You mentioned Eton mess and Victoria sponge the other day. What else did you have in mind?"

"Well, they have to be chocolate versions of those things, don't they?" Phoebe pursed her lips, then stared at the ceiling in thought. "Perhaps a Bakewell tart? Or sticky toffee pudding?"

Those were classic British desserts. I could have rattled them off more quickly, and I'm not even British. I realized that Phoebe hadn't given this subject a morsel of thought since we'd last spoken. Of course, she had a very valid excuse for that.

I remembered she was a widow now, and softened my tone.

"Why don't you have a go at making the Eton mess?" I suggested. "I'll look on to get a sense of your abilities."

"I *don't* want critiques." Phoebe's face swiveled toward me. "I got loads of critiques in the press when Primrose opened, and they didn't do a whit of good, did they?" She gave a headshake. "No. Those people didn't know what they were talking about."

"I would never critique *you*," I explained gently, startled by her defensiveness—and wondering about Primrose's turnaround. I hadn't known the chocolaterie-pâtisserie had ever struggled before now. "It's possible your technique would need adjusting, but that's not the same as criticizing *you*, personally."

"I *am* what I do, just the way I *am* Primrose," Phoebe told me crisply. "The shop and I are synonymous, aren't they? My investors didn't join in just because my chocolaterie-pâtisserie is well situated and serves good biscuits. They wanted *me*."

She had a point, of course. In today's world, people *are* their brands—especially famous people. Celebrities' images draw us to trust them, to emulate them, to want to be like them.

But I thought she was overstating her power to persuade.

"Of course. But no one expects *you* to be in the shop, day after day, serving customers and making cakes, do they?"

My attempt at conciliation earned another frosty glare. "I *am* in the shop day after day. You've seen me there yourself."

Since I'd been in London consulting for her, Phoebe had been "in the shop" for exactly fifteen minutes, I knew, three times a week, in the time slot following her favorite yoga class.

That was her schedule. She'd never once deviated from it. She couldn't stay any longer and risk letting the staff know how little expertise she truly had with chocolates and baked goods.

"Let's be real, Phoebe. Everyone knows who you are. You're not expected to be at Primrose, ruining your manicure, making dulce de leche cupcakes and peppermint white chocolate bark. You don't have to be Gemma Rose," I assured her, giving her a level look as I named Britain's most famous domestic doyenne. If the U.K. had had a sexy, seductive, finger-licking-good Martha Stewart—one who looked hot in a bikini and moaned with pleasure while tasting her own baked goods—it would have been Gemma Rose. "The world already has Gemma Rose. *You* should be yourself."

"I am far better than that tart Gemma Rose."

"I agree." I smiled. "So let's show the world!"

"Yes! Let's!" Improbably rallied, Phoebe put on her apron. She surveyed the countertop full of goods like a field general. Her eyes glowed with enthusiasm. "What do we do first, Hayden?"

Unexpected, right? Not to me. I've worked with a lot of mega-successful people, from CEOs to world-famous chefs and more. One thing the truly accomplished have in common is that they hate to be bored. But they hate being doubted even more.

I thought Phoebe was bored. She needed a kick in the pants.

I hadn't wanted to administer it, given the hard time she'd been having since Jeremy's death. But the clock was ticking.

That show on the telly wouldn't wait. Or reschedule. Frankly, getting Phoebe on TV was more of a "get" than ever. Since seeing Primrose thrive was my mission— and a successful TV appearance from Phoebe could help with that—I had to improvise.

"Why don't you start with the Eton mess?" I urged in a light tone. "What's your plan to incorporate chocolate into it?"

Typically, Eton mess was composed of layered strawberries, cream, and airy meringues, so named because it was traditionally served at Eton College during their annual cricket game against Harrow School. I could think of several ways to give Eton mess the chocolate-whisperer treatment, from adding a dollop of chocolate ganache to making the whipped cream cocoa flavored to folding chopped semi-sweet chocolate into the crispy meringues.

Phoebe's eyes were alight. "I thought I'd sprinkle chocolate shavings on top. That will be moreish, won't it?"

"Moreish" was U.K. speak for "wanting to eat more," aka tasty. It was a small change, but . . . "Let's try it and find out."

She rightly sensed I wasn't satisfied. "I could dip some of the strawberries in chocolate couverture, too. Scrumptious!"

She was thinking small. "Okay. Let's get started."

Phoebe pouted. "Oughtn't we brainstorm a while first?"

"I usually find that taking action gets the best results."

By which I really meant, *you've got to start somewhere.* Talking wasn't doing. Only *doing* would prepare her to succeed.

But Phoebe had already gotten her fill of tutoring. She gazed past me, her demeanor tense. I didn't understand. Yes, some very sensitive people assumed that anything less than a standing ovation meant condemnation of their ideas, but . . .

I realized that Phoebe wasn't sulking. She was staring at one of the free tabloid newspapers I'd picked up that morning during my usual rounds. I'd folded it to keep its sensational contents mostly private in my tote bag, but it had somehow loosened itself during my walk home to the guesthouse—and my chat with Mr. Barclay, who was still threatening to sue to gain himself some peace and quiet in the neighborhood. Apparently, he was not a fan of the Wrights' basement expansion plans, either.

Slowly, Phoebe strode toward my bag and the paper, her hand outstretched like a ghost's. She blinked. "Is that *Nicola?*"

In the nanosecond before she grabbed the paper, I realized it was. I also spotted the headline that I'd overlooked earlier.

SAUCY ASSISTANT TELLS ALL ABOUT NAUGHTY JEREMY! SEXY PARTIES! SHOCKING SECRETS! SCANDALS YOU WON'T BELIEVE ARE TRUE! FIND OUT MORE ON PAGE 10.

Both of us stared at it. A feeling of dawning disbelief stole over me, mingling with queasiness. Maybe the "clean" juice I'd tried for breakfast—full of beets, ginger, and kale—hadn't set properly with me. I felt new commiseration for Jeremy.

Phoebe was already turning the tabloid's pages. "She's writing a tell-all book!" Her face drained of color. Her fingers shook, making the paper rattle slightly. "She's going to be on television on the same morning I'm going to be on television!"

I couldn't tell if Phoebe was upset about Nicola's book or their shared TV spot. It could have been either. Or both.

"This is Claire's doing, isn't it?" Phoebe ranted,

pacing elegantly with the newspaper in hand. "That bitch! I guess she's recouped all her 'lost' money from Jeremy now, hasn't she?"

The venom in her tone startled me. "Claire?"

"Jeremy's agent. She was afraid of losing his income. Then she lost him altogether." A tiny smile quirked Phoebe's lips, as though she'd just discovered the sole upside of her husband's death: it had inconvenienced his agent. "I suppose now Claire is sitting pretty with Nicola for a client. She didn't even wait for Jeremy's body to be cold before chasing the deal, that cow."

I was so surprised to hear sophisticated Phoebe use that slur that I almost laughed. But I kept my composure instead.

I still had questions. I couldn't wait to ask them. Delicately, I glanced toward the paper, wishing I'd read it from front to back before arriving for Phoebe's tutoring session.

In a careful voice, I asked, "What scandals were there?"

SEX! SECRETS! The tabloid had promised outrage aplenty.

Phoebe tossed me a patrician look. "I will not dignify that with a response, Hayden. You're better than that, aren't you?"

I felt chastised. But I was still dying of curiosity. Exactly what, I wondered, did Jeremy's former assistant know about him?

A quick perusal of the article over Phoebe's shoulder told me the cover story had been a teaser, revealing only that "sex, secrets, and scandals!" would be forthcoming in Nicola's book.

Exactly when, I wondered further, had Claire— Jeremy's agent—put together that deal? Before Jeremy's death? Or after?

The timing made a difference—and might make Claire a suspect, depending on how lucrative the publishing contract had been. A sensational tell-all book was one thing; a sensational tell-all book about a beloved celebrity after his untimely death was another. Surely those circumstances would improve sales.

Enough to prompt a convenient murder? Maybe.

How long, I mused, had Nicola been writing her book? She would have naturally run into Claire while working for Jeremy, so making a connection with his agent wouldn't have been difficult. After that, all Nicola would have needed was material—an exposé enticing enough to fuel a deal.

It would have had to have been a real doozy of a deal to make Claire risk alienating Jeremy, her biggest client.

Claire had to be listed in Jeremy's phone. I still had it. I could call her right now. But what would I use for an excuse?

I'd like an advance copy of Nicola's book probably wouldn't fly. But at least, it occurred to me, I knew why Jeremy's former assistant hadn't jumped on my job offer at the café.

Nicola hadn't needed another lowly assistant or server job. She hadn't had to put up with abuse or being unceremoniously sacked. Not when she'd had a publishing contract on the table.

I *had* to find out more. But first, I had to get free.

"Well, shall we get baking?" I asked brightly.

Phoebe looked astounded. "After *this*? Are you mad?" She grabbed her cell phone. "I need to make some calls, don't I?"

Then, just as I'd hoped, she vanished into her town house's private salon, talking in hushed but horrified tones to whoever was on the other end of the line. I heard a raving mention of "that skank!" then made my getaway to the guesthouse.

Clearly, there'd been no love lost between Phoebe, Claire, and (maybe) Nicola. It was up to me to find out why. Stat.

Eight

Claire Evans proved to be the easiest person to start with. Jeremy's agent was so eager to bask in the limelight that she agreed to meet with me right away, largely because I'd anticipated her urge to make the most of the publicity garnered by Nicola's tell-all book and had suggested that we meet at one of London's most visible spots: a ritzy hotel at teatime.

Claire hadn't been able to resist being seen in such a prominent spot, which was how we'd come to be seated across from one another in a glorious nineteenth-century hotel tearoom. We made small talk across the starched tablecloth while mirrored walls, ornate birdcage chandeliers, tall potted palms, rococo columns, and the occasional gilded statue surrounded us.

A pianist played in the background. The tearoom's windows were arched and resplendent, accented with silk shantung draperies and golden-fringed tiebacks. The floors were polished marble. Fresh flowers were everywhere. The upholstery fabric for a single chair probably cost more than my entire wardrobe.

It was fancy. It was popular, too, full of tea takers.

I know what you must be thinking. That I, ordinary Hayden Mundy Moore, couldn't possibly clean up sufficiently to fit into such a swanky atmosphere. But I'm here to tell you that my lifetime of globe-trotting has made me into a chameleon. I don't like to blend in, but I'm perfectly capable of it.

Just as I know not to totter in shaky stilettos on Parisian cobblestones or wear a skimpy miniskirt into the Basilica San Marco in Venice, I knew better than to turn up to London's afternoon tea in jeans and a T-shirt, with kitchen clogs on my feet and my hair in a baker's bandanna. I knew to actually comb my hair and put on some lipstick, even though my usual makeup routine doesn't extend beyond much lip gloss and (maybe) mascara. I knew to put on a dress and some nice shoes, too.

Okay, so they weren't sky-high L. K. Bennett heels of the variety Phoebe and her friends favored. I would have broken my neck in those. I like to move quickly, besides. But I'd managed well enough, in my knee-length dress and ballerina flats, to make Danny do a very satisfying double take on my way out.

I'd done a pirouette, to extend the experience. He'd offered up a low wolf whistle, to meet my expectations.

"You clean up nice," he'd said, "for someone who's willing to rake cacao beans on a planation in overalls and a hat."

"Don't lose track of me, just because I look different."

"It'll take more than a dress and some lipstick to throw me off," Danny had assured me, his expression opaque. Naturally, he'd insisted on following me to my meeting. "Let's move."

I wasn't sure where *he* had "moved" to since then. I

couldn't see him anywhere at the hotel. He'd declined to put on a suit and invite Ashley to tea as a cover for shadowing me. Instead, Danny had greeted that perfectly reasonable suggestion with a dark arched eyebrow and a firmly voiced, "No way in hell."

At his look of horror, I'd almost laughed.

As the pianist's song ended, a momentary quiet settled over the tearoom. I looked at Claire Evans, then continued with my excuse for asking to meet her: a (made-up) book of my own.

"I envision the book to be an exposé of the chocolate world," I told her. "Like any luxury industry, chocolate making has its share of drama and intrigue, machinations and secrets. I've seen them all during my career. It's time to share."

"Why here? Why now?" Shrewd and tweedy, with her gray hair perfectly coiffed, Claire was in her sixties and hard to fool. She reminded me of a fast-forwarded version of London's "Sloane Rangers," girls who'd dressed in pearls, pashmina, and preppy clothes in the '80s. These days, the Duchess of Cambridge, Kate Middleton, was their goddess, with her wellies and gilets. "Why not contact someone you're familiar with in America?"

I'd anticipated that question. "I don't have an agent in the U.S. As far as 'why here' goes, I expect to be in London for quite a while yet. My parents live in Mayfair. I'm planning to spend some time with them while writing the book." At least part of that was true. I did want to see them while I was abroad. I smiled. "Besides, I like it here." That was true too.

Claire gave a narrow-eyed nod, clearly not convinced. "If your book is as scandalous as you claim, no one in the chocolate industry will ever trust you again. You'll be forced to quit."

"I'm ready for that." I wasn't at all ready for that.

It was a good thing this was just a ploy, designed to gather intel from Jeremy's agent. I would have preferred being honest, but *I suspect you of murdering your client to increase the marketability of Nicola's book* wouldn't endear me to her.

Plus, it was possible that *Nicola* had murdered Jeremy to increase the marketability of her book. She was certainly better off financially now than she'd ever been as his downtrodden assistant. I gathered that I must have glimpsed her going into that Covent Garden jeweler because she'd been buying herself a bauble to celebrate her forthcoming tell-all of Jeremy.

While I pondered the cold-bloodedness of that, Claire scanned the room. I sensed she was feeling antsy. Judging by the smell of stale cigarettes emanating from her clothes, Claire was a smoker. If I wanted to keep her interest, I needed to be more engaging. Otherwise, she'd skip afternoon tea altogether and hop onto Piccadilly Street to satisfy her nicotine craving instead.

"This is sensitive information." I didn't want to namecheck Nicola Mitchell, but she *was* the instant-book sensation of the moment. The legitimate and tabloid press had been breathless with the news of her "million pound" book deal. "I heard you were *the* person to come to with material of this sort."

Claire perked up. "You've heard about Nicola's book?"

"Of course. Everyone has." I adopted a sad mien. It wasn't difficult. I truly felt sorry about the situation. "I've met Jeremy Wright. His death was tragic. I still don't know how it could have happened, but it's made me doubly aware of how tenuous life can be. I might not have years and years ahead of me. Unless I act now, I might never get to write my . . . memoirs."

I gave that final word deliberate emphasis, making sure that Claire realized my (hypothetical) written reminiscences promised to be scandalous. I wanted to hook her quickly.

"What companies, exactly, are we discussing?" she asked.

I had her. Having already considered this, I cited some of the world's top chocolate concerns, from boutique brands to global conglomerates. "I can't disclose everything now, of course," I demurred before I got carried away. "Not without a deal in place. But I can say that what goes on is . . . surprising."

Claire leaned closer. "Are we talking about CEOs skimming profits? Managers sleeping with their secretaries? Workers sneezing on the production line? What do you have to spill?"

I hesitated. "I don't have a book outline per se. I don't want to reveal any specifics yet. I'm still planning to meet with a few other interested parties. But that doesn't mean—"

Jeremy's agent tut-tutted. "There's no need for that!"

She signaled a server who'd been lingering attentively nearby, dressed dapperly in a suit and tie. In a flash, several of his colleagues appeared, bearing the accoutrements of a cream tea—so named because it includes Britain's famed clotted cream.

At this point, I should probably clarify that, as fancy as it sounds, a "high tea" is actually much less formal than a cream tea or a full afternoon tea. A "high tea" is what working-class families have when they tuck into a late-day steak and kidney pie. An "afternoon tea" is what the Queen of England has.

Today, it was what *I* was having with Claire, too.

In the center of the table, another server placed a three-tiered silver cake stand. Its lower level contained savories—neat rectangular sandwiches such as cucumber, cress, chutney, and egg mayo, each with its crusts trimmed off. Its middle tier held those items that were neither savory nor especially sweet, such as miniature cream buns, scones, and crumpets. Its top (and most interesting to me) tier showcased bite-size petit fours, shortbread biscuits ("cookies," to you and me), and pastel-colored macarons.

You're supposed to nibble at those foodstuffs in order, from the bottom to the top. With fingers only, please—as useful as it might be, cutlery is verboten at a proper tea service.

I couldn't help thinking that some of it should have been chocolate. Someone was leaving an opportunity unclaimed here.

Delicate china bowls appeared on our table, each containing something delicious. Devonshire clotted cream. Strawberry jam. Lemon curd. White and brown sugar cubes with an accompanying pair of tiny silver tongs. Wafer-thin, almost translucent lemon slices. A tasteful silver pitcher full of fresh Guernsey milk.

The tea service itself arrived next, clad in gleaming silver plate and already warmed, with floral bone china cups and saucers beside it. Loose-leaf teas were brought after that. Oolong, Darjeeling, Lapsang souchong, Ceylon—enough to make my head spin. It was like choosing from chocolate varietals, only I'm not an expert in tea. But the server didn't know that.

"Miss? Your preference for tea?" he asked, ready to serve.

All at once, I knew exactly what to ask for. "Earl Grey. Hot. No sugar, please." Travis would have been so pleased.

While the niceties of tea service continued in a parade of ritualized brewing, waiting, pouring, and embellishing, I did my best to guide my conversation with Claire in a new direction.

It wasn't easy. DC Mishra would have had a smoother time finding out what she wanted to know from her "sources" than I ever did. I wasn't a detective. I didn't think I'd get away with acting like one. My best bet was to rely on human nature—and my own ability to create camaraderie with people I meet. I've done that for a long time, without even thinking about it. Pilots in São Paulo, jazz musicians in New Orleans, surfers in Queensland, and glassblowers in Samobor . . . they've all opened up to me for genuinely interesting and enlightening conversations.

Of course, I hadn't been trying to investigate a murder linked to any of those people. But Claire might cooperate.

Hoping she would, I gave her a direct look before tasting my tea. No pinkies in the air, either, by the way. It's just not necessary. It was delicious. I sighed, then put down my cup.

"You must have a challenging job," I said as a friendly change of subject. "All those clients, so many of them famous . . ." I shook my head in sympathy. "I know what it's like to cater to the demands of people who are used to getting their own way."

"You're not wrong about that!" Claire trilled, watching intently as the servers receded to their watchful places nearby. Surreptitiously, she slipped a flask from her purse and tipped it toward my cup with raised eyebrows. "Shall we indulge?"

I demurred. Claire added a healthy pour to her cup. Maybe she wasn't so savvy after all. It wasn't even five o'clock yet.

I'd noticed she hadn't opted for milk with her tea. No wonder. A shot of whiskey would have curdled the whole lot.

"You're sure?" She offered her flask again. I noticed it matched the tea service. "We could toast to our impending deal."

I shook my head. She tucked away her tipple, then took a healthy slurp of her Darjeeling. She sighed contentedly.

"This must have been a difficult week for you," I said.

A nod. "Indeed. It was such a shock to hear about Jeremy."

"I love his books and TV shows. Was he fun to work with?"

"Jeremy? Fun?" Claire rolled her eyes. She drank more tea, draining her cup in record time. I guessed the whiskey had cooled off her brew. A server unobtrusively poured her more. Jeremy's former agent added more whiskey, leaving her flask on the table this time. "He was fun at first. Energetic, eager to please, full of ideas and enthusiasm . . . and sex appeal. Whoo!"

Claire fanned herself, oblivious to the other tea takers turning at the sound of her excited exclamation.

"Let me tell you, Hayden. I can take people places," she assured me, eyes bright. "Before Jeremy, everyone thought no one could be more successful than Gemma Rose. She tapped a market that no one else had. She merged food and sensuality without being tacky. Especially for us Brits, that was titillating."

"I haven't heard much from her lately. Did she retire?"

"She might as well have." Blithely, Claire bit into a miniscule ham and chutney sandwich, thinking about my question while she chewed. "Jeremy eclipsed her almost immediately. Gemma Rose was popular, but Jeremy was stratospheric. Thanks to me. You see, I knew there was an appetite for a sexy male chef. Everyone else underestimated women's interest in such a thing. But especially after a certain age, women can be just as voracious as men!"

She made pantomime cougar claws and gave me a growl.

I laughed. I couldn't help it. "Equal-opportunity food voyeurism. There's nothing wrong with that, is there?"

"Not at all!" Claire emptied her second teacup. It was swiftly and attentively refilled from a freshly brewed pot. "Gemma Rose wrote that book, but Jeremy perfected it. He'd watched Gemma for years. He'd been a big fan." She gazed at the chandeliers overhead, lost in reminisces. "The day his cookbooks shot past Gemma's in total millions sold, he was so thrilled."

"I'd imagine so. That's a very big deal."

Gemma Rose had been the doyenne of British cookery for nearly a decade, I knew. She'd turned everyday cooking into irresistible foreplay. There'd never been a spoon she wouldn't lick, an olive oil bottle she wouldn't fondle, a food that hadn't compelled her to moan with pleasure. She'd created her empire based on culinary knowledge and sensuality, and she'd had the best-selling cookbooks, popular television shows, and fans to prove it. I hadn't thought about Gemma's slump in popularity as a direct result of Jeremy's ascendancy, but Claire did.

"It was because of me," Claire assured me. "I masterminded the whole thing. Jeremy's rise, his expansion to restaurants, his sold-out live tours—both here and abroad. All my ideas." She winked as she sipped from her cup. "I can do the same for you."

She was still trying to persuade me to sign with her. I appreciated her interest in me and my phantom book, but I had another agenda, stoked by what Phoebe had said about Jeremy's agent.

She was afraid of losing his income. But why? Had things gone wrong between Jeremy and Claire? Murderously wrong?

"Gemma Rose should have had *you* for an agent," I joked.

Claire blinked. "Oh, she did have me. I dropped her."

I sat up straighter. If Claire had dropped Gemma Rose as a client in favor of building Jeremy, that could have definitely stoked some ill will in the (onetime) domestic doyenne. Although it probably would have led Gemma to want to murder Claire, not Jeremy. On the other hand, Jeremy had taken Gemma's place in the upper echelons of food celebrity. That had to bother her.

"Or maybe not." Claire frowned tipsily. "I can't quite remember. It's possible Gemma is still on my roster. I'm not sure anymore. She's been in so little demand for anything substantial, ever since Hambleton & Hart switched their sponsorship to Jeremy."

Hambleton & Hart? Now I felt really alert. Also, convinced that Claire had drunk far too much whiskey in her Darjeeling. Just as I thought it, Jeremy's former agent took out her phone, snapped a selfie, then fiddled with an app for a few minutes.

Eventually, she noticed me noticing. She gave a careless wave, then set down her phone with a satisfied flourish.

"Just because I'm older doesn't mean I can't use

technology, does it? In my business, you've got to keep up."

Her phone dinged. Her gaze swerved interestedly toward it.

She picked up, obviously compelled. "To Londoners, this tearoom is instantly recognizable. Even if it wasn't, the geotagging on my selfie would let everyone know where I am."

Claire seemed satisfied to have sent out an agent Bat-Signal. Obviously, she enjoyed the attention, but I felt happier than ever that my (usually secret) job doesn't require a social-media presence. I didn't need to Tweet, Instagram, or Snapchat about my services to get clients. I just needed Travis. And me.

I didn't want to leave a consultation one day only to find myself amid paparazzi and reporters, discussing my findings.

"Hambleton & Hart worked with both Gemma and Jeremy?"

An absentminded nod. Claire typed on her phone, then focused on me again. "Product placement is a tremendous source of income for my clients. Jeremy once used a certain brand of digestive biscuits to make a crumb crust on his show." She pushed aside the sugar bowl and leaned nearer, fixing me with an intelligent look—and building suspense. "Those biscuits sold out across the entire U.K. within hours of that program airing."

That was a big accomplishment for a very modest style of cookie. Digestive biscuits were originally called that because they contain baking soda, which was once considered useful for proper digestion. But now their primary claim to fame was having a pleasant wheaty, malty flavor and a dunkable texture in tea.

I sipped my Earl Grey. "That's a lot of biscuits."

"It is!" Claire nodded. "A particular artisanal butter used in a cooking segment, a specific bottle of wine poured to drink with an on-camera meal, a relatively obscure ingredient added to a dish . . . they all represent pounds and pence to someone."

"Someone like Hambleton & Hart?" I guessed.

"They're a venerable brand." Claire broke off a piece of scone, slathered it with cream, then dabbed on some jam. "They've been around since the 1860s. They act that way, too."

She chuckled. I played along and nibbled a crumpet, wishing it was embellished with a smear of chocolate-hazelnut spread.

"They have trouble keeping up with the times?" I asked.

"Absolutely. They stuck with Gemma Rose much longer than they should have—certainly much longer than *I* advised them to."

"Well, with *your* experience," I began, flattering her.

But Claire Evans didn't require my praise. "Hambleton & Hart's core customers are young mums who want to give their children the same treats they once enjoyed. The company deals in nostalgia, low prices, and convenience. They had to be clear about that. Gemma Rose was the wrong spokesperson for them."

"Gemma *was* all about savoring the moment," I mused. "Young mothers probably don't have time to labor over homemade treats."

But Claire disagreed, keen to show her expertise. "She was about sex. The *wrong* sex. Those mums didn't want to watch Gemma Rose prancing around with her knockers out, making eyes at the camera. They wanted to watch Jeremy. *His* star was on the rise."

Claire was really loosening up now. Also, it sounded to me as though Jeremy's star hadn't merely been on the rise. It had completely obscured Gemma's. The domestic diva must have been bitter about that—about falling from public favor so quickly.

I wanted to ask about Gemma Rose personally, to get a sense of her latent violent tendencies—because that's the way I have to think about people (these days) when murder is afoot—but Claire was already moving on. At least she'd quit talking about "knockers." Her teatime nip had definitely taken effect.

"Which only made it all the more distressing when Jeremy began being difficult too," Claire moaned, looking distraught.

That was more like it. "Really? What was wrong?"

"What *wasn't* wrong?" his former agent complained loudly, drawing a few more stares from the other tearoom tables. "He demanded more money. He missed deadlines. He balked at including sponsored products in his cookery shows. He'd become intolerable."

Just as Nicola Mitchell had claimed at the café, I recalled. "He always seemed like such a friendly guy."

Claire snorted. "Of course he did. In public! In private, Jeremy was a terror. At the end, he didn't even want to be on camera. He was obsessed with his weight, his hair, his skin. He thought he was getting wrinkly. He knew he was going bald."

I remembered Jeremy's lush hair. Even in death, it had fallen perfectly around his face. He must have used some very special products to ensure manageability—to hide his bald spot.

Poor Jeremy. The more you had, the more you had to lose.

"But that's life in the public eye," Claire was saying sanguinely. "The thing is, I don't think his fans would have cared. Look at Prince William! He's certainly not possessed of a leonine mane, is he? But no one minds that. Women are very forgiving. They were attracted to Jeremy's charisma. And his physique, of course. There are Tumblr blogs devoted to his abs."

I was surprised, again, at her Internet savvy.

"He had his physical trainer to thank for that, though, right?" I suggested, tucking into my own morsel of scone, cream, and jam. It was reminiscent of strawberry shortcake. Delicious, even sans chocolate. "His trainer kept Jeremy in top shape."

"Liam Taylor?" Claire frowned. "Don't you dare mention that man to me! I doubt he has any idea of the havoc he caused, but—"

"Havoc?" I thought I knew why. I tried to look clueless, to cajole Claire into sharing more information with me. So far, I had almost everything I wanted to know—and more. I wasn't sure how to bring us back around to the subject of Nicola's book, but maybe that would have to wait for another meeting. "How's that?"

"His diet." Claire sounded disgusted. "That nonsensical 'clean eating' regimen of Liam's was going to be the death of us both, and I don't mean because I'd drop a few stone, either."

A stone was a unit of weight—roughly fourteen pounds. My mom, an avowed Anglophile, had taught me that years ago.

"Jeremy didn't look as though he needed to lose weight to me." I moved up a tier to the macarons. Mmm. "He looked fit."

"Tell that to the paparazzi. They're pitiless." Claire followed my lead, biting into a slender petit four while the pianist tinkled her way through another song. "One puffy-faced photo was all that Jeremy required to make him panic. He hired Liam, gave up bacon butties, and almost ruined the pair of us."

"How's that?" I sipped Earl Grey, still wishing there was a little something chocolaty to nosh while I listened to Claire.

"First, Jeremy refused to fulfill his cookbook contract," she told me. "He wanted his next work to focus on 'clean foods,' but his publisher wasn't interested in that foolishness. Then he objected to having sugar on set. He wouldn't allow beer adverts to be aired. Then he reneged on the Hambleton & Hart deal. He wouldn't touch their products. He said they were 'poison.'"

I widened my eyes. "Wow, that's impressive discipline."

Having seen Liam, I thought I understood why. Jeremy had probably been trying to save himself from himself—and, by extension, from Liam, Mr. "I don't tolerate doing things halfway."

"It was destructiveness," Claire disagreed, "especially given the timing. We were in the middle of filming an advert for Hambleton & Hart when Jeremy discovered his conscience. I would have had to drop him as a client if things had continued."

She gave me a self-justifying look while I digested that information. Jeremy doing an advert (a "commercial" to you and me) was news to me. "So that's what Jeremy was doing when he . . ."

Was killed? lingered between us. I couldn't say it, but I surmised that's why the guesthouse had been full of A/V equipment—equipment that was still (chillingly) in place.

"You don't have any objections to making money, do you?" Claire startled me from reliving my discovery of Jeremy's body. Evidently, she didn't want to dwell on Jeremy's death, either. "You're not secretly a Buddhist? A technophobe? A skinflint?"

"No, of course not!" I laughed, knowing I wouldn't

be making any money from my fictitious tell-all book. I felt bad about deceiving Claire, but my loyalties lay with Jeremy—and with uncovering his murderer. "That would be crazy of me."

A sigh. "If only Jeremy had had half your common sense."

Agents are paid a percentage of their clients' earnings, I knew. If Jeremy had backed out of his endorsement deal with Hambleton & Hart, it would have cost his agent a significant amount of money. Enough money to provoke an impulsive murder?

Maybe . . . if the contract had been in force when Jeremy had died *and* Hambleton & Hart had still been obligated to pay. I made a note to ask Travis to find out those details, wishing I could remember if Claire had eaten her tea sandwiches with her left hand or with her right. The killer was supposed to be left-handed, according to the police. Belatedly remembering to check, I studied her. But her hands were folded atop the table, serenely resting there, giving me no clues about her handedness.

I wished I'd checked earlier. But it's a pretty bizarre thing to do, inspecting someone to see if they're left-handed. Without that extemporaneous tip from DC Mishra's colleague, George, I wouldn't have known to look for that detail at all.

Claire didn't notice my tardy scrutiny. "So, Hayden. What are you willing to do to promote your book? I have excellent media connections. We could arrange a worldwide media tour."

That sounded horrendous to me. I smiled anyway. "I think it's too soon to discuss particulars." I finished my macaron and dabbed my mouth with my napkin, preparing to bring our meeting to a close. I didn't want to take up all of Claire's time on false pretenses. "I'll think about this and be in touch later."

I was being absolutely honest about thinking things over. Jeremy's erstwhile agent had given me a lot of food for thought.

Claire frowned. I felt momentarily alarmed. Even after more than a few whiskey-laced cups of tea, she appeared . . . formidable.

I wouldn't have wanted to cross her is what I'm saying.

But then a stir at the tearoom's entrance diverted us both.

"Darling!" A curvaceous blonde sashayed toward our table, clad in a cleavage-enhancing red jersey wrap dress with an entourage of hotel employees trailing her. "Claire, darling!"

I didn't think anyone said "darling!" Not outside of classic movies. But this woman did. It was Gemma Rose, diva extraordinaire. I was immediately struck by her magnetism.

She arrived at our table and leaned closer to greet Claire. I heard two loud, lipsticky *smacks*, then a seductive chuckle.

"Same old Claire," Gemma teased. "Whiskey at tea, love?"

Immediately, I reconsidered my limited, TV-centric notions of Gemma Rose. She might be down—and, at forty-plus, headed in the wrong direction for popular culture—but she wasn't out.

"Gemma, this is Hayden Mundy Moore, a potential client. Hayden, this is Gemma Rose." As Gemma swooped in to air-kiss me too, Claire continued. "How did you know I was here, Gemma?"

"Oh, we're friends on Nearby, darling." Gemma

raised her cell phone, indicating a social networking app. "Did you forget? I was in the neighborhood. But I'm *concerned* about you, Claire. Shouldn't you ask your doctor about those memory lapses?"

With an air of fretful inclusion, Gemma turned to me. "My grandfather had the same problem. A month later, he was living in an elder-care facility." She raised her voice toward Claire. "It was a very nice place!" Gemma shouted kindly. "Very pastel!"

Jeremy's agent frowned. But I didn't think she was senile. Even after tippling whiskey, she seemed pretty sharp to me. The shrewdness I'd noted before had returned, glimmering in Claire's eyes. I began to think she'd drawn Gemma there on purpose.

Maybe that's what she'd been doing via her selfie earlier.

Oblivious to those machinations, Gemma looked around. She seemed breathless, eager, and very proper. She definitely had that "lady in public, temptress in the bedroom" routine nailed. Most of the men in the tearoom—not that there were many, in such a feminine environment—were watching her, enthralled by her beauty and poise. She deserved more than life as a has-been.

At her show of graceful helplessness, one of her entourage added another chair to our table. Gemma took it, crossing her legs coquettishly. "You don't mind if I join you two, do you?"

"Of course not!" I waved toward our tea. I'll admit, I was a little starstruck. Like many people, I'd watched Gemma on TV. I'd bought her popular cookbooks. I'd tried out a seductive, throaty purr—similar to hers—during a chocolate-tempering demo.

The client had asked me if I were coming down with a cold.

But Gemma remained focused on Claire—and what she needed from her. Delicately, she frowned. "Did you hear from Andrew?"

"Yes. He doesn't want you back," Claire said bluntly.

I wasn't sure I should be privy to this conversation. But there was no way I was leaving. I wondered who Andrew was.

Gemma's face fell. "But Hambleton & Hart need me!"

Aha. Andrew must have something to do with them.

"Not anymore, they don't." Claire flashed me a contrite look, silently apologizing for Gemma having crashed our meeting. She signaled for the check. "Hayden, I'll call you later."

"But they *do* need me!" Gemma insisted, putting her hand on Claire's arm to detain her. "I have a new idea—a brilliant one. Now that Jeremy is gone, I thought I'd have another chance!"

Her desperate tone was unmistakable. That's when I snapped out of my fangirl trance and recognized the situation for what it was. No matter how appealing Gemma Rose might be, she'd had every reason to want Jeremy dead. He'd stolen her position. He'd taken her spot on the best-seller lists. He'd supplanted her at Hambleton & Hart. He'd cost her millions of pounds in income.

He'd replaced her in the hearts of the world's food lovers.

As far as Gemma Rose was concerned, I realized, Jeremy Wright had been an obstacle to everything she deserved.

But could she have committed murder to reclaim it?

I watched as Gemma anxiously picked up a cream

bun and bit into it, her gaze fastened on Claire as she paid for our tea.

Gemma Rose was left-handed, I saw. I had another suspect.

I'd scarcely made it two steps toward the sumptuous hotel lobby before Danny intercepted me. His long strides covered the fine Aubusson carpet at an alarming rate, making the porter and desk clerk stare . . . along with a few interested female guests.

As usual, my security expert looked *fine.* Even dressed in a pair of casual black trousers and a white shirt, Danny Jamieson was eye-catching. Without trying to, he stood out. Probably because of all the muscles, the air of command . . . and the smile.

That's what surprised me as he caught my arm. Danny didn't usually look that unabashedly happy. I couldn't help gawking.

"What happened to *you?*" I asked, noting the energy pouring off him. He looked like a kid at Christmas—a big, strong, dark, and handsome one. Okay, he looked like a full-grown man, and nothing else. "You look as though you just won the lottery."

That took him aback. He glanced at me. "You know I don't screw around with gambling. What's the matter with you?"

I'm overloaded with suspects. My brain is fried.

I shrugged and kept walking. Danny easily kept pace with me as I led us out of the upscale hotel and onto Piccadilly Street.

There, people moved just as fast as we both did. We merged with them, keeping pace with the locals and dodging tourists.

"Why didn't you tell me you were meeting Gemma Rose?"

Now it was my turn to be taken aback. "I wasn't. She crashed." He must have seen Gemma join me and Claire. "Why?"

Because . . . "You've got to keep me in the loop, Hayden."

"I just told you, I didn't know she was coming." I gave him an inquiring look. His rugged profile revealed nothing. "I'm not sure *she* knew she was coming. It looked like a last-minute thing. You must have seen the way she came into the tearoom, all breathless, as though she was afraid of missing Claire."

Danny remained mum, navigating us both through the crowd, past a Boots pharmacy and a cell phone store. He kept one hand on the small of my back, making sure no one jostled me.

He needn't have worried. People took one look at him and made a path. His default demeanor was daunting. Unapproachable.

"She *was* afraid of missing Claire," he told me.

I grinned. "Now how could you possibly know that? I know you're a ninja at shadowing me, Danny, but come on. Be serious."

"Gemma Rose got . . . waylaid on her way into the tearoom."

He made that cryptic comment and kept striding onward. But another grin broke over his face, boyish and pleased. What the . . . ?

Then I got it. "*You* waylaid her. She was late because of you?" I stared at him. "You were flirting with Gemma Rose?"

Danny shrugged. "Sometimes you've got to seize the moment."

For a few more steps, I considered that. Then, "You're a fan, aren't you?" His grin broadened in response. "Danny!"

"I may have watched a few . . . hundred . . . episodes of her show."

This was news to me. "You have a crush on Gemma Rose!" I couldn't help jabbing him in the ribs. "That's adorable."

He scowled at my teasing. "Try to rein in the squee-ing when she comes over, all right? Just be cool. No autograph requests."

I laughed. Then I realized he was serious.

"You have a date with Gemma Rose? *The* Gemma Rose? And *you*?" Danny seemed so pleased, I *almost* didn't have the heart to add, "But she's a suspect in Jeremy's murder. You can't date her."

His expression of disbelief floored me. "Yes, I can."

"No, you can't. Gemma Rose just ate a cream bun with her left hand. You know what DC George said." It occurred to me that I didn't know his last name, so I waved that off. "No. No way."

"You don't seriously suspect Gemma."

"I certainly do."

"Because she's left-handed? You're reaching." Danny tossed me a censorious look as we reached the next Underground station entrance. We made our way downstairs amid the throngs of people. "This new tactic of yours—being twice as suspicious as usual—has gone too far, if you're suspecting someone like Gemma."

I stuck to my guns. "*You* always say I'm too trusting."

"Well, now you're too suspicious." He stepped onto the escalator, leading the way for both of us. "Just back off."

I wouldn't. "Gemma Rose could have wanted Jeremy dead."

"So could anyone. So what?" We descended. Danny glanced over his broad shoulder at me. "She was carrying a purse in her right hand. That's why she ate that bun left-handed," he pointed out. "You probably didn't notice, because you were already convicting her of bludgeoning Jeremy to death." His lips quirked. "As if Gemma could even carry that heavy metlapil."

"She's a woman, not a weakling," I objected as we reached the platform. A train whizzed past, sending gusts of warm air washing over us. I squeezed shut my eyes, then refocused on Danny. "Hasn't it occurred to you that Gemma Rose might know that you're with *me*? She's smart. Maybe she's using you to find out what I've learned while investigating Jeremy's murder."

Danny's expression looked incredulous. "Not bloody likely."

"It's possible," I insisted, unmoved by his sardonic use of that British slang. I could be stubborn too. "Watch out."

"You watch out," my bodyguard shot back irritably. He didn't look at me, but most of his earlier gleefulness had left his face. "I'm seeing Gemma later, and you can't stop me."

"I'm seeing Liam later, and you can't stop me."

"I don't care about stopping you." Danny touched my elbow, steering me backward. I was dangerously close to the yellow line that marked the platform's edge. One overeager commuter, one overzealous bump, and I'd be toast. "I'm too happy to bother."

I studied him and saw that it was true. "Just be careful," I relented. We could handle an argument. We always did. "Keep an eye out for tricks. Or murder plans. Or evidence! I need some."

"I could say the same to you, about Hulk Hands."

"I don't think Liam is guilty. Just misguided about sugar."

"You've got to watch yourself," Danny told me as our Tube train arrived. "I know you wish you'd been faster off the blocks in Portland and San Fran, but you might be overcompensating for your gullible nature this time. Not everyone is a killer."

Gullible? I couldn't believe he was saying that to *me*.

"I'm not the one who's being gullible here. You are—the guy who's about to date a possible murderess." I stepped over the gap and onto the train in front of him. I grabbed the center pole with one hand, then swayed as the train left the platform. "I don't want you to wind up like Jeremy did, Danny. I mean it."

"*I* mean it," he said, finally breaking into a smile that was meant purely for me. "Just take one step back, Nancy Drew. Don't wreck this for me with Gemma Rose. We . . . have something."

He sounded so over-the-top hopeful that I thought he was joking. Then I glanced at Danny's face and knew he was serious. Uh-oh. Had my security expert just fallen for my latest suspect?

I didn't know. But it sure seemed possible.

"Fine. You can be my 'boots on the ground' with Gemma Rose," I compromised. "Let me know if she seems guilty or says anything incriminating. Tell me if she mentions murder."

Danny grinned. "Har, har. If it were that easy, anyone could do what you do—what you've already done twice now."

Twice now. He was right. But I didn't want to think about those incidents—about catching killers and everything that entailed. It was all still too unnerving.

I hadn't yet come to grips with my unwanted new role as part-time amateur sleuth.

"You'll do it?" I pushed. "You'll watch Gemma Rose for me?"

His dark look said he didn't want to. Then, "Yeah. Okay." He stared out the train's window as we reached another station. "But only to prove you wrong about Gemma. And you *are* wrong."

We'd see about that, I knew. But first, I had work to do.

Nine

The only thing I didn't learn at afternoon tea with Claire Evans, I realized as I parted ways with Danny on the street level and went to earn my chocolate-whisperer keep at Primrose, was exactly what might be in Nicola Mitchell's tell-all book.

I decided to call her. While Jeremy's former assistant and I hadn't exactly hit it off like long-lost sisters during our kaffeeklatsch, we'd had a reasonably pleasant time. Plus, I thought I knew how to persuade her. So I set up another meeting, explaining that I wanted to make good on my offer to "hook her up" with some tasty, newly enhanced treats from Primrose.

Two birds. One stone. I had to multitask these days.

From the moment I greeted Nicola—bearing chocolate caramel popcorn, double chocolate bark with salted almonds, and vivid green pistachio truffles made with Dumante liqueur, all arranged on a tray in Primrose's signature demitasse cups—she was putty in my hands. I would have liked to have credited my *fait à la maison* sweets for that fact, but I figured Nicola's newfound malleability had more to do with having just made a million pounds on her book deal than it did with my culinary wizardry.

That kind of payout would have put anyone in a good mood.

Even a murderer? Chilled to think it, I watched Nicola carefully. She dug right into the goodies—with both hands, I noticed inconclusively—doing her best to make up for lost time.

Evidently, the rigors of Jeremy's and Liam's "clean eating" regimen had really bothered Nicola. They would have bothered me too. We had that much in common. Plus, I've had dead-end jobs too—even if I didn't profit quite so handsomely from them. It was possible Nicola couldn't afford much in the way of indulgences.

Well, not until recently, at least.

"Oh, *yum!*" she exclaimed, mouth full. Her eyes rolled back in her head with pleasure. She gave a happy wiggle. "I never thought I'd be back here, but *this* is a good reason to come."

I'd joined her in Primrose's upstairs seating area—a small loft overlooking the neighborhood and its green trees. The only seating was a single café table and chair, one armchair, and a love seat–size settee, which we both squeezed onto. I'd set my tray of goodies on the loft's coffee table. Below us, the chocolaterie-pâtisserie was not quite as busy as I'd have liked.

I still hadn't made sufficient inroads training the staff. They were progressing, though. Hugh, in particular, had emerged as a leader of the group. Faintly, from the warm kitchens, I heard his distinctly accented voice shouting a command to Poppy. I felt gratified by this development. He'd gotten comfortable. Given more time, he'd master a skill he could be proud of.

In the meantime, everyone downstairs had swiftly learned to make chocolate caramel popcorn, chocolate bark, and pistachio truffles today. We'd had only a few mishaps along the way.

"Did you used to come here often?" I asked Nicola.

"Sometimes." Jeremy's former assistant bit into a truffle. She groaned with enjoyment, then waggled it toward me. "These are *really* nice. So's the popcorn. And the chocolate bark."

"Thanks, that's kind of you. It's all in a day's work, though. I had plenty of help." I indicated the kitchen downstairs, watching as Nicola swigged some fizzy, house-made lemon soda. "I appreciate your taste-testing for me. I can use the feedback. My taste isn't everyone's taste. But if you like those, please feel free to tell everyone you know," I kidded. There was nothing more valuable than authentic word of mouth. "Maybe a few strangers, too. We need more business around here."

"So I noticed." Nodding, Nicola swept her curly auburn hair from her eyes. She seemed open and eager to help. "This place used to be packed all the time. Poor Phoebe. It must be breaking her heart to see Primrose struggling after all these years."

"I think it would be, under other circumstances." When she'd hired me, she hadn't known calamity would strike. "She's managing as best she can, though. It's difficult for her."

Nicola looked skeptical. "Difficult *not* celebrating."

I was surprised she was being so cruel. I guess it showed.

"Don't get me wrong," Nicola went on. She nibbled some chocolate bark. "I like Phoebe. We were friendly when I worked for Jeremy. But he was a tyrant. And not just to me, either."

She was hinting at supposed marital troubles between Jeremy and Phoebe again. But I'd found no sign of disharmony anywhere.

"Jeremy must have had his good qualities," I argued, inhaling the buttery scents of shortbread and chocolate layer cakes that permeated Primrose. I hadn't run into Nicola while I'd been chocolate whispering at Primrose. For all I knew, Nicola had been an abysmal assistant, and Jeremy had rightly sacked her for her inadequacies. "What about his charity?"

"Jeremy's Jump Start Foundation will be getting *very* little mention in my book. You've got to stick with a theme, yeah?"

"Jeremy's giving back to the community doesn't fit?"

"Absolutely not. Jeremy was a selfish, vain control freak, and that's the story I'm sticking to." Nicola nibbled on a cluster of caramelized, chocolate-drizzled popcorn. "Even if he hadn't been, nobody wants to hear he was just a regular bloke who happened to be discovered while knocking up burgers for his friends. That's rubbish! Just between us, it's much better to say he was a gold-digging egomaniac who clawed his way to the top. Plus, now that he's gotten killed for his misdeeds?" With sham amazement, Nicola shook her head. "That's utter genius. I couldn't have made up a better plot twist if I'd tried."

Killed for his misdeeds. Was that how she'd justified bashing him in the head with that metlapil? I couldn't exactly ask Nicola that. Instead, I found another, less gritty observation. "'Gold-digging' isn't usually applied to men."

"It is when they marry the daughter of a peer." Now Nicola sounded crisp. Knowledgeable. I had the impression she was practicing for her upcoming TV appearances. "Jeremy's marriage to Phoebe benefited them both. Falling for Jeremy took Phoebe off her pedestal. It made her seem much more human than she otherwise would have, which helped make Primrose popular—at least it did. In return, Phoebe opened doors for Jeremy. He got the legitimacy he'd always wanted. Once he had it, though—"

On the verge of telling me, Nicola broke off. Her gaze wandered downstairs. From our vantage point, we could see part of the chocolaterie-pâtisserie's seating area, which contained a few customers. That was all. Not the counter, not the barista's espresso machine, not the shelves and baskets full of chocolatey baked goods and confections bagged in cellophane for takeaway.

Then I realized she was looking outside, at the sidewalk. I couldn't detect what had caught her attention. There were two mums there, holding hands with their children. Plus one dog.

I eyed that little group—and their companionable spaniel—with a pang of longing. I'm pretty happy globe-trotting. But a part of me does sometimes yearn to put down roots—to find out what it's like to have a home, a husband, a few kids, a dog . . .

"—he forgot it was Phoebe who gave it to him," Nicola continued abruptly, just as though she'd never let her attention wander. "He just took his place among the posh set and never looked back."

"It's hard to be grateful sometimes." I tore away my gaze from those women and their children. "You get used to what you have. You forget what it was like before you had it."

"Not me," Nicola swore. "I'm not *ever* doing that."

She seemed unusually fixated on class and privilege. "Did you come from a tough background too?"

I asked, thinking that might be one explanation. "From a council estate, like Jeremy?"

"No, I'm solidly middle class." Nicola narrowed her eyes. For the first time, she ignored the treats. "I didn't come here to talk about me. I thought you wanted to know about Jeremy."

"I wanted to know about Jeremy's advert," I specified. That's what I'd told her over the phone. Really, I wanted to find out what scandalous secrets her book contained. Casually, I bit into a pistachio truffle. It was delicious. "Do you know who I can contact to clear out all that A/V equipment from the Wrights' guesthouse? I'm staying there, and I'd rather—"

Not be reminded of murder every time I wander into the kitchen, I'd been about to say. But Nicola interrupted me.

"You're *staying* there? But you weren't there . . . that day."

I blinked, surprised at her alert tone. "No. You were?"

That was a new development. I'd assumed Jeremy had been alone with his killer. DC Mishra had given me no indications to the contrary. Nor had George, her colleague, when we'd spoken.

"I was around." Nicola waved vaguely. "Running errands for Jeremy. Being belittled for doing the wrong thing. The usual."

I widened my eyes. "Did you see anything suspicious?"

Nicola shook her head. "I'm not supposed to say."

"Did you talk to the police?" I pressed. "DC Mishra?"

"I guess *you* did?" Jeremy's assistant gave me a mistrustful look. "Must be tough, being a foreigner in a big city like London, suspected of murdering someone as famous as Jeremy."

I began to see why Nicola might annoy someone—

especially someone like Jeremy, who had a demanding job to do. He needed help, not backtalk. But I tried to play along, all the same.

"I'm not a suspect." *Not officially.* Frankly, I wasn't sure about that. But I *did* know that if Nicola had been with Jeremy on the day he died, she probably had some information I needed.

"I didn't do anything wrong," I added firmly. "Really."

Unbelievably, Nicola cracked a smile. "Oh, *I* know that."

Chills ran up my spine. Did she "know" that because *she'd* murdered Jeremy? Because Nicola was a crazed, taunting killer?

I choked on my next bite of popcorn. "Really?" I managed.

"Of course. Hayden, I'm practicing fielding tricky questions! See? I turned that last one straight around on you." On another loony smile, Nicola nudged me, shoulder to shoulder. "My agent told me I should prepare for tough interviews. I haven't done any yet, but there's loads of interest already. I have to be sharp, right? I have to be ready for positively anything. I have to be *watchable*, too. Hashtag Nicola Mitchell."

"Right." As she made Twitter air quotes with her fingers, I wanted to punch her. Also, tech-savvy Claire, who I knew must have been responsible for that advice. "That's really smart."

"Isn't it?" Nicola munched more chocolate bark while another customer wandered upstairs. She frowned at him. He left.

I was privately impressed by her ability to clear the loft. Could other people detect something menacing about her too? Or was I just overreacting to all the murder in the air?

"I'm *so* pleased at the reception my book news is

getting so far," Nicola ambled on in a chatty, completely friendly way. "But I didn't mean to get you caught up in it, of course. I'm so sorry. I obviously got carried away, accusing you just now."

"No problem." Maybe it was time to call it quits. But I still needed to follow up about the book in question. "So—"

"I know that you weren't the one who offed Jeremy, because I know you weren't there," Nicola said breezily before I could steer our conversation in that direction. "I was there. Jeremy was there. The crew were there. Andrew Davies too, of course."

Him again. "From Hambleton & Hart?"

Nicola nodded. "Yes. He's the CEO. He inherited the whole company from his mother's side of the family. He's a sweet man."

Hmm. I had my doubts about that. "Is he?"

Another nod, followed by what appeared to be a preoccupied smile. "Andrew took a very hands-on approach to things. He was always there when a new advert was being shot." Nicola's grin widened. "I'm definitely namedropping him in my book. Maybe I should play up that angle? Mention how Jeremy basically made a bigshot like Andrew Davies crawl on his hands and knees?"

"Maybe. What do you mean? What went on?"

"It was all to do with Jeremy not wanting to promote Hambleton & Hart anymore, despite his agreement with them. Liam had convinced him their products were 'toxic,' so . . ." Nicola gave me a "What can you do?" shrug that I completely understood. "Andrew came up with the idea of having Jeremy do the advert without actually using any of the products on camera."

I recalled the boxed Hambleton & Hart mixes that

I'd glimpsed on the guesthouse's counter. "They were backdrops?"

"They were going to be, until Liam showed up to yell at Jeremy about being a 'bad example,' especially to children."

Liam had been at the advert shoot too. Nicola hadn't included Jeremy's personal trainer in her roundup. I wondered who else she might have inadvertently omitted. Maybe she wasn't the strongest "witness" I could have consulted, but I was stuck with her. For now, Nicola was the best I could manage.

"That's when Claire stepped in to save the day," Nicola told me, looking delighted with the woman I knew she'd taken on as her agent. "She was rearranging things in the background, trying to appease both Jeremy and Liam, when she spotted that huge mortar and pestle setup. She brought it to Andrew Davies."

Mortar and pestle setup? Nicola had to be talking about the metlapil that Jeremy had been bludgeoned to death with, and its accompanying metate. It would have looked like a colossal mortar and pestle to someone unfamiliar with such kitchen equipment.

I leaned forward, riveted by Nicola's story.

"Then what happened?" I asked. "Did Andrew take it?"

Maybe the head of Hambleton & Hart was my likeliest suspect. I didn't know if there had been fingerprints on that metlapil. My impromptu tête-à-tête with the London Metropolitan Police Service hadn't reached that stage. It likely never would.

"Jeremy didn't take that thing, that's for sure." Nicola appeared to be on the verge of laughing. At my rapt interest? Was she playing me? "He wanted no part of it."

"Why not?" I asked. "Didn't he like Claire's idea?"

Nicola's only response was a coy look.

Frustrated, I sighed. "You know, I've been interviewed before. If you chop up your talking points this way, they won't be understood properly. People will take things out of context. You have to deliver the information succinctly and clearly."

That approach would definitely help *me*, at least.

"Oh." Briefly, Nicola wrinkled her forehead. She gave me an astute look. "In that case, the only person I saw touch that thing was Claire. She did it to demonstrate what Jeremy was supposed to do. Not to get ready to kill him, or anything."

"I understand." She wanted to protect her new agent.

"Honestly!" Evidently, Nicola sensed my reservations. She looked around the chocolaterie-pâtisserie, then leaned nearer on our shared settee. "See, Claire's idea was all about S.E.X. Jeremy was supposed to take that stone club thing and pretend to make something with it. But not *really* cook. You know."

I didn't. Not at all. I raised my eyebrows.

"He was supposed to get, you know, *sexy* with it. They were going to cut images of him doing *this* with shots of the food."

After another furtive look, Nicola demonstrated a salacious gesture. It was the sort of thing a man might do with his, uh, not-kitchen-related "equipment" as a means to seduce a partner.

"All while he talked about making food," Nicola added. "With the intimation that Jeremy was sexy, cooking was sexy, and Hambleton & Hart were sexy too. Sex was Claire's go-to tactic."

No kidding. "In that case, we're lucky she suggested Jeremy use a prop," I joked, having finally understood the situation. "Otherwise, who knows how risqué she'd have gotten?"

We both laughed. European advertising tends to be liberal, compared with what we might see in the U.S. Nudity is fine, for instance, usually in context to sell soap or something similar. Claire's suggestion, though, sounded practically pornographic.

Nicola sobered quickly. "Andrew Davies was *mad* for the idea. I've never seen him so excited about anything—not even Hambleton & Hart's range of banana-flavored custard cups, and those are cracking good, believe me. But Jeremy wouldn't do it."

I didn't blame him. "What happened?"

Nicola shrugged. "They argued. Jeremy stomped away. I went to soothe him. He shouted at me. I cried. He was so mean!"

"That sounds very unfair to you," I consoled her, wishing her recollections of the event weren't quite so self-centered.

"It was!" Nicola sounded outraged even now. "Very unfair."

"Is that when you made up your mind to write your book?"

I asked that question softly, carefully, concerned about spooking her before I learned what I wanted to know—when she'd written her book and when Claire had struck a deal for it.

But Nicola wasn't bothered. She was on a roll.

"No. I was well into it by then," she told me. "You don't think I stuck with that dreadful assistant job just for the dismal money, did you? I planned on writing my book about Jeremy all along, from the moment he hired me. I was just biding my time, watching him, waiting to gather sufficient material."

"Oh. Isn't that clever of you?"

Or, you know, appalling. No wonder everyone had had the impression that Nicola was mousy. She'd been staying in the background on purpose, the better to eavesdrop on Jeremy.

Confident now, she puffed up her chest. "I'm only sorry Jeremy and Phoebe hadn't had any children yet. Can you imagine the stories I would have had to tell? Talk about scandal!"

Aha. That must have been why Nicola had been watching those mums and children outside Primrose. She'd been brainstorming.

"Maybe you can get a job as a nanny next," I dead-panned.

This was so much more awful than I'd expected. Nicola seemed virtually conscienceless. I'd thought she was bitter about being sacked, sure. But that didn't explain how she'd schemed, all along, to intentionally betray someone who'd trusted her. Jeremy had deserved better than that.

"I won't need a nanny job," Nicola assured me with a telling smirk. "Not now that Jeremy's conveniently kicked it."

I felt queasy. I actually regretted every bite of chocolate I'd just eaten. That was a genuine rarity in my line of work.

Nicola noticed. Her brow creased with concern. "Too soon?"

I gave her a bewildered look. "Too soon for what?"

"Too soon to joke about Jeremy's death. I thought I'd try a lighter tone. On telly? I do want to be entertaining. Honestly, no one wants to buy a book written by a drudge, do they?"

I couldn't believe she was being so blasé about this.

"I'd go for a more subdued tone," I advised dryly. I couldn't tell if Nicola was overexcited by her own publicity or inherently tactless. "At least until after Jeremy's funeral."

It was scheduled for tomorrow, Phoebe had told me during our most recent lesson. She'd done her best to arrange a service that would be both warm and respectful—not an easy feat, given the public mourners who were anticipated to crowd the event.

Partly motivated by that fact, I was visiting Jeremy's foundation with Liam later this afternoon. I hoped he wouldn't be able to smell chocolate on my breath. Maybe I'd buy gum.

"All right." Nicola gave me a thoughtful nod. "Thanks, Hayden. You've been very helpful. Oh, and please don't tell anyone what I've told you today. I'm planning to include some of this in my book. Maybe *you'll* even make a walk-on appearance!"

I gathered that I was supposed to feel honored by that. But I didn't. "Honestly, I'd rather stay out of it. You understand."

"Not really." She glanced downstairs again, then offered me a disturbingly fixed smile. "Who doesn't like being famous?"

Well, Jeremy, for one. Despite his ambition, I couldn't help thinking that celebrity hadn't been all he'd hoped for.

I tried to laugh off the disparity between me and Nicola. "Not you, I hope! Because it sounds as though your book is going to be a fantastic success." I leaned nearer and tried to seem as awestruck as possible. "What's going to be in it, anyway? I read in the papers about wild parties, secrets, scandals . . ."

"All that and more!" Nicola promised, giving nothing away.

"Maybe you could sneak me an advance copy?" I glanced at the (now demolished) treats I'd brought. "Just between friends?"

She caught my intimation. "I would, but it's not

even fully written yet. Funny, right?" Her expression hardened. "I'm still waiting for the end of the story. I can't go forward until all the loose ends are tied up, can I? That's what I told Claire."

Loose ends. The way she said it alarmed me. I began to wonder if Nicola wanted to be famous for more than having the inside story on Jeremy's wild lifestyle and bullying ways. Seeing her just then, I wondered if Nicola wanted to be famous—at least in her own mind—for having bludgeoned Jeremy to death with "that stone club thing" and gotten safely away with it.

More than gotten away with it. Profited from it.

"Your publisher must want the book quickly, though," I conjectured, shoving away that gruesome thought. "Right? So they can benefit from all the publicity surrounding Jeremy's death?"

Nicola looked like the cat who swallowed the canary. "I don't think they'll have any trouble capitalizing on that."

"You're probably right." Danny, however, had been wrong. There was no way I could be too suspicious. Not under these circumstances. If anything, I had too many possible killers to keep up with. "Did they move fairly quickly on the contract?"

"My publisher? Gosh, I love saying that!" Nicola beamed. She squinted to remember the details. "Yes, fairly quickly. Claire said so, at least. Those big deals take time, though. There was an auction and everything. It was so exciting!"

"How did you keep it from Jeremy? He must have noticed his agent calling you, right? Didn't he wonder what was going on?"

Nicola gave a relieved giggle. "Fortunately, he was already dead. Otherwise, things would have been much trickier. But it did take a while for Claire to respond to my initial query."

Hmm. That didn't clarify the timeline at all. Claire could have considered Nicola's tell-all book without telling her. She could have hatched her own plan to kill Jeremy and boost sales, only afterward locking down the rights to his "biography."

Nicola evidently didn't sense my maudlin thoughts.

"Hey, now that we're friends, maybe you can cater an all-chocolate spread for my book launch party!" she suggested in her lilting accent. She looked irrepressible. And (maybe) super guilty? I didn't know. "That would be brilliant, yeah?"

I couldn't agree. "We'll see. If I'm still in London."

I hoped I'd be gone, having long since caught Jeremy's murderer and cleared my own name with Detective Constable Mishra.

But Nicola didn't know that. "Fab! I'll phone you!"

Then, after a few more handfuls of chocolate treats on Nicola's part, we went our separate ways, me feeling no less sure of Nicola's potential guilt . . . and her feeling no less thrilled by profiting from Jeremy's death. If that didn't make her seem remorseless and cold, then I didn't know what would.

Dancing on Jeremy's grave, I guessed. But surely it wouldn't come to that. If nothing else, Jeremy's loyal fans would make sure such a desecration didn't happen. And speaking of them . . . it was time to find out exactly why Jeremy had earned himself so many devoted admirers. It couldn't just come down to nice hair, cut abs, and a talent for sexily slicing beef, right?

With Liam by my side, I was about to find out.

Ten

I'd just tucked into a lovely forkful of creamy white-chocolate raspberry tart when the guesthouse's doorbell rang.

Liam. He was early. Uh-oh.

We'd agreed to meet at "my place" for our visit to Jeremy's charity, since its headquarters in East London were served by a complicated patchwork of public transportation. From Chelsea, we'd have needed to take two buses, an Underground train, a DLR light-rail train, *and* then walk a bit to get there, so Liam had offered to drive us both. I was glad. My world-traveler skills have a serious gap—they don't include driving on the left.

It was possible, it occurred to me as I chewed double-time and then stashed my plate of raspberry tart in the Smeg brand refrigerator, that those transportation issues might be partly responsible for keeping the people of that borough struggling. It was difficult to have a good job and a good life when you spent so much of your day making an arduous commute.

But I wasn't in London to deal with social issues. I was there—at the moment—to try to swallow my forbidden chocolate before Liam detected what I'd been up to. I'd done pretty well, so far, with my daily allotment of cardio. Running around in one of the city's green parks was an excellent stress reliever. But going without chocolate, sugar, wine, or bread? No way.

I wiped my hands on my jeans and headed for the door.

"I'll be right there!" I called, fussing with my ponytail.

I hoped Liam's abstinence from treat foods hadn't given him some kind of superhero-level detection abilities, like former smokers who could hear a cigarette being lit at fifty paces.

I didn't want to make him angry. What was I, crazy? But I also didn't want to quit chocolate. For me, *il cioccolato* answers every question.

I opened the guesthouse's door with a smile on my face, hoping to bolster my sham image of sugar-free virtuousness.

Detective Constable Satya Mishra stood there. Double uh-oh.

Stone-faced in her uniform, she confronted me. "I didn't think you'd be quite so happy to see me, Ms. Mundy Moore."

I blinked. "DC Mishra!" Instantly, my palms began to sweat. Could I dry them without looking guilty? Doubtful. "Hello!"

She gestured inside. Authoritatively. "May I come in?"

"That depends. Is this a prelude to arresting me?"

DC Mishra angled her head. "Should I arrest you?"

I gave a nervous laugh, wishing sincerely that I wasn't one of those people who feel instantaneous guilt when police officers flash their patrol-car lights behind me in traffic, even when I haven't done anything wrong. It's an automatic response, like wanting to eat chocolate when seeing it. Or shaking.

Could she see my hands trembling? I clasped them.

"Of course not. And of course, you can come in." I stepped back to allow her to enter, hoping that wasn't a dire mistake.

When in doubt, be polite. That's what my mother always said. Given that her other golden rule was *Mothers are always right,* I decided to trust Mama Mundy Moore on this one.

"What can I do for you today, Detective Constable?"

She looked amused. Then stern. "You can stop trying to do my job." Satya Mishra ambled around the guesthouse, leaving me to trail after her. She studied the furnishings, the copy of Jeremy's best-selling British cookery book I'd been reading, and the shoes I'd kicked off beside the sofa. Then she studied me. "Stop harassing people about Jeremy Wright. The department has received several complaints about your 'interference.'"

I frowned at her, unable to argue. "Who complained?"

Her stern countenance deepened. "Then you don't deny it?"

How could I? I'd done it. I'd "interfered" with everyone I could think of who might have had an opportunity, a motive, or a means to kill Jeremy. I'd be doing more of the same tomorrow and the day after, too. I picked up his cookbook, hoping to avoid squirming. I hugged it. "I can't help being curious, given the circumstances," I admitted. "But I haven't harassed anyone."

"Well, see that you don't." DC Mishra paused. Seeming on the verge of saying something else entirely, she settled for, "I know about your history—about your involvement with recent crimes in the U.S. You'll find we aren't as tolerant here."

"Oh, no?" My hairline was growing damp. I was so nervous that my hair was perspiring. Oh, god. "Why is that?"

"Solving crimes is a serious matter. It's not a hobby."

"Of course not. I realize that." I wanted to groan with frustration—at myself and at my unprepared-ness. I should have anticipated that this would happen eventually. I hadn't exactly been circumspect about questioning people. "I'm not looking for a hobby, be-lieve me. I'm busy enough as it is! I never wanted to get involved in any of this," I assured the constable, spreading my arms wide in overt innocence. "I'm just a chocolatier."

"I'm told chocolate making has its share of intrigue."

I gaped at her. That was, almost to a word, what I'd told Claire Evans during our meeting about my supposed tell-all book.

"Have I been bugged?" I asked. "I didn't do any-thing!"

"Just don't leave town. And stop talking to my witnesses."

Aha. DC Mishra must have been following me, just as Danny had been. That made sense. He hadn't met her, so he wouldn't have known to alert me. That was something else for me and my security expert to work on. You know, if we ever needed to solve a murder again. I earnestly hoped it wouldn't come to that.

"I'm sorry if I've interfered with your investiga-tion," I said in a conciliatory tone. "But DC George gave me the impression we might share information, so if you've found out anything more about Jeremy's death, I'd love to—"

She cut me off. "My colleague was misinformed."

I frowned. "Really? Because he was so"—*much more friendly and helpful than you*—"open about the investigation. I thought—"

"He's been suspended." DC Mishra gave the cookbook I'd been hugging another look. "Do we understand one another? Back off."

She raised her (intimidating) gaze to me. I tried not to quiver. But this was too important to back off from. For Jeremy.

I know I should have trusted the police. That's sensible and expected. But in case I haven't mentioned it before, the last two times this happened to me, the police assured everyone the deaths had been accidental. I'd disagreed. I'd been right.

You can understand why I'm doubtful these days about the official means of detecting murders and tracking down killers.

"I'll try not to get in your way," I promised. Then curiosity got the better of me. "Why was George suspended?"

Silence. DC Mishra examined the A/V equipment remaining in the kitchen. Then she said, "We've called someone to pick up all this gear. It should be out of your way within a few days."

She meant Hambleton & Hart. I thought it was prudent not to say so, given the circumstances. Flaunting the things I'd learned while questioning people wouldn't strengthen my case.

"Thank you," I said. "I appreciate that."

She gave a curt nod, then adjusted her baton. Police officers in Great Britain don't generally carry firearms. They're issued batons and incapacitating sprays instead. But I've had run-ins with those telescopic batons before. They scare me.

Jeremy's book slipped a few inches in my sweaty grasp. I adjusted it, catching sight of his handsome, sunlit image as I did. In the back-cover photograph, he stood in a field strewn with poppies as Phoebe clung to his side, laughing and fussing with his hair while wearing one of those floaty white dresses.

"They look so happy, don't they?" I observed wistfully.

I wished we could all just rewind and go back to that field—those days, those smiles between two people who seemed to be in love, not (according to Nicola) on the verge of divorce.

Satya Mishra's stern demeanor wavered. For a nanosecond.

"I have that book," she confided. "Jeremy's recipe for chargrilled kofta kebabs is wicked." Her smile reached me.

For a moment, we gazed at the cookbook in unison, both of us lost in memories of Jeremy. I didn't think either of us had known him particularly well— not on a personal level—but that didn't mean we didn't feel a certain fondness for him. We'd let Jeremy into our homes. Our kitchens. Our lives. That mattered.

That meant DC Mishra was at least as motivated as I was to find Jeremy's killer. Aside from it being part of her job, I thought she wanted to track down the murderer for Jeremy's sake.

I glanced away to hide my newfound affability toward the detective constable and glimpsed Phoebe through the curtained window. She stood in her garden with her arms protectively folded around herself, watching me and Satya Mishra. Phoebe was someone else who wanted to see Jeremy's death explained.

I nodded toward her. "Did you come to see Mrs. Wright?"

Satya Mishra shook herself. "No. Just you. Stay out of my case, Ms. Mundy Moore." Then she nodded. "I'll see myself out."

Then she strode to the guesthouse's door and did exactly that, passing a startled-looking Liam on the stoop as she did.

How long, I wondered, had he been lingering there? Had he overheard us? I quickly followed her there, trying to find out.

DC Mishra gave him a nod, too. "Mr. Taylor. Good day."

She knew him, then. Had she questioned him?

Liam's slightly uneasy look suggested she might have.

Tardily, he raised his arm. "Cheers, Detective Constable!"

His action drew Phoebe's gaze toward him. As it did, I saw something pass between them. Was it long-ing? Loathing? Simple joint remembrance of Jeremy? Guilt? Something else altogether?

From my angle, at least, it was impossible to tell. I hadn't stopped to think about Phoebe and Liam's relationship.

I couldn't do so then, either. Because after saying her own pleasant good-bye to the detective constable, Phoebe chose that moment to huff toward me with her patrician nose in the air.

She ignored Liam, her vaguely red-rimmed eyes fixed on me. Had she been crying? It seemed likely. With Jeremy's service happening tomorrow, Phoebe was under a great deal of stress.

"What did DC Mishra want?" she asked. "Are you all right?"

Aha. Her huffiness was concern, I realized. Maybe I'd made it into Phoebe's inner circle. "I'm fine. She just"—*wanted me to stay out of Jeremy's case*—"wanted to check on me. And let me know they'd be coming to clear away the A/V equipment soon."

I don't know why I didn't tell Phoebe I was looking into her husband's murder. Maybe because I thought it would bring up painful memories for her. Maybe because I didn't want to give her false hope. Maybe because it sounded so preposterous.

Yeah, that was definitely it. Preposterous.

Who was I to think I could track down a killer, especially ahead of the police? I'm good at making a to-die-for double-chocolate strawberry milk shake or a wildly detailed to-do list—not at sneaking around, investigating murders, or theorizing.

I was doing my best, though. It was all I could do.

"You haven't seen the papers?" Phoebe's apprehensive gaze probed mine. "There are rumors of misconduct in the police department. Several officers are being examined in the case."

As far as I was concerned, that only bolstered my position. I *had* to investigate, didn't I? Especially if the authorities couldn't be trusted to do the right thing. "Yes, I heard."

"You can't believe those rags." Liam interrupted us with a scowl. "Just look at this. I thought I was done with this."

He showed me a tabloid. I squinted. "Is that *us*?"

Irritably, Liam nodded. He crumpled the newspaper, but I could still see the paparazzi image and accompanying headline.

Friends forever? No! Jeremy's hot-to-trot trainer moves on!

Below the headline was a fuzzy photo of me and Liam, at the park, discussing my nascent healthy-living regimen. The unknown photographer had chosen the specific moment when I'd touched Liam's granite-like arm while commiserating over Jeremy's death. Without context, though, we sure looked cozy. Especially with Goldie panting at our feet. We looked like . . . well, a family.

No, we didn't, I told myself. *Toughen up, Hayden.* This was no time to indulge my occasional yearnings for a hearth and home, for a dog and a husband, for a bedroom that didn't come with an electronic keycard and a TV you could check out on.

"This is ridiculous," I told Liam. "You have a right to make a living." I transferred my gaze from the tabloid to his troubled face. "Does this kind of thing happen to you often?"

"More often than I'd like," Liam grumbled. "I'd thought it would quit." His gaze shifted to Phoebe. "You know, nowadays."

I understood. He meant, *Nowadays . . . now that Jeremy is gone.*

Or maybe he meant, *Nowadays . . . now that I took care of the problem.* It was still possible that Liam had bashed Jeremy in the head with that metlapil. Maybe because he'd been fed up with what amounted to being surveilled twenty-four hours a day?

It was creepy, I acknowledged, to know we'd been watched.

I understood, thanks to my faithful reading of those same tabloids, that Liam and Jeremy had been featured regularly. The media had followed Jeremy's unnecessary "battle to lose weight!" with tacky zeal. His "fitness quest" had been highlighted only slightly less frequently than sly shots of his "burgeoning bald spot!" and crudely circled close-ups of his barely noticeable smile lines ("new wrinkles!"). *Uh-oh*, those papers had cooed to their avid readership. *Is sexy Jeremy losing his cool?*

What I hadn't understood until now was how much Liam had disliked being in the public eye. Enough to murderously end it?

I didn't think so. If that had been the case, why would Liam have called attention to the situation by showing me that paparazzi photo of us and the accompanying article? I would have seen it eventually, when I reviewed the day's editions—something I hadn't had a chance to do yet—but he didn't know that.

"When we get to the East End, we can make out like crazy behind the scenes at Jeremy's charity function, okay?" I poked Liam, emphasizing my put-on. "If the press are this worked up about me harmlessly putting my hand on your arm at the park, that ought to really given them something to talk about."

They had to still be following us, right?

But Jeremy's former personal trainer was in no mood for kidding around. "I'm not attracted to you that way, Hayden," he said bluntly. Then, before I could reason out why, Liam turned on his heel and gestured for me to follow. "Come on. Let's go."

Eleven

I'd be lying if I said Liam's unswerving statement of non-attraction to me didn't put a damper on our outing.

It wasn't that I was attracted to Liam "in that way." I wasn't. Jeremy's former trainer was nice (mostly) and friendly (ditto) and undeniably well-built (duh), but even if Liam wasn't an unrepentant murderer, things could never work out between us.

Me, with a man who disavowed chocolate? Impossible.

I imagined myself dreaming up a scrumptious chocolate soufflé with silky chocolate sauce, a rich chocolate cookie studded with melty chocolate morsels, or an extravagant mocha ice cream pie with a chocolate-cookie crust . . . and Liam looking appalled at the whole lot. Then maybe binning all of it. (That's Britspeak for "throwing away." You know, in a bin.)

Liam would hate everything I did for a living, I knew. That meant we could never find a common ground. I wasn't going to quit working magic with

Theobroma cacao, and he wasn't going to stop believing that scrummy sugar, carbs, and alcohol were evil.

Speaking of which . . . "You ate chocolate today, didn't you?"

Liam's terse accusation caught me off guard. So did the way he glared at me while gripping the steering wheel of his modest Ford Fiesta. I'd been surprised when he'd shown up with such a non-flashy car. I'd been expecting, I don't know . . . an Aston Martin?

Surely Jeremy had paid him reasonably well, I figured.

I made a mental note to ask Liam about his car later, then addressed his question. "That tactic might work on someone else, but not me," I warned him. "I know you're just trying to change the subject." I gave him a penetrating look. "What's going on between you and Phoebe? I saw that *thing*"—I made googly eyes at him for reference—"that happened between you two earlier."

A pause. Then, "I asked you about chocolate first."

"My question is more important." I wasn't giving in. Danny had the address of the charity function. He could track me down, if need be. In the meantime, Liam couldn't very well pulverize me with both hands on the steering wheel, could he? "Isn't Phoebe coming to Jeremy's Jump Start Foundation? Are you two having a torrid affair? How many miles to the gallon does this thing get, anyway? You must enjoy excellent gas mileage."

At my trio of rapid-fire questions, Liam finally laughed.

The streets of London flashed by outside my passenger-side window, full of people, history, and life. In some parts of the city, you can actually touch sections of ancient city walls that were built by the Romans when the place was called Londinium.

It was really fascinating. Less so was Liam's stone-walling.

"I'm going to find out anyway," I pushed. "Phoebe and I are getting really close these days. I'm tutoring her in baking."

"Without tasting a scrap of chocolate?" Liam asked.

He had me. "If you and Phoebe were involved, she might need you now," I tried in a gentler tone. "You know, for comfort."

Liam arched one blond eyebrow as he stopped at a light.

"It would be equally understandable," I went on, studying his profile for signs of deception, "if you and Phoebe didn't get along. After all, she runs a bakery and chocolate shop. You wanted to get Jeremy healthy. Something had to give, right?"

I was spitballing here. As I've said, I'm a neophyte.

Liam knew it. "Phoebe didn't care about Jeremy's workouts."

I was surprised. "Did she think they were undignified?"

"She thought he was perfect, just the way he was," Liam informed me. "She never missed a chance to tell him that. Or anyone else who would stand still long enough to listen."

Aw, sweet. So much for Nicola's divorce theory. "Then why would she cheat on him?" *With you?* remained unspoken between us.

Liam swerved his car between two black cabs, then tossed me a heated look. "Phoebe was cheating on Jeremy? With who?"

He sounded convincingly infuriated by the idea. Whoops. I guessed he'd thought I'd been joking earlier and had been willing to humor me—but only to a point. *This point.* I began to have doubts about my both-hands-on-the-wheel safety philosophy.

It was possible Liam could pummel someone *and* drive responsibly around the Isle of Dogs past Canary Wharf. High rises dotted the area near the West India Docks, their names reading like a who's who of international banking, media, and professional services firms. It was ironic that just beyond them lived so many people who couldn't afford their specialties.

I could read a map. I knew we must be getting close to Jeremy's rough old neighborhood. Time was running out.

"Yes, an affair," I ventured. "With you, I'm guessing."

"With *me?*" Liam's incredulous gaze pinned me to my seat. "What makes you think I'd want anything to do with Phoebe?"

Well . . . "Right now? The fact that you're denying it so hard."

He seemed chagrinned. "I can't believe you think I'm the kind of person who would betray his friend that way."

His wounded tone got to me. I couldn't help it. I felt painfully aware that I suspected Liam might be a killer. But I didn't feel bad enough about that fact to stop questioning him.

"I'm sorry. But I heard Jeremy and Phoebe were divorcing—"

"No way." Liam shook his head. "That's not true."

He may have thrown in a few expletives, just for emphasis.

"Then he never said anything to you about marital trouble?"

"He wouldn't have had to say." Liam inched down a busy street bordered by shops. These weren't the

expensive boutiques found in K&C, though. These
were curry shops and takeaway fried-chicken restaurants, carpet shops, and small merchants offering
spices, fruits, and vegetables from sidewalk stands. "I
would have known," Liam said. "It's hard to hide anything when you're sweating through a workout. People
get honest right away, yeah?"

I considered his self-assured statement as we passed
by what I assumed were council estates—multistory
apartment buildings made of instantly recognizable
yellow-brown London stock brick and given little em-
bellishment. I glimpsed graffiti and cigarette butts, a
job center, and a health clinic. There were people of
a variety of ethnic backgrounds in the streets.

This wasn't the London of *Downton Abbey* fans. It
was the real London, lived in by real people with real,
ordinary lives.

Liam frowned my way. "You said you weren't scared."

"I'm not scared." I've been all over the world.
Poverty doesn't scare me—it makes me want to do
something to help. I knew of at least one way to do
that: by supporting Jeremy's charity. Later, I'd make a
call to Travis and transfer some funds. "I was thinking
it must have been difficult for Jeremy to make his way
out of here. He must have been quite a man."

At that, Liam smiled. "He was. He really was."

But his trainer was not as keen a student of human
nature as he wanted to believe he was, I realized. Not
if he'd studied my face just now and seen fear there.
Maybe things would have been different if I'd been
trying to knock out a few push-ups, but I doubted it.
Liam Taylor's viewpoint couldn't be relied on.

That meant I was on my own when it came to deciding who to trust in Jeremy's namesake foundation.
Because a second later . . .

"We're here!" Liam parked and turned to me, his biceps flexing as he pulled out his car keys. "Ready for this?"

We'd stopped on the street beside a park, I saw. It was a bit more run-down than the green spaces I usually frequented in London, but it was still welcomingly bordered by trees. In the distance, a crowd of children had gathered near one particular tree. Beneath it stood a table, several stacked-up cardboard boxes, and a man wearing khaki pants and a button-up shirt, along with some other adult volunteers and a few teenagers.

Liam followed my gaze. Hostility emanated from him as he squinted in the direction of that tree. "What's *he* doing here?"

"Who? Mr. Nervous over there?"

Liam looked at me blankly.

"Come on. There's no way you're not familiar with those children's books," I urged. "Mr. Men and Little Miss? They're cartoons. There must be . . . I don't know, dozens of them."

The guy under the tree was a dead ringer for the Mr. Nervous character created by Roger Hargreaves. Except he wasn't purple.

"Ah." A look of nostalgia suffused Liam's face. "I always wanted to be like Mr. Strong. He can tie knots in iron bars."

Mission accomplished. Pleased with myself for remembering the books my dad had read to me as a kid and using them—just in the nick of time—to defuse the situation, I got out of the car. I shut the dusty Fiesta's door, reflecting that it was possible that Liam didn't own a fancier car because he just wasn't a "car guy." Most likely, he usually used public transportation.

Liam slammed the other car door. He practically growled.

"*He's* leaving. Right now. I'm making well sure of it."

"Wait!" I ran after Liam as he stalked across the grass. I caught up to him and restrained him (ha! as if) with my hand on his muscular forearm. "Who is that guy?" I nodded at him.

Liam only glowered. "Don't worry. I've got this."

He walked. I chased him again, feeling the way Goldie must feel when out on a walk with him. Liam's pace was Olympics-worthy. "If you get in a fight, I'll have no ride home."

He paused to lob me a disbelieving look. "A fight? Most people don't fight with me. I'm just going to talk to him."

I had the feeling Liam's idea of "talking" primarily involved him towering over Mr. Nervous, menacing him. I glanced toward our destination, searching for inspiration. "Look, he's handing out candy to the kids in Jeremy's charity! That's not—"

Bad, I'd been about to say. But then I remembered who I was talking to. To Liam, handing out candy to kids was very bad.

There was only one thing to do: beat him there.

I silently blessed my jeans, T-shirt, and Converse All-Stars for bringing me this far. Then I took off at a run.

My tactic worked. I caught Liam by surprise and beat him to the designated tree by a good thirty seconds—maybe because he'd spent some of that time sniggering at my ungainly running. That was long enough for me to wend my way breathlessly through the assembled kids, approach Mr. Nervous, and put forward my hand.

"Hi! I'm Hayden Mundy Moore. It's nice to meet you!"

He looked up, startled. With both hands full of candy bars, he glanced from me to the open boxes that held still more candy bars. Except those weren't candy bars, I saw. They were Hambleton & Hart "vitality bars."

I'd seen those somewhere before.

"Erm, hello." Still holding those colorfully wrapped, slender bars, he pushed up his glasses. *Left-handed.* Then he hesitated with his arms in the air, plainly wondering what to do with his burden. He settled for dumping them all back into the opened box atop the stack in front of him. "I'm Andrew Davies."

While the kids nearby groaned and complained about having to wait for their "vitality bars," Andrew Davies shook my hand. Sort of. Unassumingly was how I'd describe it. His was one of the most lifeless, moist handshakes I've ever encountered. He seemed amiable enough, so I resisted the urge to wipe my hand.

"How can I help?" I asked briskly, inserting myself between Andrew and Liam. From the corner of my eye, I glimpsed Liam striding toward us with homicide in his eyes.

You know . . . figuratively speaking.

"My, aren't *you* a brash one? Not like Nicola at all." Andrew ran his gaze over me, from my sneakers to my ponytail. His ruddy cheeks colored even further, contrasting with his sandy hair. "I'd heard Jeremy had hired another assistant."

Where did everyone keep getting that idea? Did something about me radiate administrative proficiency? I doubted it. Travis, especially, would have laughed uproariously at the notion. Besides, Phoebe had confirmed that Jeremy hadn't had time to hire another assistant . . . this time.

"I'm happy to do whatever you need," I promised, leaving aside the notion of my not being Jeremy's assistant for the moment. I nodded a greeting at the other adults nearby, most of whom were clad in orange Jeremy's Jump Start Foundation T-shirts with white stylized kangaroos screen-printed on their fronts.

Before Andrew could offer me a volunteering suggestion, he glimpsed Liam. The CEO of Hambleton & Hart blanched. He stepped back in evident alarm. He tripped on a clod of grass. He yelped.

Aristocratically, of course. But still. For a man who was powerful, wealthy, and (I'm assuming) respected, Andrew Davies didn't exactly cut a dashing figure. In fact, if Jeremy Wright had had an anti-doppelganger, it would have been Andrew. They shared the same hair color, the same height and build . . . but where Jeremy had been charismatic and rough-hewn, Andrew was tentative and shambolic. He was obviously well-educated and intelligent, with a posh accent and expensive (if rumpled) preppy clothes. But his overall air of polite nervousness trumped all else.

He seemed, more than anything, utterly harmless. Which, I figured, was all the more reason to suspect him of murdering Jeremy. After all, wasn't it always the person you least suspected who turned out to be the gruesome, twisted killer?

It was almost enough to make me step out of the way and let hulking Liam commit whatever violent "talking to him" intrusion he had in mind. As you might have guessed, I couldn't do it.

What if Andrew Davies genuinely *were* harmless?

I stepped forward with my arms outstretched, ready

to run interference between Liam and Hambleton & Hart's CEO. But it turned out I didn't need to. Before Liam ever reached us . . .

"Liam! Liam!" All the kids abandoned the "vitality bar" station and swarmed the enormous personal trainer instead. They jumped up and down, waving their arms to get his attention. They dogged his footsteps like puppies. They laughed. "Liam! Hey!"

In the center of the mêlée, Mr. No Treats beamed.

He high-fived some kids and hugged others. He traded grins and laughed with joy. Amid those children of all ages, sexes, ethnic backgrounds, and family situations, Liam seemed happy.

Our eyes met over the pint-size crowd. He grinned.

His gaze swerved to Andrew Davies. Momentarily, Liam put on a scary face, then gave the CEO one of those "I'm watching you" gestures. He pointed from his eyes to Andrew's terrified face.

Andrew took another step back. "I didn't think *he'd* be coming today," he muttered, "after what happened to Jeremy."

He wasn't pleased to see his onetime spokesperson's personal trainer, either, I saw as I turned to reassure him.

I didn't know what I planned to say. *I'll protect you* sounded ludicrous, but I honestly didn't think Liam would go through me to get to Andrew Davies—no matter how much he objected to the "vitality bars" the CEO had been handing out.

That's when I remembered where I'd seen one of those "just 150 calories!" bars before. In Phoebe's cardigan pocket.

Maybe she'd attended one of Jeremy's charity events and picked up one for herself. Maybe Hambleton & Hart had given Jeremy and Phoebe boxes full of their products as thank-yous. Maybe Amelja had purchased a package of "vitality bars" to help her power through cleaning the Wrights' immense town house and Phoebe had helped herself to one. Maybe it just didn't matter.

I was grasping at straws, I realized. But DC Mishra's visit had left me feeling as though I were running out of time. If I was going to find Jeremy's killer, I had to do it quickly.

In that spirit . . . "Yes, about what happened to Jeremy," I said in a low voice, picking up where Andrew had left off. "We're putting together a memorial for him, of sorts, and I'm gathering remembrances from his friends and colleagues. I was wondering . . ." I rummaged in my handy crossbody bag and pulled out one of my Moleskine notebooks. "Would you care to share your thoughts?"

Hey, if everyone thought I was Jeremy's assistant, who was I to argue? Maybe I could use my inadvertent insider status.

Children milled around us, hollering with glee. Someone brought out a soccer ball; Liam led the kids in an impromptu match farther out in the park. The adult volunteers seemed absorbed with the foundation's shoe-donation station, a food bank offering boxes of Hambleton & Hart instant-pudding mixes, ready-bake cakes, and what appeared to be a new breakfast cereal range, plus a spot for swapping outgrown clothing and toys.

Jeremy's Foundation seemed to be doing good work.

Andrew Davies, on the other hand, appeared to be hesitating over sharing reminiscences about Jeremy. I had to goose him.

"It's going to be my final task," I confided in an

even more circumspect voice. I sighed, trying to appear on the verge of being made redundant (being "unemployed," to us Yanks). "I really want to do a good job with this. For Jeremy's sake."

"Yes, yes, of course." Andrew nearly tutted. For a fairly young man, he seemed preternaturally mature. "What do you need?"

"Well, you know . . . any last remembrances of Jeremy would be good. Thoughts of his special qualities. Amusing anecdotes."

Now Andrew seemed petrified of *me*. He licked his lips, then shifted as he studied the distant soccer game. "I'm sorry. I'm afraid I'm not especially gifted at amusing anecdotes. I'm more of an 'embarrassing mishap' sort of chap, actually."

"It could be anything, really. Anything at all." I gave him a bolstering pat on the arm. "How did you and Jeremy meet? What was he like on his final day? You were there, weren't you?"

"I'd, erm, rather not talk about that day." Andrew tugged on his collar. His face shone with perspiration. His glasses were slightly fogged. "It wasn't our finest hour together, you see."

"Oh no? That's too bad. What happened?"

He tossed me an uncertain look. I tucked my elbow beneath his arm, then led us both more deeply into the shade, where we wouldn't be disturbed. We passed clip-boarded sign-up sheets for intramural soccer, for tutoring sessions, and (for the older kids) for culinary apprenticeships at Jeremy's restaurants.

I wondered, with Jeremy gone, if there would be any more Hughs, Poppys, or Myras getting a toehold in the work world. If Jeremy had truly been responsible for the direction of his foundation—and he seemed to have been—things would change now.

"You can tell me," I promised Andrew reassuringly. "Go on."

He seemed transfixed by my hand on his arm. Maybe I'd overplayed my instincts. I wasn't exactly on Gemma Rose's level of flirtatiousness, but I do have a knack for making friends.

With a man as awkward as Andrew, too much friendly touching could be easily misinterpreted. Gently, I disentangled myself.

He blinked and blushed, fussing with his sleeve as though its expensive wrinkly fabric had unfortunately repelled me. Oddly enough, that overtly overcompensating gesture made me like him a little more.

Who hasn't felt socially awkward? Nobody, that's who.

"I apologize for surprising you this way," I told Andrew as I flipped past my notebook's list-lined pages to a clean sheet. "Ordinarily, I'd have been better prepared"—*for my imaginary job*—"but my predecessor left me quite a lot to deal with."

"Nicola. Mmm. Yes." He gave a sage nod. "I remember her."

He meant *I fancied her.* (In U.S. speak, he had a crush on her, in case you're not familiar.) I detected all the signs.

I'd been expecting *yes, mousy Nicola*, though. I regrouped.

"Nicola always took special time to speak with me."

I figured that was because she'd been pumping him for information to include in her book. I didn't want to say so.

A short distance away, the soccer game continued. Liam whooped, obviously enjoying himself. He couldn't be a killer.

"She told me how nice you always were," I improvised. In truth, she'd suggested Andrew Davies had been browbeaten by Jeremy, but he didn't need to know that. Ever. "That's why I made it a point to seek you out today. I knew you'd be able to help me with Jeremy's memorial. You know, ahead of the funeral."

A little time pressure couldn't possibly hurt, I reasoned.

"Ah, yes. Well, I'll see what I can do, shan't I?" Andrew seemed distinctly pleased that Nicola had spoken well of him. He gave me a wobbly smile. "You see, Jeremy was very important to me. To the whole Hambleton & Hart family, honestly. Ours is a very old and esteemed company. Recently, we'd encountered a few . . . problems, as any firm does. But we were counting on Jeremy to boost our flagging sales and *skyrocket us back to success!*"

He said the last in a chipper tone, with a goofily awkward fist-pump gesture to go along with it. I felt positive Andrew had practiced both in a mirror at home for quite some time.

Inevitably, I liked him even more because of it. What can I say? Travis and Danny aren't completely wrong about me. I do have a soft spot for the underdogs of the world. Despite Andrew Davies's position of affluence and authority, he seemed hapless.

"I'm afraid we're in a bit of a pickle now, though." He leaned nearer to me with a confidential air. "With Jeremy gone, that is. He wasn't always the easiest man to get along with. He had a bit of a temper. I'm afraid, regrettably, so do I." Andrew gave me a sheepish look. "But he was also brilliant and funny and terribly, terribly talented. Just terrific at making food seem irresistible. I'd staked my reputation with my shareholders on Jeremy's cooperation—that's how highly I thought of him."

"I'm sorry things didn't work out. What will you do now?"

I felt genuinely concerned about him. Shareholders could be sharks. Andrew Davies didn't seem up to battling them for long.

"Oh, well, erm, we'll think of something, won't we?" Andrew gave me a jolly laugh that wasn't the least bit convincing. The breeze lifted his wispy, sandy hair, revealing a burgeoning bald spot at his crown. "You don't maintain a company for more than a hundred and fifty years without having a few tricks up your sleeve, do you?"

"No, I guess not." I almost volunteered to consult with Hambleton & Hart for him. They had chocolate . . . - ish products. Maybe I could help. But that would blow my cover. "You'll manage!"

Now we were both doing it. The faux-jolly routine.

For a moment, we watched the activity around us. More of the older children—teenagers and young adults—had arrived now. They were chatting with volunteers, practicing knife skills at a portable chef's kitchen setup, trying on much-needed new shoes.

Andrew turned to me. "How is Phoebe holding up?"

I hesitated, wondering how Jeremy's wife was supposed to fit into my fake personal assistant shtick. I frowned, fumbling.

"I'd assume she's been directing your efforts in Jeremy's absence?" Andrew's voice broke on his former spokesperson's name. Gruffly, he cleared his throat. "She's faring well?"

"Well enough," I hedged. "Do you know one another?"

A vague wave. "We run in the same circles, don't we?"

"Of course." I should have anticipated that. "It's

been very difficult for Phoebe, naturally. She *so* loved Jeremy."

As I said it, I watched Andrew's face, hoping to glimpse what he thought of their marriage. Nicola was biased. Liam was too fond of his own "expertise" in reading people to be reliable.

"Ah, that's where you've gone a bit wrong," Andrew said.

This was it. Jeremy's and Phoebe's plans to divorce were about to be confirmed—and by an unbiased third party, too.

"Jeremy *so* loved *her*," Andrew corrected me, eyes twinkling.

Hmm. I couldn't guess why he looked so pleased. Maybe he was simply a nice guy who was happy to see someone else happy.

Whatever the explanation was, I'd learned all I was likely to from Hambleton & Hart's CEO. I wrote a few scribbles in my notebook to bolster my spur-of-the-moment cover story, then prepared to volunteer my genuine help with the foundation.

Wanting to make a graceful exit (and, okay, feeling guilty for having taken advantage of Andrew Davies's kindly nature), I nodded to the soccer match. "Are you going to join the game?"

For a moment, he appeared to ponder it. With unambiguous satisfaction, he watched the Jump Start kids chase the ball, then clump up to kick it. An instant later, Liam hove into view, shouting coach-like encouragement. "Go on, my son!" he yelled.

Liam's typically British shout of encouragement (roughly, "Attaboy!" to you and me) seemed to break Andrew's spell.

"No," he mused, "I'm more of a cricket man, myself."

I didn't wonder, what with Liam waiting there to crush him—all for the innocent "crime" of handing out "junky" health food.

But I didn't want to let on that I suspected Andrew was (reasonably) afraid of Liam. "Oh, sure." I nodded. "Remind me, is cricket the one with the ball and the scrum, or the bats?"

Andrew treated me to the same indulgent look that Danny sometimes did when I tried to talk about sports with him. I like football—I'm *passionate* about football—but everything else to do with balls, courts, nets, and scoring leaves me cold.

"Rugby is the former," he told me. "Cricket is the latter."

Maybe, I thought, I should broaden my horizons. If I were to continue sleuthing—however unwillingly—I might need to know such things. There were a lot of sports fans in the world. Talking about games was an easy way to bond with people.

Andrew glanced at me. I must not have appeared suitably impressed, because he added, "I'm one *hell* of a batsman."

Taken aback by his very crisp swearing, I remained mum. What was the correct response to that? *Congratulations!* felt wrong. *Wow!* was probably overstating things. *Way to go?*

"That's the hitter," he informed me, crossing his arms as he watched Liam and the kids play. "I can knock it straight down the lines, right past the bowler, and clear out of the park."

"Good for you!" I said, having settled on that a moment ago. But I doubted I sounded convincing. Because I'd just recognized Andrew Davies from the cell phone photo that Ashley, the intern-turned-journalist we'd met at the pub, had been showing around. She must have heard he was a suspect in Jeremy's murder and had been trying to gather information about him.

That was pretty incriminating on its own. But combined with having just heard that same man brag about how hard he could swing a bat, only days after Jeremy had been bludgeoned to death with a very bat-like instrument?

Well, that was significant, for sure.

It looked as though it didn't matter how many suspects I already had or how tricky it was to deal with them. Because I'd just found another one in mild-mannered Andrew Davies, all the same.

Twelve

On the day of Jeremy's funeral, Primrose was closed. All of Jeremy's restaurants were closed too at all of their locations throughout the United Kingdom. The services were to be held in Kent, where Jeremy was to be interred near his parents' home.

Phoebe had hoped that the location—more distant from London—might discourage all but the most fervent of Jeremy's fans from crowding in and disturbing his family and friends. I could see from news reports online and on television that her hopes had been dashed straightaway. Thousands swamped the small country church where Jeremy's mourners had gathered, turning the somber proceedings into a muddle of paparazzi and helicopters.

I felt sorry for Phoebe. For everyone who'd been close to Jeremy. But that didn't change my plans. I couldn't let it.

I switched off the TV and turned to Danny. "Let's go."

He frowned. "Let's not and say we did."

"We'll never get another chance like this one. Everyone is gone for the day—including most of my suspects—and I'm not expected at Primrose to work my chocolate magic or teach all the bakers the difference between beating, creaming, and stirring."

In case you're curious, beating something incorporates air into the mixture. Creaming continues this process long enough to dissolve granular ingredients. Stirring, on the other hand, simply combines components. For instance, you'd beat egg whites for angel-food cakes (delicious with cocoa added!), cream butter and sugar for layer cakes (chocolate, for the win!), and stir wet ingredients into dry for pancakes (chocolate chip, maybe?).

There's a reason my consultation services are in demand, and it's not because baking—or working with chocolate—is easy. It's not. It requires patience, attention to detail, and a willingness to step outside your comfort zone in order to learn.

That's exactly what I planned to do today, while everyone was gone at Jeremy's funeral. I hadn't attended because I hadn't been invited. That wasn't surprising; I hadn't really known Jeremy—at least not while he'd been alive, I hadn't. Now that he was gone, I was beginning to get a good sense of who he'd been.

As far as I could tell, Jeremy had been boisterous and bold, softhearted and generous. He'd been brave enough to leave his rough old neighborhood and smart enough to thrive when he had. He'd been loving and sensual, hot-tempered and faithful, and when it came to finding justice for his murder, I couldn't let anything stop me. Not Satya Mishra. Not fear. Not propriety.

Not even Danny, who was currently giving me side-eye from his position on our guesthouse's sofa, surrounded by tottering stacks of Jeremy's hardbound published cookbooks. I'd been combing through

them in my off-hours, looking for clues. So far, all I'd
learned was that Jeremy *had* been sexy. For real. And
that he'd included far too many people in his multiple cookery books—from publicans like the one
who'd given me that personal dimpled pub glass to so-
cialites to fishermen to teenage girls on Brighton Pier
in summertime—for me to possibly narrow down any
further suspects. Jeremy had left no stone unturned
when it came to his culinary curiosity. Now I wanted
to do the same for him.

The "no stone left unturned" part, I mean. Not the
culinary curiosity part. What I'm saying is, I needed to
investigate further. Impatiently, I looked out the
window. "It's go time!"

My enthusiasm left my sometime partner in crime
unmoved.

"We agreed it would be a good idea to sneak into
Phoebe's town house and have a look around while
she's gone, remember?" I reminded him. "That's where
Jeremy lived—where he sometimes worked. Who
knows? We might find something incriminating."

I was hoping for a concrete link to one of my
suspects—something that might hint at *why* someone
had attacked Jeremy.

"We might find ourselves arrested." Danny's lazy
gaze met mine. "DC Mishra has been watching you.
Don't be stupid."

"The police are dealing with the crowds at Jeremy's
funeral," I argued. "This is Satya's perfect opportunity
to watch all her suspects. She has access I don't have.
Isn't that what happens on those TV crime shows?
They always case the funeral."

He gave me an engaging grin. "Look who's an
expert now."

I wasn't sure if he was flattering me or teasing me.

With Danny, you never knew. You just had to give as good as you got.

"Fine." I held out my hand. "Give me your . . . you know, lock-picking stuff, and I'll do this myself. You can stay here."

That moved him. With unfair muscular grace, my security expert rose from the sofa. He stretched, flashing an expanse of perfectly taut midsection as his shirt rode up. I followed the view down to the waistband of his low-slung jeans—where things started to get interesting—then deliberately looked away.

I didn't need trouble. I had enough to deal with already.

"I don't carry that stuff anymore," Danny told me. "Bump keys and torsion wrenches aren't popular with customs agents."

"Pshaw. You're not scared of those guys."

"Besides, I've gone legit, remember?" His eyes dared me to challenge him on that familiar claim. "If it weren't for you, I wouldn't have done anything remotely shady for years now."

I wanted to be indignant, but I couldn't. Danny *had* come to my aid lately, under some legally shaky circumstances. I'd needed him. He'd delivered. But that didn't mean he was unscrupulous. Far from it. My sometime bodyguard was merely loyal. To me.

I didn't want to take advantage of that, but . . . "How else am I supposed to get in there?" I gestured toward the Wrights' town house, across the grass and up the walk from us. "I'm up to my eyeballs in suspects, but I don't have any real evidence."

"What makes you think you'll find any in there?"

"Intuition. Optimism." I pinwheeled my arm. "Desperation?"

He looked away, predictably unconvinced. Danny

deals in facts, not feelings. That's why he doesn't like gambling. He knows the odds are against him, so he'd rather not get involved.

Or maybe he just doesn't want to feel that momentary burst of hopefulness as the cards are dealt or the wheels spin. I do, on the other hand. I love feeling that I've risked something and won. Maybe that's why I didn't mind the risks involved in trying to find Jeremy's killer. In the end, it would all be worthwhile.

So, I hoped, would sneaking into the Wrights' town house.

"You're not going to give up, are you?" Danny asked.

I grinned. "Did you just meet me?"

"Point made." He looked through the window at the garden. As expected, everything looked calm. "Let's get this over with."

Getting inside the town house was the easy part. Finding anything useful once we'd sneaked in was another story.

Until Danny and I entered via the back-terrace door that day, I hadn't seen much more than the kitchen. Thanks to Phoebe's ongoing baking tutorials, I'd seen a lot of that. Not surprisingly, the rest of the place was just as well-appointed, full of expensive-looking (but sedate) furniture, tasteful fabric-covered walls, acres of painted moldings and trim, plentiful antiques, and framed original artwork. I might have guessed that Phoebe would have traditional taste in furnishings.

In short, it looked exactly the way you'd expect an old Georgian town house in Chelsea to look, right down to the wall sconces, gleaming hardwood floors, and hand-tufted rugs.

We made short work of examining the place, starting with the salon ("living room," to you and me) and continuing down the corridor to the formal dining room, butler's pantry, and what must have been Jeremy's office. Its oak-paneled walls were full of Jeremy's framed cookbook covers, photos of him and Phoebe with other celebrities, and a variety of awards and honors. Jeremy's laptop computer was on the desk where he'd left it, right next to a reproduction Rodin sculpture. A plastic bottle of Hambleton & Hart "vitality water" stood nearby, half full, as though Jeremy might wander in at any moment and finish it.

Unexpectedly moved by those remnants of Jeremy's life, I paused. Behind me, Danny flipped through an old-fashioned filing cabinet, methodically searching for anything that seemed out of place. He knew how to look without anyone detecting. I mostly scanned the rooms we were in, trying to spot incongruities.

That bottle of specialty water was one. I knew Phoebe had had Amelja in for her routine cleaning sessions since Jeremy's death. Maybe the housekeeper was supposed to overlook this room?

If so, why? I turned to Danny. "Hey, if you got rich tomorrow, would you hire someone to clean house for you?"

"Depends." He examined a paper. "How big is the house?"

I glanced at the town house's ornate ceiling medallion, estimating. I was no realtor, but . . . "A few thousand square feet."

"Nah. I wouldn't want a stranger going through my stuff."

Bingo. "I'd be willing to bet Jeremy wouldn't have, either." He and Danny had come from similar hardscrabble backgrounds. They might have comparable attitudes about things. "That means this would be an excellent place to hide something."

"No kidding, Sherlock. That's why we're here."

"Of course, you'd have to know someone might guess that."

Danny went back to searching in earnest. "Here we go."

"Which means you purposely *wouldn't* hide anything in here." I looked around, giving Jeremy's office close scrutiny anyway.

"Right. Except?"

"Except anyone with a reason to search would probably know that, which means you might be safe hiding something in here."

Danny straightened with his hands on his hips. "I hate to bust up all your illusions, but most people don't think much beyond the first step, if that. Let's just stick to the plan."

We did. I searched Jeremy's laptop for clues. The device conveniently recognized that it was in proximity to Jeremy's cell phone (in my bag) and unlocked itself without a password, but my search through his e-mails and files turned up nothing.

Danny and I ascended the baroque carved-oak staircase to the first floor (meaning "second floor" to us Yanks). As I stepped onto the upper landing, the floorboard creaked. I froze.

Behind me, Danny did too. We both strained to hear.

Which was silly. What were we listening for, exactly? No one was around. There was no reason to be on the lookout.

Except that's when we heard it. Very faintly.

The sound of pop music filtered from the master

suite. It sounded muted, but it was definitely there. Was someone home?

I shook my head, trying to hear anything more. Nada.

"Phoebe must have left a radio on, that's all," I muttered to Danny. "She can't be home, and no one else lives here."

"We don't live here, either, but we're here."

"It'll be fine," I assured us both, then kept going.

Alarmed nonetheless, we searched through the other upstairs bedrooms swiftly. I turned up a risqué book, but nothing more.

"Shouldn't there at least be a safe?" I asked Danny.

But he was peering down the hallway toward the master suite, clearly concerned. "We should leave. I heard something."

"Yeah, the radio, remember?" I marched straight toward the suite, fueled by the likelihood of finding something useful in the town house's most private spaces. "Just don't turn off the radio when we get in the bedroom, or we'll give ourselves away." I tossed him a grin. "No matter how much you hate pop music."

So far, our investigation wouldn't have survived a good police detective's scrutiny, much less one of those forensics evidence-gathering teams. We'd left fingerprints all over the place. But I couldn't see why that would matter. DC Mishra and her colleagues at the London Metropolitan Police Service had already done all the double-checking they planned to do here.

"Remember the other, smaller bedroom?" I reminded Danny as I strode down the long, artwork-decorated hallway. "It definitely looked as though someone had been sleeping in there."

"My money's on guests. It's a guest room."

"I think it was Jeremy. If he and Phoebe were having

marital troubles, it's not a stretch to think that they'd use separate bedrooms." It was still possible there was a third party in their marriage—someone Jeremy had been sleeping with. He did have a sexy reputation. To bolster my argument, I added, "The bed linens were all rumpled, as though that room was off-limits to housekeeping. That's exactly the way Jeremy would have wanted it if he'd been using that room as a crash pad."

I'd been looking over my shoulder at Danny as I said it, which probably explained why I didn't see what Danny saw.

Specifically, what made him put on his "tough guy" face. He only used that expression when confronting problems. That meant there were problems, I saw as I swiveled to look—specifically (and funnily enough) problems of the housekeeping nature.

Phoebe's young Polish housekeeper, Amelja, stood in the doorway to the master suite. She'd been wearing earbuds. Music still blasted from them, which explained what we'd faintly heard earlier. Now they hung around her neck—right below, I couldn't help noticing, her quizzical and irked-looking face.

"He did want it that way," Amelja informed me tartly.

Oh no. What were we supposed to do now? We'd been caught red-handed. As far as I'd been able to tell, Amelja was loyal to the Wrights. She would almost certainly tell her boss (aka Phoebe) that we'd been there, snooping all over the town house.

Apprehensively, I glanced at Danny. He gave me the equivalent of a facial shrug, indicating that this one was on me. I understood why. This excursion had been my idea. Plus, Danny wasn't the kind of man to take down a twentysomething working woman with violence just because she was inconvenient.

Maybe Danny really had gone straight, as he'd said.

On the other hand, it occurred to me, at least now we had firm verification from Amelja that Jeremy and Phoebe had used separate bedrooms. That didn't signal marital bliss, did it?

Wishing we could have at least searched the master suite before being found out, I glanced behind Amelja. There were ball gowns and shoes scattering the floor of Phoebe's bedroom. Under one particularly gauzy purple number, I spotted a cardboard box.

There was no way Phoebe routinely decorated with cardboard.

I dragged my gaze back toward my own position. That's when I got a closer look at Phoebe's housekeeper . . . and her feet.

"Jeremy was a little unconventional," I said. "But Phoebe isn't. Does she encourage you to wear her shoes while cleaning?"

Amelja started. Shamefacedly, she looked down at the (probably) thousand-pound slingbacks on her feet. "Erm . . . ."

But I didn't have time for that particularly British version of "um." I had to get out of this predicament.

"I won't tell Phoebe that I saw all of . . . this," I volunteered with a wave toward the gowns and shoes, "if you don't tell her that I was late picking up the donations she's making."

I held my breath, hoping my hunches—that those cardboard boxes contained things Phoebe was discarding, and that Amelja had been indulging in a major (forbidden) gown-and-shoe try-on session— were correct. It was possible that Phoebe had simply had trouble deciding which designer ball gown to wear to Jeremy's funeral today and had flung all those things about in a frenzy before leaving. It was possible that Phoebe was notoriously slobby, prone to strewing her bedroom with clothes and shoes on a daily basis. It was possible that Amelja hadn't taken advantage of her boss's absence—for the entire day—to indulge in a little Cinderella time. And, I theorized further, possible that she didn't have the cell phone selfie pics to prove it.

"I'll bet your Facebook account was hilarious today."

Behind me, Danny cleared his throat. I turned— and Amelja glanced up toward him—to see him holding up his own phone.

On its screen was Facebook's unmistakable signature blue layout, loaded with multiple photos of Amelja. She was wearing that filmy purple gown and a tiara, holding a feather duster.

I raised my brows at Danny in surprise. He shrugged.

"Just because I have muscles, I'm some kind of meathead?"

I knew he wasn't. But I was still taken aback by his preparedness. It looked as though I wasn't the only one who'd wanted to step up my game. He must have researched everyone who had a connection to Jeremy, both virtually and physically.

"If you'll excuse me . . ." I gestured to move past Amelja. She stepped aside quite readily, her gaze fixed on Danny's phone.

"I was only having a bit of fun," the housekeeper said.

She was young enough to be defiant and old enough to be scared. I didn't doubt Phoebe would have sacked her for this.

"That's fine. Your secret's safe with me." I hefted that cardboard box, then took a sneaky look around. Aside from the dresses and shoes spilling from Phoebe's (astonishingly well-appointed) closet, everything appeared to be in order. There was a small sitting area with an antique desk I was dying to search, but I couldn't think of an excuse to do that. "Thanks, Amelja."

I edged past her with the cardboard box in my arms, the tinny sounds of earbud-based pop music serenading my steps. That explained why Amelja hadn't heard Danny and me rummaging around. She'd had the volume cranked so high, a British Airways jet could have landed outside in the garden without her noticing.

Danny had put away his phone. Chivalrously, he took the box from me. He shot me a puzzled glance as he discerned its relatively light weight for its size. I hadn't been similarly confused. I'd seen—and Danny hadn't—the other side of Phoebe's immense closet. Everything that had belonged to Jeremy was gone.

It seemed a little premature for Phoebe to have cleaned out Jeremy's things—or, more likely, have asked Amelja to do so—but it wasn't up to me to judge how a wife grieved for her husband. Maybe Phoebe simply wanted to keep busy, to avoid getting lost in her sadness. Maybe someone had approached her from a worthy charity that needed menswear, and she hadn't had the heart to refuse. Maybe she merely wanted more closet space for herself.

"That's the last box," Amelja informed us as we prepared to get the heck out of there before something else went wrong. She nodded toward the staircase. "I already took the rest downstairs earlier, before I got"—

carried away trying on Phoebe's clothes—"busy with other things. You'll take care of all of them?"

I tried to seem as though I'd expected that. "No worries."

Phoebe's housekeeper looked relived. "That saves me a trip, then. It's not my job to carry boxes around, but the church wouldn't send anyone to pick them up on such short notice."

Aha. Now I knew where everything was supposed to go.

"I'll make sure it all gets to its proper destination," I promised, meaning it. First, I'd have a look for any clues, then I'd transport Jeremy's things to the church. "I'm on it."

I might as well make the most of my excuse for being there, I figured, no matter how fabricated it might have been.

With her hands already raised to replace her earbuds, Amelja shook her head at me. "You're different from Jeremy's other assistants," she said. "Too bad he didn't find you first."

I was getting fed up with being mistaken for Jeremy's personal assistant. Not that there's anything wrong with that job, but Amelja had seen me tutoring Phoebe in baking. Did she think I was just that multitalented? Or did she think I was just that friendly with Phoebe? Also, exactly how many assistants did Jeremy regularly churn through, anyway? Had he been *that* bad?

But all I said was, "Oh? Why's that?"

"Because *you* weren't likely to get in trouble sleeping with him, were you?" Amelja's eyes sparkled as she pointed her thumb at Danny. "Not with a hunk o' man like him waiting at home."

She gave my security expert a cheeky wink, then

went back to "cleaning"—aka trying on all of Phoebe's fanciest clothes.

Me? And Danny? I might have blushed. I know I felt a little flustered as I turned toward the stairs. Just because I've known Danny a long time doesn't mean I don't have eyes. I can see that he's good-looking. I can *feel* that he's special—brave, strong, sometimes funny and often brilliant, always willing to help . . .

"Remember, Amelja," he said behind me, using his most Travis-like throaty tone, "we won't tell if you won't."

The housekeeper giggled, reminding me how young she was. She was attractive, too. *She* might have tempted Jeremy to be indiscreet . . . to have a reason to sleep in the guest bedroom. Maybe that was why Amelja was interested in Jeremy's love life?

It was impossible to know why the housekeeper had speculated about Jeremy's relationships with his assistants. I didn't think he'd slept with Nicola, but . . . who knew? A woman scorned might have had good reason to write a tell-all bio.

Either way, we hustled downstairs and got out of there. I was pretty sure, if we didn't, that I might have a heart attack.

Safely back in the guesthouse, we stared at the box.

I sort of felt like giggling, Amelja style, myself. I couldn't help it. Sometimes that's how stress affects me. Big blubbery tears or helpless hysterical laughter—that's how your favorite chocolate whisperer tends to react to nerve-wracking situations. I swigged some water—non-fancy, non "vitality" style water, you should note—then picked up my plate, which held a slice of white-chocolate raspberry tart. I forked up a mouthful, frowning at that cardboard box. We probably shouldn't have filched it.

We probably should have taken it straight to the church.

But this was just a temporary delay, I reminded myself. It was for a good cause, too—finding Jeremy's murderer. It couldn't be for anything else. It wasn't as though Danny would want to pinch any of Jeremy's cast-off clothes. All the other boxes, which we'd rapidly sorted through, had contained items that had definitely belonged to Jeremy Wright. All of them were too loud, too short, and too tight in the shoulders to fit my bodyguard.

"This isn't cool, picking through a dead man's clothes," Danny complained, glowering at the box. "I feel dirty."

Honestly, I did, too. But I couldn't quit. "This is the last one," I inveigled, having swallowed my bite of tart. I'd offered a slice to Danny. He, being him, had passed. "After this, we'll tape them all back up and take them to the church."

"You don't think that will look suspicious?"

"Phoebe isn't going to check with the rector to find out who delivered all the boxes. She has people to take care of things like that for her." In this case, Amelja. "Plus, you might have noticed Phoebe's a little preoccupied lately. She'll be glad to have this off her hands." Privately, I knew she was freaking out about her upcoming TV appearance, too. The addition of Nicola to the lineup had lent a distressing new edge to her already fearful anticipation. "Let's just finish this."

I put down my plate and dug into the box. We hadn't found anything notable in the others—just a bunch of Oxford-cloth button-up shirts, some trousers and jeans, argyle sweaters, belts and men's socks, a disturbingly large number of trainers ("sneakers," to those who don't live abroad), and T-shirts.

I opened the final box, expecting more of the same. Instead, I found toiletries. Men's toiletries. Shaving soap, razors, a popular brand of sensitive toothpaste, expensive department-store wrinkle reducer and antioxidant creams, and hair products.

I examined them all. "These must have set him back a few quid," I said, recognizing the brands. Jeremy *had* been vain—or at least unquestionably interested in keeping his sexy image intact. I couldn't really blame him for that. I pawed further. "Aha. *Here* are the rest of the clothes." I pulled out crisp-looking athletic socks and running shorts, a pair of unworn Y-fronts (you might know them as tighty-whities, or traditional men's underwear) and a pair of . . . "Ugh!" Recognizing it, I dropped it. "A thong?"

Yep. That was taking "sexy" several miles too far.

Danny grabbed that stretchy, barely there garment. "Jeremy really was itty-bitty. I could hardly fit my bait and tackle in these." He tested the elastic, then tossed it onto the pile. "Nope. Definitely not enough room for the old frank and beans."

"Danny!" I made a face. "Show a little respect."

But he was kidding, and I was laughing, and a second later, we'd lost it completely. I had a go at shouting "frank and beans!" Danny encouraged me by making funny faces. Maybe you had to be there, but it was hilarious—and just what I needed.

See what I mean? Danny always has my back . . . in more ways than one. For as long as I've known him, Danny has made me laugh.

Officially, of course, we were both going straight to hell for mocking the clothing choices of a dead man.

But in the meantime, I felt better about what we were doing.

"Maybe the thong was a gift," Danny suggested, packing up.

"From someone who hated him," I agreed, helping him return things to the box. I grabbed the briefs, then paused. "You know, all the rest of the underwear were boxers. Or boxer briefs."

"He probably bought those by mistake." Danny's nod prompted me to deposit those tighty-whities into the box where they belonged. "Sometimes you grab a three-pack off the shelf, it turns out to be the wrong kind . . . who's going to return underwear?"

"Sure." *Except I doubted millionaire Jeremy Wright bought his "pants" by the three-pack wrapped in plastic.* I didn't want to make Danny feel self-conscious about his purchasing habits, though. He sometimes has an ax to grind about wealth. "Maybe."

Danny stopped packing and studied me. For a second, I thought he'd detected my difference of opinion about Jeremy's underwear-buying habits. I didn't want that. But that wasn't it.

"Hey, keep your chin up," my security expert told me with a reassuring nudge to my shoulder. He grinned. "If this were easy, everyone would be finding murderers in their spare time."

"Yeah. Woohoo! Yay, me!" Joking, I waved my arm like Andrew Davies.

My go-get-'em gesture had exactly as much believability as the Hambleton & Hart CEO's had (meaning, none), but Danny seemed to buy it anyway. That made it all worthwhile. I didn't want my pal to know I was struggling. I wanted to sleuth effortlessly, like a modern-day Miss Marple, no matter what the reality was.

Maybe Mr. Barclay was right, it occurred to me. Maybe we American's always *were* "whooping over this, that, and the other." Even when we had no real reason for such enthusiasm.

Maybe that was because, like me, sometimes we had no other leads and didn't know what else to do. I was at a dead end.

It was time to go back to chocolate whispering. Maybe while I was tempering chocolate and baking real molten chocolate cakes, another approach would occur to me. In the meantime, since the chocolaterie-pâtisserie was officially closed today . . .

"Have you ever been to the Tower of London?" I asked Danny. "Tower Bridge? Piccadilly Circus? Greenwich? We've got all day. We might as well act like tourists while we're here, right?"

To my surprise, my (usually) taciturn security expert agreed. "Hand me a Union Jack T-shirt, a basket of fish and chips, and a map of the Underground, and let's go."

Thirteen

Despite the rollicking time that Danny and I had while seeing the Big Smoke as tourists—ending our spontaneous tour of London in the same friendly pub that had been Jeremy's local—my security expert wasn't up for more of the same the next day.

"I have . . . things to do," Danny told me cryptically. He gave me a hawk-eyed look. "You'll be okay without me today?"

I nodded. "I'm just going into Primrose for a while, then I have a tutoring session with Phoebe. She insisted on it."

It was back to the grind for me, now that Jeremy's funeral was over with. Today's tabloids had had a particularly vicious take on the memorial service and the people who'd attended it—including Liam, Andrew Davies, Claire Evans, and several prominent Londoners—probably owing to the difficulty the media had had while covering the event. Numerous members of the London Metropolitan Police Service had been there for crowd control, as it turned out, so Danny and I had chosen an opportune day for our search of the Wrights' town house. Since it hadn't turned up anything noteworthy, I was happy we hadn't risked much.

Danny examined me. "That's all that's on your agenda?"

"Well, that and a workout with Liam at The Green Park," I amended. Sometimes I thought Danny and Travis kept better track of my schedule than I did. Or maybe I just wasn't looking forward to another round of wind sprints, burpees, and push-ups.

Yeah, that was probably it. One had been enough for me.

Danny's expression sobered. "I'll catch up to you by then."

"You don't seriously think Liam would hurt me, do you?"

"He's too big and dangerous to overlook."

"You're just saying that because *you're* too big and dangerous to overlook. Besides, you don't fool me," I told Danny with a grin as I slung on my crossbody bag and gathered my chocolatier gear in preparation for my travels. "You just don't want me to know that you'll be shadowing me, probably all day."

"That's not it."

"Would you tell me if it were?"

Danny had no answer for that. That's how I knew I had him.

"Cheerio!" I told him. "Try to stay out of trouble."

"That's easy when *you're* not around." He beat me to the guesthouse's door and held it open for me. He was being gallant—just as he'd been when he'd forgone his turn in the four-poster bed (again) so I could be comfy. "*You* stay out of trouble."

"I would if I could," I told him truthfully.

Then we both sailed out into another (this time, drizzly) English summertime morning, ready to take

on chocolate whispering (for me) and . . . something
mysterious (for him).

I hadn't been at Primrose ten minutes before Hugh
had another outburst. They were starting to become
problematic.

I didn't understand it. Most of the time, the tattooed and lanky baker was a hard worker, jocular—if
coarse—and dedicated. But some of the time, when
things didn't go exactly right . . .

"Bloody hell!" Hugh shouted. "This is bollocks!"

A loud clatter shot through the chocolaterie-
pâtisserie's kitchen. Pans hit the floor. Chocolate
splattered everywhere.

Poppy squealed. "Hugh! Watch it, will you?"

Everyone else stepped back. Hugh stalked through
the kitchen, then gave another shove to a stack of
sheet pans.

"Hey! I just prepped those!" Myra objected, hands
on hips.

The rest of the bakers watched, openmouthed, as
Hugh paced back and forth. Thick dark chocolate
slowly dripped from his prep table. It pooled beneath
a wide stainless steel bowl and an overturned pot.
Once-simmering water sloshed beneath it all.

Hugh had upturned a bain-marie, I saw. He'd been
melting chocolate for mendiants. Evidently, something had gone wrong.

"So?" Hugh snarled, daring anyone to object. He
glanced at his upended bain-marie setup, then frowned
more fiercely. "What kind of wanker melts chocolate
for a living, anyway?"

"The kind of wanker who does nothing but whinge
the moment things go wrong, apparently!" Myra said

heatedly, striding over to her dropped sheet pans. "Pick those up, right now."

Hugh glared at her. "Piss off. I ain't your servant."

"What's got into you lately?" Myra gave him a questioning look. "You knocked them down. Now you should pick them up."

Hugh dug in his heels. "*You* should shut up," he said with narrowed eyes, "before you get yourself in trouble."

"Ooh, look who's so tough." Poppy stepped up to stand beside Myra. "Picking on a pair of girls. Nice, Hugh."

But despite their bravado, both of them jumped back a pace as Hugh suddenly approached them, his hands balled into fists.

"You aren't any better than me, Poppy," he said in a low voice. "We both started at the same time, back when Phoebe cleared house. So don't go getting all high and mighty, you—"

That was where I stepped in, before names could be called.

I knew that Hugh wasn't the only apprentice at the bakery. Just before I'd arrived in London, Phoebe had replaced all of her previous chocolatiers and bakers. She'd claimed that she'd wanted to give the participants of Jeremy's foundation a fresh start. And, you know, maybe net some positive publicity for Primrose, while she was at it—which she'd done. It hadn't been enough, but I'm used to that. By the time my clients call me, they've usually tried any number of things to salvage their floundering chocolate businesses, usually without success.

Hers had been an understandable impulse—and Phoebe had helped find good jobs for the workers she'd replaced—but she hadn't thought it through.

Like so many things in her life, it was supposed to have simply succeeded, one way or another. If I'd led a similarly charmed existence, like Phoebe, I might have done the same thing. But since I haven't, I got down to work.

I faced Hugh squarely. "What's the matter?"

"My chocolate seized." He may or may not have heaped in several expletives to make his point. Okay, he definitely did.

Hugh was nothing if not outspoken. Occasionally, abrasive. Most often, though, he was perfectly charming and likable. Being an apprentice can be challenging. Everyone is very aware that they're theoretically on probation. They might fail at any time.

"Seizing is no big deal." I looked around at the mess. "It happens sometimes, but it certainly doesn't warrant this. Clean up, redo Myra's sheet pans for her, then see me," I told him in a pacifying tone. "I'll walk you through it, step by step."

He shook his head and crossed his arms. "I'm not a baby."

This time, he added an even rawer expletive.

I straightened to my full five-foot-six or so, then met him toe-to-toe. I might not be big, but I'm strong, stubborn, and unafraid to tangle with belligerent bakery staff. Bullies and troublemakers populate restaurant kitchens worldwide. You can't show fear. If the average line cook thinks he's intimidated you, you're toast. Besides, I've faced down honest-to-God murderers and lived to tell (you) about it. Hugh didn't worry me.

"Then stop acting like a baby and get to work," I told him. "Be an adult. Take responsibility for what you did."

My serious tone finally broke through. Hugh's

lower lip actually wobbled. I could have sworn he almost cried.

Maybe I didn't need to work out later. I'd already (figuratively) bench-pressed a surly, tantrum-prone baker.

But since it wouldn't do any good to push Hugh further, I turned to everyone else next. It was a deliberate act, designed to show Hugh and the rest of the Primrose staff that I trusted Hugh to do the right thing. Just as I trusted them to work hard.

"Let's have a progress report from the rest of you." I headed for another baker's station, inhaling chocolate as I did so. "How are the triple chocolate biscotti coming along?"

Even as I said it, I felt Hugh's scowling attention follow me. But as I examined the biscotti in question, then showed the baker how to diagonally slice her cookie logs into batons for their second baking—the one that makes them crunchy enough to dip—I heard the clatter of pans. Then the swish of a mop.

Hugh was cleaning up, I saw from the corner of my eye.

We'd finally turned a corner at Primrose, I realized. Sometimes things got worse before they got better. But you have to persevere. You never know when you're on the verge of a breakthrough—when the very next thing you try is the thing that succeeds . . . the thing that would have never happened if you'd quit.

I'd needed Hugh's full cooperation, and I'd gotten it. I needed to find out who'd killed Jeremy Wright— and remove myself from suspicion, in the process—and I was doing that, too.

I couldn't stop. For Jeremy's sake, I had to keep

going. No matter how little evidence or how many suspects I had just then.

Reminded of all the proof I still didn't have, I headed back to see Hugh. His eyes still looked suspiciously red-rimmed—he was, after all, a young man trying to learn a difficult new job—but he'd calmed down by the time I reached him. He'd already set up a new bain-marie by balancing another wide stainless steel bowl atop a pan full of barely simmering water. He was adding chopped chocolate to the bowl, preparing to temper it.

If he didn't, I'd explained to the Primrose staff, the chocolate would never set. Any confections made from it might bloom. They'd definitely look dull. They'd melt much too easily.

You know that gloss and depth that well-made chocolate has? That faint *snap* when you break off a piece? That's the result of skilled tempering—bringing chocolate to the correct temperatures to align its various crystalline structures. I know that doesn't sound delicious, but it's important. Without tempering, no one would ever have eaten a delicious Mexican *chocolatina* flavored with cinnamon, almonds, and vanilla, or a Belgian *chocolade* with its signature praliné center made of caramelized ground nuts.

Hugh didn't acknowledge me. Not right away. For the first few moments, we worked side by side, me chopping the rest of his allotted chocolate block into the tiny shards that would make up his "seeding" chocolate for a later stage of the tempering process, and him studiously watching his instant thermometer.

At last, Hugh nodded at the temperature. "That's it."

Surreptitiously, I sneaked a peek, then gave a slight nod. One of the things that's fiddly about tempering chocolate is that different varieties of chocolate melt at different rates. Harder Malaysian cacao takes longer; softer Brazilian takes less time. Unless you know your chocolate's origins, it's tricky.

Wordlessly, I stepped back to let Hugh add some of the waiting seeding chocolate. That unmelted chocolate would cool the mixture just enough. After that, Hugh would increase the temperature again, until most of the beta crystals reached a uniformly small size. That homogeneity was what would give the resulting tempered chocolate its unique capability to be dipped, molded in bars, or used to coat Primrose's chocolate biscotti.

With all the seed chocolate added, we both held our breath. Then, beneath his bandanna, Hugh's face brightened. "Whew!" He peered into the bowl, then gave me a relieved look. "That's not what happened last time. This looks loads better already."

"Last time, did it go all grainy? Dull? Hard to stir?"

He nodded. "It seized up like a mother—"

I stopped him before he could finish that obscenity. I'm not squeamish about profanity, but some of the bakers were.

We were, after all, working in a family business.

"That happens," I told Hugh, fighting an urge to clean some of the splattered chocolate from his chef's whites. In some ways, he seemed like a little boy—a gigantic, broad-shouldered, profane little boy. Hugh was easily angered, but just as easily soothed. He could have been my younger brother. You know, if I had one. "Most likely some water found its way into your first batch of chocolate and bollixed up the works," I explained. "If that happens, the chocolate isn't ruined—"

Hugh's sheepish expression told me he'd thought otherwise.

"—but it's no good for couverture." For coating or

molding. "If it's seized, you can sometimes bring it back, though."

"I tried to fix it by pouring in boiling water," Hugh told me. "I thought it made sense. Something hot plus something hot."

I understood the impulse. "When tempering, water is your mortal enemy, no matter how hot it is. You can sometimes smooth things out by adding a tiny bit of oil or melting in some more chocolate. It won't behave the same way, but it's still fine for baking or making chocolate sauce. Next time, just ask, okay?"

Hugh crossed his arms. "You would've chewed my arse off."

"Not likely. Teaching is what I'm here for."

He shook his head. "*Everybody* has other things they want."

"I want to create superstar chocolates. That's it." *And find out who bludgeoned Jeremy.* "How about you? What do you want?" I watched him gauge his chocolate's temperature again. "Why did you come to work at Primrose? You must've had choices."

His derisive chuckle disagreed. "I've never had those."

"You will if you stick with this." I wanted to encourage him. Who knew the hardships Hugh had overcome to be there? "A baker can find work anywhere. A chocolatier can too, especially in Europe. There, the chocolate-making tradition goes way back."

Hugh twisted his mouth with doubtfulness. "Me? In some posh place where the chocolates cost a fiver each? Not likely."

"It could happen. Look how well Jeremy did."

Hugh's gaze turned murky. "Yeah. Not so well, after all."

Oops. *I meant before he was killed.* "I meant that Jeremy came from a tough background, and he succeeded wildly." I nudged Hugh. "Big house, nice wife, lavish parties on the weekend. Not bad." I injected a casual note into my voice. "I heard you went to a few of those parties. Were they as wild as everyone says?"

Meaning, *as wild as cranky Ellis Barclay says?* I still wanted to know if Jeremy's neighbor had had a valid complaint.

Hugh glared at his chocolate. "How would I know?"

"Someone told me you delivered party supplies for Jeremy." I held my breath, then dived in. "Were you there . . . that night?"

"What kind of bloody question is that?" Hugh shot me an irate look. "What are you doing, writing a book, like Nicola?"

In the face of his angry questions, I held my ground. But it wasn't easy. I kind of wished Danny were there for backup.

Also . . . Hugh knew Nicola? I wondered why. And how well.

"No, I'm not writing a book. But if you were there—"

"I've got to concentrate on this chocolate, yeah?" Hugh barked at me, wiping his hands on his apron. "What are you doing distracting me, anyway? You're a shit teacher in a shit bakery!"

Whoa. So this was what it was like being the subject of Hugh's rage. I went still, momentarily shocked by his hostility.

"That's enough, Hugh." Phoebe strode forward, elegant in a pair of black trousers paired with a flowy black top and strappy black sandals. Her jewelry gleamed; her expression brooked no disagreement. "Come with me, please," she directed serenely.

Of course she had every expectation of compliance. She was the Honourable Phoebe Wright. Primrose didn't exist without her.

I'd been so busy trying to tease information from Hugh that I hadn't noticed her arrival. Phoebe was right on time, though, I noted with a swift glance at the clock. This was her post-yoga window, although her outfit suggested she hadn't gotten her namaste on today. Worriedly, I glanced at my consultee's face, wondering if (a) she knew I'd sneaked into her house and/or (b) she was on the verge of ending our consultation on the spot.

Arguing with Hugh wouldn't help my case, that's for sure.

Phoebe looked right at me. Her placid face gave no clues.

"Now, please." She directed that command at Hugh, then swiveled on her fancy heels and glided toward the back room.

All the bakers had gone deathly silent. Hugh included.

He glanced at me with murder in his expression. Also, a great deal of self-righteousness. *See?* his face seemed to say. *This is what happens when people like me dare to feel hopeful.*

I knew that Danny would have agreed with the sentiment.

Every sign pointed to Hugh being sacked on the spot. The chocolaterie-pâtisserie suddenly felt too quiet. Like a wake.

I couldn't let him lose his job. "I'll talk to Phoebe."

"No, I'll do it." Hugh held up his hand to stop me. He set aside his mop and bucket, then straightened his head kerchief. His eyebrow piercing caught the light. "Be a man, right?"

Argh. He had to reference my earlier lecture *now*?

I couldn't disagree, though. Hugh *was* a grown man. If necessary, I promised myself, I'd talk with Phoebe later myself. I'd make sure she knew that I'd pushed Hugh into his outburst. I'd explain that he was a promising baker, a valuable employee.

I stood pinned in place as Hugh jerked up his chin and strode away to meet his fate. I could see his hands shaking; I could see Phoebe waiting for him in her office, regal and sure.

Whatever she said to him was too low to hear clearly. The most terrifying people are always the quietest, aren't they? My own father tends to get *more* silent, *more* calm, the angrier he gets. Try explaining *that* to six-year-old me. You can't do it.

Down the passageway in her office, Phoebe reached up to touch Hugh's head kerchief. She seemed to be indicating that he should take it off, like a supplicant come to see the queen.

Well. That wasn't a very nice thought, was it? Annoyed with myself for thinking that about Phoebe— and worse, for believing it might be true—I turned away. I didn't want to see any more.

I turned to address the others. This might not have had anything to do with chocolate explicitly, but it was my job to lead them. Myra, Poppy, and the others would have questions.

Specifically, questions about why Hugh was already emerging from Phoebe's office, his bandanna held in his tattooed fist.

We all gaped as the gangly baker strode through the kitchen. He didn't look at any of us. If he'd been sacked, it had happened in record time, remorselessly and quietly.

"Hugh? What happened?" Myra kneaded her chef's jacket.

"Are you all right, Hugh?" Poppy crowded in. "Can I help?"

The other bakers clustered around, fretful and curious.

Hugh held up his arm but didn't break stride. For an instant, his gaze flashed to meet mine. "See you around, yeah?"

Then he pushed open the back door and stepped outside. I didn't know if he'd quit, was fired, or (I couldn't help thinking) had maybe stabbed Phoebe in her office with his knife.

I should have checked his combat boot for its telltale shaft. Hugh had never liked kitchen clogs; he wore his boots.

"I'd feel a right tosser in those things," he'd said.

Left behind in the chocolaterie-pâtisserie's kitchen, we all looked at each other. I wasn't sure what to do. Call DC Mishra? I didn't want to be suspected of another murder, just because I'd been standing nearby. On the other hand, there were witnesses this time. Everyone knew I hadn't attacked Phoebe.

I put on a smile and hooked my thumb toward the office, not wanting to alarm the others. "I'll just go check on Phoebe."

Poppy snorted. "Yeah, right. Check on *her*, why don't you?"

Myra's mutinous gaze hit me. "Are you with *us* or her?"

"Hugh's the one who needs checking on," someone else said.

What could I say? *I'm worried your boss might be dead* wouldn't fly. *I think Hugh might have killed Jeremy?* Nope.

I was spared by Phoebe sticking her head out of her office, then high-handedly signaling to me. "Hayden, please come here."

I sagged with relief. Suddenly, I had everyone's sympathy.

"Never mind." Morosely, Myra turned away. "Good luck."

"Yeah, nice knowing you," Poppy added. "Sorry, Hayden."

So, haughtily summoned, I headed back to see Phoebe. I'd never been fired from a consultation before. Not ever. How would I explain this to Danny? Worse, to Travis? He'd be disconsolate.

There was only one way to approach this. Diplomatically.

If I got fired from my chocolate-whisperer consultation at Primrose, how would I investigate Jeremy's murder? I knew Danny and Travis would say this was proof I shouldn't investigate any murders (they were in unprecedented agreement on that subject), but I was already knee-deep into this one. I couldn't stop now.

I went in, closed the door, and faced Phoebe.

"I think you may have misunderstood about Hugh," I began.

If I was going down, I intended to go down swinging.

"Hugh? This isn't about Hugh." Phoebe looked briefly nonplussed, but that didn't last long. She regrouped, clasping her hands equably atop her desk. I envied her composure. "I spoke with Andrew Davies at the service yesterday. He wanted to know where to find the memorial to Jeremy you'd put together?"

I blanched. "Oh, that." I laughed, buying time to

think. I couldn't tell Phoebe about my investigation, could I? No. "Mr. Davies and I met at Jeremy's charity, and he assumed I was Jeremy's assistant. I didn't want to embarrass him, so . . ."

"Ah." Phoebe nodded, instantly understanding. The British yen to avoid embarrassment at all costs ran deep. "I see."

"I'm afraid there isn't really any memorial."

"*I* know that." Phoebe's brittle tone stood at odds with her elegant appearance. She was, hands down, the world's most graceful widow. For a moment, she looked wistful. "It would have been nice, though, wouldn't it? A fine remembrance of Jeremy?"

"I think everyone's remembering him in their own way."

"Yes, well . . . they would, wouldn't they?" My consultee looked up at me with polite smile. "You mustn't be afraid to be tough with the staff here, Hayden. I need your leadership, now more than ever." She paused. "I also need your tutoring. Otherwise . . ."

You'd be fired. I didn't doubt that's what she meant.

Duly warned, I nodded. "Hugh surprised me, that's all. He really is a good worker. Smart and capable, and very helpful with the other bakers. Confectionary isn't his forte, but he—"

"Hugh won't be giving you any more trouble." Phoebe sorted through some papers on her desk, clearly finished with our conversation. Then she glanced up as though struck by another thought. "I was wondering . . . do you still have Jeremy's phone?"

I did. "It's in my bag, in my locker." At Primrose, all the staff used lockers during working hours. It was standard. "I'll get it for you right away, as soon as we're done here."

I'd gotten all the information I could cull from it anyway.

"That would be acceptable."

"I'm sorry I didn't return it before. I've been"—*busy using it to investigate your husband's death*—"absentminded lately."

"Haven't we all?" Phoebe sighed. Then she sharpened. "You'll need to pull yourself together, won't you? It won't do for me to have lessons from someone who isn't up to the task."

Her condescending tone bothered me. I didn't doubt that Hugh had quit the moment Phoebe had gotten all queenly with him.

But I didn't have the luxury of storming out of Primrose, the way Hugh had done. I had a job to do— one I took pride in doing well. Aside from that, I needed access to the people who'd been in Jeremy's life. Otherwise, I'd never solve his murder.

"I'm completely up to the task," I assured her. "In fact, why don't I show you our new range of cookies? There are triple-chocolate biscotti, Devil's-food chocolate chip, fudgy brownie bites, cocoa shortbread, hazelnut chocolate-drop cookies with caramel centers, peanut butter–filled chocolate . . . They've been very popular with the chocolaterie-pâtisserie's customers."

"Another time." Phoebe gave me an indifferent wave. "I have things to do. I've let some tasks linger uncompleted for far too long now, haven't I?"

It had been less than a week since Jeremy's death. I didn't think that qualified as "far too long." But all I said was, "We're still on for our baking lesson this afternoon, then?"

"Of course, Hayden. I'm not an idiot, am I?"

Well . . . since Phoebe hadn't fired me? No.

I smiled at her. "Of course not."

"Then I'll see you this afternoon," she confirmed, going back to her documents. "We'll make a Bakewell tart today. A chocolate version, of course. You'll know how to do that."

I did. We were fine, then. But since I couldn't leave well enough alone, I had to get the last word. Blame pride. Blame leftover adrenaline from dealing with Hugh. Or just blame the chocolate, butter, and sugar fumes wafting through Primrose. Those were decadent enough to have scrambled anyone's senses.

Whatever was responsible, next I heard myself say . . .

"I'm not an idiot, either," I told Phoebe in a cautionary tone, wanting the respect I'd earned. I hadn't gotten my chocolate-whisperer cred by being mediocre. I was the best in the world. The *only* in the world. If Phoebe wanted help, I was her best option. "You should remember that, Phoebe."

Then I turned without waiting for a response and sailed away . . . not nearly as graciously as Phoebe had done earlier, but it felt pretty darn satisfying to leave her gawking, all the same.

Fourteen

"... and then *I* said, *'I'm* not an idiot, either.'" I lowered into another squat, my thighs trembling. After only half an hour or so of working out with Liam, my muscles burned—even muscles I hadn't been aware of having, until now. I lifted myself again. *Ah.* "You should have seen Phoebe's face. She was gobsmacked."

"I doubt anyone ever talks to Phoebe that way." Liam urged me down into another shaky squat. "Or ever has done, actually."

All around us, Londoners reveled in The Green Park on a summer afternoon. Some filled its classic, awning-striped deck chairs, enjoying the newly blue skies and meager sunshine. Others relaxed on the rolling grass or atop picnic blankets. The unluckiest ones followed the paths winding amid the tall London plane trees, scurrying from Buckingham Palace and St. James's Park on one side of the royal park to the Tube station that lay on the other. That's where I'd be, once I'd finished training with Jeremy—on the Underground, headed back to Chelsea.

"Maybe Jeremy did," I fished. I was tired, sure. But

not too tired to try to wrangle useful information from him. "He was Phoebe's husband. He didn't have to worry about her firing him."

"Humph." Liam gave me a sardonic look. "You've never been married, have you? My mates who have tell a different story."

"I've come close." I grunted with effort. "Three times."

He grinned. "Close only counts in horseshoes and hand grenades." The trainer raised his brows. "Three times, though?"

I nodded, then switched to performing a plank at Liam's silent request. By now, I'd come to understand his signals.

I didn't like them, necessarily. But I understood them.

"Unfortunately, I have a weakness for the same kind of man," I explained, wishing I'd wiped my sweaty forehead before embarking on my plank. I still had almost a full minute to go. The grass prickled my palms. My knees quaked. "Tall, good-looking, home-body types—you know, guys who want to settle down."

Liam was squinting toward the bushes that lined the park's fence along Piccadilly. Tardily, he realized I'd quit speaking.

"Those kind of guys really exist?" he asked.

I gave a rueful grin. "I've turned three of them into the wild myself." Perspiration dripped from my chin. Gross. Liam's workouts were really hard. "I wasn't ready to settle down."

"Maybe you weren't ready to settle down with *them*," Liam suggested, gently touching me with his strong hands—a reminder for me to keep my back flat. "You travel all the time, right? A guy who likes to stay at home sounds like a wonky fit to me."

I disagreed. "But that's what I *want*. Someone who's secure. Someone who's dependable. Someone who won't—"

"Gallivant off across the globe? Like you do?"

He had me. We'd gotten friendly enough that I'd explained my traveling to him. "Okay, so I have a 'type.' Big deal." I focused on my plank for a few more seconds. "I bet you do, too."

Liam allowed me to relax between sets. For a nanosecond.

"Not really." He shrugged. "I'm pretty open."

"No, you're not. You just think you are. Everyone has a type. They want their partner to tick all the checkboxes."

Again, I caught Liam looking into the bushes. What the . . . ?

He frowned, then shook himself. "Speak for yourself. That's too limiting, if you ask me. You've got to try new things!"

He trod to his trainer's bag of tricks, then took out some small blocks. Recognizing them, I groaned. This was the part of our workout where Liam set up those blocks, then I sprinted from one to the other, developing quickness and stamina. Ugh.

I wished I'd eaten more than a fruit salad with hazelnut vinaigrette, leafy greens, and crunchy cacao nibs for lunch. With a chocolate éclair from Le Pain Quotidien for dessert as a chaser, of course, because . . . well, I'd needed to power up, right?

Why wasn't chocolate some kind of superfood? (It's not, despite what you may have heard. Sure, it contains antioxidant flavonoids plus beneficial phytochemicals, but that's no excuse to pack away pounds of it—to my eternal regret.) I'd already had a lecture from Liam about not having quit my favorite treats.

He'd known—or had accurately guessed—my transgressions.

I didn't think I was that transparent. Maybe I was wrong.

"Most 'new things' are superficial," I argued. "Blond instead of brunette, tall instead of short. That doesn't count."

Unfazed, Liam went on setting out his blocks. "I'll bet you a tenner that your guys all looked the same, too."

I laughed, ready to take that wager. Then I realized . . .

My three ex-fiancés pretty much *had* looked the same. Hmm.

There was no way I was admitting defeat. "What do you keep looking for in the bushes?" I asked instead, dabbing my brow.

Liam's face darkened. "Paparazzi. I hate those guys."

Aha. I scanned the perimeter. "Did you see someone?"

"Don't worry about it. We're almost done here."

"Does that mean I get to skip the sprinting drill?"

Liam laughed. "You'd be gutted if you missed that one, wouldn't you? It's your favorite."

I slumped, eyeing those blocks with well-deserved enmity.

But that only made Liam laugh harder. "Best shape of your life, remember?" A clap. "You don't want to miss that marathon!"

His jolly reminder of my initial excuse for seeing him hit home. He was right. I couldn't quit. Not because I truly wanted to sweat, ache, and stride for more than twenty miles, but because I still didn't know why Jeremy had been killed. I *had* to be getting close. I just needed to make a few more connections.

"Regular exercise is good for mental functioning,"

Liam urged, leaning over in his usual coach's stance with his hands on his musclebound thighs, ready to watch me. "Mood, too."

Mood? Hah. Grumpily, I considered flipping him "the vees" (a two-finger salute similar to the middle-finger gesture in the U.S.), just to prove my mood was going to be a challenging one.

But then I realized I wasn't mad at Liam. I was mad at myself. Mad for not having succeeded yet. Mad for dreading a dumb physical fitness drill. There were people across the park—in a group with a trainer similar to mine—doing it. Why not me?

I dug in. "Are you still talking? Put down those blocks."

Liam recognized my newfound grit and smiled. "That's the way! Don't let anything hold you back! Push through it!"

Or bludgeon it? I couldn't help thinking as I prepared to run. Because no matter how likable Liam was, there was still a big question mark hanging over my trainer's head. He could have killed Jeremy. He could have been cunning enough to hide it from everyone. He could be playing me right now. How would I know?

I wouldn't. But I still vowed to keep searching.

Beside me, Liam blew his whistle. "Go go go!"

Okay. Head down, I ran straight toward the blocks at top speed (for me, at least). If any of the tabloid press snapped photos today, they'd capture a very sticky and winded (but very accomplished) Hayden Mundy Moore in their telephoto lenses.

Our workout session had ended when I finally spotted them: members of the tabloid press, crowded at one side of the ornate wrought-iron and gilt-painted fence protecting the queen's park. Some had cameras. Others had phones. A few even had notebooks.

It should have been illegal to prey on Liam so mercilessly, especially when all he wanted to do was earn a living—something that (for him) necessarily happened outdoors. Our sessions weren't free; I wanted to help Liam, now that Jeremy was no longer in the picture. Britain's sexiest chef might as well have been there, though, for all the interest Liam and I merited.

After we said our good-byes, I scoured the press with a shaming glare, then slung on my bag and headed toward Green Park station. Fortunately for me, the park fence would keep the reporters at bay long enough for me to make my way safely underground. Not that *I* was of particular interest, but it was hard to guess what a bunch of opportunistic tabloid journalists might do. It wasn't as if they had to tell the truth.

Liam had headed in the opposite direction, toward Hyde Park Corner. At least we had divide-and-conquer on our side.

Feeling optimistic, I delved into the station. Even in the middle of the day, its central ticket hall swarmed with people, from clumps of bewildered tourists to Transport for London employees to fast-walking Londoners and buskers on their way into the tunnels to their official performing positions.

All the amenities in the station didn't ameliorate the crowding, either. There were ticket machines and wall maps, a dry cleaner and a kiosk selling candy and newspapers, a small branch of Marks & Spencer, plus multiple entrances and exits. I pushed through the crowd, headed for the row of ticket barriers.

That's when I saw them. The same tabloid press members.

They swarmed down the street-side entrances, opposite from the park-side entrance I'd used, moving in a chattering crowd. It was evident that something had happened to rouse them.

It couldn't be me. Could it? I seriously doubted it.

I touched my card and dashed through the ticket barrier in my workout clothes and sneakers, feeling like the fox in one of those old-timey foxhunts—albeit one that was ponytailed and vaguely achy. In front of me, various escalators led down to the different Tube lines. In my rush, I forgot which one I needed.

I was standing there trying to remember which way to go, being buffeted by the crowd while listening to those tabloid reporters shouting to each other behind me, when someone grabbed me. I felt myself being yanked sideways, away from the crowd.

Instinctively, I pushed away whoever had grabbed me. It was never good, I knew, to be separated from the safety of numbers.

"Whoa, Hayden! Calm down!" Ashley Fowler, the reporter from Jeremy's local pub, chuckled as she held out her palms in a peacekeeping gesture. "These Tube stations are crazy, am I right? I've almost gotten trampled bunches of times already."

I stared at her in confusion while people zoomed past us, headed for the trains. "Ashley? What are you doing here?"

Her eyes looked manic. Or, you know, just excited.

"There's been an arrest in the case!" she gushed. "I'm on my way down to the scene right now, with everyone else. I saw you over here, nearly getting crushed, and stopped to help."

I couldn't believe it. "An arrest? In Jeremy's murder?"

Her nod was emphatic. She looked *thrilled*. "I'm finally going to get out of this place! Can you believe it? I'm so *sick* of quiet people and museums and stake-outs and the *food*. Ohmigod! It's so awful, I can't even believe it." She moved closer to me, farther from the stream of commuters. "Did you know they have a thing called 'mushy peas' here? And they actually *eat* it? Ugh!"

I didn't care about food. Not with Jeremy's murderer on the hook. I grabbed Ashley, willing her to focus. "Who was it?"

She was busy waving to someone in the press corps. "Huh?"

"Who killed Jeremy?" I nearly shrieked over the mêlée.

"Oh, that. Yeah." Ashley gave a trilling laugh. "It was the personal assistant who did it. Jeremy's, I mean. She confessed."

Confessed? I was galvanized—and, for once, happy *not* to have been confused with one of Jeremy's many personal assistants. Maybe I hadn't even met this one. It was possible.

"Who?" I pressed inane Ashley. "What was her name?"

"The book writer. You know." Ashley frowned. "Nicole?"

"Nicola Mitchell? Nicola *confessed?* But why would she?"

When she had every reason to stay mum and sell books?

I never had a chance to ask. "Sorry, gotta run!" Ashley warbled. "You'll read about it all in the papers tomorrow!"

She waved me off and bolted for one of the escalators, following the last of the pushy reporters to . . . the police station, I guessed? I didn't know. But I did know there was no way in the world I was continuing with my regularly scheduled day now.

I was following Ashley—and, as it turned out, Nicola.

Finally, Jeremy's murderer had been caught. Unbelievable. There were zero chances of me waiting to read about it tomorrow.

I'd underestimated the journalists, I learned as I made it down to the platform level. It was easy enough to follow them. Heck, if ditzy Ashley could do it, I absolutely could do it.

The trouble was, there's a certain art to catching a train on the London Underground. You're supposed to queue along the platform, which is generally long enough and wide enough to fit a train car's worth of people. Then, as the train arrives, you stand to one side of the open doors so passengers can disembark. Then—and only then—are you supposed to board the train yourself.

Evidently, London's tabloid journalists did not adhere to this etiquette. The platform was already busy; they only added to the mayhem. A few of the earliest arrivers had caught a previous train—probably by pushing willy-nilly onto it—but there were still plenty of volatile people jamming the platform, pacing its length in search of better positions. Some elbowed aside the people who'd been waiting, earning themselves disgruntled looks from the locals.

No one actually objected, of course. But there was much frowning, muttering, and tut-tutting in the reporters' wakes.

Oblivious to the safety protocol suggested by the yellow painted line at the platform's edge, they crowded right on top of it, even while the last train whooshed away into the tunnel. Another would be along in two minutes, so I did the same thing.

The tumult on the platform was deafening. To all sides of me, people yelled and jockeyed for position. Someone's elbow gouged me. I tottered, then reclaimed my position. I haven't made my way through transit systems all around the world—the U-Bahn, the Metros of Paris, Tokyo, and Shanghai, the Chicago "L," and more—by being passive. I knew better than to stand meekly.

I wanted to get to the police station and find out what had really happened with Nicola Mitchell. Like, yesterday.

I'd just staked out my own square foot of space when my phone buzzed. I fished it out of my crossbody bag while peering down the tunnel to look for the next train. I was getting on it.

In front of me, a huge advertising poster pushed "city breaks" to Brittany. Beside me, a hardened commuter stood, with his laptop bag secured on the floor between his feet, reading a copy of the *Financial Times*. Unlike the shifting, squirming mass of reporters to my left, he wasn't likely to budge. I edged closer to use him for a shield during the few moments I'd be distracted by looking at my phone, then peered at the screen.

There were three recent missed calls from Travis. They must not have rung through while I'd been underground. There was also a new text message from my financial adviser. I opened it.

Watch out for Andrew Davies, he'd typed. *H&H had insurance on Jeremy. Dead or disabled meant compensatory payout. Broken contract did not.*

That was interesting news. If I understood correctly,

Travis's findings meant that while Andrew Davies *had* needed Jeremy to "skyrocket" his family's company "back to success!" Andrew had also had an escape hatch: that insurance policy.

Even now, shambolic Andrew might be pocketing the disbursement that Hambleton & Hart were due because of their spokesperson's death. I didn't know if such corporate arrangements were typical, but it made sense. Hambleton & Hart would have wanted to protect their (expensive) investment in (unpredictable) Jeremy, by whatever means possible.

Leave it to Travis to dig up all the (legal and/or fiduciary) dirt. I'd need to call him to clarify this, but in the meantime, I smiled fondly as I looked at his text again.

Travis wrote text messages as though he were paying by the word. He might as well have used Morse code—his missives were sometimes that concise. On the other hand, he had spelled out *compensatory* correctly, just like the financial genius he was. That was impressive. In true Travis fashion, he hadn't buried the lede, either. He'd barreled right into his suspicions of Andrew Davies, then followed up with a reasonable rationale.

In his own way, Travis had my back too, every bit as much as Danny always did. Travis cared. That meant a lot to me.

On the other hand, we had a confessed killer now. Nicola. That meant that Andrew Davies's potential motive for potentially murdering Jeremy—their advert argument—didn't matter anymore.

A rumble drew my attention back to the tunnel. I glanced briefly down it, glimpsed the train's lights, then looked back at my phone. I needed to stash it before everyone pushed forward to board. If I lost it,

I'd lose touch with Travis. Even divided by several time zones and a raging air-travel phobia, we were—

Slipping. Flailing. *Pushed?* My heart shot to my throat as I tried to keep my balance. The train's approach grew louder.

Hot air buffeted me. The din of the crowd confused me.

One thing was sure: if I fell on the tracks, I was dead. That oncoming train's driver would never have time to stop.

I didn't want to die. But I was *falling*, shaky and queasy.

Suddenly, the strap to my crossbody bag yanked higher, to my throat. I was choking, held in a hideous suspended state at the platform's dangerous edge, eyes widening as I saw the train.

It looked huge. And fast. *Oh, God.* I thrashed my arms, trying to grab hold of something. *Anything.* I felt clothes, brushed someone's arm, heard startled cries as people around me finally realized what was happening. This was it. The end.

Someone wrapped an arm around my waist and pulled me to safety, just in time.

My rescuer gave a final mighty tug as the Underground train pulled in. My knees gave way as it whizzed past within inches of my face. The rest of me flew backward. I stumbled, then fell.

Instinctively, I covered my head with my arms so I wouldn't be trampled. My rescuer was already on the job. He hauled me up like a rag doll, then surfed the crowd to the refuge of the platform's tiled wall a few feet away. There, I gazed at the yellow-lettered WAY OUT sign without comprehension. For the moment, I was nothing but nerve endings, alive with panic.

The disembarking passengers pushed outward. The newly boarding passengers—including the journalists—surged forward.

I pushed away. "I've got to get on that train."

It felt critical that I do so. The strap of my cross-body bag inexplicably waylaid me. Impatiently, I yanked at it with my shaky fingers, trying to get free. Confounded by its twists and turns, I followed its length to the person who'd rescued me.

Danny. Of course.

"You're going to have to catch the next one," he said, finally relinquishing my bag's strap. His palm was scraped raw.

The look in his eyes was inexplicable to me. So were the standard directional signs, the bright adverts, the people . . .

I was a mess. "You finally saved me," I wheezed. "On time!"

If I haven't told you, Danny is a chronic latecomer. He's prone to arriving an hour late for . . . everything. Also, I realized numbly, *now* I understood his expression. He looked . . . wounded.

"Yeah," he said drily. "It took me a couple of seconds to realize what was happening and react. Sorry about the delay."

I'd meant that he hadn't been there for some dangerous incidents in the past, not *this* one. I was already sorry I'd blurted out that observation, too. But Danny didn't address my growing remorse, even though I knew he must have sensed it.

With his eyes smoky, he adjusted my bag's strap so it lay where it was meant to, snugly across my chest and shoulder.

Hazily, I caught on. "You rescued me . . . *with my bag?*"

He nodded. "It was all I could reach. At first."

Dazedly, I stared down at it. "Good job, bag." Shakily, I patted it, thankful for its near-constant presence in my life. "This is the same bag Travis surprised me with as a gift in Portland," I reminded Danny, dizzy with relief. "I'll have to tell him he rescued me from being smashed by a Tube train."

Danny's lips tightened. "Yeah. You tell Harvard that."

He gave me another evaluative look, then turned away.

I had to follow him. *Thank him.*

"Wait!" I yelled. "What are you—"*Doing here?* "Whoa."

Unable to finish, I stopped with my hand to my head. I felt awash with vertigo. My knees threatened to buckle again. I sagged against the nearest wall as exasperated commuters coursed past, caring only that I was between them and the next train.

I'd almost been killed. The stark reality of it scared me.

What was I doing, messing around with murder? This wasn't what normal people did. I needed to stick to chocolate. Period.

Danny's big-booted feet entered my downcast field of vision. He put his hand on my arm. "Let's get you out of here."

"I can't. I'm supposed to be—" I broke off, uncertain what to say next. *Headed to the police station?* There had to be many of them in London. I wasn't sure which one the reporters had gone to. I looked at Danny. "Nicola confessed."

He arched his brows. "The one with the skeevy book?"

I nodded, still feeling nauseated. I didn't want to be

sick in an Underground station, but any movement seemed to make things worse. My knees still felt unsteady, my hands shaky.

Helpless for the moment, I looked up at Danny.

Something passed between us. Something tender. I knew, when the chips were down, that Danny cared about me. But *this* was—

"Ahem." The sound of a man deliberately and loudly clearing his throat broke into my thoughts. "Terribly sorry, but is this yours? I saw you go down back there and managed to grab it."

My phone. I took it from the stranger's hand and clasped it in my own, stupidly grateful to have it. "Thank you so much."

At the familiar feel of my phone in my hand, I felt my throat close. My eyes filled with uncontrollable tears. Uh-oh.

Saved from death? *Fine.* Reunited with phone? *Waterworks.*

This had obviously affected me more than I wanted to admit.

The good Samaritan glanced anxiously from me to Danny and back again. He leaned in. "Are you quite all right? Do you need anything? Anything at all? Can I call a member of staff?"

"No, no thank you." I dashed my tears, feeling dopey and embarrassed. "I'm fine, honestly. Just a little overwhelmed."

He hesitated. "Are you utterly sure? It's no trouble."

Danny put his arm around me. "She said she's fine."

My phone's rescuer nodded. "All right then. Be careful!"

He strode away, wearing a trench coat and carrying a brown laptop bag. Almost instantly, he was swallowed up by the crowd.

The way he disappeared made me bawl a little harder.

Danny saw. He hugged me closer against his broad, strong chest, then gave me an unmistakable "cheer up" squeeze. "It's all fun and games until someone almost gets killed, right?"

This time, I laughed through my tears. I had to get a grip.

"What are you even doing here?" I asked my security expert.

"I said I'd be there when you were working out with Liam."

"Yeah, but I didn't see you."

Danny gave me a long look. "You weren't supposed to."

His sardonic tone smoothed away some of my weepiness. His earlier hurt feelings seemed to have mended somewhat, but that didn't let me off the hook for what I'd said. Feeling sorry about that all over again, I looked up. "I'm sorry, Danny. About what I said before, about you 'finally' saving me. I didn't—"

"Don't worry about it." He let me go. "It's all good."

"But it's not all good! I hurt your feelings."

"I deserved it." Danny obviously didn't intend to admit having anything as mushy as feelings. "I'd followed you to the platform, but then I got separated from you in the crowd. I'd just managed to reach you when I saw you start falling."

I shuddered at the memory. "One second I was fine, just looking at the train coming down the tunnel, and the next—"

"I grabbed your bag, but it almost wasn't enough."

That effort had cost him, too. "How's your hand?"

Danny hid its abraded surface inside his fist. "Fine."

I didn't believe him. I unfolded his fist and looked. "You're bleeding! We should get this looked at right away."

He pulled away. "I've had worse." His concerned gaze roamed over me, just as intensely as it had before. "How are you?"

"Anxious to get to the police station." Tentatively, I pushed away from the wall, then stood on my own. I still felt wobbly, but I could walk. I couldn't help grinning at my own tottering steps. "You wouldn't believe how a near-death experience messes with your ability to do the little things, like walk and think," I cracked, fighting an urge to grab Danny for support.

He stuck close to me anyway, just in case. "You know," he mused, "I think my hand does need medical attention."

His disingenuous tone hit me like a record scratch. That wasn't the way my old pal usually talked to me. Then I got it.

"I'm going to see Nicola," I warned, realizing he didn't really want medical care. He wanted to save me. All over again. From . . . *everything.* "I have to. After all the effort I've expended trying to track down Jeremy's killer? After all we've both done?" I went for drama. "After I nearly got killed?"

"That's all the more reason you shouldn't go."

I frowned. "Someone just bumped me, that's all." I hoped.

"Someone could have pushed you," Danny maintained darkly. "The platform was crowded. No one would have seen. They would have melted into the crowd right afterward. They could have slipped into another tunnel or even gotten on the next train."

I envisioned someone pushing me to my (almost

certain) death, then blithely boarding a Tube train to Westminster.

It was too absurd. "Nobody wants to *kill* me."

Danny's face disagreed. "It wouldn't be the first time."

He was referring to the other times I'd been hurt on my unofficial, nonchocolate-whispering murder investigations. In hindsight, they seemed ludicrous. At the time? Critically important and perfectly reasonable, under the circumstances.

"All right. Let's say someone *did* push me on purpose."

Danny crossed his arms over his brawny chest. "And?"

I tried not to look at his bulging biceps. This was no time to be distracted, no matter how many caring looks he'd given me today. Things that happened during emergencies didn't count.

"And I'm fine! See?" I performed an unsteady twirl on the nearly unoccupied platform. Between Tube trains, it emptied almost completely. "No lasting harm done." I knew that wouldn't be enough for Danny, so I added, "Did you *see* anyone push me? No. I was standing too close to the edge, that's all, trying to be first to board the next train. Next time, I'll be more careful."

There. All sorted. I felt marginally better already.

"Who are you trying to convince? Me? Or you?"

He was too astute for his own good. "Nicola confessed, Danny! I want to know what she said. Don't you? We're wasting time. If she's at the same police station as DC Mishra—"

"Hayden, it's over," Danny said in a low voice. "This

time, you didn't get the bad guy. You weren't really supposed to."

I gawked as he started walking toward the escalators, leaving me no choice but to follow. I strode after him, feeling uncertain. Was this really about me not wanting to admit defeat?

"Hey! What do you mean, I wasn't 'supposed to'?"

All right. Maybe it *was* about that. A little bit.

Danny stepped onto the escalator with me right behind him. "You're a chocolate expert. You're a *great* chocolate expert."

"But I'm not a detective. Is that it?"

He was silent as we ascended. Then, "Those other times were flukes." His voice was gentle but firm. "Travis thinks so too."

"You agree with Travis about this?" That was . . . disturbing. The two men in my life almost never agreed about anything. "You talked with Travis about this? When? What else don't I know?"

I didn't like thinking that they collaborated about me. If two people as different as Danny and Travis were in cahoots . . .

"We talk when necessary." Danny turned to make sure I made it safely off at the top of the escalator. "We talk about you."

"Oh yeah?" I turned the opposite direction. "Well, talk about me heading to the police station alone, then. I'm going."

Danny sighed, then trotted after me. "Hold up. You're emotional right now. You're not thinking straight. Just let me—"

I shoved away his comforting hand. The din of the station continued around us, now that we'd reached the ticket hall.

A woman with a little girl cast us a curious look.

"Let you do what, Danny? Huh?" I waved my arm with dismay. "Tell me that I shouldn't be doing this because I'm not an expert at it? That I just almost got killed for nothing?"

His eyes wised up. "You do think you were pushed."

"Of course I think I was pushed!" I hadn't wanted to admit it before, but now I was angry. Angry at whoever had gone after me. Angry at myself for being vulnerable. Angry at Danny for pointing out the truth. Despite my efforts, I was out of my depth when it came to this. "That *can't* have been a coincidence. Someone doesn't want me looking into Jeremy's murder."

"But you're not going to quit," Danny surmised.

This time, it was my turn to toss *him* a long, knowing look. I have to say, it felt strangely satisfying. No wonder he pulled that maneuver with me so often.

"I'm going to be more careful," I acknowledged. As I'd told Phoebe, I wasn't an idiot. "But no, I'm not going to quit."

"What if Nicola really did do it?" he asked, reasonably enough. "There probably aren't two murderers to track down."

I squared my shoulders. "Then I guess I'll be done with the investigation. This time." I still hoped there wouldn't be a next time. "Let's find out what Nicola had to say to the police. Both of us. Deal?"

"Deal," Danny said. Then we went to find out if my sleuthing was over . . . or had just gotten a lot more complicated.

Fifteen

Complicated won.

Danny and I made it to the police station just in time to catch a commotion in front of the building. Almost immediately, it became obvious that Nicola's supposed "confession" wasn't what it had appeared to be—most obviously because she was free.

Wearing an unassuming yellow dress that beautifully accented her porcelain skin, blue eyes, and long auburn braid, Jeremy's former assistant stood amid a mob of media types. Some took photographs; others filmed or recorded Nicola as she spoke.

She definitely had not been arrested for murder.

"You can be sure this travesty of justice will appear in my book," she was saying, scanning the crowd with tear-filled eyes. "This is only the latest of several indignities I've had to suffer because of Jeremy Wright. The world should know the truth!"

Amid the babble of shouted questions that came next from the assembled journalists, I looked askance at Danny. His mistrust of the situation was plain on his beard-shadowed face.

We edged closer, me still in my workout clothes and

Danny in his jeans, white shirt, and overall pugnacious attitude.

"Nicola! Nicola! The *Independent* here," someone yelled.

Graciously, she acknowledged that reporter with raised brows. I was amazed how poised Nicola had become since our last meeting. Then she'd blurted out statements erratically, with none of the self-control she exhibited now, in a more demanding situation. Had Nicola been using me for media practice, as she'd semi-jokingly claimed? Or had she been fooling me all along?

It was hard to know who the real Nicola Mitchell was. Mousy or outspoken? Awkward or composed? Ill-treated or murderous?

"We know now that Jeremy mistreated you terribly," the reporter said. "Do you believe that justice has prevailed?"

The reporter meant, I deduced, that Jeremy's murder could have been a sort of justice for her, his "tormented" assistant.

To her credit, Nicola recognized a trap when she saw one. "I believe justice *will* prevail, once DC Mishra and the London Metropolitan Police Service have finished their work."

Tardily, I glimpsed Satya Mishra standing to Nicola's left. On her right, Claire Evans typed on her cell phone. As though sensing my attention, Nicola's agent glanced up. She saw me.

She nodded, then somberly resumed listening to her client.

After a few more questions, Nicola seemed to sway. Claire handed her a tissue for her teary eyes. Nicola dabbed at them.

She did so, I saw, much more prettily than I had earlier, when I'd almost been flattened by an Underground train.

"I'm afraid that's . . . all I can answer for right now. I'm sorry," Nicola said in a broken voice. "Thank you all so much for listening to me. For being there for me. For helping me set the record straight about Jeremy. His death was tragic, but his life was . . . monstrous." She shuddered theatrically. "Soon, you'll all understand that, just as intimately as you possibly can."

As a teaser of her forthcoming book, that statement naturally incited a new frenzy of questions. But doe-eyed Nicola could only turn fraily to Claire. Her agent expertly put Nicola in the hands of the detective constable. DC Mishra ushered Nicola back into the station. Claire cleared away all the media, good-naturedly sharing good-byes with reporters as she did.

I gaped at the measure of influence she had on them. It was obvious that Claire had experience handling the press. I wondered how many times she'd used those skills on Jeremy's behalf—and how many times, perhaps purposely, she hadn't.

Surely, if Claire was on such good terms with the media, she could have prevented some of those damaging stories from surfacing—about Jeremy's weight, his bald spot, his wrinkles.

Unware of my speculation, Jeremy's former agent lit a cigarette. She took a long, obviously satisfying drag, then exhaled a plume of smoke into the cloudy (again) afternoon.

The exodus of the press left Danny and me exposed. Claire noticed and strode over in her immaculate gray business suit.

I was about to greet her when she embraced Danny.

Cooing with pleasure, she gave him double air-kisses on each cheek.

"Danny! Fancy seeing you here. Ready to go again tomorrow?"

I gawked. I'd been unaware they'd known one another. It hadn't been me Claire had nodded at earlier. It had been Danny.

"Believe me," he said, "I'll go as long as you need me to."

At his unmistakably promising tone, my stupefaction doubled. A glance at Danny clarified nothing—and I didn't have time to be subtle—so I stuck out my hand to Jeremy's agent.

"Hi, Claire." I nodded at my musclebound security expert. "That sounded mysterious. What's going on between you two?"

They both clammed up. I swear it.

Were Danny and Claire . . . an item? I knew he was open-minded and she was interested in sex, but I just didn't believe either of them would take things that far.

"You'll find out!" Claire trilled teasingly. "Eventually."

Danny shifted, looking as uncomfortable as I'd seen him.

I watched them both. "I think I'm finding out now."

It was hard not to stare openmouthed. Claire had to be twenty-five years Danny's senior, if not thirty. What could they possibly have in common, except (as Nicola would have said) S.E.X.? How had that happened? And why was Danny always getting lucky while I was globe-trotting from place to place, fixing up chocolate indulgences and trying my hardest to solve murders?

Claire smiled at me. "You're so funny, Hayden. I'm looking forward to representing your exposé." She dragged on her cigarette. "With your voice, it's bound to be a terrific hit."

Oh yeah. My supposed potboiler about the chocolate biz. I'd forgotten all about it. "I'm still looking into my options."

"Of course you are. Of course. Don't delay too long, though!" Claire leaned forward in confidence, then waved her cigarette toward the front of the police station where Nicola had held the media captivated. "You see what I can do, obviously."

"Nicola's arrest?" I played dumb, but I had my suspicions about what had taken place today. "Or her press conference?"

The agent puffed on her cigarette. "Someone tipped the police that Nicola had killed Jeremy. Can you imagine that?"

I nodded. "It's fortunate she was ready to come down to the station and clear up the misunderstanding—fortunate that the media responded so quickly. That was quite a speech she gave."

Claire looked pleased. "Yes, Nicola did a fine job, didn't she? The story will be in all the papers tomorrow, and on all the morning television news shows, too. Almost everyone needs media coaching, but Nicola is an exception. She came to me with a very clear vision of what she could do. I do wish her book about poor Jeremy wasn't necessary, you know, but since it is . . ."

Adroitly, Jeremy's former agent let that statement trail away. I'd misjudged Claire, I realized, and her willingness to profit from Jeremy's death. She was smart. And ruthless.

"Anyway, must dash." Claire dropped her smoldering cigarette, then crushed it beneath the sole of one of her slingbacks. "Kisses, Danny!" she cooed. "Bye, Hayden!"

After her lovey-dovey farewell, I turned to my body-guard and crossed my arms. "I can't wait to hear you explain this."

His outrageously oblivious expression didn't fool me.

"I'm keeping an eye on things," he said. "Like you wanted."

Mmm-hmm. "Is that what the kids are calling it these days?"

He caught on. "You must have bumped your head when you fell on the platform," Danny deadpanned. "You're imagining things."

I didn't think so. "Do you have to have every woman who throws herself at you?" That was the way I envisioned the scenario, at least. "You could be a little more discriminating."

He laughed. "You could be a little less uptight."

"What, me?" I nearly howled with disbelief. "Nope. Nice try. This is about you." I studied him. "Maybe I'll ask Travis."

Danny looked amused. "What makes you think he'd know anything about me?" *Short of my tax return,* his grin added.

I dug out my phone. "You two are pals now, re-member?"

I was on the verge of dialing when I spied my broken screen. Also, Danny chose that moment to cover my hand with his.

"I'm not indiscriminate. I'm not sleeping with Mrs. Robinson, either." Except he used a much blunter term than that. "All this stuff going on, and you're worried about my sex life?"

"It doesn't matter to me who you sleep with." I yanked away my hand and squinted at my damaged phone. "You're your own man. I pay you to protect me, not to—" *Sleep with me?* Argh, where was I going with this? I jerked up my head. "Just watch yourself."

"You watch yourself."

"Be sure to use protection. Don't break any hearts." He gave a dazzling smile. "I wouldn't know how."

That's what he thought. That was the thing about Danny, though. That was what saved him from being insufferable. He truly didn't understand how appealing he could be. How desirable. There were compelling reasons women wanted him.

"How to use protection, I mean. What's that mean?" His eyes sparkled as he joked with me. "I break hearts constantly."

I couldn't help laughing. "I need to talk to DC Mishra."

"But I'm really interested in discussing my love life now," Danny said with elaborate artlessness. "How will I know when a woman is 'the one'? How many 'ones' can one man have? Help a guy out, Hayden. You seem to have opinions you want to share."

I raised my palm in surrender. "Forget I mentioned it."

His laughter rang out, startling two police officers who'd just left the station. "Yeah," Danny said, "I thought so."

I harrumphed and turned away. "I'm going in. You coming?"

My sometime bodyguard gave the police station a guarded look. Given his past, Danny and the authorities don't get along.

"Yeah, okay." He set his chin stubbornly. For me. "Okay."

I commiserated. "You said 'okay' twice."

"That's how much I mean it."

"It's all right." I touched the back of his injured

hand. "Why don't you go have your palm looked at while I'm in there?"

"Why don't I go to the corner pub and have a pint?"

"Because that won't fix up your injury. You know, the one you got because you were saving my life?" Suddenly feeling overcome with gratitude, I flung my arms around him. I sniffled so I wouldn't cry again. "Thanks, Danny. I owe you one."

His arms encircled me. "You owe me dozens. You just don't know it," he assured me as he stepped away. His head was down, so I couldn't see his face. "You never see me, remember?"

He might have a point. For all I knew, Danny had been trailing behind me for years, taking out bad guys and making sure I didn't wander off cliffs. For all I knew, he might be habitually late because he was always busy looking out for *me.*

I knew he was loyal. And skilled. I also knew he never wanted to talk about the things he did for me. That was his way.

"Go have a pint and celebrate, then." I aimed my chin at the nearest pub, a lively place on the corner. "I'll be there soon." I gave him a serious look. "Then we'll fix your hand."

My longtime friend gave me a mocking salute. "Yes, ma'am."

Two minutes later, I was inside the station. I headed straight for the reception desk—then stopped short in surprise.

I recognized the officer on duty. "George! How are you?"

I thought you'd been suspended pending a misconduct investigation whirled through my mind. I opted not to say it.

"Well, if it isn't Ms. Hayden Mundy Moore." George gave me a jovial look. He seemed none the worse for wear after his suspension. "Have you come to see DC Mishra? I'll fetch her for you."

"No! No, thanks." I smoothed over my protest with a smile. "Actually, I'm here to report an assault." I couldn't get over his presence there. I guessed he'd been absolved of suspicion.

I wished I could say the same thing about my own suspects in Jeremy's murder. Even if Nicola really had confessed to killing her boss today, plenty of people still looked guilty.

"An assault? Oh no. That's a shame, isn't it?" With a cheerfulness that belied his words, George took out some forms. "Now, who was attacked?" he asked concernedly. "And where?"

I assumed he thought I'd witnessed a crime. But that wasn't the case at all. "I was," I told him. "On the Underground."

"You don't say?" George quit writing. "Well, that's another story altogether, isn't it? You're a principal suspect!"

Before I could object, he went to collect DC Mishra. I hoped I hadn't inadvertently made myself appear even guiltier somehow. I really liked that four-poster bed at the guesthouse. I didn't want to spend the night in a London jail instead.

". . . but this is the real deal, innit?" The gray-haired publican at The Fat Squirrel flipped his pub towel over his shoulder. He nodded at me and Danny. "Not like them corporate pubs you see sproutin' up all over the place nowadays." He frowned. "No, this place has been here since Tudor times."

It looked it too—all dark polished oak, creaky floors, and well-used taps on the kegs of lager, ale, and hearty stout.

I nodded, happy to listen to him boast. I'd had an arduous meeting with Satya Mishra, during which she'd done everything from accuse me of wasting police resources to faking a crime to wanting "as much attention as poor Nicola Mitchell got today."

Suffice it to say, the detective constable hadn't been a sympathetic listener—probably because she'd just been duped by whoever had phoned in that bogus "tip" involving Nicola.

I would have been short-tempered too.

But now it was happy hour, and all the pubs were filling up. Danny and I were two of the few customers who'd opted to sit inside with our lagers, rather than stand outside and revel in the good weather. Since I hadn't been able to persuade Danny to do more than wash his abraded hand . . . well, why not linger and enjoy a pint? I was interested in what the pub owner had to say.

There was nothing like a publican's pleasantries to help pass the time. No one else did small talk quite the same way.

"We've even got ourselves a smugglers' tunnel, down in the basement," the barman confided next with a mischievous twinkle in his eyes, handily proving my theory just as I thought of it.

I gave him what he wanted. "I don't believe a word of it!"

"It's true! All owing to us being close up to the Thames. See, back in the day, almost everything came in by ship. But it was expensive to bring in cargo, on account of taxes and all that."

"Not much has changed there." Danny played along, too.

"Right. So smugglers would wait till the middle of the night, then slide right into their secret quays, down from the patrolled harbor, to unload their cargo without nobody seein'."

"Then they'd come in here for a drink?" I supposed.

"Bang on!" The publican looked pleased. I had the sense he told this story to all the tourists. "They'd sneak their goods right through the tunnel, up to here, then meet their buyers."

Danny took another drink of lager. Then, "I heard those were Roundhead escape tunnels, used during the Civil War, so the Parliamentarians could get away from Charles I's Royalists."

I stared at him. He gave me one of those looks.

Just because I have muscles, his expression said, *I'm some kind of meathead?* I remembered him saying that when we'd run into Amelja at the Wrights' town house. I should have known by now not to pigeonhole my longtime buddy. Danny was multifaceted.

"Sure, sure!" the publican hastened to add. "Them, too."

Most of my half pint was gone. I could have polished off a full, I realized, but I didn't want to get pissed. (That's not what you're thinking—it's Brit for "drunk.") Either way, I was already feeling better about the harrowing events of the day.

"Why were they called Roundheads?" I asked Danny, peering at his skull. "Everybody's got a round head, don't they?"

"Unlike the froufrou 'divine right of kings' crowd, with their long, flowing ringlets, the Roundheads had short hair. Practical hair." Danny didn't notice me glancing meaningfully at his own militarily cropped dark haircut. "The Cavaliers had influence, so their slur stuck. That, or the Parliamentarians owned it." He swigged more beer, then grinned at me. "Probably that."

"You've got a unique take on history," I told him. "Leave it to you to side with the underdogs in a three-hundred-year-old war."

"Well, they won, now didn't they?" the publican argued, pulling me another lager. He set it down. "That's not so bad."

I couldn't argue. My grip on British history was too tenuous for that. I'm a chocolate whisperer, not a professor. I'm a world traveler, not a historian. So I raised my glass. "To The Fat Squirrel's secret tunnel, for helping the rebels win!"

We toasted, then happily drank.

"That's boring stuff, though," the barman said affably. "The smuggler story is a bit more popular with most tourists."

"We're not 'most tourists,'" Danny pointed out.

"How about showing it to us?" I asked. "Can we see it?"

"My tunnel?" The publican started. "Oh, erm . . . well, right at the moment, it's all blocked up with some kegs of Guinness."

"Mmm-hmm." I shot him a dubious look. He laughed.

"Don't go spoilin' my fun, now. Or runnin' off to Twitter to tell the whole world The Fat Squirrel's a big, fat sham."

"I won't. I promise." I crossed my heart. His banter was just what I'd needed today. "Your secret's safe with me."

The publican shot Danny a wary glance. "What about him?"

I guessed Danny looked less upright than I did.

"He can keep a secret, too," I assured the barman. Reminded of my sometime security expert's most recent secret, I nudged Danny. "Especially when it's got to do with the ladies."

The barman perked up. "You're on the pull, are ya?"

That slang for "picking up interested ladies" was lost on Danny, but not on me. "He doesn't need to be. Ladies pull him."

"Yep. That was me in my younger days." With a smile, the publican gazed at the busy pub. "Now too, if I get a chance."

He spotted a woman nearing the bar and made his excuses.

Duty called. For the proprietor of The Fat Squirrel and us too. I looked at Danny. "Are you going to tell Travis, or am I?"

He understood me immediately. He shook his head. "Not me."

I didn't want to do it, either. The news of my trainward push would only upset my financial adviser. The minute Travis heard I'd run into more trouble, he'd scour his sources for two tickets stateside. He'd already been upset that I'd encountered another murder in London. If I told him *I'd* been a target?

I shivered, not wanting to think about it.

"It has to be you," Danny advised. "If it's me, I'll never hear the end of it. I was supposed to protect you, remember?"

"You *did* protect me. If not for you—" I shivered again. Then I gave my friend an earnest look. "You saved my life."

He cracked a wry grin. "That's not the way Harvard will see it. By this time tomorrow, he'll have spreadsheets and graphs proving what a useless waste of financial resources I am."

Danny wasn't wild about being on my payroll. I'd wanted him on retainer after San Francisco, partly to keep him away from his bad-influence buddies and partly to keep me safe. Travis had disagreed, partly out of contrariness (I was sure) and partly out of frugality. Despite spoiling me sometimes, Travis takes seriously his duty to watch out for my financial well-being.

We'd disagreed. We'd argued. I'd won. End of story.

"Travis cares about me, that's all," I reminded Danny.

And *that's* why I knew I had to tell him. Now, not later.

With a resigned sigh, I rummaged for my wallet. I took out twenty quid (twenty pounds, technically) and left it on the bar.

"Wish me luck." I wielded my cracked phone. "Time to find out if this thing still works. I'll be back in a few minutes."

"Stay within sight of the window." Danny nodded at it. Then he thought better of his advice. "On second thought, I'm coming with you." He thumbed through his own wallet and withdrew a few pound notes— enough to cover both our drinks. Then he tucked my money into the side pocket of my bag. "You might need that."

He was so predictable. It didn't matter what I could afford. Danny wanted to treat us both. I tried not to grin.

"Yeah, to buy *you* drinks tomorrow." I nodded good-bye to the friendly publican. "One of these days, you'll forget to insist on treating me. Then you'll sleep in that four-poster."

"Not alone, I won't. That's a girly bed. Times a hundred."

"Then you'd sleep in it with company?" I wasn't sure if I could stomach inviting venal Claire for a sleepover with my bodyguard, even if that's what he was hinting at. "Is that it?"

We made it to the door. Danny stopped to let me go first, the way he usually did, but I must have been tipsy. We wound up chest-to-chest in the tight entryway, staring at each other.

His suggestive look wasn't lost on me.

"'With company'?" he repeated roughly. "Is that an offer?"

For one recklessly overheated moment, I considered it. I honestly did. My shared past with Danny tugged at me, tossing up memories of wanting, waiting, giving in . . . wising up.

If there'd ever been a time I might have weakened, that was it. Hard on the heels of almost dying, I felt all too aware of how fragile life could be—how important it was to seize it.

But I'd made it through other dangerous situations without losing my mind over Danny. I could do the same thing tonight.

"When it is," I told him, "I won't be half that coy."

Then I gave him a pat on the chest and headed off to a more private spot next to one of those iconic Royal Mail postboxes to make my call. I pulled out my phone. I took a deep breath.

I considered the intense "pillar box red" color of that antique mailbox. I thought about the royal insignia stamped on it, dating from the 1870s, according to the inscribed year. I recognized I was stalling about calling Travis with my news.

I realized, too late, that I'd said *when it is* to Danny just now. Not *if it is* an invitation to share my bed or *it will never be* an invitation to share my bed. But when. *When it is.*

Shoving aside that troubling realization, I dialed. My phone *did* work. Hurray! I listened to its ringing while Danny paced around at exactly the distance *not* to overhear my conversation.

It connected. "Hey, Travis," I said breezily. "Guess what?"

As breaking-bad-news tactics went, it might work. Maybe if I sounded super-duper *alive,* Travis wouldn't react too badly.

Maybe.

But I wasn't counting on it.

I should have known my supersmart keeper was already on the job. "Hayden," he said in that extra-sexy, extra-perceptive voice of his, "next time you feel a need to file a police report, let me know. As a legal expert, I might have pertinent advice."

His hard retort didn't fool me. I considered, *You're a lawyer, too?* But I settled for, "I love you, too, Travis."

Silence. Then, "You're all right? You're not hurt?"

That was more like it. Inexplicably, at the sound of Travis's gruff questions, tears sprang to my eyes. Feeling foolish, I swiped them away. I managed a smile. It felt good.

"Getting better all the time," I promised.

I really meant it too. Thanks to him.

Sixteen

For the next few days, I was swamped with work. Things were picking up at Primrose—the chocolaterie-pâtisserie was featured in a travel magazine, which gave its business a major boost—and all the bakers and chocolatiers were doing well. The brigade of prams and stockbrokers from The City picked up, as well, which I found encouraging. It wasn't enough that one-off travelers visited Primrose. For the place to really thrive, Londoners had to embrace it themselves. Quite suddenly, it seemed they were.

Phoebe was pleased with the shop's progress. So was I, as a matter of fact. In only a few weeks, I'd taken a crew of novices from East London and turned them into a competent, close-knit workforce. It wasn't what I usually do when taking on a chocolate-whispering consultation—ordinarily, I'm more about refining existing techniques and adding creativity, not training beginning workers from scratch—but it felt like a major accomplishment, all the same. Whatever got the job done, right?

Unfortunately, Hugh never returned. I tried to

salvage his job by taking up his case with Phoebe, but she wasn't having it.

"We can't afford any disruptions among our staff, now can we, Hayden?" she'd said finitely. "Especially not with my television appearance coming up in a matter of days. Focus!"

Her rallying cry of "Focus!"—delivered with a goofily inelegant arm thrust—had been strangely reminiscent of Andrew Davies, I'd thought. But maybe that wasn't too surprising. As the head of Hambleton & Hart had told me himself, he and Phoebe did "run in the same circles." Maybe, in their posh, public-school crowd, that gesture was super cool. Who knew?

For the rest of our phone call, Travis had reacted reasonably well to the news of what had happened to me on the Tube platform. First he got mad. Then he lectured me. Then he told me how much he worried about me (aww). Then he described the odds of such an event being genuinely accidental (pretty good, actually) versus the probability of it happening to me again, depending on how often I used the London Underground.

He'd said some truly unprintable things about Danny, for having allowed me to slip away from him in the first place.

Then he'd said some incredibly nice things about Danny, for saving my life in the end. Then Travis had hung up. Abruptly.

I would never understand the relationship (if you could call it that) between the two men in my life. It was . . . inexplicable.

So was the express-delivered package I received the next day—until I opened it to find a pristine version of my old phone. Unpacking it like a kid at Christmas, I'd discovered . . .

"It already has all my stuff on it!" I'd shown the screen to Danny. "See? Isn't that thoughtful? Travis is a genius."

My security expert had been about to leave for another mysterious appointment. "Harvard knows how to spend money and use a cell phone OS. So what?" he'd grumbled before leaving.

I'd been reminded that I still didn't know exactly how Danny was "keeping an eye on things," as he'd promised. I'd also remembered—via that technical sounding "OS" comeback he'd tossed out—that there was more to my longtime friend than meets the eye. Danny might look like a thug, but he isn't. Not really.

My first call on that shiny new phone had been from Nicola.

"Hayden, how *are* you?" Jeremy's former assistant had oozed disingenuousness, just as she'd done at her staged "press conference" at the police station. "Are you well? Is everything going simply marvelously? Claire told me *you're* writing a book!"

Unhappily, I tried to change the subject.

But Nicola persisted. "You've got to be careful," she warned. "Claire is quite busy with *me* at the mo, and there are only so many hours in the day, aren't there?" A tinkling laugh.

I'd gripped the phone, frowning. Was that a threat? Was Nicola suggesting that she'd kill me to keep Claire for herself?

I might be jumping at shadows, but I still wasn't sure of Nicola's capacity for wrongdoing. She didn't seem physically capable of pushing me off a train platform. On the other hand, all she'd have needed was a momentary imbalance, and I wasn't exactly the

Incredible Hulk myself. I would have been easy to push. I was just lucky that whoever *had* pushed me had delivered a glancing, destabilizing bump, rather than a direct hard shove.

"Anyway," she chattered, "the reason I'm phoning is that I wanted to discuss my book launch party. You *are* willing to cater it with some delicious Primrose goodies, aren't you?"

"We'll see. Gotta run!" I blurted out. "Sorry! Bye!"

I hung up. And that—for the moment—was that.

Claire also phoned me. Multiple times. I ditched every last call. I didn't want to lie to Jeremy's former agent about my nonexistent chocolate industry tell-all book. But until I could connect Claire to Jeremy's murder (or not), I wasn't keen to come face-to-face with her mercenary nature, either.

Eventually, things came down to the wire. With my consultation at Primrose essentially completed— except for the obligatory report—and only one day remaining until Phoebe's TV appearance, I felt no closer to finding out who had bludgeoned Jeremy to death than I had before. My suspects were all arrayed. The trouble was, I still couldn't connect all the dots between any particular one of them and Jeremy. I had my theories, but—

"Hayden!" Commandingly, Phoebe snapped her fingers beneath my nose. "You're woolgathering again, aren't you? That simply won't do. If I'm to perform this recipe flawlessly on telly tomorrow, I'll need *you* to pay attention and do your job."

I shook myself into alertness. "I'm sorry, Phoebe." I scanned the fancy quartz countertops of her expansive kitchen, trying not to lock eyes with Amelja, who was dusting in the adjoining dining room, obviously eavesdropping. "Where were we?"

"I was making this Victoria sponge." Phoebe's voice was tart as she gestured to her cooling vanilla cake layers. Later, we would fill them with raspberry jam and—in place of the usual whipped double cream— white chocolate buttercream. *"You* were staring into space, just as you've done most of the morning."

Aha. She wasn't finished berating me, then. Okay.

"Again, I'm very sorry, Phoebe." I knew she was anxious about her upcoming TV appearance. Her curtness had only grown as each day had brought it closer. "You'll be fine on TV. Don't worry about a thing. Your buttercream looks wonderful!"

My consultee frowned into the stainless-steel bowl of her professional-caliber standing mixer. "White chocolate is awfully plebeian, isn't it? I'm not sure this is sophisticated enough. Perhaps I should go with the chocolate sticky-toffee pudding."

"That *was* tasty," I agreed. If you're not familiar, it's essentially what Americans would call a "pudding cake," served with toffee (caramel) sauce. It was an especially beloved, homey British dessert. For our version, we'd added melted chocolate to the cake batter, then added a garnish of chocolate curls. "You were very good at making the chocolate curls, too."

"Don't condescend to *me,*" Phoebe snapped. "A child could make chocolate curls! I *must* be impressive tomorrow. I'm not sure you comprehend what's at stake. Primrose is my life!"

I nodded, calling on the reserves of patience I've built over my years of chocolate whispering. Aside from expertise with all varieties of chocolates, my job also demands that I possess scrupulous attention to detail, a thick skin for criticism, and an excellent memory. Right now, my memory was reminding me that in just a few days, I'd be leaving London (and Phoebe) behind.

Until then, I'd simply have to make the best of things.

"Primrose is doing much better now," I reminded Phoebe.

She looked unsure. "That could go away at any moment. My shop did well straight out of the gate, with extensive press coverage and heaps of people queuing, and then everyone got bored. They moved on to the next thing, didn't they?" Phoebe's voice rose as she grew increasingly red in the face. "Well, this time, *I'll* be the next thing! I will not have it any other way!"

Buffeted by her shrieking, I stepped back. Amelja stared.

"You can't simply will yourself into success," I reminded Phoebe in a consoling tone, knowing that her heartbreak over Jeremy must be affecting her composure. "The vagaries of the business being what they are, none of us can do that. Being a restaurateur is challenging. But with a little extra practice—"

Phoebe scoffed. "Perhaps if you had done your job properly, things would not feel quite so dire just now, would they?"

That stung. Probably because I *had* neglected my work, just a skosh, while looking into Jeremy's death. I wasn't proud of that fact, but I'd thought I'd compensated for it pretty well.

Judging by Phoebe's reaction? Maybe not.

"It was *so* much effort for me to get here. What if I can't succeed? The only thing that saved me before was Jeremy!" Phoebe informed me in a shattered voice. "The love everyone felt for him transferred to me, too. It grounded me, *and* Primrose. All of us basked in his glow, didn't we? But now that he's gone—"

She broke off and started to weep. I felt sorry for her—and struck by the poetry of the way she'd described her husband.

Maybe I was being too hard on Phoebe. Maybe I was a snob . . . about snobs. I didn't like her much, and she probably knew it. Just when she was having the worst time of her life, too.

Contritely, I stepped forward to give her a hug.

I caught Amelja's suddenly alarmed expression and stopped.

Phoebe's housekeeper was right. What was I doing, offering an unsolicited hug to someone like Phoebe? I patted her arm.

"Everything will be fine," I said. "You'll be wonderful. By this time tomorrow, you'll be the talk of London. I promise!"

The TV segment was being taped remotely at Primrose, to give the chocolaterie-pâtisserie an added boost of publicity. Even though I wouldn't be on camera, I'd already helped the staff bake chocolate goodies for the TV show's cast and crew.

Phoebe sniffed. "Do you truly think so? Honestly?" She gave me an attentive look. "Don't muck about with me, Hayden. I simply do not have the time for any shenanigans right now."

"Of course." She (obviously) had enough on her mind already, so I decided to take charge. I wanted to end things with Phoebe on a positive note. "You'll make that chocolate Bakewell tart. You did a wonderful job with that, remember?"

Another sniffle. A nod. "Yes. Yes, I did, didn't I?"

"Yes." It *had* been delicious. Rather than using the typical shortcrust pastry for that multilayered tart, we'd made a crumb crust out of chocolate digestive biscuits. Then we'd prebaked it, spooned in layers of blackcurrant jam and traditional almond frangipane—the latter augmented with melted chocolate—and baked it some more. We'd split on adding a top layer of confectioner's sugar icing. I'd thought it was too sweet. "Everyone loved it."

We'd paraded her Bakewell tart to Primrose, at Phoebe's instigation, to show it off to the staff. They'd ooed and aahed.

You know . . . all except Hugh, of course. I wondered how he was.

"And you really, truly think I'll be good?" Phoebe pushed.

I was starting to feel frustrated. If the Honourable Phoebe Wright had self-confidence issues, it wasn't my job to solve them. "You'll be wonderful," I assured her. "So let's make the show version of the Bakewell tart"—the one to be revealed at the end of the segment—"and get that much squared away. The more prepared you are for tomorrow, the better you'll feel."

To my relief, Phoebe agreed. We rustled up all the supplies and ingredients to accommodate our change of plans, then got busy making the Bakewell tart. We crushed biscuits, spooned jam, made frangipane . . . before too much time had elapsed, we'd made a delightful dessert. The whole kitchen was redolent of sugar, butter, almonds, and chocolate. I could have dived right in.

I glanced up to see if Phoebe was as pleased as I was. I couldn't tell, because she was staring outside, looking annoyed.

My long day (so far) was stretching out even longer. I fought an urge to snap my fingers in her face. I'm not proud of it, but it's true. Even chocolate experts have limits.

"Who is *that*?" She narrowed her eyes. "And why are they going into my guesthouse?" Phoebe snatched off her recently delivered (couture) apron and hurled it onto the counter. "Honestly, Hayden, if you've invited more guests to stay—"

Rather than complete that ominous-sounding warning, Phoebe marched out onto the terrace and straight toward the guesthouse.

Amelja followed with her duster. So (sans duster) did I.

By the time I caught up to them, hurrying in the wake of Phoebe's indignation, there was nothing to do but goggle.

In all honesty, you would have done the same thing.

"That's beautiful!" Andrew Davies shouted, his voice carrying. "*Yes!* Keep going, just like that. Don't stop!"

The focus of his ecstasy became clear as I skidded to a halt just inside the guesthouse's doorway. Peering past Phoebe and Amelja—who stood there staring—I spotted several members of a film crew, one person who looked like an accountant (I've spent enough time envisioning Travis to know what they look like), and Claire Evans. Plus Gemma Rose, the U.K.'s favorite (former) culinary temptress. Alongside her, being filmed, was . . .

"*Danny*?" I gawked at my pal-slash-bodyguard. I glimpsed him smack in the middle of the set. "What are you doing here?"

It wasn't immediately obvious. Especially given the fact that he was shirtless—dressed in jeans, a pair of work boots, a yellow high-vis safety vest . . . and nothing else. From the kitchen counter, Danny gave me an unreadable look. He opened his mouth.

I expected to hear "I picked up some freelance security work with Gemma Rose." Or "I'm keeping an eye on things, like you said."

Instead, I heard, "He's working! I should think that would be obvious to all involved." Andrew Davies rolled his eyes at me after interrupting with that derisive put-down. Then he turned back to Danny and Gemma. "Keep going, you two! Just as you were before! Let's finish this so we can go on to the last setup."

I reeled at the scathing tone that Hambleton & Hart's CEO had used with me. In direct contrast to his unassuming manner at Jeremy's Jump Start Foundation, Andrew Davies was an entirely different man when he was in his element (in charge) at work.

No wonder he and Jeremy had argued about their commercial.

Despite Andrew's clear directions, though, Gemma hesitated. She was dressed in costume, too, but her outfit featured even less clothing than Danny's did. Still bodacious at forty-plus, Gemma wore a skimpy minidress, pearls, and high-heeled pumps.

From her feet to her wild bed-head hair, she looked . . . well, ready to do a lot more than cook, despite the big wooden spoon in her hand and the pot simmering on the stove behind her.

The whole tableau was discernable at a glance. Gemma was a (sexy) housewife, caught in the act of making dinner. Danny was a (sexy) builder—one who seemed to have come in to share "a cuppa" with Gemma and then gotten seductively carried away.

The teacup and saucer beside his low-riding jeans

gave that away. So did the fact that we three—Phoebe, Amelja, and I—had caught them in a clinch so hot it should have been smoking.

No wonder Andrew had been excited. I would have been, too.

I mean by capturing such a scene on film, of course. It was evident that's what they were up to: an advert, just like the one Jeremy had been filming when he died. The stove and countertop were littered with boxes of Hambleton & Hart snack foods, cake mixes, "vitality waters," and ready-to-eat treats.

There were workers, lights, and music, too—a soundtrack for the ad. No wonder no one had come to pick up the A/V equipment, I realized, as DC Mishra had assured me they would do. I'd noticed, but I hadn't wanted to inquire and risk annoying her.

"Gemma! Don't go ditzy on me now!" Andrew instructed. "Look at Danny. He's sexy, right? *Yes.* He's feeding you some *delicious* Dreamy Delight. You *love* its chocolaty flavor. Go on, then!"

Despite the whole absurd scenario, I couldn't help grinning at Andrew's use of the word "chocolaty." That's *not* the same as "chocolate." I doubted their desserts contained any of that.

Picking up where she'd left off before the distraction of our interruption had intervened, Gemma did as she was told. She shook out her long, blond hair, then resumed her cheesecake pose on the countertop. Danny stepped between her lithe, bare legs, then gave her a smile and fed her a spoonful of Dreamy Delight.

I'd have bet a thousand pounds it was ninety percent air, suspended in a mixture of cheap sweeteners, waxy vegetable fat, and artificial flavoring. But

Gemma's carnal moan of pleasure made a lie of everything I knew. I almost wanted a taste.

"Yes! *Yes!*" Andrew shouted, completely ignoring us now. He had the same air of privilege Phoebe did. "Danny, take off your hi-vis, mate. Go on." He gave a roar of delight. "Brilliant!"

To my amazement, Danny did as he was told to. He shucked his faux safety gear in a single, muscle-rippling gesture, then went back to his next task: body-painting Gemma with pink frosting swiped from a package of Hambleton & Hart's Strawberry-Crème Flavored Heavenly Slices. It looked like . . . fun.

Next to me, Amelja agreed. She gave me a wink, then went back to watching with her duster propped on her hip, forgotten.

I couldn't believe how at ease Danny seemed on camera. He was every bit a match for Gemma, who was plainly an experienced professional. She turned this way and that, always keeping her "good side" to the light as she writhed in pretend bliss.

Across the room, Claire supervised the proceedings with her phone in hand. She seemed delighted by this turn of events.

Why shouldn't she be? I wondered. Making this deal happen must have been why Claire had lured Gemma to afternoon tea via the Nearby app. Claire had probably already made contact with Andrew Davies and had wanted to keep Gemma sufficiently humbled so the necessary negotiations would be short but sweet.

Claire, it occurred to me, was being paid twice for the same job. Plus netting a big profit on Nicola's book deal. For her, Jeremy's death had definitely worked out advantageously.

"That's right!" Andrew encouraged. "That's the way! Yes!" He turned to the rest of the crew, making it plain that he was more than a guest on the set. He was in command. "Now, *you*. Go!"

He pointed to a woman holding a script near a mic.

"Have *everything* you desire," she breathed into the mic, clearly performing a professional voice-over. "Hambleton & Hart. Why not try the full range? It's *so* easy . . . and *so satisfying*."

Her final moan reverberated through the microphone. A beat later, the music resumed. *Wow*. If this had been an old movie, I couldn't help thinking, everyone watching would have lit up a postcoital cigarette. Her tone was *that* overtly suggestive. I could see why Jeremy's sexy image had fit the company's new advertising theme. And why Andrew Davies had loved Claire's lewd idea involving the metlapil and Jeremy's . . . manipulation of it.

"That's it!" Andrew yelled as someone else fussed with the sound system. "That's a wrap on this setup! We've got it!"

The crew erupted in applause. Weirdly, no one whooped.

I expected Phoebe to barrel forward with guns blazing. She'd been on the warpath all day, to the point where she'd out-grumped old Mr. Barclay next door. But amazingly, she didn't.

"Andrew!" she sailed toward him with her arms outstretched, a gracious smile on her face. "I'm terribly sorry I wasn't here to greet you earlier. Everything looks splendid, doesn't it?"

If Phoebe was bothered by being in the same place where her husband had recently been bludgeoned to death, it didn't show.

They traded air-kisses *and* an almost embrace. Cheeky.

"Thank you so much for allowing us to finish filming." Andrew beamed at her. Then he perked up as Gemma came forward. "Ah, Gemma. You know Phoebe, don't you? If not, please allow me to present the Honourable Phoebe Wright." Unbelievably, he bowed.

In unison, Amelja and I moved closer. All we needed was a bucket of popcorn to complete the fireworks show we expected.

Blue-collar Gemma versus blue-blooded Phoebe? Those two women could not have been more different. It was catfight time.

But we were disappointed. "I'm so sorry for your loss." Solemnly, Gemma grasped Phoebe's hands. "Poor, poor Phoebe."

Aha. I understood why Phoebe tolerated her so cordially. I was pretty sure I'd heard her scornfully refer to Gemma Rose as "that tart" not too many days earlier. But Phoebe was nothing if not willing to be fêted, adored, or properly sympathized with.

"Can it really have been so long?" Phoebe marveled in her turn. "Gemma, you look younger and better than ever, don't you?"

Her refined exclamation sounded . . . believable. Warm, even. I was surprised. Even more so when I heard next, "You'll have to tell me *all* your secrets, won't you? Please, please do!"

The two women giggled together, then veered off toward a corner of the busy guesthouse kitchen to trade compliments.

As they did, Danny approached, carrying a prop safety helmet. He'd pulled on a token Hambleton &

Hart "gimme" T-shirt over his bare chest, but all I could see were acres of abs.

He'd looked good with his shirt off is what I'm saying.

I smiled. "So, you've found a new career, huh?"

My bodyguard gave me a sheepish look. "It was Gemma's idea. She called me after we ran into each other at the hotel where you and Claire had tea and pitched it to me. I said I thought it sounded like fun, so she and Claire pitched it to Andrew. He agreed, everyone else came on board, and here we are."

"You look"—I squinted, deliberating trying not to openly ogle my bodyguard—"as though you're having a good time. I guess this is your idea of 'keeping an eye on things'?"

Danny nodded. "You're wrong to suspect Gemma."

"I suppose her bodaciousness has nothing to do with that opinion?"

He grinned. "It has *everything* to do with it. Are you kidding me?" He watched her with Phoebe. "I've had a major crush on Gemma Rose for . . . hell, I don't know how long. She's sweet."

"Sure, she is. She's covered in pink strawberry icing."

"She's fallen on some hard times," Danny reminded me. "I wanted to help. Now, partly thanks to me, Hambleton & Hart is going to sponsor her new cooking show and her next cookbook."

"Along with doing the ads? Wow, that must be lucrative."

My buddy nodded, then gave Gemma a fond look. "They're a weird pair, Gemma and Phoebe." He shrugged. "They go way back, but you probably already know that. Travis must have told you."

He hadn't. I tilted my head quizzically. "Told me what?"

"That Gemma was a principal investor in Primrose.

Back then, she had money to burn." Danny gave me a cocky look. "Who else would invest in *chocolate?* Ugh." He gave a teasing grimace.

But this was no time for Danny's incomprehensible dislike of sweets. "Why didn't you tell me about this?" I asked him. "A connection between Gemma and Phoebe could be significant."

"For your 'investigation'?" Danny said that with a lowered voice—and skeptically raised brows. "Come on. We've been over this. The chances of you finding out who iced Jeremy are—"

"Getting worse every moment *you* keep something from me," I interrupted. "I don't care how sweet she is, Danny. Don't you see? Now that Jeremy is gone, Gemma Rose has *everything* she ever wanted. Everything *he* took from her when he succeeded."

Danny's doubtful expression deepened. "She deserves it."

I followed his gaze to the spot where Gemma was— or where she had been a second ago. Now she was walking away, wiping off frosting as she went. She handed her towel to her companion.

Liam Taylor. I shot a questioning glance at Danny.

"He trains her. You don't get to be that hot without work."

I almost smacked him. "Danny! Why didn't you tell me?"

Stubbornly, he compressed his mouth. That's when I knew.

"You didn't think I could do it, did you?" I accused. "Not again. You thought I didn't need to know about Phoebe and Liam's connections to Gemma because my 'investigation' didn't matter."

Danny's apologetic gaze told me all I needed to

know. "The police are on it this time," he said. "Let them handle it."

"Right, by arresting *me*. Did you forget that part?"

I frowned at him, willing him to back me up. As usual.

Danny only shook his head. "If they were going to arrest you, they would have done it by now. The police don't screw around."

I frowned at him, unable to come up with a suitable rejoinder. I wasn't the one who'd been in jail. That was *him*.

A long time ago, but still. Danny knew about that stuff.

Annoyed and hurt, I deepened my frown. What else could I do? I was stuck. But my salvation, conversation-wise, was at hand.

When I say that I realized—in the next two minutes—who murdered Britain's sexiest chef and why, you won't believe me.

But I swear, that's exactly what happened.

It hit me just after Gemma wriggled into a slinky cocktail gown, the advert crew got ready for the next setup, and someone turned on the music again. This time, it was a song overlaid with party sounds: laughter, conversation, clinking glasses . . . the works. Danny got into a suit, then joined Gemma in the kitchen.

That's when I finally made the connection I'd needed.

At long last, I knew who'd killed Jeremy Wright.

I knew how they'd (almost) gotten away with it, too.

Seventeen

The first thing I did was tell Travis.

I slipped away from the Hambleton & Hart taping at the guesthouse, walked down the block while pulling out my brand-new cell phone, then called my financial adviser with my theory.

Why not Danny? Partly because he was on the set, and I couldn't wait. Partly because—when it comes to logic—Travis is the king. Partly because I'm impatient. I may have told you that, in my head, the wheels never quit spinning, whether it's a new way of making chocolate mousse (with water instead of cream—believe me, it works!) or staging a trial run of what sounded like a pretty kooky theory to explain a murder and subsequent alibi.

To his credit, Travis listened all the way through without interrupting. He's *excellent* at that. Only afterward did I hear him typing in the background—probably searching for plane tickets with an immediate departure from London.

"You're going to have to leave." My sexy-voiced keeper had a way of making fleeing sound like an unbeatable idea. "Now."

"Not yet." I shook my head, even though Travis couldn't see me. I was fortunate that Phoebe and I had been working on her baking tutorial for quite a while today—and that we'd watched the Hambleton & Hart advert filming for three-quarters of an hour after that—so that it wasn't the middle of the night for Travis. "If I leave now, it will be too obvious. If I flee, *someone else* might flee," I suggested, "if you catch my drift."

Generously, my financial adviser didn't remind me that he, as a proven mastermind, *always* caught my drift. Instead, Travis quit typing. "If someone there suddenly turns up with travel plans to Caracas or Guanacaste, get out *immediately.*"

"Are those hot new destinations or something?" I smiled. "Travis, have you been looking into beating your travel phobia?"

He squashed that idea. "Neither Venezuela nor Costa Rica has an extradition agreement with the United Kingdom. There are other countries with the same status, of course, but looking at available flight paths, those two appear most pertinent."

Aha. That meant that my suspect could board a plane—at Gatwick, Heathrow, Stansted, London City, Luton, or another smaller, private airport—and get away with murder. Literally.

I shook my head. "As far as I know, no one has any travel plans. Everything's been building toward me finishing my chocolate consultation at Primrose, Phoebe filming her TV appearance, Nicola launching her book, Gemma turning Danny into the next 'Old Spice man'-style advertising sensation, and Claire profiting wherever possible." I threw in mentions of Andrew Davies, Liam Taylor, and Amelja, too. "Anyway, I want to be here to see justice done," I told Travis. "I've worked hard for it."

"It *will* be unique to see the police sweep in to save the day this time," my financial adviser mused. "I'm glad you're not going rogue, Hayden. I would have advised against it. Again."

Again. In my own defense, the last couple of times I'd been involved in something criminal, the authorities had been two steps behind the culprit—*too* far behind for my own safety. We both knew that. But this time, I had to agree with Travis.

I envisioned him in his high-rise office building in Seattle, looking out over Puget Sound. Cradling the phone with one hand and loosening his tie with the other. Getting ready, at long last, to tell me *exactly* what he was wearing right now.

"Just keep your distance," Travis said instead, his tone gravelly with concern. "I don't want you to get hurt."

"Aw, Travis. I didn't know you cared," I joked.

There was a meaningful silence as I waited for him to laugh. Except he didn't. I paced worriedly, frowning at the iconic British telephone box I'd chosen as my stopping point for this conversation as though I was unhappy with that crimson Art Moderne–style kiosk, its tidy panes of glass, and its gold bas-relief crown motif. Some tourists slowed, wanting a photo of it.

I stepped aside to let them. Travis cleared his throat.

"If you don't know I care by now," he said in a carefully casual tone, "then I've done a terrible job of communicating."

Whoops. "I was only joking." Unable to stop, I added, "I'm the one who keeps professing my undying love for you, Travis."

More silence. Then he remembered. "That's right.

The other day, after your Tube train incident," he recalled. "You know as well as I do things that happen during emergencies don't count."

It was, to a word, exactly what I'd thought when Danny and I had shared that moment down on the Underground platform, when we'd both looked at each other and felt . . . something significant.

"I do know that," I said contritely. Crisply. I watched a few Londoners striding toward home, carrying newspapers and laptop bags and cell phones. "I'm a little on edge right now."

It was too little, too late. I think we both knew it.

"Hey, it's not every day you turn in a murderer," he said.

"I hope it's the *last* day I turn in a murderer." I paced, smiling at the outlandishness of that statement. However bizarre my circumstances were, I had to deal with them. "I'll let you know what happens. You know, unless I get killed or something."

This time, there was no delay. "Not funny. Be careful."

"I'll be careful."

"Be more than careful."

"Yes, sir." I didn't think Travis had caught up to my new reality yet. But I had. Or at least I was making strides in that direction. What I'd been through was unprecedented. None of us had been ready for it, including Travis. But we were adjusting.

"You're headed to the police station next?" Travis asked.

"I think that's for the best." Still pacing, I wandered to the phone box again. As a piece of history, it was unmatched. As a useful public utility? Not so much. Not many people used phone booths anymore. But I hoped that bit of English heritage would stick around awhile. "I can offer proof. The police should take me seriously—even if DC Mishra has her doubts about my motives."

"I'll vouch for you," my keeper said reliably.

I appreciated his loyalty, but . . . "I doubt even you could sway the detective constable from her opinion. She's pretty tough." I had to admire a woman who was making her way in what had to be a male-dominated field. All the same, maybe I'd seek out George to give my statement to. "She's . . . tenacious."

"Hmm." Travis's sexy murmur rumbled over the line. "Sounds a lot like someone else I know. She works with chocolate. She's pretty incredible at a lot of things, actually. You know her?"

His playful tone made me quit pacing. Suddenly, I *really* wished I was anywhere but London, embroiled in another murder.

"I've got to run." I cut short our banter. More than anything, I wanted to cling to the phone and forget about everything while listening to Travis and his sensual rumble. I would have settled for my financial adviser's take on the ABCs, if it came down to it. But time was wasting. "It's obvious no one is planning to confess to Jeremy's murder anytime soon, so . . ."

Travis caught my hint. "Good luck, Hayden. I mean it."

I swallowed hard. "I'll give the police your number if I need someone to vouch for my good character, okay?"

"Already done." I could practically hear him smile across the phone lines. "Why do you think you're not already arrested?"

I laughed. "You're smart, Trav, but you're not omniscient."

He laughed too. "That's what you think. Talk to you soon."

His sign-off was as good as a vote of confidence. If

my financial adviser had doubted my ability to get this done, he would have kept me on the line, trying to talk me into another course of action. Going to the police was the (only) smart move.

I shot Danny a text message, then headed over there.

It wasn't until I was safely on the Tube train, recalling my conversation with my keeper, that I remembered what I'd said.

Trav. I'd called him *Trav.* More significantly, he'd let me.

Next time, I promised myself, I was asking about his dog.

I'll spare you the details of my appointment with George.

He, as predicted, was a *lot* more amenable to hearing my theory than DC Mishra would have been, though. Which wasn't to say that Satya Mishra *didn't* wander by and shoot me one of her typically hostile looks (she did), but she seemed about as eager to engage with me as I'd expected (meaning, not at all eager).

I'm pretty outgoing. Ordinarily, I make friends easily, which is helpful in my line of work. I don't usually run into people to whom I can't relate (at all), but the detective constable was one of the few and the proud. She did *not* like me.

Since I half suspected DC Mishra was still hoping to find a reason to arrest me, I have to say the feeling was mutual.

I skedaddled out of the station as soon as possible, then spent the evening in a state of anticipation. Everything would be ending *very* soon now. I had the

assurance of the London Metropolitan Police Service
on that. Still, I felt trapped.

I couldn't leave, for the reasons I'd told Travis: I
didn't want to spook Jeremy's murderer. I couldn't
just behave as though everything was A-OK, either,
though. I do *not* have much of a poker face, just FYI.
In the end, I sequestered myself in the guesthouse
and baked chocolate chip cookies.

That's right. When the pressure is on, your gridskipping chocolate whisperer gets out the flour,
butter, sugar, and chocolate (natch) and goes to town.
By the time midnight rolled around, I was pulling
another batch of my personal king of cookies from
the deluxe (but not *too* deluxe) oven. The scents of
melted chocolate and caramelized sugar filled the
kitchen.

I waved my oven mitt, fanning those aromas toward
Danny.

"Cut it out!" he grumbled, casting me a look that
reminded me how much he'd rather have had fish
and chips. "Have you lost your mind? I know you're
worried, but this isn't the answer."

"Chocolate chip cookies are *always* the answer."

He eyed the cooling racks full of dozens of cookies.
I *may* have done test runs of several variations—
chocolate chip with walnuts, with pecans and whiskey-
soaked golden raisins, with hazelnuts and dried
cherries, with white chocolate chunks, with oats, with
peanut butter . . . It had been a very long evening.

"How will you know when it's all over with?" Danny
asked.

That was the tricky bit. "The arrest isn't happening
until tomorrow," I confessed. "Did I forget to tell you
that part?"

His glower confirmed that I *had* "forgotten." I'll

spare you the swearword he followed up with. Danny was even worse at waiting around than I was. We both like being on the move.

"It's a strategy," I explained, having been over this while at the police department. "There are multiple forces at work here. There are legal issues involved, warrants to be obtained . . ."

I trailed off, not one hundred percent clear on the legal details. Frankly, I'd been trading evil eyes with DC Mishra during the legalese-filled part of my visit. I'd only snapped to later.

"You can't just barrel in there and start shooting," I reminded Danny, admiring my nicely golden-brown cookies. I inhaled deeply, savoring their calming, delicious smell. "This isn't the movies. This is real life. This is the way it is."

Full of waiting around. I wasn't wild about it, either.

Nervously, I puttered around, moving cookies from sheet pan to cooling rack, then from cooling rack to serving tray. I'd found one of those three-tiered stands in one of the cupboards. Each of its three levels was chockablock with cookies now.

I put my hands on my hips and surveyed the results of my evening's labor. "Maybe a batch with olive oil and sea salt?"

There are innumerable variations on the king of cookies. That's why they're the king of cookies. But for that latest variation, I would need mild olive oil and flaky fleur de sel.

I opened the nearest cupboard door and started searching.

"Are you going to eat any of those?" Danny wanted to know.

I shrugged. "I doubt it. I feel pretty wound up at

the moment." I nudged a pan nearer to him. "You go ahead, though."

With knowing eyes, my security expert watched me. "It's not too late to take things into our own hands, you know. We might be able to extract a confession. That would move things along."

"So would my murder, if things went wrong." I shuddered as I envisioned that grisly scenario. "Let's just wait this out."

Danny frowned. So did I. Our gazes met. They held.

We both knew of one thing that would distract us for sure.

Fortunately, that's when my cell phone rang.

"Maybe they moved early." I grabbed it and answered.

Danny started pacing at the same moment I heard Constable George's jocular voice on the other end. "We're on," he said in an excited, confidential tone. "It's definitely happening tomorrow. So I would suggest you avoid Primrose at all costs."

I caught his meaning instantly. "You're doing it at the TV taping? But there'll be so many people there," I reminded him.

All of the chocolaterie-pâtisserie's crew would be present behind the scenes. So would Phoebe (of course), the TV film crew, Nicola and Claire . . . and Andrew Davies from Hambleton & Hart, if what I'd overheard him saying earlier was correct.

"That's the whole idea," George informed me. "No place to run, no place to hide. Instant coverage on the telly, too."

Aha. The police department had taken a drubbing in the press for not having already captured Jeremy's killer, I knew. I'd read the papers; they undoubtedly had too. They probably wanted to capitalize on the ready-made publicity on offer.

"Well, if you're sure," I hedged, glancing at Danny.

He was busy scanning the guesthouse, making sure we were safe. That was my security expert for you—making things secure.

"Just sit tight," George urged. "We have to do this right."

I felt a sudden burst of nostalgia for the times I'd gone in after a killer with a half-formed plan, a bit of intuition, and a lot of luck on my side. But that was foolish, wasn't it?

It was. Travis would have agreed. Danny too, despite his earlier comment about our potential ability to move things along ourselves. We both knew this was (still) the smart way to go.

I inhaled, then nodded. "Okay. Thanks, George."

Then I hung up the phone and looked at Danny. "There's someplace we have to be," I told him. "And it's not here."

Then I grabbed a jacket and my bag, and we were on our way.

It's important, in life, to have allies. I have Danny and Travis. I have my mom and dad. I have friends scattered worldwide, people I trust from Monte Carlo to Oamaru. I value their support, and I treasure the special qualities they bring to my life—things like humor, expertise, and the ability to bake Belgian gaufres (sugar-studded waffles) to the perfect shade of golden brown and the ideal level of crispiness.

But not everyone is as lucky as I am. Not everyone has someone they can count on. That's why I found myself, with Danny steadfastly and pugnaciously by my side, back in the East End.

That rough neighborhood looked no quainter or cheerier in the dark, I can tell you that. Long past midnight, the council estate where Jeremy Wright had grown up to become one of the world's most famous culinary celebrities was partly deserted.

Except for the extra-shady parts, where we were going.

As we made our way down the darkened street, past bits of trash, to one of the pubs I'd heard about while consulting at Primrose, Danny cocked his dark eyebrow at me. "Are you sure about this?" he asked, keeping a watchful eye around us.

I nodded, then kept going. I won't tell you I wasn't nervous; I was. Gridskipping doesn't make you immune to danger.

In some ways, though, staying alone in our guesthouse with nothing to do except wait might have been pretty dangerous for Danny and me, too . . . if you catch my drift. That had been a pretty loaded look we'd exchanged, right before George's call.

Taming our boredom by testing out that four-poster would have been stupid *and* dangerous. Plus, this was productive.

"I'm sure." I found the place I wanted, then opened the front door. Inside, it couldn't have been more different from The Fat Squirrel. The pub we'd entered had none of that place's charm or antiquity. Its barman had none of the same bonhomie.

Danny backed me up, but I took the lead. Maybe I'm crazy. Or just really eager not to wind up in bed with Danny again.

I spotted the person I was looking for in the corner,

playing darts. He flung one as we approached. It hit its mark.

"Nice one." I nodded at Hugh Menadue. "How are you, Hugh?"

His friends howled with annoyance, berating Hugh for the interruption in their game. He shrugged, obviously used to their abuse. It seemed to all be in good fun. You know, with knives.

I glanced downward. Hugh still carried his in his boot.

Danny stood behind me, probably looking fearsome. It was his specialty in situations like this. Given his background, he has no trouble pulling it off. He means business. It shows.

The lanky, tattooed baker rolled his eyes at me. "Listen good, all right? If you're lookin' to bring me back to work, you can just piss off. I'm finished with all that stuff."

You've probably guessed that he didn't say "stuff."

"I'm not here to rehire you," I told him, trying not to breathe in too deeply. I'm no fussbudget, but Hugh's local pub didn't smell like roses and sugar cookies. It smelled like cut-rate beer, cheap perfume, and the sweat of hard-working men. "I'm here because I like you, Hugh. You're young and dumb, and you're going to make some mistakes because of that, but—"

"Oi!" He balled his hands in fists. "I ain't dumb!"

"—but that doesn't mean you should pay for what someone else did," I finished calmly. "Unless you want to do that?"

His frown expanded as he edged us both toward an empty table. I went willingly, but Danny got between us for one long, tense minute. Whatever stare-off they had had, it improved Hugh's willingness to listen by a factor of ten. *Thanks, Danny.*

"Look, I didn't do nothin'." Hugh pounded his chest, his expression fierce. "And I don't want anybody sayin' I did."

I believed him. Almost. "In this case, doing 'nothing' is almost as bad as doing 'something'." I leaned nearer, avoiding a puddle of spilled lager on the scarred table. "I know you know what I mean." I hardened my expression, hoping to make an impression on him. "Go to the police. Tell them what you know—"

Hugh gave a bitter laugh. He looked away. "Yeah, right. As if them lot are going to listen to somebody like me."

"—or be charged as an accessory to murder. *Jeremy's* murder." I kept my gaze fixed on his troubled face. I thought I was getting through to him. "You liked Jeremy. He was good to you. He gave you extra work, delivering things for his parties."

Hugh's lip wobbled. I knew I'd struck a nerve. He might be used to acting tough, but this was a different story. This was *murder.* There was no finessing this—no talking big and smashing up pans. Myra had been right when she'd noticed changes in him.

What's got into you lately? she'd asked Hugh after he'd had his chocolate-spilling tirade at Primrose. It had been a cogent observation because of just one word: *lately.*

That single word had told me that Hugh's short-temperedness was something new. I'd followed up with some questions later, of course, but I'd had my suspicions then. Now, with (almost) all the dots connected for me, I thought I knew why he'd been upset.

"Jeremy liked you. He wanted to help you." I raised

my voice to be heard amid the pub's noise. "How did you repay him?"

We both knew. I saw the guilt in Hugh's rawboned face.

"You know what?" Hugh inhaled. His cheeks were mottled, his hair askew, as though he'd spent the night yanking his hand through it with worry. Now, he slapped both big hands on the table. He gave me a killing look, then swore. "You don't know a bloody thing about anything. If you did, you'd be down at the police station, 'stead of slummin' it around here. So get out."

He pointed two fingers at me, then added a heap of additional swearing. I'll leave out the details, but I flinched.

Danny started looking unhappy. That wasn't good. That meant he was on the cusp of interfering but was controlling himself for my sake. I appreciated his ferocity, but I had to be braver.

"I *was* down at the police station," I informed Hugh. I wasn't proud that my voice shook as I did so, but it was a dangerous crowd and a treacherous situation. "They know what I know. Now, so do you." I slid out of the booth, then stood. "They'll be moving in soon. Don't make this any worse than it already is," I advised Hugh. "You want to be smart? Save yourself— as much as you can—while you still can. Tonight."

Whatever cooperation Hugh offered, it wouldn't be enough to absolve him of guilt, I knew. But it would help bring about some justice for a man who really had been kind to him—Jeremy. It would strengthen the police's case when they made their arrest.

I was shaking when Danny took my arm. "Let's go."

"Hang on. I have one more thing to say." I wheeled

around with Danny at my back. Hugh lounged at the pub table with fear in his eyes and a wobbly smirk on his face. I tried to remember the time when I *hadn't* known what I did now. I succeeded well enough to soften my voice. "You could have made it," I told Hugh, thinking of our work together. "You really had talent."

Then I nodded at Danny and we made our getaway.

With a little luck, Hugh wouldn't be doing the same thing tonight, via one of the Venezuelan or Costa Rican flights that Travis had told me about. I didn't want Hugh to get away.

I only wanted him not to suffer *too* much for this.

"'Someplace we have to be,' huh?" Danny mimicked as we reached the sidewalk outside. He shook his head. "You're still a softy, Hayden. No matter how much you want to deny it."

"Hey, I successfully suspected everyone, didn't I?"

"Yeah. Even when you shouldn't have."

I knew he was thinking of Gemma Rose. "You're only saying that because you have a big, fat crush on Jeremy's competition."

Danny obviously didn't want to discuss that. Instead, he hooked his thumb toward the pub as we strode away from it.

"That was a gutsy move back there. Dumb, but gutsy." His dark-eyed, sideways glance wasn't exactly schmaltzy, but his sardonic grin warmed me, anyway. "What's next on the agenda? Taunting an MMA fighter? Jumping into a shark tank? Skydiving?"

"Running with the bulls in Pamplona. There's nothing like a good *encierro*, right?" He knew I was kidding. It was the adrenaline talking. I want the *toros bravos* to be left alone. I shivered as we strode along. I watched as a car approached.

A police car. I froze. Was that DC Mishra behind the wheel?

Danny saw. "Just keep moving." He grabbed my hand and pulled. "There are probably patrols around here all the time."

We veered around a corner and cut between two buildings. Within moments, I already felt lost. But my bodyguard was on it.

"That looked like DC Mishra," I protested. "Do you think she's following me?" I craned my neck, half expecting to see her in pursuit with her antagonistic expression and department-issued baton at the ready. "Maybe *she's* the one who should have been suspended in the police misconduct enquiry, not George."

If Satya Mishra were corrupt, I figured, it would explain her suspicion of me.

"You're only saying that because she doesn't like you," Danny said in a reasonable tone, this time offering *me* an unsolicited reality check. "It happens. Get over it."

I examined his profile as we reached our parked car. We'd borrowed Liam's, after offering up a plausible excuse. Jeremy's former trainer had seemed deeply interested in the imminent arrest of Jeremy's killer. I thought I knew the reason for that.

In the meantime, I'd decided, we'd needed a car. Liam had been the only person I knew of in London who had one available.

"Yeah, okay. Good enough," I agreed. In the end, it didn't matter who liked me or not. I was fine. "After tomorrow, DC Mishra and I will never have to see one another again, anyway."

I hoped. Danny opened the car doors. He got behind the wheel and started the engine while I slid inside.

"Buckle up," I urged. "Let's lose her."

"*You* lose her." Danny sounded amused at my zeal for movie-style car capers. "Right after *you* learn to drive on the left."

Point noted. Maybe I was a little overwrought after our adventure with Hugh. On the other hand . . . "When did *you* learn to drive on the left, anyway? You're from L.A., not Leicester."

As far as I knew, this was a new item on his résumé. Either that, or he was planning to expand his security business and start protecting British film and television stars.

He put the car in motion. "Anyplace else you want to go?"

I guessed he didn't want to discuss his expanding skill set.

"No, that's it." I shook my head. "Back to the guest-house."

Danny shot me an ambiguous look. "Are you sure about that?"

No. Of course I wasn't. Hanging around in our posh accommodations with nothing to do but wait? That was a recipe for trouble. "Let's just go," I pushed, hoping for the best.

He heard the *no* in my voice, but there was no help for it. Until tomorrow, we were joined at the hip. All night long.

Eighteen

Danny and I made it through the night. Just barely.

Fortunately, we had all those chocolate chip cookies I'd baked for a distraction. Neither of us could resist by the time we got back from seeing Hugh. We each took a couple and then went our separate ways, me to the guesthouse's bedroom and Danny to his spot on the sofa. I heard him firing up *Antiques Roadshow* on his laptop; he probably heard me typing my Primrose chocolate report on my own laptop into the wee hours of the morning.

I'd found the cure to my chronic procrastination, I'd realized at around two AM. All I needed was something even *more* critical to avoid—other than report writing—and voilà!

Job done. No more procrastination troubles. No app needed.

After completing the last pages, I finally fell asleep. But my idyll didn't last. The next thing I knew, Danny was there.

Looking unreasonably alert—given the circumstances and the fraught night we'd just spent—he waved a cup of coffee in front of my nose. *Mmm.* Yum.

He set it down on the nightstand and then stared at me with his hands on his jeans-clad hips.

"What if you're wrong about trusting Hugh?" Danny asked.

I had the impression he'd waited hours to ask me that question. I doubted he'd slept well, either. Groggily, I lifted my gaze to his chest. He was wearing a Union Jack T-shirt.

Ha. I guessed that was my security expert's send-off to the U.K. After today's . . . events . . . were completed, we were both leaving—him, back to the states, and me, to France to see my parents at their castle archaeological site. With only a Eurostar ride between us, it would have been criminal not to make the trip.

Speaking of criminal . . . "I'm not wrong about trusting Hugh."

"You can't know that. You worked with him for a month."

"I'm good at reading people." I sat up and grabbed the cup of coffee. Mindful of the four-poster's fancy bedding, I brought that lifesaving elixir to my nose. I inhaled. Double *mmm*.

I'm an expert at chocolate, but coffee is a close runner-up. I enjoyed a careful (but very fortifying) sip.

"If you were *that* good at reading people, you would have realized who done it on day one," Danny argued. "You didn't."

"Be reasonable. I needed proof." I swallowed more coffee, then studied my longtime pal. "What's up with you, anyway?"

He paced across the bedroom, full of coiled-up energy. He glanced out the window at the Wrights' flowery garden beyond, frowned, then went on striding across the rug. He sighed.

"I had a . . . tip last night," Danny told me.

"A 'tip'?" I raised my brows. "From whom?"

"I'd rather not say."

"From Gemma, then."

He cast me a beleaguered look. "It doesn't matter who."

"*Definitely* from Gemma, then. What did she say?"

Danny scowled at me. "You're going to be biased."

"You're already biased. Can't you hear yourself?" I relaxed my tone, then tried again. "Has it occurred to you that Gemma might be misleading you on purpose to protect Phoebe? They were pretty chummy yesterday, remember? They go way back, those two."

That's right. To protect *Phoebe*. That's what I said.

Because *she'd* killed Jeremy. I knew it. I could prove it.

Now all that remained was seeing her arrested for it. That eventuality was what had kept me pinned to the guesthouse all night. I hadn't wanted to alert the Honourable that I was on to her. If anyone had the means to flee the country, it was Phoebe.

"Gemma was only pretending to like Phoebe yesterday," Danny informed me. "She was being polite. She's a nice person."

"Or she's a liar." I shrugged. "It happens."

Danny looked away. "Gemma says that Hugh and Phoebe were—"

"Lovers. I know," I interrupted. "Those Y-fronts, that thong—those were both Hugh's." I still wished I'd never found those intimate items, much less touched them. Ugh. "Phoebe thought she could get rid of them by mixing them with Jeremy's things. But that underwear wasn't Jeremy's style *or*"—more importantly—"his size. Those things were definitely Hugh's."

Danny's crack about his "frank and beans" had made me realize that. Now, though, my security expert gave me a dour look. Under the best of circumstances, he was hard to convince.

I had the fix for that. "It all fits, Danny. Phoebe has a 'type.'" *Just like I do.* My conversation with Liam while working out at The Green Park—about my three (nearly identical) ex-fiancés—had reminded me of that . . . and made me expand my theory. "Jeremy was Phoebe's type, especially when they met. But Hugh is like a younger, hotter, edgier—and more malleable— Jeremy." I angled my head at Danny. "Don't tell me you can't see it."

"Yeah." He squinted at the ceiling. Nodded. "I guess so."

I *knew* so. "Phoebe did the same thing men have done for millennia. She traded up for a younger, sexier model of the husband she already had. She did it because she could."

She'd done it, I'd understood further, as part of her revitalization and publicity plan for Primrose. She'd glimpsed Hugh at one of Jeremy's Jump Start Foundation events, been smitten with him, then restaffed the chocolaterie-pâtisserie with novice bakers as an excuse to be around him more often.

It all made sense. Even Hugh's cooperation with the plan did. Phoebe was attractive. Attentive. Able to give a hard-luck bloke like Hugh the life he'd only dreamed of—the life she'd once given Jeremy . . . until he'd become too demanding and too plagued by his own insecurities to put up with anymore.

Jeremy truly had been vain, I'd realized. But Phoebe had been worse. She'd needed validation from every corner—proof of her authority, her success, her desirability . . . everything. She'd gotten some of that validation from Hugh and the rest from

Primrose. Phoebe had meant it when she'd said she *was* her shop.

Its gradual decline had mirrored her feelings about her own life. Coupled with the rift that must have been growing between her and Jeremy, it had all been too much.

It seemed absurd that someone as privileged as Phoebe could have felt so insecure. But she had. I'd seen it every day, when I'd tutored her in baking— when I'd tried to prepare her for TV. Phoebe had been touchy about the least little correction.

Hugh had been the balm for Phoebe's battered ego. But when Jeremy had stumbled upon Phoebe and Hugh together—*intimately together*—and had suddenly had grounds for an acrimonious divorce, the situation must have gotten ugly. Jeremy must have threatened, I'd reasoned, to expose Phoebe's infidelity. News of that perfidy—especially with someone as low-brow as Hugh—would have cost the Honourable years' worth of public goodwill.

She'd wanted a harmless fling. Instead, she'd taken on a starring role as Jeremy's tragic widow.

The only thing that saved me before was Jeremy! Phoebe had told me yesterday. *The love everyone felt for him transferred to me, too. It grounded me, and Primrose. All of us basked in his glow, didn't we?* She'd broken off and started to weep.

But not because she'd missed Jeremy, I'd realized. Because she'd feared missing out on the adoration that the British public—and people around the world—had felt for her husband. She'd never wanted to lose that overwhelming admiration.

Reminders of it had been there every day, in the tabloid reporters and in the legitimate journalists who'd waited outside the town house's door. In the sad fans who'd swarmed Jeremy's funeral. In the friends—like Gemma—who'd seen Phoebe as a heart-broken widow and had wanted to console her.

"That doesn't mean Phoebe bludgeoned Jeremy to death so she could be with Hugh," Danny said. "I'm not sure she could do it."

"Physically?" Realizing that we'd likely be at this a while, I slipped out of bed and pulled on a pair of jeans beneath the T-shirt I'd slept in. Tactfully, my old pal glanced away. "You have a point. Jeremy was strong, and Phoebe is much too slight to take him on face-to-face. But he was struck from behind."

That much had been evident to the police from the gruesome murder scene I'd stumbled upon in the guesthouse's kitchen. I simply hadn't wanted to dwell on that—just the way I hadn't wanted to dwell on the significance of Jeremy's flawless hair.

Even in death, his hair had been perfectly arranged. But that hadn't been a fluke, I'd realized. After Phoebe had killed Jeremy, she must have looked at him. She must have known he'd be discovered. She must have knelt beside his lifeless body and then done the same thing she always did—the same thing I'd seen her do in countless photos in Jeremy's cook-books. She must have arranged his hair to help cover his burgeoning bald spot.

I doubted she'd even thought about that habitual gesture of hers—or about the teensy bit of caring that must have prompted it. I hadn't dwelled on it, either—until I'd glimpsed Phoebe making the same gesture with Hugh, at Primrose, on the day he'd left for good, when I'd thought Phoebe had fired him.

Actually, I suspected now, Hugh had quit. His reaction at Phoebe's tender gesture had been telling. He'd been disgusted, I thought now. By Phoebe, by himself, by what they'd done together. By what he'd known about Jeremy's death. That's why Hugh had been so uncharacteristically short-tempered. That's why he'd refused to reminisce about Jeremy along with everyone else.

"Jeremy was probably drunk when Phoebe attacked him." I busied myself with getting dressed. "We know he spent a lot of time down at his local." I glanced at the old-fashioned dimpled pub glass that the publican had given us to return "to his missus," which I'd left on a side table. I'd hesitated giving it to Phoebe, as I'd promised. At first, I'd thought my reticence had to do with not wanting to see Phoebe refuse to fit Jeremy's personalized pub glass into her décor. But then I realized I simply hadn't wanted Phoebe to have it—in case it really had meant something to her husband. "Andrew Davies told me everyone went down to the pub to try to mend fences after their advert shoot on the day Jeremy died. Jeremy must have come here after."

"And found Phoebe here with Hugh?" Danny guessed.

I nodded. "I suspect so. I think Phoebe and Hugh were meeting regularly, probably whenever Hugh delivered new 'party supplies.'" Those parties really had happened, but they'd taken place at Phoebe's instigation, not Jeremy's, as a cover for her liaisons with Hugh. "Jeremy must have surprised them together."

"That's still no reason to beat him to death." Danny swore, shaking his head. "To have planned something like that—"

"I don't think it was planned," I disagreed, downing more coffee. "I think it was a spur-of-the-moment thing. A real crime of passion. It probably happened during an argument. Maybe Jeremy insulted Phoebe. Maybe Jeremy punched Hugh. Maybe Jeremy begged Phoebe to come back to him. Maybe he threatened them both. Who knows? But once Phoebe delivered that first blow from behind, knocking Jeremy to the floor, the rest would have been easy." I shuddered. "You know, if you were a killer."

"And Hugh just stood by watching?"

I didn't know. "I don't think so. I hope not. Either way, even if Hugh didn't help Phoebe beat Jeremy to death, he definitely knew she did it. That's what ultimately ended their fling. He just couldn't handle knowing who Phoebe really was. That's why I thought we had a chance last night, trying to get Hugh to confess. If he does it *before* Phoebe is arrested, it might help his case," I pointed out. "Otherwise, it looks as though Hugh conspired with Phoebe to kill her husband."

Danny made a face. "Gemma thinks Hugh will warn Phoebe."

"You told her about our plan?" I cried. "Danny!"

"I trust her," he said stubbornly. "She knows Phoebe."

"And does she 'know' Phoebe is capable of murder?"

"She thinks it's possible, yeah." My security expert caught my exasperated, concerned look and frowned at me. "I called her last night. I had to do *something* besides . . . well, you know."

Join you in your snazzy four-poster bed was what I assumed.

I relented. "Just as long as Gemma doesn't warn Phoebe—" I broke off, considering it. "You don't think she will, do you?"

Danny studied me. "No." But he didn't sound certain. As though realizing it, he rushed on. "We can't be sure about Phoebe," he insisted. "She has a confirmed alibi, remember? The police checked. Everyone said Phoebe was at some chichi party on the night Jeremy was killed. Eyewitnesses vouched for her."

I arched my eyebrow at him. "Now who's being naïve?"

He scowled. *Not me,* his expression said. "Police," Danny reiterated. "Eyewitnesses. *Proof.* What have you got?"

"Plenty. But before I remind you, let's break this down," I hedged. "You honestly don't believe any of Phoebe's upper-crust friends would have lied to protect her? Or maybe just not have noticed whether she was at that party the entire night or not?"

I knew Phoebe had been there for part of the evening. She'd been there when the police had come to tell her that her husband was dead. She'd even convincingly collapsed at the news.

"Yeah, I think they would have lied to cover for Phoebe." Danny conceded that argument, then gave me the ghost of a smile. "But I'm a cynic. I think everyone is willing to lie."

I'd already known that about him. But our differences weren't the point here. The chronology of the evening was.

What came next was the clincher—the linchpin that had pulled together everything else, last night at the advert taping. If I'd had my old phone with its cracked screen, I'd have brandished it to make my theory more airtight. But since I'd already surrendered it as evidence to Constable George . . .

"You might be right about that," I told Danny willingly enough, "but those lies from Phoebe's friends won't be enough to save her. Not when I've got the phone call that Phoebe made to me on that night, moments after Jeremy was killed, asking me to rush over to Primrose and make sure the chocolaterie-pâtisserie was locked—something she'd never asked me to do before then."

Danny gave me a blank look. "So?"

"So Phoebe knew I was staying here at the guesthouse—the scene of the crime," I reminded him. "But she didn't know when I'd be home. She must have wanted to make sure she—and maybe Hugh—could get away and set up alibis before I arrived. So Phoebe called me and sent me on a wild-goose chase to the shop."

I hadn't even batted an eyelash at her request, I recalled. At the time, I'd become so used to Phoebe being difficult and autocratic that I'd accepted her demand as par for the course.

As it turned out, it had been anything but routine.

"By the time I arrived to find Jeremy's body," I continued, "Phoebe was gone, safely at her party, establishing an alibi."

"Which the police accepted," Danny pointed out. "So why don't you? Phones are portable these days, you know. Phoebe could have called you from the party to send you to Primrose."

"She could have," I agreed, "but she didn't. I know because of the music. Because of the party sounds. Because of the chattering and glass clinking and all the rest. They were exactly the same as the background noises playing during your second Hambleton & Hart advert yesterday. Exactly the same."

That's when everything had clicked into place for me. I'd heard that same set of inauthentic party sounds, and I'd known.

I'd known that Phoebe had killed Jeremy. I'd

known that she'd used me and my errand to Primrose to help cover for it.

"Phoebe had heard that track before," Danny mused, "sometime while Jeremy had been filming. So she turned on the A/V equipment and played it, knowing you'd think she was at her party—when really it was moments after she'd killed Jeremy."

I nodded, unable to stop picturing the scene. The truth was . . . *chilling*. Even more so than I'd expected it to be.

I couldn't believe I'd given a phony statement myself about Phoebe's whereabouts that night. I thought I'd been being truthful, when instead, I'd been purposely deceived. By Phoebe.

"I don't know why Phoebe thought it would be perfectly fine to frame *me*, but she did," I added, still miffed about that. "Unfortunately for her, she picked the wrong chocolate whisperer to throw to the wolves." Phoebe must have known I'd become the police's top suspect after I'd found Jeremy, but she hadn't cared. "If not for her 'clever' strategy of calling me to send me to Primrose—if not for her augmenting her call with that soundtrack—I would have had a much harder time figuring it out."

"Phoebe should have tried harder to get rid of that A/V equipment when you asked about it." Danny grinned. "It doesn't pay to get between you and your to-do list. Everyone knows that."

We both looked at the corner where the equipment had previously stood, along with the lights and boom mics and all the rest. The people from Hambleton & Hart had taken it away yesterday, after Danny and Gemma's advert shoot had finished. I imagined now that it was only a matter of time before the

London Metropolitan Police Service arrived to take possession of all of it as evidence.

"I wish I hadn't been so swayed by the promise of that claw-footed tub and four-poster bed," I grumbled, only semi-jokingly. "If I hadn't been staying here in the guesthouse in the first place, I wouldn't have had to be involved at all."

Danny gave me a knowing look. "You would have been involved. You would have made sure of it. At this point? Yeah."

He was probably right. "Well . . . there really weren't any other lodgings available." *Thanks, Wimbledon.* "So there's that."

I didn't want anyone thinking I *wanted* to sleuth around. Especially Danny. He was endangered by my "investigations." Risking myself was one thing. Risking my loved ones (and Danny definitely counted as one of those) was something else.

Speaking of which . . . "Anyway, you should probably go say good-bye to Gemma. Travis is booking you a ticket for tonight."

"Are you nuts? I'm not leaving you here by yourself."

"I'll be fine. Phoebe is at the TV taping at Primrose, remember? She won't ever be coming home from it, either."

Danny scrutinized me. "You don't want to go?"

"To watch Phoebe be arrested?" The idea of seeing justice done did appeal to me, but I couldn't do it. "If Phoebe sees me at the chocolaterie-pâtisserie, she'll know something's up. I already told her I was leaving to visit my parents today." I pointed at myself. "No poker face at all, remember?"

I'd thought it was prudent to cook up an excuse in advance. I'd barely been able to eke out the words last night—not while looking her in the face and knowing what she'd done to Jeremy.

"Are you really leaving to visit your parents today?"

"What do you think?"

"I think . . ." My security expert studied me. For a heartbeat, I feared he'd detect the truth—that I was sending him away on purpose until all this was over. "You really are." He grinned. "You've got 'chocolate croissant' written all over your face."

"I do love those." I shooed him, wondering if my ability to bluff had grown alongside my newfound skepticism. "So go on."

Danny hesitated. "What are you going to do?"

Call George and find out why nothing's happened yet.

A glance at the clock told me it was past time for Phoebe to have been arrested. Things must be happening at that moment.

"I'm going to pack." I shrugged. "I don't have much, but everything I own fits in those two bags. I'm taking them."

My musclebound buddy still didn't budge. "If you're sure . . ."

"Danny! Just go. I have my phone, thanks to Travis." That would help prod him along. "I'll call you if anything happens."

I pulled out my new phone as assurance. Danny shot it a disgruntled look. "Tell Captain Calculator he got you last year's model. I would have gone for the latest and greatest."

"You *are* the latest and greatest. Get lost so I can pack."

It only took one little shove and another sworn reassurance to make it happen. Danny finally set up a rendezvous with Gemma Rose over the phone and then left. I watched every step as he swaggered across the Wrights' garden and out the back gate.

Then I dialed my phone and called George. Again.

The things a person collects while globe-trotting are pretty esoteric, I reflected as I went through my packing ritual after Danny left. Innumerable plastic baggies (some of them spares) to ensure I made it through airport security. Odd bits and pieces from hotel amenity packs (hello, miniature sewing kits). So many tiny shampoo bottles I could have opened a boutique.

Sorting through everything, I methodically set aside the discards as I went. The toiletries I'd donate to a women's and children's shelter—they can always use soap, toothpaste, and all the rest. The other things . . . well, how many eye masks can one person use, anyway? And those foam earplugs they give you on international flights—do those things multiply in a Dopp kit?

Adding to the usual detritus were items unique to my profession. Chocolates of all types were crammed into my single wheelie bag and accompanying duffel. There were dark-chocolate samples slipped into the interior pockets, single-origin varietals tucked into the side pockets, and elegantly wrapped assorted bonbons wedged ignobly next to my spare shoes. (Don't worry; both were wrapped.) There were chocolates from abroad, chocolates from Lemaître in the Marin Headlands, and chocolates from the Cartorama food cart pod in Portland, Oregon. There were powdered hot-chocolate mixes from a potential consultation client and raw cacao beans from a grateful past consultee.

It's not that I'm a pack rat. Far from it. But lately I'd been traveling from place to place with even less of a break than usual. My luggage was starting to show the strain.

With nothing but time on my hands, I did my best to focus on whittling down my unwanted collection of confectionary and knickknacks. There was a tiny chocolate knife with a cartoon kitten on it (China), a packet of chocolate-covered seaweed (Korea), and a random, bullet-shaped N_2O charger (U.K.). Not much bigger than a lipstick container, it could work magic.

You know those pressurized containers of "whipped topping" found in the supermarket's cold case? With a special cream whipper that uses nitrous-oxide cartridges, you can make your own (dairy) whipped cream, complete with fancy swirls and loops.

That didn't explain why *I* had an orphan charger (the cartridge) and no special cream whipper to hold it, though. I frowned at it, unsure where it had come from. Primrose? The chocolaterie-pâtisserie used cream whippers to top desserts. Whatever . . . I had to ditch it. Eurostar security—like airport security— frowns on pressurized gasses. I didn't want to wind up surrounded by angry guys with guns, refused boarding privileges.

With a sigh, I set aside the N_2O charger, then glanced outside. No sign of Danny. I looked at my phone. No word from George. I hadn't been able to reach him earlier, but I'd left him an urgent message to call me when things were wrapped up.

Back to sorting. I separated all the edible items, then set them aside for donation to Jeremy's Jump Start Foundation. The kids might not go wild for the chocolate-covered seaweed (you never knew), but they might like some of the rest of the candy. I'd already arranged for a big endowment via Travis. Sometimes, though, there was nothing like an in-person donation of goods.

Just as I was about to run out of diversionary tactics, I felt something between the lining and the outside fabric at the bottom of my bag. I fished around and pulled out a baggie full of white powder. At the sight of it, my heart almost stopped.

Not for the reasons you're thinking, though. This wasn't anything illicit or illegal (at least as far as I knew). It was a bag full of powdered caffeine. I'd used it to help create caffeinated "nutraceutical" truffles at Lemaître Chocolates.

My job there had gone horribly awry (to say the least). I'd forgotten I'd even had that bag. When used inexpertly, its contents were nearly as lethal as the powdered cocaine it resembled—that's why I'd grabbed it one night from the ballroom kitchen at the chocolate-themed Lemaître resort spa. I'd wanted to make sure no one (else) was hurt by accidentally using it.

Awash in sadness at the memories evoked by that overlooked bag, I stared at it. I missed Adrienne, one of my coworkers in San Francisco. I missed not having personal knowledge, as I did these days, of how horrible people could be to one another.

I wasn't sure what to do with it, though. If Amelja found that bag while cleaning the guesthouse after I left, she might get in trouble just by having it. If I tried taking it with me . . .

From the corner of my eye, I glimpsed Phoebe.

She passed by the bedroom window and strode

down the garden path without a care in the world, plainly not arrested.

Oh, God. What had happened? I stared at her, feeling my heart start to race. I gripped the baggie I'd been holding, no longer worried about powdered caffeine and its proper disposal.

I had to leave. Could I slip out without her seeing me?

I gauged my chances and quickly decided against trying. The Wrights' town-house terrace was faced with pristine windows. Through them, I knew, the whole yard could be seen. Even though Phoebe didn't know *I'd* turned her in to the police, she might still be dangerous. I already knew she was prone to deadly impulsiveness. *To murder.* What if, as Danny had suggested, Hugh had warned Phoebe about . . . everything (me)? Or what if, as I'd hypothesized, Gemma had warned Phoebe about everything (still me)? I had to get out without her seeing me. Somehow.

No. I had to call George. Maybe Phoebe had slipped away from him before he and his colleagues could arrest her?

Partway through dialing, I felt my hair stand up on the back of my neck. Abruptly, I hung up my cell phone. I'd already called George. Multiple times. Something had obviously gone wrong. Maybe that something wrong had to do with George.

Maybe Constable George really *was* the corrupt officer. Maybe he'd been suspended from the department for good reason.

Whether he had or not, I couldn't trust him. With my mind racing, I hauled in a breath and dialed Satya Mishra. The detective constable had given me her number when she'd warned me to not leave London. I hoped now that she'd pick up my call.

She didn't. *Oh, God.* I left her a (possibly incoherent) message, then bolted to my feet. My breath felt strangled. My heart still clattered wildly in my chest. Should I call Danny?

Except I couldn't wait for my security expert to get there, I saw as I peeked out the other window and glimpsed Phoebe in the town house. She'd taken out her own (designer) luggage. She was currently scurrying around, packing it with far less deliberation and organization than I'd just employed.

I'd have bet a million pounds she was headed for Venezuela or Costa Rica—or any other sunny non-extradition country.

I had to *do* something. At the best of times, I'm no good at waiting—my long night with Danny was proof of that. If I didn't act, Phoebe Wright would get away with murder. Jeremy's murder.

I stuffed a few things into my trusty crossbody bag, then slung it over my shoulder as though I were on the verge of leaving. I picked up the folder containing my consultation report, put on a smile, and then headed toward the town house.

I didn't know if my plan would work, but it was all I had.

Nineteen

I knocked on the terrace door.

Phoebe startled, then stared in my direction. For a second, I thought I saw murderous intentions cross her face. Then I realized that the Honourable always looked slightly annoyed.

There was nothing special about this situation except that now I knew Phoebe was a murderer. Other than that? Piece of cake.

I flexed my grip on my report folder, trying to keep my hand from shaking as I watched Phoebe glide gracefully across the dining area. She frowned at me through the terrace door.

It would have been her right to simply ignore me.

I gave her my biggest, cheesiest American grin and waved my folder. "I forgot to give you my chocolate consultation report!"

That did it. With evident reluctance, Phoebe opened the door. "Hayden, shouldn't you be on your way to France by now?"

"Yes, and I would have been too." Ignoring all the expected British etiquette, I barged inside. "But there's been a strike. You know French rail workers! I've been delayed." I gave her an elaborately disgruntled face. "Better to wait here, I figured, than cram in with everyone else at St. Pancras, right?"

At my boldfaced lie, Phoebe didn't even blink. "Oh, that *is* tiresome, isn't it? That's so selfish of them, to inconvenience everyone that way. They should all be sacked, wouldn't you say?"

I wouldn't. But I should have known someone like Phoebe wouldn't be a supporter of workers' rights. While it was true that travel abroad and in France itself was sometimes disrupted by unionized workers, all they wanted was fair treatment. But I wasn't there to debate social and economic issues, was I?

I was there to keep Phoebe from getting away. Somehow.

First, I tried stalling her. "How did it go today?"

While you weren't being arrested by the police?

"Oh, brilliant!" Phoebe bustled around some more, gathering paperwork and stuffing it into her luggage. She was not an organized packer—probably because she usually had Amelja to do such things for her. "You should have been there. The reception was very positive. The Bakewell tart was a tremendous success."

"I'm happy to hear it." I wasn't. "How were the hosts?"

"Tediously chipper, as always. But that's their job, isn't it?" She scrutinized her luggage, then glanced up at me. "I'm terribly sorry, but I'm in a bit of a rush. If you'll just put down that report someplace, I'm sure I'll get to it later. Just be a dear, won't you? Right there is fine."

Her elegant wave indicated the dining table. I was being dismissed, I realized, and my report along with it.

I held onto it. "There are some things we should discuss," I spitballed. "Some procedural improvements, product ideas—"

Phoebe stood still, a perplexed frown on her face. "What part of 'I'm in a bit of a rush' don't you understand?"

"Oh!" I laughed. "Sorry. Are you taking a trip too?"

Her curt nod confirmed it. I swallowed hard, unable to stop picturing her with that metlapil in hand, sneaking up on Jeremy.

"Yes, and I'm running late, thanks to that television show." Phoebe smacked down a printed boarding pass. CARACAS leaped out at me from the destination line. "Excuse me," she said.

She brushed past me, leaving me clutching my report folder and my bag. Two steps away, Phoebe stopped. She turned to me.

She'd caught me. I laughed again, then gestured at her paperwork. "Venezuela is nice this time of year," I improvised.

"Oh?" Her eyebrows arched. "Have you been?"

"Of course, to visit cacao plantations." I launched into a dialogue about cacao fruit. "The people are very friendly."

"Ah." Phoebe accepted my story. "Well, won't that be nice?"

As she hurried into the next room to get something else, I finally had my chance. Keeping my ears open for sounds of her return, I sneaked closer to her bag. I pulled out that N_2O cartridge, a jar of artisanal hot-fudge sauce, and the caffeine.

The first would make sure that Phoebe wasn't allowed past security and onto the plane. The second (a liquid, believe it or not, according to the authorities) would make sure that her luggage was flagged for inspection. The third would make sure that if the first two failed, all hope wasn't lost. It would require expert (and time-consuming) verification at the airport security gate to prove that Phoebe wasn't smuggling cocaine.

I tucked everything close together into Phoebe's luggage. I was betting by the size of it that this was a carry-on item. With the click-click of Phoebe's high-heeled sandals coming ever closer, I hastily covered the cartridge, the hot-fudge sauce, and the baggie of powdered caffeine with some filmy silk clothes of Phoebe's. They would turn into a wrinkled mess if she ever made it to Caracas. It was obvious she'd never been there.

It was equally obvious, unfortunately, why she was going now. As I gave a final covering yank, my cell phone rang.

It sounded like a rocket firing. I jumped and yelped.

I almost knocked the whole bag off the tabletop. My heart leaped into my chest, pounding even faster. I hurled my hand upward, hoping I wasn't having a stress-induced heart attack.

Nonchalantly, Phoebe click-clicked in. "Aren't you going to answer that?" She smiled. "I can never ignore a ringing phone."

Her insouciance completely spooked me. How could she be so carefree, knowing she'd coldly bludgeoned her husband to death?

Because she knew she was about to get away with it, I answered myself, then glanced anxiously at my phone screen.

It was DC Mishra. My hand shook even harder. I felt Phoebe's curious scrutiny and knew I had to be smart.

More than anything, I wanted to answer the detective constable's call and scream, "Come to Phoebe's! Come quick! She's getting away!"

I forced down my panic and returned Phoebe's smile. "It's just my financial adviser, calling about my next chocolate-whisperer job." *As if I would ever refuse a call from Travis.* I clicked the button to send it to voice mail. "We'll talk later."

The screen went dark. My heart sank along with it.

"All right. Well, thank you, Hayden." Phoebe strode to me with her hand extended. Her jewels gleamed. So did her eyes. I thought I saw madness there. "I appreciate your help very much."

She was saying good-bye. Maybe I could still delay her. With any luck, the London Metropolitan Police were on their way.

For real, this time. I devoutly hoped so. *Come on, Satya.*

"Maybe we can share a cab?" I suggested. "I should probably be heading to the station by now, anyway. I'll just get my things." I wheeled around as though intending to do so. I'd already packed, so I could bluff convincingly. "I won't be long."

Phoebe sniffed. "I don't travel to Heathrow by cab," she told me in a dismissive tone. "I have a private car for that."

Bingo. Heathrow. "That sounds great! You won't mind giving me a ride to St. Pancras, will you? It's awfully kind of you."

She glanced at the clock. "I'm afraid that won't be possible." No longer interested in having a cordial farewell, Phoebe zipped her luggage. She added it to a larger suitcase—one she must have wheeled in while

I'd been trying to booby-trap her carry-on—then picked up her phone. She dialed. "I'm ready."

She was getting away. "Don't go yet!" I yelped.

Okay, so it wasn't smooth. I'm new at this, re-member?

Archly, Phoebe confronted me. "If you're hoping to wangle a reference from me, I'm afraid you're spoiling your chances." She shook her head. "Mr. Barclay is correct about you brash Americans. You simply don't know when to call it a day, do you?"

Was that a threat? Nervously, I stepped backward.

After all, Phoebe had handled her luggage with ease. It was possible that she was stronger than she looked. There we were, too, in a kitchen full of knives and meat mallets. Yikes.

I sneaked a glance at my phone, desperate to press that voice-mail icon and find out what DC Mishra had had to say.

I didn't. "It's just that I'm so sad our consultation is finished," I dithered. "I've grown very fond of Primrose."

Phoebe flattened her mouth. "Yes, well, haven't we all?" She took my arm and walked me to the terrace doors. "Good-bye."

It was the most amiable bum's rush I've ever re-ceived.

"Won't you miss the chocolaterie-pâtisserie when you're in Caracas?" I was all but clutching the door-jamb in my efforts not to be dismissed. "How will the bakers get on while you're gone?"

Phoebe gave me a chilly smile, then opened the door. I wished I'd glimpsed police cars and diligent officers outside.

"That's really none of your concern now, is it?" she said.

She was right. And I was out of delay tactics.

"You're right." I considered shaking Phoebe's hand, but I couldn't bear to touch her. Although I did wonder, once again, if she was a lefty . . . the killer's handedness. She had to be. Forcibly, I switched gears. "Have a nice trip, Phoebe. Bye!"

Then I hurried across the terrace and onto the garden path, hoping against hope that Phoebe wasn't a secret knife thrower. If piercing glares counted, I was sure she'd have been an ace.

I banged into the guesthouse and grabbed my cell phone.

DC Mishra answered on the first ring. "It's Heathrow," I told her. "Phoebe is taking a flight from Heathrow to Caracas."

The significance of that destination wasn't lost on the savvy detective constable. Neither was my belated call.

"We're on our way," Satya said. I heard talking, traffic, background noises—enough to give me hope. "Just sit tight." There was a pause. Then, "Don't leave town, Ms. Mundy Moore."

Danny was there when the police arrived to pick me up. He wasn't happy about having missed my showdown (such as it was) with Phoebe. He wasn't overjoyed about riding to the police station with me, either. These days, my security expert prefers to avoid run-ins with the authorities. But he did it. For me.

Satya Mishra was there to greet us when we arrived.

The detective constable shook Danny's hand first, then turned to me.

"I want you to know, you're not being arrested," she said.

I'm not embarrassed to say that I sagged with relief. I guessed the specter of jail time had been haunting me more than I'd been willing to admit. But I recovered quickly enough.

Quickly enough to cut straight to the point, at least.

"I hope you've arrested Phoebe."

DC Mishra smiled. "Come into my office and we'll talk."

Danny and I followed her there. As we did, I aimed an inquiring glance at the front desk. "Where's Constable George?"

"We'll get to that." Satya ushered us inside, then shut the office door behind us. At her desk, she steepled her hands. "You *were* a suspect. You should know that. Given your history, that was unavoidable. You should avoid these situations in future."

I nodded. "I'd like to do that, believe me."

A scanty smile enlivened her face. Then she got back down to business. "We weren't sure we would catch up to Mrs. Wright at Heathrow. As you know, traffic can be horrendous in London. While we can alert the security officers to detain someone, that wasn't necessary in this case." DC Mishra pinned me with a stern look. "You wouldn't happen to know how 300 milliliters of unallowable liquid, one N_2O cartridge, and an undisclosed quantity of powdered caffeine came to be in Mrs. Wright's hand baggage, would you?"

Danny gave me an alarmed look. But I knew it was time to come clean. "I planted them on her, to delay her at security."

For a moment, DC Mishra was somber. Then, "Good work. That was quick thinking on your part. I don't approve of your being involved, of course. That is the department's official stance, and I support it wholeheartedly. I have to say, though . . . without your intervention, we would not have caught her in time."

I straightened in my dingy desk chair. "Really?"

"Really," Satya confirmed. "We were certain that Jeremy Wright's murderer had to be one of three people." She caught my expectant look and shook her head. "I'm not telling you who those people were. Suffice it to say that Ms. Wright was one of them." She gave me a wry look. "A tip? It's often the spouse."

Nodding, I filed away that helpful hint. Not that I wanted to be in the position of tracking down a killer again. I didn't. But it's always good to expand your knowledge base, right?

"Between the statement and evidence you provided and the evidence we'd compiled, we were able to obtain a confession."

"From Phoebe?" I almost wished I'd been there for that.

A nod. "And a corroborating confession from Hugh Menadue. He came in to see us very late last night."

I shot Danny a triumphant glance. *Told you so.* I'd been right to have faith. "I hope this won't be too hard on him."

"It will be." DC Mishra frowned. "But Mr. Menadue's cooperation has already helped us build our case against Mrs. Wright." She stacked some papers on her desk, then looked up. "I apologize for what you've experienced with Constable Smith."

I blinked. "Who?"

"George," Danny told me. He appeared no less comfortable to be an invited guest of the police than he would have been as a suspect. "Constable Smith *was* the crooked one." He gave DC Mishra an unyielding look. "She used you to get to him."

The detective constable didn't deny it. "Mrs. Wright has powerful friends—including members of the police department," she explained. "I had to use Constable Smith to expose them before I could build an unassailable case in Jeremy's murder."

"Otherwise, Phoebe would have gone free," I surmised.

Her nod confirmed it. "Thanks to you, now she won't."

"That's why Phoebe wasn't arrested at the TV taping." With new concern, I looked to DC Mishra. "My phone? My evidence? I gave everything to Constable George, along with my statement."

"We got it. We were watching him." She consulted her paperwork. "We got the A/V equipment from the Hambleton & Hart filming, too. George and his associates had taken it elsewhere."

"Wow." I shook my head. "George was always so nice to me."

"Niceness doesn't mean anything, Ms. Mundy Moore."

Danny eyed her with new respect. "That's what I keep telling her." He actually smiled. "She doesn't ever listen."

I had to stand up for myself. "The world needs nice people," I pointed out. "People who don't bludgeon someone to death. People who don't try to push other people into trains."

"Ah." Satya appeared to remember something. "About that—"

I listened, eager to learn who'd tried to kill me.

"It was an accident," she informed me. "We reviewed the CCTV footage. Someone bumped you in the crowd. As far as we could tell, they didn't know they'd done it. It was a chain reaction—one person bumping another, and another, and so on."

So I hadn't been forcibly discouraged from looking into a murder. Not this time, at least. That was food for thought.

In the future, I'd have to be careful not to over-react.

Although even if I *had* overdramatized that push on the Tube platform, I'd still have been right about everything else.

"That's a relief. Thanks for letting me know." I reviewed everything in my mind, knowing this might be my only chance to hear the official explanation for what had happened. "Are you sure you can't tell me who your three final suspects were?"

Satya Mishra looked amused. "I can tell you who it wasn't."

I swear, Danny and I both leaned forward while the detective constable began ticking off suspects on her fingers.

"It wasn't Ellis Barclay next door," she said. "He was seen in his box at the symphony on the night Jeremy died. It wasn't Nicola Mitchell. She didn't like Jeremy, but she never handled the murder weapon. We did have forensic evidence from it."

I hadn't had access to that. I frowned, considering it. My prints must have been all over that metlapil, along with Phoebe's. Maybe Hugh's, too. I pegged *us* as the "final three."

"It wasn't Claire Evans. She was having dinner with Andrew Davies, trying to smooth over things for Jeremy at Hambleton & Hart. They'd gone to the restaurant directly from the pub in Chelsea. The staff at both locations confirmed it."

"Well, the staff would have no reason to lie for them."

"No. Who else?" DC Mishra frowned. "It wasn't Liam Taylor—he was at the dog track, cashing in winnings. Those funds are tracked and verifiable. Unfortunately, he lost not long after."

Aha. A gambling habit would explain Liam's modest car—not to mention Goldie, the lovable retired greyhound he'd adopted.

It was too bad *I* didn't have police-style access to alibis, forensic evidence, and witness interviews. If DC Mishra hadn't been so hostile to me from the moment we met, I might have been able to finagle some information from her. Next time, I decided, I needed to make friends with the investigating officer.

What was I saying? I *really* hoped there would never be a next time when it came to me and murder investigations.

"It wasn't Amelja, the Wrights' housekeeper," the detective constable continued crisply. "We confirmed her presence at her second job, a part-time position at a hotel in Kensington."

Two jobs? Poor Amelja. That couldn't be easy.

Danny cleared his throat. "What about Gemma Rose?"

Satya glanced at him. "Never seriously a suspect."

I frowned at the two of them, half suspecting they were colluding with each other, just to pester me. "Why not?"

"She was on a flight home from America when Jeremy was killed. However motivated she was, she couldn't have done it."

I was impressed by DC Mishra's resources. I could never hope to match things like forensic evidence and flight rosters.

Satya noticed. "Don't be too hard on yourself, Ms. Mundy Moore. Without your intuition, your presence, and your wits—"

I shot Danny a proud glance, then perked up my ears.

"—and your utter disregard for my instructions to you, we would not have solved Jeremy's murder." The detective constable leaned across her desk, scowling. "Do *not* interfere again."

"But you just said it worked," I protested.

"Maybe the third time's the charm," Danny cracked.

But DC Mishra wasn't entertained. "This is a dangerous pastime you've picked up. I strongly advise against it."

"Well, I wouldn't call it a 'pastime' per se," I argued. "More of a sixth sense for murder that I'm developing, whether I want to or not. It's coming along slowly. It's similar to my sense for when a particular chocolate is right—you know, for a truffle or a—" I caught her quelling look and zipped it. One thing still bugged me, though. "Is Phoebe Wright left-handed?"

Satya looked confused. "Maybe. I'm not sure. Why?"

"Because I was told that whoever had killed Jeremy was—"

Left-handed. I broke off, belatedly understanding. George.

He'd purposely misinformed me, to throw me off the trail.

More than ever, I believed Phoebe's influence would have helped her get away with murdering her husband . . . if not for me.

And Danny. He sat beside me wearing an uneasy look.

I could have hugged him for having accompanied me there.

"You're free to go," DC Mishra said, scattering my fond thoughts of my longtime pal. She folded her hands. "Unless you have further questions for me, we're finished here."

Danny shot to his feet. "Have a nice day, DC Mishra."

I tried for a more lingering departure. "I'll be just across the Channel, in France, if you need anything else."

A faint smile. "We won't."

"I promise I won't make a habit of this," I went on.

Meaning murder, of course. All I wanted was to take my dozens of chocolate chip cookies (and all that international chocolate) to Jeremy's Jump Start Foundation and be on my way.

"See that you don't," the detective constable said.

"And Phoebe won't be released from jail?" I pressed.

I'd be having nightmares about metlapil-wielding daughters of British peers for weeks. I suspected there would be a lot of handily distracting chocolate whispering in the days to come.

I had to call Travis and line up something new right away.

"Mrs. Wright will not go free," Satya reiterated with a sigh. "Not if I have anything to say about it." Bluntly, she added, "Do you need help finding your way out?"

"No, we've got it covered." Danny grabbed me and bolted.

In the hallway, I protested. "Danny! We were talking."

"No, you were fishing." He strode onward, holding my hand to keep me with him. "Nobody's going to congratulate you."

I slowed. Was that what I was after? Had I been fishing for accolades? If I was, it was understandable. I'd risked murder.

"Travis will congratulate me." I cheered up at the

thought. "He always knows what to say." More importantly . . . "And how to say it." I couldn't wait to hear his sexy tones, telling me how brave I'd been, how clever, how determined and how persistent.

The minute we reached the sidewalk, Danny stopped. He faced me. He cleared his throat. He wore the deepest possible frown.

"Congratulations," he said roughly. "You did it."

I smiled. "There. Was that so hard?"

He didn't quit frowning. "Given the circumstances? Yes."

I examined his face. "I knew it. You only said that to beat Travis to the punch, didn't you?" With an annoyed exclamation, I swatted his arm. "Danny! You're supposed to mean it."

"I mean everything I say to you," he said.

"That's more like it. Come on." I started walking toward the closest Tube station. I'd glimpsed an iconic roundel nearby, and I refused to be scared away from such a useful form of transportation. Although, since my push had been accidental—

"You mean too much to me to keep risking you like this," Danny said from behind me. Too late, I realized he hadn't followed me. "If you keep this up," he warned, "I'll quit."

What? I turned to face him, openmouthed. "Quit? You can't quit. You're just upset." Right? "You don't mean that."

He crossed his arms. I couldn't read his face. "Try me."

I didn't want to. "Fortunately for us," I said, "that won't be an issue, since I'm not running into any more murders."

Danny gave me a cynical look—the same look he'd been giving me for years now, for just as long as we'd known one another. He didn't back down or agree. But then, I hadn't expected him to.

I could always count on him for sheer stubbornness.

Well, I could match him on that. "I sneaked Jeremy's dimpled pub mug out of the guesthouse in my luggage. I'm going to give it to Liam. I think he'd appreciate the keepsake."

Danny only looked at me. I thought he was waiting for me to cave in to his (unlikely to be enforced) demand. But I wouldn't.

A tense moment ticked past between us. We both stood there.

Finally, Danny sighed. "I'm the one with the shady past, here. If you start stealing things, where does that leave me?"

At his grudging acceptance of my change of subject, I almost went weak with relief. I guessed a part of me *had* feared he meant that threat. But Danny *not* help if I were in trouble?

It was unthinkable. Both of us knew it.

"My little slip leaves you reformed, just the way I like it." I gestured for him to catch up. Together, we walked. "What else do I have to do?" I mused, taking in the only-in-London mixture of skyscrapers, centuries-old buildings, Routemaster buses, and black cabs. "Oh yeah. Call Claire and tell her I *won't* be writing a tell-all book about the chocolate industry."

"At the commercial taping with Gemma, Claire asked me if 'chocolate whispering' was a real job," Danny confided with a twinkle in his eye. "I told her you made it up."

"*You* made it up! *You* came up with the name, too. Remember?"

Danny offered me an exaggeratedly thoughtful

look. He furrowed his brows in confusion. "No, I don't remember that."

"Yes, you do. That night in New York, when we decided I could make a living at chocolate? You said I'd be great!"

Doubtfully, my security expert shook his head. "Nah, that doesn't sound like me. You must be thinking of Harvard."

"It was you." I knew it was. "I remember as if it happened yesterday. Danny, I'm doing this job because of *you*."

There were a few other factors at work, of course. But my longtime friend and sometime source of frustration was the main reason I'd found my purpose in life. I owed him for that.

I *always* would owe him for that. Just as much as I owed wonderful Uncle Ross for giving me the world in a suitcase.

But Danny wasn't in the mood for reminiscing with me. Probably because he'd just threatened (inconceivably) to quit.

If you keep this up, I'll quit.

I just couldn't believe it. Maybe he was feeling grumpy.

"Gemma is planning to buy out Phoebe's share of Primrose," he said affably, shooting down my "grumpy" supposition with his hand on the small of my back as we headed down into the station. "She told me so last night. She has enough money now. So if you're worried about the chocolaterie-pâtisserie continuing . . . don't."

"I wasn't even thinking about that," I said honestly.

Danny gave me a skeptical look as we neared the ticket barriers. "You were there a whole month. I know you, remember? I know when you're worried about the people you care about."

Yeah—and I'd known Danny a lot longer.

But I didn't want to think about whatever lay ahead of us—up to and including the danger of losing Danny to another (implausible) murder. Just then, all I wanted was to unwind before running my errands, catching my Eurostar train, and visiting my parents. All I wanted was to move on. As usual.

I may have told you before that I like being on the move.

Playfully, I nudged Danny. "Hey, you wanna go celebrate? We did this together, you know—you, me, and Travis." *As usual.* "I know a place near here that serves a wicked ice cream sundae."

"Oh no." With faux alarm, my security expert held up his palms. "Here it comes. Don't do it, Hayden. Just don't."

"It's got Tahitian vanilla-bean ice cream, dark-chocolate ice cream, and hand-churned cookie-dough ice cream," I said as we reached the escalators. "It's drizzled with bourbon caramel, espresso ganache, *and* house-made white-chocolate whipped cream—"

Danny covered his ears with his hands. "I'm not listening."

"—with a cherry on top and loads of homemade chocolate jimmies." I smiled broadly at him. "Did you know you can make your own jimmies? All you need are confectioner's sugar, a little liquid, some flavoring of your choice, and something—"

To bind it with, I was about to say. But Danny stopped me.

"If I say I'll try it, will you stop describing it?"

"But describing it"—*anticipating it*—"is the best part!"

He shook his head with evident disagreement. But once on the escalator, he grinned up at me. "Don't ever change, Hayden."

"Who, me?" I feigned surprise. "I won't. Count on it."

The only trouble was, I was afraid I already had.

If another unlikely murder came up, I'd change even more.

But until then, I owed Danny an ice-cream sundae to remember. "You'll never forget this," I told him. "Never."

"Yeah," he joked. "That's what I'm afraid of."

I scoffed. "You're not afraid of anything."

I was. Now. But I knew how to put that out of my mind.

I'm a world-traveling expert in chocolate, remember? If *I* can't successfully distract myself with myriad destinations and hundreds of pounds of *Theobroma cacao* at my disposal, who can?

So I grabbed Danny's arm and led us both in the direction I wanted to go. For now, at least, I was still in the driver's seat. Even if I couldn't (yet) drive on the left, I was planning to take control—starting with a scrumptious ice-cream sundae, continuing with a phone call check-in to Travis, and ending . . . ?

Well, *that* I didn't know yet, I acknowledged to myself as the people of London raced past. But I *did* know that I couldn't wait to find out.

DOUBLE CHOCOLATE STOUT COOKIES

½ cup (room temperature) butter
½ cup brown sugar
¼ cup granulated sugar
2 teaspoons vanilla extract
1 egg
1½ cups flour
⅓ cup cocoa powder
¾ teaspoons kosher salt
1 teaspoon baking powder
6 ounces Guinness or other stout
12 ounces semi-sweet chocolate chips

GET READY: Preheat oven to 375°.

MAKE COOKIES: In a large bowl, beat butter with brown sugar and granulated sugar until light and fluffy, about 3 minutes. Add vanilla extract and egg; beat to combine.

In a medium bowl, whisk together flour, cocoa powder, salt, and baking powder. Add dry flour/cocoa mixture to creamy butter/sugar mixture in thirds, alternating with the stout.

Fold in the chocolate chips; stir just until combined.

SHAPE & BAKE COOKIES: Chill the dough for 15 minutes, then scoop rounded spoonfuls onto greased or parchment-lined baking sheets, spacing them about 2 inches apart. (A #20 portion scoop—which holds 3 tablespoons—is handy here.) Flatten cookies slightly. Bake for 10–13 minutes, until just set. Cool and enjoy!

Notes from Hayden

Guinness works well in this recipe and is widely available across the U.S. Or go for a specialty stout like Triple Chocoholic from Saltaire Brewery in the U.K. Either one will have a roasted malt flavor that will add extra pizazz to your cookies. These are traditional chocolate chip cookies' double-dark older brother— the one who's always getting into trouble!

STRAWBERRY-CHOCOLATE ETON MESS

   whites of 4 eggs (save yolks for another recipe)
   1 cup granulated sugar
   3 tablespoons cocoa powder
   2 ounces chopped bittersweet chocolate
   1 pound strawberries, hulled and sliced
   3 tablespoons granulated sugar
   1 cup heavy whipping cream
   2 tablespoons granulated sugar
   1 tablespoon cocoa powder
   1 teaspoon vanilla extract

GET READY: Preheat oven to 350°. Prepare a bain-marie by filling a small saucepan with a few inches of water and bringing to a boil; reduce to a very low simmer, then proceed with meringues.

MAKE THE CHOCOLATE MERINGUES: In a heatproof stainless-steel bowl, whisk together egg whites and 1 cup sugar. Set over bain-marie, making sure the bottom of the bowl doesn't touch the water. Whisk frequently until all sugar granules are dissolved.

Remove mixture from the heat, then beat on high speed with a whisk attachment or beaters until the meringue is stiff and glossy, about 5 minutes. Sift over the cocoa powder, add the finely chopped chocolate, then gently fold together.

Scoop rounded spoonfuls of the mixture onto a parchment-lined baking sheet to make individual meringues. Bake for 8 minutes; rotate baking sheet and bake for an additional 8 minutes, until meringues look puffy and slightly cracked. Cool completely.

MAKE THE STRAWBERRIES: In a medium bowl, stir together strawberries and 3 tablespoons granulated sugar. Let macerate for at least 20 minutes, until juicy and delicious.

MAKE THE COCOA WHIPPED CREAM: Whip together heavy cream, sugar, cocoa, and vanilla with a mixer until soft peaks form.

TO MAKE THE STRAWBERRY-CHOCOLATE ETON MESS: Crumble the cooled meringues into a mixing bowl. Gently fold in the strawberries and cocoa whipped cream, mixing just until barely combined. Divide among 8 serving dishes, garnish with additional sliced strawberries and/or chocolate curls, then enjoy right away!

Notes from Hayden

Think of this as a British version of strawberry
shortcake—with a chocolaty twist! Like Italian tira-
misu, this layered dessert full of meringue pieces,
whipped cream, and sweet strawberries is more than
the sum of its parts. Sure, it's messy—but only in the
most delectable way! It's easiest to make with a standing mixer and whisk attachment, but you can use a
handheld mixer—just remember you'll need to beat
the meringue a bit longer.

GOLDIE'S
CHOCOLATE STICKY TOFFEE
PUDDING CAKE

  8 ounces bittersweet chocolate, melted and
cooled
  1¼ cups boiling water
  ⅔ cups chopped dates
  ½ cup softened butter
  ¾ cup brown sugar
  3 eggs
  1½ cups flour
  1 teaspoon baking soda
  1 teaspoon baking powder
  ½ cup Lyle's Golden Syrup
  ¾ cup brown sugar
  ¼ cup butter
  ½ cup heavy whipping cream
  1 teaspoon vanilla extract

GET READY: Preheat oven to 350°. Grease an 8-inch
square baking dish, line the bottom with parchment

paper, then set aside. In a small saucepan, combine 1¼ cups boiling water with dates; simmer over very low heat for 10 minutes, then set aside.

MAKE CAKE: In a large bowl, cream butter with brown sugar until light and fluffy. Beat in the eggs, one at a time, then mix in the melted bittersweet chocolate.

Sift together the flour, baking soda, and baking powder. Stir into the butter/chocolate mixture. Add the dates and their soaking liquid, then stir just until combined. Pour the mixture into the prepared baking dish, then bake for 50 minutes until the cake feels springy to the touch or a toothpick inserted into the center comes out clean.

MAKE TOFFEE SAUCE: In a small saucepan, combine golden syrup, brown sugar, butter, cream, and vanilla. Bring to a boil, then simmer gently for 4–5 minutes, stirring often.

SERVE: Serve the cake warm with hot toffee sauce. Add a scoop of vanilla ice cream for an extra-decadent treat!

Notes from Hayden

This recipe might sound complicated, but it really isn't! Lyle's Golden Syrup has a light caramel flavor and is irreplaceable in this recipe. It's been made by the British company Tate & Lyle's since 1881 and was first called "Goldie," just like Liam's dog!

CHOCOLATE BAKEWELL TART

1¾ cups digestive biscuit crumbs
¼ cup granulated sugar
¼ teaspoon salt
4 tablespoons butter, melted
5 tablespoons blackcurrant jam, well stirred
¾ cup butter
¾ cup + 2 tablespoons granulated sugar
3 eggs
½ teaspoon almond extract (optional)
8 ounces chopped blanched almonds
8 ounces ground almonds
6 ounces bittersweet chocolate, melted and
   cooled

GET READY: Preheat oven to 350°.

MAKE THE BISCUIT BASE: In a medium bowl, combine biscuit crumbs, ¼ cup sugar, salt, and melted butter. Stir to combine, then pour into a 9-inch springform pan and press into an even layer. Bake for 7 minutes, until very lightly crispy. Set aside to cool.

Carefully spread the jam in a thin layer over the cooled biscuit base (an offset spatula is handy for this), spreading almost to the sides of the pan—leave an approximate 1-inch border so the jam doesn't bubble over the edge.

MAKE THE CHOCOLATE ALMOND FRANGIPANE FILLING: In a medium bowl, beat together ¾ cup butter and ¾ cup + 2 tablespoons sugar until combined. Add the eggs, one at a time, beating well after each addition. Add the almond extract (if using;

vanilla extract makes a good substitution). Add the chopped and ground almonds; stir well. Pour mixture into the prepared, jam-filled crust.

Dollop the melted chocolate on top, then use the edge of a knife to swirl it lightly into the mixture for a "marbled" effect. Place in the oven and bake for 35–40 minutes, until the almond/chocolate mixture has set but the filling is still slightly wobbly in the center. Cool completely on a wire rack.

To serve, slice the tart into individual portions, then plate and enjoy with a dollop of whipped cream and/or additional jam.

Notes from Hayden

The pièce de résistance of Phoebe's appearance on "telly" can be yours, too! If you can't find digestive biscuits, substitute an equal amount of shortbread cookies, graham crackers, or even animal crackers. Or, for a real chocolate extravaganza, use chocolate wafers. Use any flavor of jam you like (blackcurrant is my fave, but it's hard to find outside the U.K.), such as raspberry, strawberry, or apricot.

Grab These Cozy Mysteries
from
Kensington Books